Praise for *Saving Miss Oliver's*

"Some are called to serve in schools. Some are called to write. Davenport is called to both." —Annie Dillard

"From the very first paragraphs, *Saving Miss Oliver's* is an engaging read and is very highly recommended to all general fiction readers..." —*Midwest Book Review*

"There are moments here that indicate that Davenport, who, as his bio notes, 'had a long career in education,' was probably an excellent teacher, like a scene in which Francis explicates a Robert Frost poem with his class, and there are some wonderful students, like the head of the school newspaper who is conducting research about the sex lives of students... A book for anyone who's wondered about the inner workings and worries of a school administration." —*Kirkus Reviews*

"Stephen Davenport has written a first novel that resonated with me. *Saving Miss Oliver's* is about the change of leadership at a small private girls' school, but it could as easily have been any change of leadership anywhere... This book kept me happily entertained from beginning to end." —*Bookloons*

"Steve Davenport is a consummate schoolmaster and a gifted writer. In this splendid first novel, Davenport builds on all the other exceptional 'school' novels: *The Prime of Miss Jean Brodie*, *The Rector of Justin*, *The Headmaster's Papers* and *The River King*. *Saving Miss Oliver's* is a must read for anyone who appreciates the seasons of a school's life and the lives of people who make schools work." —Peter Buttenheim, Sanford School, Hockessin, DE

"Steve Davenport's novel is fast-paced, entertaining and singularly evocative of the pressure-cooker atmosphere of a boarding school. Steve knows schools, and he brings us face to face with their passions, their absurdities and their virtues—especially when it comes to schools for girls." —Rachel Belash, Former Head of Miss Porter's School, Farmington, CT

NO IVORY TOWER

NO IVORY TOWER

A Novel

STEPHEN DAVENPORT

This is a work of fiction. Any resemblance to real people or schools of any of the characters or schools in the novel is coincidental and unintended.

Cover image: Ivailo Nikolov/Shutterstock.com

Library of Congress Cataloging-in-Publication Data is on file

ISBN 9781513262024 (paperback) | 9781513262048 (ebook) | 9781513262031 (hardbound)

Published by West Margin Press®

WestMarginPress.com

Proudly distributed by Ingram Publisher Services

WEST MARGIN PRESS
Publishing Director: Jennifer Newens
Marketing Manager: Angela Zbornik
Editor: Olivia Ngai
Design & Production: Rachel Lopez Metzger

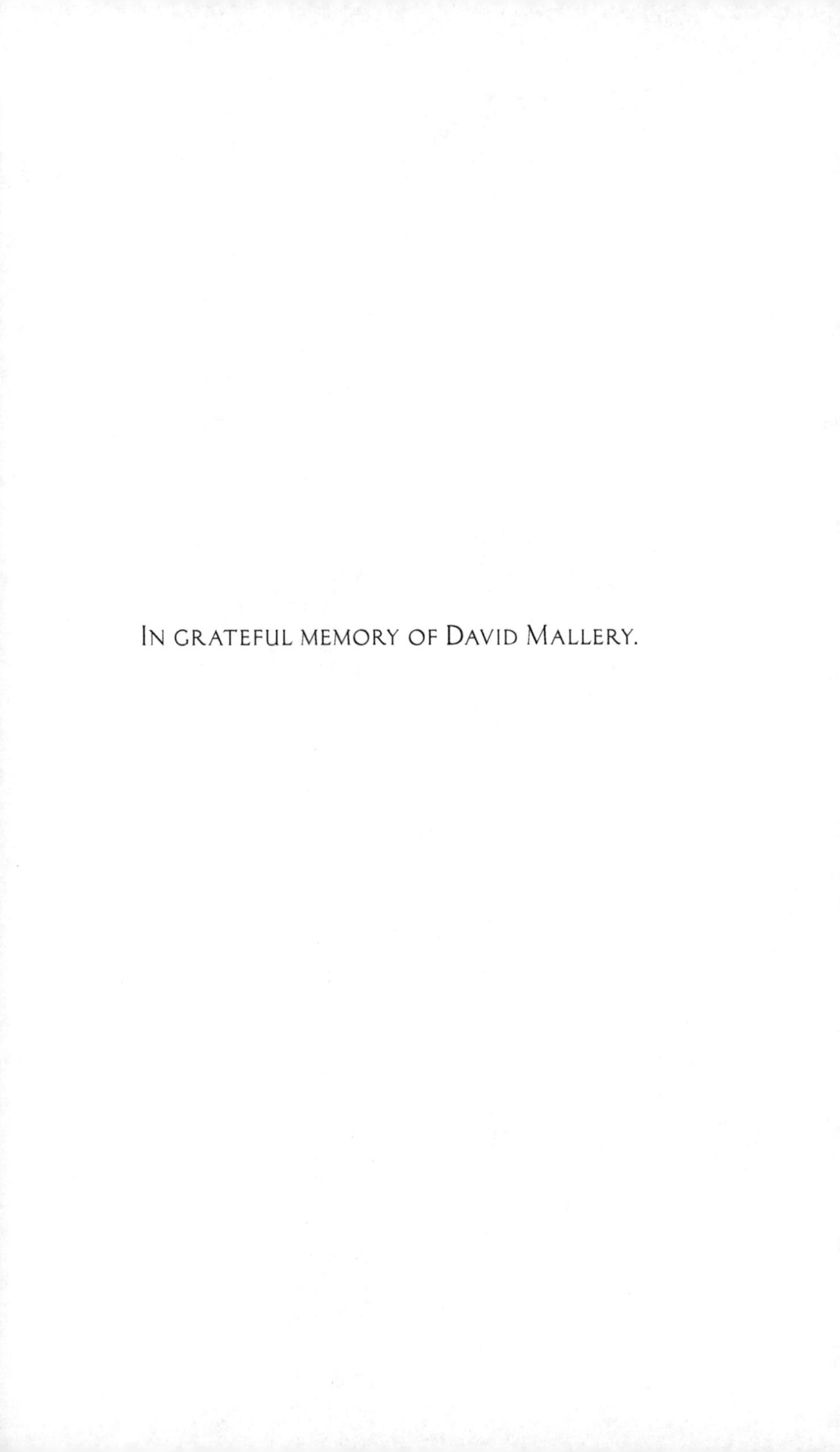

In grateful memory of David Mallery.

ONE

Gregory van Buren, teacher of English, was more respected than beloved. His students would no more dare to be one minute late for his class than write *different* when they meant *various*, or use *annihilate* for *destroy*, and when someone used *lay* for the act of reclining in the present tense, he would actually lie down on the floor and deliver a lecture about transitive and intransitive verbs.

So Gregory's heart sang when Rachel Bickham, his brand-new boss, started the first faculty meeting of the 1992 school year exactly at nine. It sang still more when she paused, mid-sentence in her start-of-year speech, and gave a look with precisely the right amount of amazement in it at the several teachers who straggled in at one minute after. It seemed an eternity before they found their seats and she resumed her sentence. Oh how he did enjoy their discomfiture! *This is Miss Oliver's School for Girls!* he wanted to shout, *not a used car lot.*

He was also delighted by the way Rachel dressed: in a red silk blouse that set off her brown skin, a silver necklace, a gray skirt, and stockings. Stockings! Half the faculty were wearing shorts, some not even socks. Yes, he knew it was still summer—the Monday before Labor Day weekend—and the girls wouldn't arrive until a week from Wednesday, but don't try to convince him that people in sloppy clothes don't do sloppy work. He was wearing his summer-weight blue blazer, the single-breasted one, a tie, and freshly pressed khaki trousers. He liked it too that Rachel stood up to make her talk, that she was tall—an asset for a leader—and that she moved her hands through the air as she talked—comely, long-fingered hands, the palms lighter in color than the rest of her.

Please, don't say how grateful to have been appointed you are, he thought, and she didn't, and his heart lifted still more. Why should she be grateful? It was the other way around. So what if she was only thirty-five? As the chair of the Science Department *and* director of Athletics, she had proven to be the best leader available at the end of last school year, just two months ago, when Fred Kindler, that honorable man, suddenly resigned after only one year in office.

Just thinking about how Fred Kindler had been treated made Gregory feel ashamed. Fred had been appointed to save the school from imminent financial collapse. Parents, and even some of the alumnae, were not sending their daughters because they had heard the school was so broke it might actually have to close—so the under-enrollment grew worse. When under-enrollment had caused the problem in the first place. The possibility of closing grew even more probable, and then rumors flew around that Fred Kindler planned to solve the problem *by admitting boys.* So he challenged the alumnae to save their beloved school and its sacred mission of empowering young women by raising the necessary money and persuading the parents of every high school *girl* they knew to send their daughter to Miss Oliver's School for *Girls.* The alumnae's response was clear: *not until you go away.* So he resigned, and right away the alumnae started to raise money and recruit girls—enough to keep the school alive.

But Gregory's shame over the way the school had behaved was matched by his pride in Rachel for her response when the board chair offered her the position of interim headmistress while they looked for a permanent one. Oh, but didn't she surprise them! "I won't be your head just because I'm convenient," she had said. "You've got to want me enough now to want me permanently." How about that for nerve? And if anyone tried to mess with her the way they messed with Fred Kindler, they'd have Gregory van Buren to answer to.

Rachel sat down and turned the meeting over to Gregory's colleague, Francis Plummer, who seemed rather pale and tired for a man who'd been on vacation all summer. Gregory, who remembered how he'd felt when his wife divorced him years ago, was sure Francis was grieving over the separation from his wife, Peggy, the school's librarian. The rumor was she'd kicked him out of the apartment next to the dorm they parented. It made everybody sad, especially the girls in the dorm, to think of them living apart. Gregory didn't believe they'd ever get back together. Francis had rebelled against the leadership of Fred Kindler, and Peggy had gone out of her way to support Fred. In Gregory's view, that was enough to rend them asunder forever.

But Francis maintained his involved presence, no matter the state of his marriage. Indeed he drew all faculty eyes to him now as he stood up, seeming quite small after Rachel's tall presence. He looked directly at Gregory. Almost everybody thought Francis was the best English teacher in the school, if not the world, and Gregory the second best by just a little.

"I do hope this satisfies your questions about our young artist Claire Nelson's academic schedule," Francis said to Gregory, referring to a student who had transferred last year for mysterious reasons into Miss Oliver's from her school in New York City in the middle of her senior year. Right away some of the faculty had felt that was going to be trouble. Within days of attending the chair of Art Eudora Easter's painting class, Claire had discovered a prodigious artistic talent. Rachel invited her back for another year in order to build a sufficient portfolio to gain entrance to the Rhode Island School of Design. Not everyone thought that was a good idea.

"Yes, I do hope to be satisfied," Gregory said, returning Francis stare.

Francis looked surprised. He'd expected a long speech in ponderous syntax from Gregory. He didn't know that his colleague had resolved to be as self-disciplined in his speech as he was sure Rachel would be in everything.

Eyes went back and forth between him and Gregory. "We have decided that almost her entire time will be spent on her art," Francis said. "She'll elect two other courses from English and history."

"But she's abysmal in math."

Francis smiled. "If she needs an accountant to register sales of her pictures, she'll hire one." Some of the faculty laughed.

"We?" Gregory said. "Shouldn't we have conferred?"

"I thought about that," Francis said, smiling more broadly now.

"And?"

"I decided it wasn't necessary."

Gregory smiled too. He'd made his point. "I thought so," he said, and Francis sat down.

It was a wonder that two so different models for students of how to be in the world could be contained in so small an institution as Miss Oliver's School for Girls. Gregory was tall, always impeccably dressed, and formal, a believer in authority. Francis Plummer was short, slightly pudgy, and indifferently attired. Gregory was a devout Catholic, and Francis a Pagan, having been converted from his father's Episcopal faith by an equal measure of affinity to the way he thought Native Americans viewed the world and a strong dose of rebelliousness. Gregory kept a discernible distance from his students—and, some would say, from the literature he presented to them. He thought of it as the world's possession, not his, and he showed it to them analytically, letting them decide for themselves if they would fall in love with it, as he had so long ago that he couldn't remember. At graduation time, more girls asked Francis to confer their diplomas on them than all the other teachers combined, but only one or two girls would ask Gregory. The poems he chose to honor them were never easy to understand, and when he hugged them, which he did only because graduation hugs were a sacred tradition at Miss Oliver's School for Girls, he was so shy of contact, he'd stick his butt out so far behind himself that people laughed and said he looked like he was wearing a bustle.

Everything that happened in Gregory's classes was an exercise in critical thinking, and everything in Francis's an exercise in engagement. Francis was passionate and demonstrative, and he wasn't about to let the students decide whether they would fall in love with literature. The alumnae loved him for this as fervently as they disliked Fred Kindler for coming in from the outside, a perfect stranger. Every move Fred Kindler had made seemed to generate the same question: *how dare you think you could understand us?*

Francis Plummer was the face of the school. In the classroom he was as powerful and larger than life as Superman; outside the classroom, quiet, small, and unobtrusive. Many years ago, the students took to calling him Clark Kent, generating a mystique that'd been building for decades. That this very unathletic man spent weekends running dangerous rapids in the springtime when the water was high only added to the legend.

Thus Francis Plummer was vastly more powerful than Gregory

van Buren in the school's fraught politics that Rachel Bickham would have to manage. Gregory had arrived thirty-three years ago, right after his wife divorced him, and proceeded to live a monkish life on campus. But Francis and his wife Peggy, the school's beloved librarian, had come a year earlier, directly from their honeymoon, and right away the then-headmistress, Marjorie Boyd, a brilliant, charismatic educator, admired by all, feared by many, beloved by some, put Francis Plummer at her right hand—though only unofficially, for she was too authoritarian to delegate *officially* anything to anybody. Francis was passionately loyal to her. Some would say he'd made her his surrogate parent, and when the board finally dismissed her after her own thirty-five-year tenure, for paying too little attention to the school's increasingly precarious financial condition, Francis's resentment over her dismissal led to his rebellion against her successor, Fred Kindler, until, too late, he realized how unwisely he had been acting. Francis felt guilty for this now, and though he was worried that Rachel was too young and inexperienced to succeed in so difficult a job, he was resolved to do everything he could to support this new headmistress, including, as everyone expected, taking the leadership of the academic program off her hands to lighten her load. Francis would be the first dean of academics in the history of Miss Oliver's School for Girls.

Near the end of the meeting, Rachel announced that the evening study-time supervision in the dormitories would be extended by a half hour, as Gregory and Francis had both advised. The chair of Foreign Languages, well known for her defense of workers' rights, didn't think it was fair to add to the teachers' duties after the contracts had been signed. "All the assistant dorm heads would like to have a meeting with you this afternoon," she said to Rachel.

"Oh, I never meet people in groups," Rachel responded without a second of hesitation, and everyone looked at each other, and Gregory said quite loudly while pretending to murmur, "Hear, hear." And right then and there Rachel adjourned the meeting at precisely the scheduled time, a first in years.

Gregory wanted to stand up and cheer. He was sure Miss Oliver's School for Girls was back on course.

And Francis was grateful for this promptness. He often joked that when it came to his time to die, he hoped the passing would occur during a faculty meeting so the transition between being alive and being dead would be imperceptible.

What Francis and Gregory didn't know was that there was another reason, beyond her ingrained punctiliousness about schedules, for Rachel's adjourning the meeting right on time: she had a powerful desire to her to talk to her husband. And he was about to leave for Chicago.

TWO

Rachel Bickham didn't wait long enough to cross the campus from the faculty room to her office to call her husband so that the conversation would be private. She was afraid she would miss him if she did. So she called him from the faculty room the instant the meeting was over, while the teachers were still there. She'd talk quietly so they wouldn't hear. And anyway, she didn't have anything really private to tell him. She just wanted to hear his voice.

She had gotten up at dawn that morning because her husband, Bob Perrine, the CEO and founder of Best Sports Inc., with stores in New York City and Chicago, had begged her not to leave him alone yesterday in their New York City apartment, which he kept to be near his office and where they'd spent the weekend together. Then, after four hours of driving through the Bronx into Connecticut and north along the Connecticut River, she had returned to Miss Oliver's School for Girls on the bank of that river, bursting with eagerness to get to work. She'd gone straight to the faculty meeting.

The first thing she would tell Bob, as she had promised him she would even though he hadn't asked her to, was that she had arrived safely. She was feeling a little remorse for having been so preoccupied by the faculty meeting that was about to start—*her very first one*—that she'd forgotten to call him when she'd arrived on campus. First she would apologize, and then he'd forgive her and tell her he was glad he didn't need to worry anymore, and then she'd tell him how lovely the white clapboard buildings of the campus looked in the morning sun, how the dew sparkled on the lawns, and how the mist was rising off the river.

She didn't realize she was holding her breath, praying she wasn't too late while the phone rang on the other end of the line. After what seemed to be forever, his secretary answered, and Rachel knew he'd already left to catch his plane. It was his private number. His secretary never picked it up unless he wasn't there, and when she did, Rachel always felt resentful of her, though she knew that made no sense. "Oh well, I'll call him later," she told the secretary, but the morning that had seemed so bright had lost its luster.

So instead, the first thing she would do would be to call the new board chair Milton Perkins and get everything squared away by doing what she should have done on the day she was appointed. She would ask him to propose to the board that her title *Headmistress* be changed to *Head of School.* Certainly, Milton Perkins would understand how dated *mistress* was, and that, for a girls' school with a newly appointed African American head, the term had an especially nasty ring. A year ago she had been on the verge of advising her predecessor, Fred Kindler, to make the same request, *headmaster* being even more out of tune than *headmistress*, but she refrained because she thought him too preoccupied trying to win over a disapproving community, busily traveling around the country and assuring the alumnae that he had *not* been brought in specifically to build up the enrollment by allowing boys into the school, the mere idea of which drove everybody crazy. And of course another damning issue for Fred had been his gender. Rachel had begun to think that if she had persuaded her friend to change his title, it might have changed attitudes just enough to save him his job. He would still be the head of the school and she still the chair of Science and director of Athletics.

But Fred wasn't the head anymore because he'd offered his resignation when he realized which way the wind was blowing—and Milton Perkins had said, "You're a hell of a guy, Fred. Almost everybody else would have to be told."

What happened next was a secret that Rachel and Milton Perkins would rather die than not keep: the executive committee of the board asked Francis Plummer to be the interim head, but he refused because he understood they were offended by his refusal to support Kindler. They were choosing him only because the alumnae would follow him. Besides, his replacing Kindler, if only for a year, would embitter Peggy still more.

Just the thought that she would soon be talking with Milton

Perkins began to brighten Rachel's spirits again and melt away her dispiriting concern for having been the second choice. When Fred Kindler had resigned, the then-board chair Alan Travelers resigned too because he was tarred with all the same brushes that Fred Kindler was, especially the rumor of the Plan to Admit Boys. Perkins, whose three daughters had graduated from Miss Oliver's, had assumed the chair in his place. He was everything Rachel was not: white, rich, elderly, retired, Republican; but they'd liked each other from the moment he'd offered her the interim headship last June after Francis had refused it, and she'd heard herself say, "I'm not going to be your head just because I'm convenient. You've got to want me enough now to want me permanently." The idea had just come to her. It was outrageous. "Jesus!" Perkins had said, but he had already started to grin, loving her moxie, and she had answered, "You don't want to be picking a new head every year." His grin had gotten even broader and his face lit up. "You obviously agree," she then noted. "You bet I do!" he had replied.

Now she was halfway across the lawn to her office, planning the day, her disappointment about the conversation with Bob that hadn't happened fading further into background. First she'd persuade Milton Perkins of the importance of changing her title to Head of School, then she'd call Francis Plummer in to her office and give him the good news she knew he must have been expecting: *you are, as of right now, the dean of academics.* She and Milton Perkins agreed that without the right people around her, she wouldn't last any longer in her job than Fred Kindler had. She would do everything she needed to do to avoid his fate. From the instant she had been appointed to hold the school in her hands as its head, she'd fallen more and more in love with it. And she was no longer just Rachel Bickham. She was *Head of School* Rachel Bickham. It wasn't a promotion she had received; it was a new identity. Asleep or awake, she'd already begun to wear the school like a coat around herself. To lose it would be a cruel diminishment she couldn't begin to imagine, a death in minor key.

But here was this talented, passionate man ready to serve at her right hand and help her succeed. How lucky could she get? She would create this new title just for him, thus expanding and making official the leadership he had been providing unofficially for years as the school's most influential teacher. Rachel would have made the appointment early in the summer, very soon after being made the head, if she had not had to leave the campus right after graduation. Months before being appointed, she had accepted a critical leadership job at Aim High, a highly successful summer program for low-income kids in Oakland, California. She didn't even consider breaking this commitment. She had missed the relatively calm summer when Francis would have advised her on all the complex issues that can undo a leader before she's hardly begun. And she hadn't been able to start the search for a business manager to replace the one whom Fred Kindler had fired.

She wasn't daunted though—not with the prospect of Francis Plummer at her right hand, and Milton Perkins supporting her as the chair of the board of trustees. Besides, she was a quick study, and she loved to work.

On the steps up to the door of the Administration Building she stopped and turned around, obeying a surprising impulse to gaze at the campus she had just crossed. It was as if she saw it for the very first time: across the wide, green lawns, the four dormitories, in new white paint applied over the summer, were aligned in a semicircle embracing a new library with a steeple that, like its predecessor, contained a bell that rang just once a year in June at noon to mark the beginning of the graduation ceremony. To its right was the classroom building, and to its left the Art Building and the Science Building, and beyond these, the gym, and then the athletic fields, and beyond those, more green lawns sweeping down to the river. She stood very still, taking all this in, and it came to her as it never really had before: *she was in charge of this*. It felt just right, so right, that she declared out loud, as if to an assembled multitude, "This is where I belong, right here."

The declaration had come to her unbidden, without thought, just as those other words had a few minutes ago in the faculty meeting. She'd had no idea that she never saw people in groups until she had announced the fact and drawn to herself every atom of power in the room. So who could blame her right then for suspecting she had all the right instincts for her job? Besides, everybody who works in schools is optimistic in September when every single day of the new school year is still before them, a clean white sheet of paper.

And who could blame her, right then, for expecting she could have everything she wanted? After all, *everything* was only three desires, each connected to the other: First, to survive as the head of this school she was in love with and respected more than any other, the most effective instrument she could imagine for the empowerment of young women. Second, to keep a happy marriage with a husband whose job was just as consuming as hers. Third, to be a mother, and soon.

MOMENTS LATER, RACHEL was greeted at the door of her office by her secretary, Margaret Rice, who told her that her father had called.

"So early!"

"He's lonely, I guess," Margaret offered. She was a tall, large-boned, black-haired woman in her fifties. Margaret's and Rachel's memories of losing their mothers to breast cancer when they both were very young had already built a sisterhood between them.

"I called you last night," Margaret said. "I thought you might like to come over for supper."

"Thanks. That would have been nice, but I wasn't home."

"You stayed with Bob?"

"Yes, I did."

Margaret frowned. "Really? Just how early did you have to get up?"

"I like the early mornings," Rachel said, careful not to sound defensive. She asked Margaret to call Milton Perkins and set up the time for them to talk on the phone, and to make an appointment with Francis Plummer in her office, and then she entered her office and closed the door.

Rachel had arranged her office so that her desk was to the right of the door as you entered. To the right of her desk, big French doors looked out on the campus. She had placed a circle of chairs in the center for the efficient conduct of school business, and against the back wall a commodious sofa for those who wanted to mix business with conversations, including students who simply wanted to chat—which Rachel swore to herself she would always find time for no matter how busy she was.

That morning the sun flooded in through the doors, lighting above the sofa on a picture painted by Claire Nelson, whose schedule Francis Plummer had arranged, of the ancient copper beech which stood in front of the Administration Building, a motherly presence. The tree had grown there since the time when a Pequot Indian village stood on the ground now occupied by the campus, and sometimes, passing under its branches, Rachel would apologize to the people she imagined sitting in its shade. Now, paused inside the doorway of her office, she remembered telling Claire that she was the most artistically talented student she'd ever known. Rachel liked to think Claire painted the picture in thanks for Rachel's trusting her to manage the burden that talent always brings, for the school's admitting her, a girl with a troubled past, in the middle of her senior year and letting her stay on for an additional year so she would have time to build a portfolio for admission to the Rhode Island School of Design. For Nan White, the admissions director, Claire had painted a picture of the gates to the school.

Claire had no brothers and sisters. Her mother had abandoned her when she was eight years old, and Claire's father, an investment banker, had just been transferred to London. He needed a safe place for his beautiful and precocious daughter who, according to the headmaster of her private day school in Manhattan, had "ventured into sexual activity." Obviously, Miss Oliver's, tucked away in a boring suburb and devoid of boys, was the right environment for Claire. After only a few days at her new school, Claire, like a child bringing her artwork home from school for her mother to post on the refrigerator, had invited Rachel to the Art Building to see one of the very first paintings she had made. It was of two little girls on a beach, holding hands, clinging to each other, an endless ocean behind them. To Rachel, it spoke so powerfully of loneliness, she had to look away.

Now Rachel lingered in her office, her eyes focused on the picture of the copper beech, for once obeying her mother's dictum: *Be still! How long do you think you will be here?* And it came to her that because Claire hadn't touched a paintbrush before enrolling in the school, she could stand for every student the school had ever taught. Rachel would never say in public such a thing about one girl out of so many, but just the same it felt like truth. Nor would she say in public—she would barely confess it to herself—that her hunger to be a mother had focused on Claire whom she had allowed deeper into her heart than any other girl in the school. Rachel's mother had clung to her family through unspeakable pain, as long as she could. But here was a child whose mom had walked away on purpose.

Rachel sat down at her desk and reached for the phone.

THREE

"Well, has the shoe dropped yet?" Rachel's father asked. He'd picked up the phone on the very first ring.

"No, Dad, it's only August," she reminded him. She knew better than to claim that shoes don't always have to drop.

"When it does, it will be some issue you didn't know was out there," her father said. He felt a powerful empathy for Fred Kindler and was sure that the brevity of his tenure was the result of the latest dogma: *everybody gets to have an opinion whether they know anything or not.* He should know. He'd lost the presidency of a small liberal arts college in Ohio because he hadn't been sufficiently eager to lead by persuasion in an institution where the faculty had tenure and he did not.

Rachel had had a lot of practice leading her father away from subjects she didn't feel like talking about, so it was easy to get him to ask for news about her husband's career. One of the many things in her life she was grateful for was the respect and affection her husband and her father felt for each other and how they always seemed to agree. Bob happened to be a white person—generating casual, indeed pleased, acceptance by most of the community of Miss Oliver's School for Girls while, to no one's surprise, in the larger community the reaction was far from universal. Rachel told her father about Bob's plan to expand Best Sports and how hard he was working.

"Good news," her father said. "I'm happy for him."

"I am too, Dad," Rachel said just as Margaret opened the door and poked her head inside. Rachel assumed she was going to tell her Milton Perkins was on the phone. "Dad, I have to go," she said.

"Well, then go," he said huffily into the phone. "But remember, it's only August—not too late to tell the board you've changed your mind." Then he hung up.

Margaret told Rachel that Milton had decided to come to school to talk with her face to face rather than just on the phone, and that he'd be here in just a few minutes. "Good," Rachel said, her prospects for the morning brightening still more. "When's my meeting with Francis?"

"Not today." Margaret flushed, as if slightly embarrassed, or feeling a surge of happiness. Rachel couldn't tell. "He left. He'll be back for the first day of classes."

"Left?"

Margaret nodded. "He and Peggy. To the Cape. They'll be with their son, Sidney. A family celebration, I guess. He wants you to know, he's moving back in with Peggy. Isn't that wonderful? What a great way to start the year!"

Rachel agreed that it was. So what if she had to wait till the first day of classes to appoint Francis? Everybody had been afraid the Plummers were going to divorce. The hot contention between them as leaders of the pro- and anti-Kindler factions had brought to the surface the grievance of their religious differences they had been burying in years of overwork. Everybody knew Peggy was a devout Episcopalian, deeply involved in the local parish, and that Francis never accompanied her to church. He didn't hide the fact that he saw divinity differently from his wife: in nature, "just like the Pequot People who once lived right here." Every once in a while in class he would talk about a transcendent, egoless moment when he was a little boy fishing with his father and an ancient turtle had swum up from the bottom of the lake and presented itself to just him. "My father saw him but didn't *see*," he would say. "*Here I am*, the turtle's message was as we stared at each other, and I felt myself melt into him and him into me and both of us into everything. Then the turtle sank back down out of sight and I was me again, though I didn't want to be, and my father was my father, an *other*, and everything was *else*."

When Fred Kindler arrived early in the summer one year ago and Francis fled to California ostensibly as the faculty advisor to a school-sponsored archaeological dig on an ancient Native American village where a housing tract was about to blossom, Francis had claimed he was on a vision quest. But Peggy had claimed it was part of a crack-up, a mid-life crisis, which, if he weren't so immature, would have happened earlier. What he was really doing was running away from his responsibility to show Fred Kindler where all the rocks and shoals were. God knows there were plenty of them.

Rachel remembered the sudden silence that had come over the faculty room last year, soon after a mysterious fire had destroyed the library, when Fred Kindler announced that there would be a substitute co-dorm parent, named Patience Sommers, to partner with Peggy in what had been the Plummers' dorm for thirty-four years. Everyone had looked down at the floor rather than let their eyes meet either Peggy's or Francis's, who were sitting as far apart from each other as they could get. It had just become clear that there was too much bitterness between them to work together. Peggy believed that Francis agreed with the opinion, widely expressed by the student council, to which Francis was the advisor, that the fire that consumed the library was a sacred fire because it also consumed the Pequot Indian artifacts which Peggy had reverently curated. It was Peggy who had created the display and provided it the most prominent space in her library. She also collaborated with interested members of the faculty to use the display as stimulus for creating the school's celebrated comparative anthropology course. Paradoxically, it was the respect for other cultures engendered by that course that inspired the student council's assertion to the board, signed by almost every student in the school, that Miss Oliver's had no right to possess what rightfully belonged to conquered Native Americans. Francis didn't deny that he agreed with the recommendation. It was the last straw for Peggy. She told him to leave. He moved off campus. Thanks to Fred Kindler's sensitiveness, the announcement that Patience Sommers would replace Francis was the last item on the agenda. The faculty room had never emptied so fast.

Now, thanks largely to the imagination and skillful work of Fred Kindler and Peggy Plummer, there was a new library with a wing owned jointly by the Pequot Nation and Miss Oliver's arraying a more extensive, richer display of artifacts owned by the Pequot Nation, one of whose officials sat on the board of Miss Oliver's. Rachel was as happy for herself as for the Plummers. Francis would be even more powerful in his new position with his marriage on the mend.

"All right then, please set up a meeting with Patience Sommers," Rachel said.

"Not necessary," Margaret said. "The Plummers already told Patience she wouldn't be needed anymore. They hoped you wouldn't mind. They felt it should come from them." "Of course I don't mind," Rachel said, but as soon as the words were out, she knew she did. It was her prerogative, not theirs, to make such decisions. She felt a twitch of resentment.

"Their car was packed and ready to go when I called," Margaret said. "They want to get to know each other again, I guess. They've done all their prep for starting school. They've been here for years, they don't need the time."

Rachel frowned. "Even so, don't you think they should have asked me if they could leave?"

Margaret flushed again. "Yes, and I told them so, but obviously they didn't agree," she said, and in the heavy silence that followed, Rachel wondered if Margaret was embarrassed for her new boss's lack of authority or for the Plummers' behavior. Then Margaret's face lighted up with relief: the subject was about to be changed. She gestured toward the French doors and said, "Here comes Milton now."

Rachel turned, relieved too, and watched Milton Perkins's thin, slightly stooped frame come toward her across the lawn, wearing a shirt and tie even on this warm summer day. She went out through the doors to meet him. He already knew she liked to walk by the river. They headed that way together.

"What's on your mind?" he asked, sparing her the usual how-are-you exchange. She told him the good news about the Plummers.

"Really? Back together? I didn't think that was going to happen."

"Neither did I, and neither did Margaret."

"Well, I have to say I'm glad we were wrong," he said.

"The whole school's going to be glad, especially the girls in their dorm," Rachel said. "I was going to appoint him today, but he and Peggy went to the Cape. They want to get to know each other again," she added, quoting Margaret.

He didn't answer, just nodded his head. She was surprised. She wondered if he'd guessed that the Plummers hadn't sought her permission to leave before the weekend began.

When they had reached the trail along the river, he put his hands on his hips. "This is a nice place to walk." Indeed it was. The trail followed the edge of a bluff into an open field, high above where the river broadened. There was no wind that day, and the water below them was placid, a big, smooth heave on the way to the Sound. It always settled Rachel's mind to walk along there where the river would still be running long after she was gone.

"We ought to sell this waterfront land," Milton Perkins said out of nowhere. Rachel couldn't tell whether he was actually serious. Maybe he was just pushing her buttons. There was a wide streak of irreverence in the man. There had been glee in his eyes when he had talked to the faculty and made up a story of a survey he'd recently read that showed that the IQs of liberals averaged twenty-five points lower than those of conservatives did.

She turned to him and said, "If we sold this land, every girl in this school would leave here straight for Hotchkiss. And the alumnae would give all their money to Wellesley and Smith."

He grinned. "Then we'd fill the school with girls who wouldn't miss it. We'd have enough money to pay off the accumulated deficit."

She didn't answer. She was right and so was he. The school had failed to make budget for the last four years of Marjorie Boyd's tenure. The total accumulation was one million and two hundred thousand dollars. The board had pledged to find the money to pay down the loan that covered it. The deadline was in three years, four hundred thousand dollars a year. If they failed to meet it, the bank would raise the interest rate, maybe even call the loan. The school would be out of cash.

They came to where the trail ran down off the bluff to a little beach. She sensed that it was too steep for his old legs, so she pretended she'd had enough walking. They turned around and started back, and just before they arrived at his car, he told her to make sure she dropped everything over the Labor Day weekend so she'd be rested up "when school starts and everything hits the fan." She told him she would. She and her husband and siblings and dad were going to spend the weekend at their family place on Martha's Vineyard.

Just as he was about to get in his car, she remembered what she'd had Margaret call him for.

"You really care what your title is?" His tone was incredulous.

"I do," she said. She wasn't about to try persuasion. There wasn't a PC bone in his body.

"Well then, I'll take care of it." He was looking over her shoulder at something behind her. She turned around. Gregory van Buren, still in his blue blazer, was just disappearing into the library. "What about him?" Milton Perkins said.

Rachel didn't answer.

"I understand," Milton Perkins said. "Plummer's the one with the most charisma—and the alumnae expect it." Then he got in his car and drove away.

FOUR

It was three o'clock in the morning and Mitch Michaels was wide awake.

Ordinarily, the two Vicodins he had swallowed at midnight would have taken him all the way to six o'clock, and then there would be the limo ride to the studio where, as soon as he leaned forward into the mike, he'd imagine all those people nodding their heads, guys mostly, driving to work all over the country, their shoulders relaxing because they were hearing what they already believed, and his pain would melt away. But there was no show today because it was a holiday weekend and he was not in his New York apartment. He was in his summer house on the beach in Madison, Connecticut, and without the daily morning rage vent to look forward to, and with the disturbing presence of Claire Nelson, his daughter's long-legged, willowy guest with the raven hair and deep-set innocent eyes, who was sleeping just down the hall, he knew that if he didn't take another pill in another half an hour, the electricity that was then a mounting tingle at both sides of his lower back would pulse down through his buttocks and explode in his hamstrings and toes like bombs going off every minute and a half. Ninety seconds exactly. He'd counted them. It never varied. The worst part was waiting in between.

He didn't need to turn the light on to find his way down the hall to the bathroom past the room where his daughter Amy and Claire were sleeping, because it was just a little shingled cottage, which he and his wife had bought for seventy-five thousand dollars when he was still a sportscaster. Seventy-five thousand! It was worth six hundred thousand now. He knew because he'd had to pay her half that to buy his half from her when they divorced—which he was happy to do—until he figured out that it made her rich enough to enroll their daughter in that school. "How would you feel," he'd asked on his show, pretending he was talking about some other family, "if you had no say in what kind of a school your daughter goes to?"—forgetting that most of his listeners sent their kids to public schools and didn't have any say either. The more he'd learned about Miss Oliver's School for Girls in Amy's freshman year—how the students address their teachers by their first names (or even nicknames!), how the kids are allowed to dress like savages and read books like *Catch-22* (as if they knew enough by then to know why we fought that war and what guys died for)—the more cheated he felt. It didn't help that his ex-wife, as sole guardian of his daughter, in total control of when and if he could visit with her, had obtained a court order prohibiting him from stepping foot on the campus.

In the bathroom, he opened the medicine cabinet and reached behind the row of bottles containing aspirin and ibuprofen and vitamin C and Barbasol shaving cream to where the one containing the Vicodin pretended to hide, and he opened it and shucked two into his palm. Only ten left. He put one back and swallowed the other. He'd learned to take them without water because water was not always handy, and besides, if he drank water now, he'd have to get up and pee when what he needed was to be obliterated in sleep. The doctor in Madison didn't know there was a doctor in New York who filled out prescriptions too—or pretended he didn't anyway.

On the shelf beside the sink sat his daughter's guest's toilet kit. *Toilet.* What a nasty name for what was in there: toothbrush, toothpaste—lipstick maybe? What else? He reached, touched the soft leather, ran his fingers where the zipper was slightly opened, then, shamed, pulled his hand away. Never before in his life had he imagined that a teenager would stir him. Girls that age, especially if they were as beautiful as this one, were people you needed to protect! He didn't understand that this one's ability to stir feelings very near to lust in him was a purposeful application of power, in this case just for the hell of it, and he was as addicted to being around power as he was to painkillers—because maybe they were the same. But he did understand that when the Vicodin kicked in and he was back in bed in the dark, not counting the seconds until the next explosion, he might dream of her, and because he hoped he wouldn't and still wanted to, he was shamed still more.

On Thursday, Amy and her mother had driven from their home on Long Island to meet Claire at JFK, where she'd flown in from London. They spent the day and that night in the City—Mom's treat—all three in the same hotel room. Yesterday morning, Amy's mother had put them on the train in Grand Central Station; he'd picked them up an hour and a half later at the New Haven railroad station. They were still glowing from their New York City fun. Claire's dad, a VP of an NYC investment bank, recently transferred to the London office, was busy that weekend, Amy had explained, and Claire, whose mother had abandoned the family when Claire was eight years old, didn't want to be in London alone, so Amy invited Claire to spend the weekend. Afterward, Amy's mom would drive them both to Miss Oliver's.

Typical of Amy: innocent, naive, kindness personified, but he also knew that she'd never spend a whole long weekend alone with her dad. "Just don't listen to my show," he told her every time she let him call her on the phone. "Just forget that part of me, and we can like each other again." He was that straight with her. "No," she said. Every time. "No way. You stop, and then we will." That made him love her all the more. So when she announced Claire was visiting, he'd said, "Of course, you can bring a friend."

They'd gone straight from the railroad station to the house, put on their bathing suits, and walked to the beach across the front lawn in bare feet, and he remembered when Amy was just five years old and she stepped on a bee; it stung her and he carried her back to the house, feeling her arms around his neck, and he put ice on it and it stopped hurting just like he told her it would. It was one of those times when he was almost crazy with happiness, but now they couldn't go swimming because the water was full of jellyfish, which happened more and more now in August than it ever did before, and so they had sat on a blanket in the hot sun while he tried to keep his eyes off Claire as she talked about her life in London. "Oh, I'd love to go to England," Amy had said—an enchanted sophomore to a post-graduate student. He'd coached her in T-ball and early volleyball, and now, in her one-piece modest bathing suit, he saw she didn't have that chubbiness anymore and wondered if she was wearing it so she wouldn't have to listen to him disapprove.

Now, with the pill inside him, he turned out the bathroom light and headed down the hall to his room where he'd get back in bed and tell himself not to worry about whether or not he'd be able to sleep. Over and over *Don't worry* he'd think, *Don't worry, don't worry, because what do you think is keeping you awake? Worrying about whether you can sleep, that's what. Well then, stop worrying, idiot! Just lie there if you have to, it's not the end of the world*, but he'd already turned around. He went back into the bathroom, and this time when he turned on the light, the glare off the tiles was an explosion in his eyes. He opened the medicine cabinet, found the bottle of Ambien, squinted hard at the label to make sure that's what it was, and swallowed two, imagining them landing on the Vicodin, and, just to be sure, popped a Benadryl. Then he turned out the light and it was somehow darker than it was before, like the inside of a camera, or the bottom of the ocean, and he had to feel his way with his hands on the walls, his fingertips along the grooves in the old-fashioned tongue-and-groove paneling that still smelled like just-cut trees and the door behind which his daughter and Claire Nelson slept, where he wanted to stop and listen to them breathe, but he didn't. Moonlight shone through the windows in his room, his big empty bed right there in the middle. He climbed up into it, and few minutes later he was on the thin line between sleeping and waking, wondering if he would ever cross over. And then oblivion.

When he got up at seven he felt relieved, maybe even proud, that he'd managed not to dream of Claire, and he didn't swallow any pills, just black coffee, and took a long walk on the beach to kill time until Amy and Claire woke up. An hour later when he returned they were still asleep, obviously, being teenagers. So he mowed the lawn, the big green sward in front of the cottage that swept down to the seawall. He figured the roar of the lawn mower engine would do it, but at nine o'clock they still hadn't appeared downstairs. He was tempted to climb the stairs and wake them, but he was afraid to annoy his daughter. As soon as they did wake up, he'd propose they go sailing. It was one of those blue-skied September days you get only once in a while and you remember forever, the air light and buoyant, and everything sparkling, the Sound as blue as the sky with little whitecaps. If they got going early enough, they could take a lunch and sail all the way across the Sound to Long Island and back on the southwest wind, a broad reach in both directions. In the meantime, he might as well mow the back lawn too. He liked the mindless back-and-forth; it soothed him. So he cranked up the mower again and set to work. The scent of the honeysuckle that trailed up the trestles on the back of the cottage drifted to him and he was almost happy, thinking of how Harry Truman mowed his own lawn in Missouri even though he'd been the president of the United States, and Ronald Regan cutting brush in California.

The window of the room where Amy and Claire slept looked out over the back lawn, and so he left the mower's engine on and parked it in neutral right below the window, where it roared for at least a half an hour while he raked up the cut grass, a finishing touch he'd never done before and never would again. After he saw through the kitchen window that the girls had at last come downstairs to the kitchen, he went on raking to show them the reason the mower was still roaring—and sending exhaust fumes through the open kitchen window into the house—was that he had simply forgotten to turn it off, and that it was very important to get all this grass raked up. But they weren't even aware he was raking the grass. Sitting at the kitchen table, side by side, their backs were to the window.

"Oh, you're up!" he said, sauntering into the kitchen a few minutes later. He was still holding the rake, as if he'd forgotten it was in his hand.

"Why didn't you just come upstairs and wake us up?" Amy stared at him. "Don't you think that would that would have been better?" Her irritation frightened him. Claire looked at him, then back to Amy by her side, then back to him, like someone watching a play.

He felt his face get red and turned away, and carefully leaned the rake against the wall in a corner, as if that was why he'd brought it in. "I thought we might go sailing," he said, still facing away.

They didn't answer. He turned around. Amy and Claire were looking at each other. Claire was wearing blue pajamas. Amy was in pajamas too, he supposed, but he didn't know what color because they were underneath a robe. "We could take a lunch," he said. Claire turned her gaze from Amy's face to his. "How about you, Claire," he said, "would you like to go sailing?"

Claire held his gaze just to see if she could, though she'd never admit to herself that's what she was she was doing. When he couldn't hold his gaze on her any longer and had to look away, she turned to Amy and nodded her head.

"All right then, let's go sailing," Amy said.

It was too late now to sail all the way across the Sound to Long Island and back. He wasn't surprised by how disappointed he was. They'd sail east instead, toward the mouth of the Connecticut River.

They bought sandwiches and cokes for lunch at the grocery store by the marina in Clinton where he kept his boat, a thirty-two-foot sloop, which when it was still true he'd named *Amy's Delight*. It had two bunks and a head, and a tiny galley below. He was well aware that if Amy were the same age as Claire, who'd be a college girl if she were not doing an extra year at that school he hated, he would have bought beers instead of cokes. Amy wore his black L.L. Bean woolen shirt over her bathing suit. It dwarfed her, coming down to her knees, and made her look younger than she was, a middle school kid instead of a high school sophomore. That was all right with him. She could stay that age forever. Claire wore his big red hoodie. It covered her down to just below her bikini bottom because she was that much taller, and it made her long legs look as naked as they really were. It was hard not to imagine that the hoodie was all she wore.

They jumped down into the boat and Claire said, "I don't know a thing about sailing," and had the good sense to climb halfway down the companionway to get out of the way. Amy went forward, like he'd trained her to do before the trouble between him and her mom, to take the clips off the furled jib and then came aft, and they hauled it up together, and then she helped him haul the main sail halyard. Then he turned to her and said exactly what he knew she knew he would say: "Will you take us out, Amy?" And as if no misery had ever happened between them, she smiled and said she would, and gave that little funny salute he'd taught her, and there was such a hot red surge of love for her like a live thing rising in his chest that he thought he'd never be able to breathe again, his eyes flooding and his lip quivering, and he turned away so she wouldn't see a grown man crying and jumped up on the dock to cast off the lines.

He took the stern line off the cleat on the float and flipped it to Amy, who, sitting at the tiller, coiled it at her feet while he went forward to cast the bow line off. Claire still stood in the companionway, a mere passenger, nowhere near center stage, just watching. He uncleated the bow line, pushed hard on the nose of the boat to swing it away from the dock, and jumped onboard, and Amy pushed the boom and the tiller hard to the left and jibed expertly around in the very narrow space of the crowded marina to head for open water.

Anybody else would have used the motor.

As soon as they were past the jetty, a strong wind heeled the boat way over and he was glad to see that Claire, still standing in the companionway, was scared. He sat down on the bench on the windward side, just forward of his daughter, and said, "She'll go a little faster if we tighten it a bit," meaning closer to the wind, but what he really wanted was to heel even more and scare Claire more. He wanted water coming over the lee rail into the cockpit. He wanted her to lose her composure, but you might say he just wanted to show off for her.

Amy nodded her head, and pushed the tiller down and he pulled the main sheet in a little further and adjusted the jib sheets, and *Amy's Delight* came up still closer to the wind and heeled still further over. Water did come in now over the lee rail, sloshing in the cockpit before exiting through the scuppers, and Claire, feeling much too close to the down side of the boat, abandoned the companionway and climbed up the slant to the windward side and sat down next to him, bracing her feet against the floor of the cockpit to keep from sliding down off the bench. There were bands of paleness on the tops of her feet where her sandal straps had prevented the sun, "Isn't this fun!" he said, and Claire nodded her head and tried to smile.

They sailed like this for another half an hour or so until they were several miles out from the Connecticut shore. Amy said, "Now, Dad, is it time, do you think?" raising her voice over the sibilance of the rushing water and the wind and the throb of the windward stay, and he nodded his head to say, *Yes it is time*—because even if it wasn't time yet for them to come around and get the sail on the other side and start the long slide downwind toward the Connecticut River, this was one day he wouldn't correct her. He uncleated the sheets and Amy pushed the tiller way down, and the boat first heeled even further over so that Claire grabbed his hand and said, "Oh!" Then the boat righted itself as it swung and there was the lovely shuddering of the sails as the boom came over, and they were going downwind now, even faster, and except for the fact that Claire wasn't scared anymore because the boat was upright with the main on one side and the jib on the other, Mitch Michaels, who hadn't dropped a pill since three in the morning, was as happy as he'd been in years.

So happy, in fact, that he forgot all about the tendency of the wind to fade on summer afternoons and ultimately cease all together—which is what happened that Saturday afternoon of the Labor Day weekend a few hours later, just as they were about to poke into the mouth of the Connecticut River. The sail that had been so taut went almost slack and the boat slowed. Amy didn't even ask him whether she should come about and head for home; she just did. "We should have headed for New Haven instead," she said. If they had, they would have tacked upwind while the wind was strong, and come home downwind when it was weak. Now they had to do the opposite. They both hated to use the motor.

Soon the wind died altogether, and *Amy's Delight* lost all way, rolling in the swell, the boom swinging back and forth, and it was suddenly hot and misty, the sky turning from blue to white, and even the Sound itself succumbed to lassitude. He started the motor, and Amy put it into gear and steered straight for home, and the exhaust from the motor, with no wind to blow it away, hovered around them, stinking.

Even so, Mitch was still happy. These things happen when you go sailing. But then Amy asked Claire, over the throb of the motor, if, since sailing wasn't fun anymore, would she like to sunbathe "up there," pointing to the deck forward of the cabin. Claire didn't answer right away, glancing at him, catching his eye, asking, without saying, *Would you mind?* Of course he minded. Who knew how long it would be before he had Amy's company again? But he said, "I'll take the tiller." He could have put the automatic pilot on and gone forward with them, but he wasn't invited.

He moved over and took the tiller from Amy, and the girls took a step forward. "Wait!" he said, and reached into a cutty built into the bench and pulled out a tube of sunblock. "You better put some more on," he said, holding the tube out. He knew it was silly to try to postpone Amy's going up forward and leaving him alone. How long does it take to put sunblock on? Amy took her L.L. Bean shirt off and Claire took the sunblock from him and handed it to her. Amy rubbed the sunblock on her arms and, bending over, the front of her legs. Then she handed the tube to Claire and turned around, and Claire applied the stuff to the back of Amy's shoulders and legs. It wasn't so long ago that it was still okay for him to do this for her.

"Now you," Amy said, and turned around and took the tube from Claire. He could swear that Claire turned her head to make sure he was looking before she peeled his big red hoodie up over her head. Claire bent over, reached her two arms up to her shoulders, and pulled the hoodie up, slowly, slowly, he thought, to tease him, he was sure, while his daughter watched him watch, and there Claire was seconds later, tall, flat bellied in her tiny bikini bottom and thin top that didn't cover the rounded tops of her breasts, about as naked as you can get and still be in a bathing suit. She didn't glance at him now; that would have been too obvious. If any other girl her age, even one just as pretty, tried to do this to him, he'd laugh and tell her to put her clothes back on, but there was something knowing about this one, something that made her older than her nineteen years.

Claire took the sunblock tube from Amy. She said, "I'll put this on up there," pointing forward where they would sunbathe. He knew she knew perfectly well what she had been doing. Maybe she was beginning to have second thoughts.

"But what about you, Dad?" Amy asked. "Shouldn't you put some on too?"

He shook his head. "Never use the stuff." It was true. He didn't wear a helmet when he rode his bike either. And once when the buzzer in his brand-new BMW told him to put his seatbelt on, he smashed his hand against the dashboard so hard trying to shut it up, he sprained his wrist. He could actually laugh at himself about stuff like that, but he wasn't laughing now. He'd been played like a fish. The two girls went forward, and he took the sails down and steered for home.

The girls came aft just as he nosed the boat into its berth and shut the motor off. Amy jumped off to tie up. Claire gathered up the remains of the lunch. He handed her the hoodie without saying anything, and she put it on. He wanted to say, *Don't you ever try that again*, but he would have needed the upper hand for that.

By the time they got back to the cottage it was almost seven o'clock. His back was beginning to hurt again. It would only get worse. He wanted to go upstairs into the bathroom and take a Vicodin, but the girls went straight there to shower, so he poured himself a vodka on the rocks and went out on the porch where he put charcoal in the grill and lighted it off. They'd have steak. Amy could make the salad.

But the charcoal wouldn't burn. It just sat there as if it wasn't supposed to. He blew on it and rearranged it, getting his hands all black and sooty, and it still wouldn't burn. First the goddamn wind went down, and now the fucking grill didn't work! He gave the grill a petulant kick, almost knocking it over as the two girls appeared on the porch, looking fresh from their showers, dressed almost alike in cut-off jeans and T-shirts. Amy stayed back. She knew better than to talk to her dad when he was like this.

Claire stepped forward. "Can I help?"

"No! I can do it myself," he said, picking up the can of lighter fluid and leaning over the grill.

"Dad, don't!" Amy said. Too late. Her father squirted much more lighter fluid than he was supposed to on the charcoal.

"Watch out!" Claire lunged forward and pulled him back just before the stuff exploded and a jet of flame leaped up. It would have burned him. "Are you all right?"

"Of course I'm alright. Can't you see it's burning?" he said.

Claire laughed as if she thought he was joking.

"Dad, I'll make the salad," Amy said.

He went back into the kitchen, poured himself another vodka and took it upstairs into the bathroom to get the Vicodin. It was still steamy from the girls' showers. Draped over the shower stall door were his daughter's one-piece bathing suit and the tiny top and thonglike bottom of Claire's bikini. Did they shower together? He was very careful not to imagine his daughter naked in the shower, but there was Claire, nude, soaping herself, as clear in his imagination as if she had actually been there. Right then and there, he decided to find a way to make her leave that school. No way was he going to let her corrupt his daughter. He put the pill in his mouth and washed it down with the vodka. Then he combed his hair as best he could since he couldn't see himself clearly in the fogged-up mirror and went downstairs and poured another vodka. He took the steak out of the refrigerator and went outside and put it on the grill while the girls set the table. With the pill and the vodka in him and a decision made, he felt a little better. He guessed that he'd been coming to that decision all along.

He went to bed early that night, almost right after dinner. He wouldn't have if he'd had Amy to himself, but it was obvious she was a whole lot more interested in this older girl—who actually lived in a foreign country!—than she was in him. Upstairs in his bed, he tried to read but fell asleep with his clothes still on, and dreamed that he wasn't asleep—that he was wide awake in his bed and the window was open and the two girls were talking on the porch right below the window.

I didn't do it with any boys, one voice said.

With who then?

A teacher.

Claire!

And then he dreamed he was only dreaming. When he woke up the moon was shining through the window and a breeze had come up fluttering the curtains. He took off his clothes and put on his pajamas and went into the bathroom where the bathing suits still hung and swallowed an Ambien. It was three in the morning. No voices rose from the porch below.

In the morning at breakfast he said, "Claire?" his voice casual. He'd had a good night's sleep, he was feeling fine, and when Claire looked up, he said, "Tell me, why did you leave that other school in the middle of your senior year?"

"Because my father was transferred to London," Claire answered, her expression blank.

But he wasn't watching Claire's face. He was watching his daughter watching Claire. It was obvious by her expression he hadn't been dreaming. He had his ammunition now.

There were lots of ways of finding out things people would prefer to keep secret, and he was good at all of them. All he needed to find out whether Claire had told the truth or had made up the story to impress his daughter was to get his hands on the faculty list of Central Park Academy at the beginning of the previous year, and the revised one that would have been distributed after Christmas vacation.

How hard could that be for a man with his connections?

FIVE

On the same Friday that Mitch Michaels started to host his daughter and Claire Nelson in Madison, Connecticut, Rachel Bickham drove from the campus of Miss Oliver's School for Girls to Woods Hole, Massachusetts, and joined her father, brother and sister on the ferry dock for Martha's Vineyard. There, just as he always did, her father sighed as if he'd just heard news rescuing him from some unbearable fate, and announced, "This is where vacation begins." As usual, he spoke for all of them. It was always the same: after the rush to get everything done so they could leave their work, after the packing, after the turning around and driving for miles to be sure all the burners on the stove were out, after fighting through the monstrous Cape Cod weekend traffic, they'd stand on the dock in the salty air clutching their tickets while the tension rose out of them, released to the sky where the gulls called and floated. That Labor Day weekend Friday, each coming from a different place, they arrived almost simultaneously a half an hour before the five-o'clock evening boat. First they exchanged the usual hugs; then they told each other how great each looked, and then they gushed over Rachel's brother's bouncy almost-spaniel puppy he'd just rescued from the pound, and then, surreptitiously, they began looking at the oncoming crowd and beyond it to the parking lot for Rachel's husband.

It wasn't as if her brother and sister didn't understand that Bob might have felt he couldn't leave his work to get there on time, or even not at all. Everybody in her family also worked very hard, each a high achiever like their dad, like leftist versions of Condoleezza Rice. Rachel's brother, DuBois Bickham, was by day a public defender, by night the author under a pen name of money-making detective novels; her sister, Marian Anderson Bickham, was a community organizer in Detroit, a protégé of a prodigy of Saul Alinsky. She was tone deaf, believe it or not, a condition she confessed only half in jest that she assumed on purpose to claim her own identity.

Rachel didn't carry the burden of a provocative name because she was the youngest and her mother had insisted this last child would have a neutral one. Her father used to remind her, though, that Rachel was a biblical name, heavy with implication. Her mother had been a stay-at-home mom until Rachel entered New York City's Stuyvesant High School, where, before he became a famous author, Frank McCourt was everybody's favorite teacher. From then until her death, her mother was a kindergarten teacher.

Ten minutes after they had greeted each other, and after DuBois's puppy had lifted his leg all over Marian's suitcases and she had forgiven both the dog and her brother and claimed that from now on the puppy's name was Bags, Bob still had not arrived. The boat coming from the Vineyard was now at least two-thirds of the way across the Sound. They watched it move the rest of the way and tie up, and he still wasn't there. The passengers trooped off, looking jealous of the people waiting to board, whose time on the Island was all still before them, and who now surged forward. Rachel and her family hung back, risking their favorite seats topside along the rail. She put up her hands and pushed them forward and her father, resisting, frowned. He was about to ask, "Shouldn't you wait for him?" But Marian put her hand on his elbow, sent him a warning look, and tugged him toward the gangplank.

Martha's Vineyard was special to Bob and Rachel also because it was where they had first met, seven years before, at a five-kilometer race to raise funds for a cause neither of them could remember. The woman Bob was dating then had invited him to spend the weekend with her and her family at their summer place—a sign that the romance had progressed to a critical point—and she had talked him into running with her in the race. Though the only thing Bob claimed to hate more than running was dieting, he agreed—another sign the romance was at a critical point. Bob played good tennis when he had the time, which was hardly ever, and he admitted to having been a fullback in high school, but a runner he was definitely not. He and his date showed up at the starting point at the same time as Rachel did. Bob's date was as tall as Rachel, and blond like him. Though also as tall as Rachel, Bob would be willing to describe himself as a little tubby in the middle and with thick legs. Even his face was round.

They started out together, running side by side, his date in the middle between them. Rachel was still sleepy that morning from staying up late, so she ran at their easy pace. Besides, Bob kept glancing at her. Clearly he liked her looks, and she didn't think his were too bad either. They chatted as they ran along for a while, and then Rachel quickened the pace. After all, they were warmed up by then, and when your legs were as long as Rachel's it was uncomfortable to run as slowly as Bob and his date. Pretty soon the date wasn't quite keeping up, and Rachel was telling Bob about the places they were passing through, like a tour guide, including her family's cottage as they passed by it, and with his date no longer between them, they ran closer to each other. About halfway through she said, "By the way, my name's Rachel Bickham."

He was sufficiently winded now to have difficulty saying, "Mine's Bob Perrine."

"That's a nice name," she said, and for the next mile or so, she did all the talking. She tried to fool herself that she was just being nice, but she knew she was really showing off, and by practically killing himself to keep up with her, so was he. In Edgartown, they crossed the finish line at last and she turned to give him a high five, but he was bent way over, his hands on his hips, gasping. His date wasn't even in sight. "Oh dear!" she said, managing not to laugh. "Did I run too fast?" He shook his head, still bent over. She wanted to say something funny about white guys being just as bad at running as jumping, but she decided she didn't know him well enough yet. So instead, she said, "I don't think I should be here when your date shows up." He nodded his head up and down this time, but she didn't budge.

Finally, he was able to stand up straight. He looked down the road. His date was staggering around the corner. "Yes, you better go," he said. "But I know where you live."

She giggled and said, "I know, I made sure," then she turned away and ran up a side street toward home at a much faster pace than they'd run together. The next day, he called her from the public phone at the ferry dock.

Their first date was the next weekend in Boston where she was finishing her doctorate, and where he was raising the funds to start Best Sports. In the restaurant, which was all brown walls and red carpets and smelled like the ocean, his blue eyes never left her face, and he kept his hands very still when he talked, while she, as, usual, waved hers through the air. The next night they went to the movies. They started to hold hands the minute the lights went down.

Now, seven years later, Rachel's father and brother and sister got their favorite seats on the ferry after all, overlooking the stern where she could keep watching the dock and the parking lot. Bob still wasn't there. A minute later the long whistle blew, the thrum of the propellers increased, the boat vibrated, the water boiled at the stern, and then she saw him sprint out of the building where they sold the tickets. He ran awkwardly, leaning to one side carrying his suitcase. The boat started to move. A deckhand put up his hand to tell him stop, but he threw his suitcase onto the boat over the gap that was getting bigger and bigger, and leaped after it, landing clumsily on his feet like third-string basketball player surprised to have come down with a rebound. The crowd cheered. Not Rachel. At that moment she wished he was still in New York. She had left her work on time to make sure she didn't miss the boat. What made him think his job was bigger than hers?

By the time they sat down to dinner that evening, Rachel had forgiven Bob. The atmosphere was too loaded with anticipation of the long weekend, and of memories of all the days here they'd never have again, to hold on to tiresome resentments. The menu was what it always was for the first dinner: spaghetti, the sauce straight out of a can, bolstered with hamburger and mushrooms, and a salad. That's what Rachel's mother had always prepared for the first meal because they always arrived too late for anything fancier. And, for this dinner, like for every first dinner since she died, they left her chair at one end of the long table empty. There'd been no decision to do so; no one in the family had ever said one word about it. They just did.

Rachel and her brother and sister never sat down at that table for the first meal of the stay without reliving, however subliminally, their mother getting up suddenly from her chair and running down the hall, getting to the bathroom just in time. They remembered it as if it had happened every night during their mother's siege of chemo. Their father would freeze in his chair and then he'd get up and follow her into the bathroom so he could hold her head and the three kids would be the frozen ones now, while they looked in each other's eyes across the table and heard the sounds of their mother throwing up on the other side of the bathroom door. There must have been something in the shape of that hall that amplified sound, a kind of horn—or maybe the sound no one wanted to hear was the one that was always the loudest.

A few minutes later, their parents would return and take their places as if nothing had happened, and her father would urge his children to eat, trying to keep a sense of normalcy, they understood, even Rachel, the youngest of the three. Her breasts had budded years before, but now where her mother's soft bosom had been there was only flatness. Soon she'd lie on her back in the dark of her coffin deep under the ground, and so Rachel slept with every light in her room on, and didn't stop until her freshman year at Smith where her roommate said she could only sleep in the dark.

Rachel's mother would pretend she'd never left the table and resume the conversation right where it had been interrupted and Rachel still wondered how in the world she could remember. Her father would interrupt her and urge his children to eat again, but he couldn't eat either. It was a wonder that the whole family didn't waste away as fast as Rachel's mother did—while the family dog got fatter and fatter.

Maybe that's why, all those years later when her ardent husband kissed her breasts in bed that night, Rachel felt a wave of a feeling she couldn't name—a surprising mixture of fear and disgust. He sensed it right away. He didn't speak. He turned the light out and she lay down and he pulled the covers up over her and when she started to cry, he put his arms around her. They both sensed she wasn't crying only for her mother. It was just time for her to cry, that's all, and so she did. They both knew that people who don't cry every once in a while haven't the foggiest idea what's going on. He held her tight until he fell asleep.

In the morning they awoke to perfect weather, so clear they could see individual people in a sailboat at least a mile out from shore, the color of each person's hair and what they were wearing. Rachel's mother had believed such gifts from the god of vacations heralded storms. She'd look up at the sky, observe there were no clouds, and advise her family to have fun on the beach while the sun is still shining "because this one is a weather breeder." Rachel couldn't remember her ever being right. And if she was, it didn't make any difference: rainy days in the cottage were cozy with driftwood burning in the fireplace, Parcheesi and Monopoly. (It wasn't against the rules to cheat.) And books! Everybody in her family loved to read. They'd sit, engrossed by stories in the living room with its wicker chairs and tongue-and-groove paneled walls and the black-and-white drawings of yachts in harbor, while the rain pattered on the roof and the fire crackled and the wind rattled the shutters.

Their mother had found the drawings in a flea market. Their father would have preferred brand-new pictures to grace the walls of the cottage, but their mother never got used to having whatever she wanted, let alone this capacious, gray-shingled "cottage," part of Martha's Vineyard enclave of affluent African Americans. Now their father treasured those pictures. They caught him looking at them again and again, as if he'd never seen them before.

It didn't rain a drop that weekend, all three days as perfect as the first. No Parcheesi, no Monopoly, they didn't read a line. They spent the mornings playing doubles on a neighbor's clay court, four at a time until each had served a game, while the fifth took turns on the sidelines holding Bags's leash so he wouldn't chase the balls. The afternoons they spent on the beach. Evenings gin and tonic, dinner, then long talks over too much wine. Rachel and her husband were always the first to go upstairs to bed.

On their last night, already nostalgic, Rachel took a long hot shower to wash the ocean salt away while her naked husband waited for her in bed. Then she put perfume on in the places he liked her to, opened the medicine cabinet above the sink, and took down the little striped purse in which she kept her diaphragm. Last winter, after six years of marriage, they had decided to have a child, but in June she still wasn't pregnant and then she was suddenly appointed head of school. They made the common-sense decision that she wouldn't get pregnant until she'd been in office long enough to feel comfortable about taking a maternity leave. But she was thirty-five. Her time was running short. Or was it her mother's empty chair that made her want to make a child right this minute for herself and a grandchild for her dad?

She opened the purse and took out the case. In her hands its round smoothness felt like some kind of shellfish made in a lab. Inside, the diaphragm looked altogether too much like the rubber dam her dentist used for her root canals. She thought of all the ardent little swimmers that had raced each other toward it, only to crash into it and die like thwarted salmon. She opened the bathroom door and stepped naked into the bedroom. Her husband's eyes lighted up. She lifted her hand, the round rubber thing held between thumb and forefinger as if it were maybe just a little bit poisonous. "Let's just see what happens instead," she said.

He sat bolt upright. "What?"

"Just this once." She let her hand drop down to her side. His eyes followed. She stood still so he would see her instead, naked, facing him. His eyes moved down from her face and over her body, lingering; his Adam's apple jumped, his face softened, seeming to melt, as it did when he was aroused. "I'm sick of planning," she murmured, fervent now, as aroused as he, and turned around to go into the bathroom and put the thing back in the cabinet. She gave a little booty shake to try to make him laugh, and with the door still open so he could see, she put the diaphragm back in its shell, the shell into the striped purse, the purse back into the cabinet. They were going to make love her way, or not at all.

Then she crossed the room to him, lifted the sheet, slid in, and pressing herself against his side, she threw her arm across his chest. "You are too," she said. "Admit it."

"I am what?"

"Never mind," she said, raising herself above him. She lay down on top of him, and aimed her lips for his, but he turned his face. She missed, kissing him on his cheek. He was even more aroused now. That was obvious. She put her tongue in his ear, but he kept his head sideways on the pillow. She was suddenly as furious as she was horny, and she rolled off him onto her side, facing away.

"Oh, Rach!" he said. "A baby right now is the last—"

"Don't say a word!" she hissed. "Just don't."

He was very still. She waited for him to beg her to get up, go back into the bathroom, put the damn thing in, and start all over, but he said nothing and they lay in the dark on their backs not touching, watching a glimmer of moonlight that played on the ceiling, and listening to the distant surf.

THE HONEYSUCKLE SMELL at the front door of the Head's House, to which she returned on Monday, made Rachel want to cry. The vines ran up a trellis on the front of the Island cottage too, and yesterday all the windows were open and the same sweet, heavy summertime smell was rushing in when she saw her father straightening the pictures of yachts in harbor on the wall for the second time that day, and she touched him on the shoulder, just the end of her fingers lightly there.

She shook her head to clear the memory away. She had work to do. She'd go in, change into running clothes, take a run, then come back and shower and get to her office. She pushed the door open. It was dark inside, all the shades down, and cool after the humid air outside. And big. Too big for her right then—commodious enough for a head with a spouse and several kids. All of a sudden she didn't want to be alone in it, even for the few minutes it would take to change to running clothes. She put down her suitcase in the foyer, turned around, and headed for her office.

The campus was empty. All afternoon, working in her office, Rachel waited for the phone to ring. Twice she reached for it to make the call to Bob. Each time, she stopped before she picked up the receiver. *You're being dumb*, she told herself. *What difference does it make who calls first?* Still she didn't call, and when she was hungry at dinnertime, she went to a restaurant in the nearby village of Fieldington to eat. She still didn't want to be alone in her house. The hostess seated her at a table next to a middle-aged couple. Rachel took comfort in the fact that they hardly said a word to one other.

Back on campus, the lights were on in Eudora Easter's apartment. Eudora was the chair of the Art Department, twenty years older than Rachel, and the only other black woman on the staff. Rachel stopped the car by the side of the drive and crossed the lawn in the twilight, hungry for her company. Their friendship had blossomed at the end of last year when Eudora had gone out of her way to thank Rachel for daring to break precedent by allowing Claire Nelson to stay another year. Eudora had been on the faculty forever—only one year fewer than the Plummers. During all that time, no girl had ever stayed on after her senior year. "But you gave me the chance to do what needs to be done to make sure that enormous talent of hers gets a foundation," she told Rachel. "I don't trust anybody more than I trust myself to make that happen." Eudora dressed in costumes that, no matter how outlandish, always seemed just right for her. She was a large woman with a round, soft body and a beautiful face whom Marjorie Boyd had hired when Eudora was still thin—right after her husband drowned absurdly in a swamp during a Reserve Marine Corps exercise two weeks after their honeymoon—and since then she had given up dieting.

But before Rachel was halfway across the lawn, the lights went out in Eudora's living room in the front and, an instant later, came on in the backroom Eudora had converted into her private studio. Rachel turned around and walked back to her car. She knew better than to intrude on Eudora's painting time.

On the other side of the lawn, the lights in Francis and Peggy Plummer's apartment were out. The Plummers and Eudora had lived just across a small lawn from each other all those years. It warmed Rachel to think about the deep Plummer-Easter friendship. She figured the Plummers were still driving home from the Cape and wondered what they were saying to each other after living apart for almost half a year.

Home at last, she went straight upstairs, turned on all the lights in her bedroom, got in bed to watch the Red Sox game, and promptly fell asleep. She woke up long after the game was over, switched off the TV and the lights, and lay back down in the dark, wondering what it had been like for her dad getting in bed alone the first time after her mother died. She saw an enormous darkness in which her father reached to touch the empty space beside him. She wasn't surprised; it had happened every first night she was alone again after a weekend with her husband.

But this time it was different: she got up out of the bed and padded down the hall in her bare feet to one of the other bedrooms, climbed up into a single bed, surprised at herself for being so weird, and promptly fell asleep again.

ON TUESDAY MORNING the sky was blue, the air fresh, a perfect September day. The faculty would return; the campus would be busy again. And this morning she would interview a candidate for business manager to replace the geriatric, incompetent, beloved man whom Marjorie Boyd should have let go but didn't, leaving that nasty job to Fred Kindler. The business manager was also the chief financial officer in Rachel's scheme, a critical part of the team she needed to create around herself. Maybe this was the one.

He was a retired CFO of a successful mail-order business who'd grown sick of playing golf all day. His CV and references convinced her he had the necessary sophistication to think outside of the box about the finances of what was actually the combination of a school, a hotel, and a kind of orphanage. So, before she broached the subject of the school's history of poor discipline regarding finance, and the one-million-two-hundred-thousand-dollar accumulated deficit, Rachel asked him some questions about how he would interact with the faculty. She explained that the teachers savored their autonomy and had a tendency to hold their issues as more important than "business" ones, and was about to tell him she could use some help in modifying this aspect of the culture, when he interrupted her and went on and on about how *if you just give people the data they always catch on to the truth.* She waited for a chance to tell him that she agreed—unless the data came via the way he was pontificating at her now, but he just kept on going, and by the time he finished, she was pretty sure he didn't have what it takes to be the business manager of Miss Oliver's School for Girls.

She gave him one more chance. "Our teachers can be a bit resentful of all the people they know who have twice the money and half the brains," she said. "How would you react to that?" She was hoping for a laugh. Instead he got a little huffy right there in his chair, and it crossed her mind to suggest he check with her husband: maybe the sporting good business could use his expertise. Instead she told him she would get back to him and stood up. He left, shaking his head.

The next day the students arrived.

SIX

It was the vodka, Claire Nelson thought, walking toward Rachel Bickham's office on the first day of school. Without the vodka, she never would have told. Did Amy's father leave the bottle out on the counter when he stumbled off to bed just so he could sneak downstairs and out onto the porch and catch her giving a drink to Amy? He was weird enough. What would he have said when he found out Amy was only drinking tonic? But he never did come downstairs and so she poured another vodka tonic for herself and another straight tonic for Amy and then another and another.

And then they ate the ice cream.

"Ice cream and vodka!" Amy said. "Good nutrition makes you strong." She had no idea there was no vodka in her tonic. "Only forty billion calories," she giggled. They fed each other chocolate ice cream until it was all gone. It was smeary on their faces, and there were hundreds and hundreds of stars in the black above them, and the soft air carried the rich smell of Long Island Sound up to them from the beach. So maybe it wasn't imagined alcohol that Amy was drunk on, maybe it was her happiness. "We're going to do this every Labor Day weekend until we are a hundred and ten years old," she said to Claire. "You and me. Promise?"

Claire burped. "Abshiludely!" She crossed her heart, and burped again, this time on purpose.

"Oh yes!" Amy said. "And always for dessert a burping contest!"

"Until the day we die!" Claire said. She stood up, opened her mouth, and spread her arms, a singer about to perform, and burped a perfectly satisfactory burp, and Amy responded with a louder one, which Claire tried to exceed in volume and length, but nothing came out. She swallowed air until it hurt and tried to expel it, but it got stuck somewhere down there, and then Amy stood up, leaned over, and, sticking her butt way out behind her, produced not a burp but instead an explosive, heroic, and very loud fart into the silence. Both girls dived to the floor. They were laughing too hard to stand.

When the laughter subsided, they spread their arms out, their fingers touching, and looked up at the stars, and while Amy was thinking how much fun it was, how liberating, to act like a jerk, to be an asshole on purpose, just for the fun of it, like boys do when they want to fool around, Claire felt that sudden lightness she always got when the *Oh what the hell* words came up in her brain like headlines, and she knew right then she was going to tell Amy everything.

Amy had said, "I won't ever tell." But that's what Claire had said. And look what had happened! Twice now, once last year, and now this.

But last year's confession—was that what it was?—was different from telling Amy. Karen Benjamin, the editor of the *Clarion*, the student newspaper, had been working on an article about the sexual activity of Miss Oliver's students, and Karen, who was about the naivest person the world, needed Claire's help. Karen needed to know that stuff like this happened if she were going to get the article right—even though both Karen and Claire knew that Mr. van Buren, the paper's faculty mentor, was much too smart even to think about letting them print it. During their discussions, Claire had blurted out the scandal—maybe just to see how shocked Karen could be. But Karen was ethical—she wanted a journalist's career, and that meant keeping secrets. Karen wouldn't break her promise not to tell any more than Amy would. Besides, Karen had graduated in June and gone off to college where there were other things to think about.

What was she going to tell Rachel about first? The thing she did with the teacher? Had telling Amy been practice for that? Or was it not telling Nan White, the admissions director, last year when she was admitted—even though that was her father's responsibility, because he was the grown-up? But she never expected that much integrity from her father, and she was sick of feeling guilty. She couldn't talk to her father about it any more than she could to Mr. Gaylord Frothingham, the headmaster who'd caught them. He'd made it perfectly clear to Nan White that Claire had been sexually active. That was the term, those were the words: *sexually active*, like she did it jumping up and down, in a gym, maybe with lots of boys when she'd never actually done it with any boy in her whole life—and her father was being transferred to London, so they needed a boarding school, especially one without any boys. He just didn't say sexually active with whom, that's all, and who could blame him? He needed to get rid of the teacher and keep everything quiet. Mr. Alford, only twenty-three years old. His first year of teaching. She had no idea where he went. Or what he told his wife when she asked him why he was fired.

One thing she did know: Amy was the only girl she'd want to have a burping contest with every Labor Day weekend for the rest of her life. It wasn't coincidence that their fingers touched when they lay on their backs and looked up at the stars. They both had reached for each other's hand. *Like sisters.* Maybe it was even lonelier to be ashamed of a father when all he needed was for you to love him back than to have a mother who ran away and a father who's too busy. Amy had planned to spend the second half of the academic year on exchange at St Anne's School in England, but she'd decided to wait till next year so she and Claire could be together this year while Claire was still at Miss O's. Only sisters do things like that for each other.

CLAIRE WAS HALFWAY across the lawn, getting closer, getting nervous. Did she dare? Up ahead, that tree she'd painted. Her teacher, Eudora Easter, a perfect name for her, a black lady too, built like a snowman, said, "Paint what you see," but Claire didn't, she painted what the tree made her think about instead. What she felt while she watched it grow. *Because if you can see it, why bother painting it?* That's why Rachel loved it so.

No, she didn't have the nerve. No way she was going to tell. Stop and turn around. Rachel was never going to find out, she didn't need to tell her first.

Too late. Rachel was waving to her. *Well, I'll just say hello.*

HOW BEAUTIFUL SHE is! Rachel thought. She would have been hurt if Claire had pretended she hadn't seen her waving. She opened the

French doors and stood in them, watching Claire come toward her across the lawn. For any other girl, she might have waited at her desk, but it was hard not to stare at Claire. She had presence, a power to draw attention, and to get what she wanted at the moment, part instinctive, part calculated, Rachel thought, that emanated from an unruly will and stunning, good looks. If anyone needed guidance, it was Claire.

And any other girl would be coming through Margaret's anteroom, but Rachel liked to think every girl on that campus had an adult she could go to as a surrogate parent, and she was glad to be that person for Claire. Since when does a child need to check with a secretary to talk with her mom?

A moment later, as Claire came through the French doors, Rachel reached to hug her, but Claire hesitated. Surprised, and a little bit hurt, Rachel kept reaching and hugged her anyway.

Claire turned full circle, after Rachel let her go, looking around the office, and Rachel realized she was trying to decide whether to sit on the chairs, for business, in the center of the room, or the sofa, for just visiting, under her art. Before she had been appointed head, Rachel had organized her office in the Science Building the same way: businesslike chairs and table in the center, comfy sofa against the back wall. Soon after Claire was admitted last January, she had started to spend some free time in Rachel's office. She always headed straight for the sofa and plunked herself down. Some nights she would bring her books and do her homework on the sofa while Rachel worked at her desk. Rachel had confessed to her that she had no desire to take her work home to an empty house.

Rachel put her hand on Claire's elbow and led her away from the chairs to the sofa, and pulled a chair up close for herself. "It's good to see you again, Claire. Did you have a good summer?"

"It was okay." Claire's face was blank.

"Did you get some art done?"

"Yeah, some." Claire looked out the doors, fidgeting.

"Paintings? Drawings?"

"Just drawings. "

"I'd love to see them."

Claire shrugged. "Okay."

Rachel waited, not wanting to prod anymore, but Claire still offered nothing. Her eyes refused to meet Rachel's, and at last Rachel understood she'd have to be direct. "What's up, Claire?'" she said, speaking very gently. "What's on your mind?"

"Nothing. I just came to say hello."

Rachel smiled. "We already did that."

Claire tried to grin. It came out as a smirk. "Okay, let's say hello again then."

"Come on, Claire. This is me. Rachel. I'm not the sheriff."

"I know," Claire murmured.

"Well then?"

Now Claire looked like a person counting to three. She took a big breath and said, "I didn't do it with a lot of boys. I didn't do it with any boys."

It took a moment for Rachel to absorb this news. Then she reached and took both of Claire's hands in hers, flooded with motherly protective love. This was not the first time a girl had come out to her. Boys, too, in her other school. That was the kind of person she was—and what place could be safer than this? Why didn't that headmaster just say it?

Claire frowned. "No, Rachel," she murmured. "A man."

"A man?"

Claire nodded. "A teacher."

Rachel pulled her hands away. It was a while before she found her voice. "A *teacher*, Claire? Really?"

Claire kept her eyes on Rachel's and didn't answer.

"Oh my goodness!" Rachel said. She stared at Claire, and, horrified, saw a classroom, empty of students except for Claire standing in the center like an actress in a soap opera, watching the open door. Rachel couldn't tell whether Claire's expression was provocative or curious or regretful. And was she waiting for the teacher to enter through that door, or was it after *it* had happened and she was watching him escape?

"Yeah, a teacher," Claire murmured, bringing Rachel back. Her tone was matter of fact, resigned. "Now you know."

Rachel looked down at her desk. There was a tiny scar in the varnished surface she'd never noticed before. Claire continued, "I'm sorry. I should have told Nan White. My father and my headmaster should have too."

Rachel willed herself to look up from the scratch. It had begun to look like a child's drawing of a bird flying up near a big yellow sun. "But if it hadn't happened, there wouldn't have been anything to tell." She didn't want to talk about Claire's not telling. That was beside the point.

"But I really am sorry," Claire said.

Rachel put up her hand. "Who was this teacher?"

Claire stared. "I'm not going to tell you that!"

"Oh, Claire, I don't want his *name*. How old was he?"

"Twenty-five, maybe twenty-six," Claire said, shrugging and adding several years. Then, after a pause, "Maybe I should find a school in London. Maybe you shouldn't have started a post-graduate program just for me."

"Please, Claire. Don't try to change the subject."

"But what if someone finds out?"

"Claire! You didn't hear me."

"But that *is* the subject," Claire insisted.

"No, Claire. What you and the teacher did. That's what we need to talk about."

Claire turned her face away from Rachel.

"Isn't it?"

Claire said nothing, still looking away.

"Please look at me. I'm talking to you."

Claire slowly turned her face to Rachel. She wore a stubborn look.

"Tell me one thing," Rachel said. "Did you let it happen, or did you make it happen?"

Claire shrugged. "I don't know."

"I think you do."

Claire sighed, exasperated. "Okay—both."

"Both, really?"

Claire dropped her head. She seemed relieved to surrender at last "No, just me."

"Why?"

Claire hesitated.

"Claire?"

"All right. Because I could." Claire still refused to look up at Rachel.

"I thought that might be the case," Rachel said. "I'm glad you understand this much." And when Claire didn't speak, she added, "You know, we would have let you in if you'd told us when you applied."

Claire nodded her head, then looked up at Rachel at last.

"We really would have, you know."

"I know that now."

"But you didn't then. I understand, Claire. But if we had known that you were hiding something, we had the right to know—"

"You wouldn't have."

Rachel nodded. "Maybe not."

"Especially since I was eighteen. It wasn't a crime."

"Really, Claire? Did you know that then?"

Claire flushed.

"I bet he didn't either. He had other things on his mind," Rachel said, bitterly. "What happened to him?"

"I don't know. He just disappeared."

"Probably to Australia. Maybe Mars."

"You think so?"

"Oh, Claire, don't pretend you don't know he was disappeared. I would have sent him to a whole other galaxy if I'd been his headmaster. Yes, you were eighteen, and you knew what you were doing, but he was older than that and a teacher, with a teacher's authority, doing the worst thing a teacher can do, and he knew he was doing it. You understand?"

"Yes."

"Good, but it doesn't let you off the hook, does it? Did your father sue the school?"

Claire shook her head.

"See? He didn't because it might have come out if he had."

Claire didn't answer.

"I'm glad you've told me, Claire. It's a start—"

"You're not the only one I told," Claire blurted.

Rachel didn't answer. Claire had answered the question she had planned to ask next. She was now aware of a headache throbbing, and her neck felt stiff.

"Two people," Claire said. "They both said they wouldn't tell. One's the best friend I have in the school. The other's already graduated."

"That's good news," Rachel said, relieved that the second girl was no longer in the school. "It's really confidential, isn't it, Claire? Nobody's business. Make sure your friend still in the school understands."

"I told you. I already did," Claire said, and started to cry. "She's the best friend I have anywhere, not just in the school."

"So you thought you'd get it off your chest by telling her?"

Claire shook her head.

"Well, then you wanted to impress her, maybe?"

"I don't know. What difference does it make? I just did."

Oh all right, Rachel thought, giving up for now. *Half the time adults don't have any idea why they're doing what they're doing. So why should children?*

"Oh, I just wish I hadn't done it!" Claire said through her sobs.

Rachel wondered if Claire's tears were authentic—or was she like an actress in a movie whose director says, "Cry." She was irritated now—at herself as much as at Claire. Something was very wrong about the way she was handling this. She stood up, told Claire to stay there until she got settled, and went out through the door to walk by the river—until she felt settled too.

RACHEL'S EVERY INSTINCT told her that casual sex was wrong. Plain and simple: wrong, especially for kids. Call her an old-fashioned woman, she didn't care. *Nothing* about each person in the world should ever be treated casually. If she didn't believe that, then how could she believe anyone was worth teaching? So why wouldn't she be especially heartsick about a kid having sex with a *teacher*, and also especially since the kid in question was Claire? And even more especially since she was sure Claire had been the initiator. Yes, Claire was the victim too, but so was teacher. That this wasn't the first time such a thing had happened, and it wouldn't be the last, only made it more painful for Rachel.

Rachel remembered again how touched she'd been when Claire wanted her to see her first real painting. They had only known each other for a couple of days. Claire was indirect about it, as if she were actually a shy person. She started the conversation by talking about how Eudora Easter had begun the first class of the new semester by simply telling the girls to start drawing.

The girls had stared at Eudora. "Draw what?"

Eudora smiled. "How about this?" She put her hands on her hips, turned her head to one side, and pointed her chin skyward: an African Queen. Round and soft, at least two hundred pounds. Red beret, red sneakers, big pendant earrings golden against her black shiny skin. "Or something out there," she said, changing her pose to point out the window. "Or something in here," pointing to the left side of her voluminous chest, "or here," touching her forehead.

"But you keep moving," someone said. "And we don't know how."

Eudora said, "Just start."

Claire told Rachel she already had. "Everything went quiet," she said. "And I didn't draw Eudora, I drew my mother. Isn't that silly? I could hardly remember what she looked like. It's in the studio if you want to see it."

So in her next free moment, Rachel had crossed the campus to Eudora's studio. "I know why you're here," Eudora said. She pointed to the wall where she'd posted the picture. She didn't need to. It had already drawn Rachel's attention.

Claire had turned the sheet of paper sideways to make it horizontal and then cut it in half lengthwise to make it long and thin. A long, narrow beach stretched along that horizontal. Two little girls walked holding hands toward the right margin. In a few more steps they would disappear. Behind them, the ocean, the horizon, the sky, each long and thin and horizontal. "Look!" Eudora said. "There's no real foreground. Everything recedes."

Rachel didn't answer. She wouldn't have been able to describe what she was feeling without sounding crazy. All she knew was she was intensely alive and profoundly lonely at the same time. She wondered, after Claire learned the skills to go with her talent, would her pictures still be as primal as this? How did she know to make mother and daughter the same age, collapsing time?

"This is why I do what I do," Eudora had said.

Now, as Rachel walked on the bluff above the river, some clouds, moving fast, crossed the sun and a cool wind came up, roughing the water below her, which was suddenly gray like November, and Rachel realized why she had suddenly felt something was wrong in the way she was reacting to what she was already thinking of as Claire's Confession: it wasn't the head of school's business. It was Kevina Rugoff's, a psychologist, the school counselor, appointed specifically to help kids and their families negotiate situations like Claire's. Rachel needed to put Claire under Kevina Rugoff's attention and focus on the care of the school.

That realization should have left her the mental room to consider the media's delight in finding nasty stories about scandals at "elitist" private schools, a head of school's nightmare: the baby aborted in a dorm, for instance, found in a plastic bag under the would-be mother's bed; the teacher who invited the students in his dorm to his apartment for pizza—and pornographic movies.

But her feelings for Claire blinded Rachel. Claire needed a mom more than she needed a shrink, and Rachel was the closest thing to a mom Claire would ever have.

Rachel would have to call the head of Central Park Academy, Claire's New York City school. *Is it true that one of your teachers had sex with your former student, Claire Nelson?* She could think of a million people to whom it would be easier to pose the question to which she already knew the answer than to this sixty-year-old man. *She did! Then why didn't you tell me?* As if she didn't know. The only time she'd spent with Gaylord Frothingham was when they had served together on an ad hoc committee of the National Association of Independent Schools. During lunch, he had assumed that everybody was as fascinated by his detailed analysis of the last two centuries of Harvard-Yale football games as he was. Nevertheless, she was sure he would be more ahead of the times than she was about the problem she was calling him about, much less easily perturbed. She turned around and hurried back to her office. When she got there, Claire had left.

CLAIRE HAD STOPPED crying right after Rachel left her alone. That didn't mean she'd been faking the tears, she told herself. No, she stopped crying because, as she watched Rachel pass under the copper beech and across the lawns toward the river, it sank in that Rachel hadn't seemed worried that the story would come out and hurt the school. So if Rachel wasn't worried, why should she be, and how did she ever get up the nerve to say, *Maybe I should find a school in London?* No school in London, or anywhere else, would ever have a teacher like Eudora Easter. And now she didn't have to feel guilty anymore about not telling. That was for her dad and old Mr. Gaylord Frothingham to feel.

She stood up from the sofa and went out the way she came, grateful for the privilege. She'd known all along she did what she did with poor Mr. Alford because she needed to prove she could.

He was just out of college, twenty-three years old, only five years older than she had been—and everybody knows girls mature faster than boys. She was still wondering how dumb can a school administration get, to give a brand-new teacher *seniors* to teach. He'd ask a question and all the class would raise their hands and wave them as if they were going to die if he didn't give them a chance to show how deeply they were reading his assignments, and whoever he called on would give the dumbest possible answer, and they'd all agree, talking all at once, shouting at each other, going on and on, sometimes for the whole period. Claire began to feel sorry for him. One day she gave him a good answer. Everybody stared at her. She stared right back. One of the boys said that was the wrong answer and started to propose an absurd one. "Stop," she told him. "You're boring me." He stopped and looked around the room. No one said anything, and they never played that game on poor Mr. Alford again. Claire relived that moment over and over. She'd discovered something about herself she hadn't known was there. After class Mr. Alford thanked her, apologizing for not controlling her classmates.

That afternoon, walking home after school, she discovered that his route to where he lived was the same as hers when she saw him walking in the same direction ahead of her. The oh-what-the-hell feeling rushed up in her and she walked fast and caught up with him just as he turned from the sidewalk onto the steps of the brownstone house where he lived. "Remember that book you said you'd lend me? Can I pick it up now?"

That was the first time. They both regretted it and agreed it would never happen again. But her power over his resistance was intoxicating. It was the same newly discovered power that made the boy shut up. So it happened again. And then again. For six weeks, on Friday afternoons, after they thought everyone had left the school—until old Mr. Gaylord Frothingham discovered them. He'd stayed late and was going around making sure all the lights were off. If only they had gone to Mr. Alford's house, like the first time. But that would have required planning, an admission of intention, instead of pretending, each time, that they were caught in a spontaneous whirlwind they never would have submitted to, if they'd had time to think.

Claire shook her head. She'd think more about all this later. Right now she had to hurry to get to class.

But passing under the branches of the copper beech as Rachel had, she couldn't keep herself from slowing down. What would the tree look like, she suddenly needed to know, if she were sitting down, looking up at it, the way Rachel said she thought the Pequots must have done? The question made her sad, wondering if those people knew what was going to happen to them. She'd find the answer by coming back in the winter and sitting down on the ground and painting what she felt when all the leaves had fallen off and died and the branches were bare against the sky. It would be a different painting from the one she'd painted for Rachel.

Thus decided, she hurried on, looking back only once to see how the morning light washed across the coppery leaves.

"Yes, it's important," Rachel told Gaylord Frothingham's secretary. "Very."

"Important enough to interrupt his vacation? He's in Paris. It's his last day. Our school starts next week."

Rachel hesitated, knowing how much she would hate to have her vacation broken into with the kind of questions she needed to ask. "Well, I guess it is," the secretary said, interpreting the silence.

Rachel gave her direct number, and not five minutes later her phone rang.

"Rachel?" he said. "Rachel Bickham?" The wariness in his voice was louder than his words.

"Hello, Mr. Frothingham. Sorry to interrupt your vacation."

"That's all right. I'm here in our hotel room, resting. My wife's at the Louvre looking at pictures. She can look at them forever. Museums exhaust me right away. They're worse than faculty meetings. How's everything in Connecticut?"

"Fine, Mr. Frothingham, everything's fine. But there's one thing I want to talk about."

"Well, good. Because if everything's fine then perhaps we should both hang up."

"Mr. Frothingham—"

"I'm Gaylord. And you're Rachel, and please, let's both hang up."

Rachel shook her head as if he could see her from across the ocean. "I have a question. It's about Claire Nelson."

"Oh Rachel, I wish you were better at taking hints!"

"Is there anything about her I should know that I don't?"

"Please. Don't ask that question."

"Mr. Frothingham! I already have."

"Well, let's just pretend you didn't. It would be so much better for you and your school. She's graduated. She's gone. Why in the world do you want to know?"

"She isn't gone. She's back for a post-graduate—"

"She is! Oh my! Then you really don't want to know."

"But she told me already. She confessed. I just want to know if there's anything else I need to know."

"She told you? When?"

"This morning."

"This morning! That's wonderful."

"Wonderful?"

"Because last January when you admitted her is a long time ago. Which means when you admitted her you didn't know. Rachel, you're in good shape. And besides, I've taken care of everything. Everything. Our school is in Manhattan, you know. New York City.

Right, Rachel? Believe me, we're way ahead of you on stuff like this. She's a good girl. She needed to confess. Fine, she did, and that's the end of it. Because she's also very smart."

Rachel didn't say anything. She agreed: the less she knew, the better.

"I'm going to walk to the Louvre to get my wife, now," Gaylord Frothingham said. "Whether or not she's through. It's aperitif time in Paris. She'll have the goose liver. I'll have a glass of wine and forget this conversation ever happened. All right, Rachel?" Before she could answer, he hung up.

Rachel called Milton Perkins to share this news with him—without, of course, identifying Claire. She knew he could figure out who the student was, but she also knew the people you can trust with a secret are the same people who don't ever want to know what they don't need to know, and they had agreed that when it wasn't clear whether to share information or not, they would. No surprises between them, ever.

He was silent for a long time when she finished telling him. He had three daughters who had graduated from the school. That they loved Miss Oliver's School for Girls was the reason he did too. No one would be more determined than he to protect the school's reputation. "Thank you for telling me," he said at last. "The rest of the board doesn't need to know—unless something happens, which I don't think it will." Then, after a pause, he added, "But they will want to know why you started a post-graduate program on your own. That's a board decision."

Rachel was stunned. It hadn't occurred to her.

"You'll remember next time," Milton Perkins said.

SEVEN

The next morning, the first day of classes, Francis Plummer awoke to a big surprise: the air around him was not aglitter, shimmery with expectation the way it always had been on the first day of classes. It was simply air. He sat up straight and leaned back against the headboard.

He wanted to tell Peggy, but even if he didn't feel shy in their bed after months of not being allowed in it, he wouldn't. She might think he was having another crack-up. Or the second chapter of the same one. And anyway, she was still asleep, her arm across her eyes.

So he got up and went into their bathroom, took a shower, shaved, and brushed his teeth. When he came back naked into their bedroom and put on his new khaki trousers and new shirt and tie, laid out for him last night in readiness for this day, Peggy had turned over, facing the other way, still asleep. He went into the kitchen and made the coffee, where Levi, their dog, greeted him with less effusiveness than usual, it seemed: just one thump of his tail on the floor and a return to sleep.

Right after the electric percolator had its little orgasm and the coffee was ready, he heard the shower going. At last, Peggy was up. He went to the front door, opened it and bent to pick up her *New York Times*, and brought it back and placed it on the kitchen table for her. She practically memorized it every morning, and she ate breakfast too. He never did. He liked to start the morning's classes caffeinated, empty, like a jock before a game, not satisfied. And he never read the *Times* until after lunch. To go to class stuffed with random irritations and bits of passing interest would be like trying to pray, or meditate, while someone was screaming in your ear.

He turned on the front stove burner, the medium one, as she had instructed him about four billion times, and heated the pan slowly as the manufacturer instructed—even though that was bullshit just to make the pan special, which it wasn't—it was a *frying pan*, for crying out loud—and broke two eggs in it scrambling with a fork, the way she liked it. He sliced a bagel, plain, without poppy seeds, because after you've reached fifty you could get diverticulitis if little things like poppy seeds got stuck in your intestines.

She appeared just as he was sliding the eggs for her onto a plate next to the bagel, wearing a green terrycloth bathrobe he'd never seen on her before. It looked like a big towel with sleeves. Its unfamiliarity made him sad. Her hair, still wet and shiny from the shower, had thin strips of gray against the black. She'd pin it up before she went to her library. "Good morning," she murmured.

Good morning. Like what you might say to the mail carrier? Or two strangers passing in an office doorway? "Good morning," he answered, and she sat down at the table and ran her fingers through her hair. He put the plate down before her.

She looked down at it, unmoving. Then she looked up at him. "Like old times," she said. It sounded more like a question than a statement. He poured her coffee. She began to eat. He sat down across the table and watched.

The sound of several showers going at once, of adolescent murmurs and soft footfalls on the other side of the wall telling him the girls were getting up, brought him the same neutral feeling that had surprised him awakening. He wondered if this would happen again tomorrow. He knew Peggy had heard the girls getting up too; she'd been listening for it just as unconsciously as he had. If she hadn't heard the sounds, she would be up from the table by now, gone through the door into the dorm, still in her new green robe, making sure they all got up. Old times for sure.

He wanted even more now to tell her about how he'd felt when he woke up. But he didn't know how such a sense of loss could be described when September's air rushed at them through the open windows. It heralded autumn's gold and hung on to summer all at once, distilling what he most loved about the world. He stood from the table, took Peggy's finished plate to the sink, then came back to her, bending down to kiss her goodbye—until they'd meet again at noon in the dining room. He looked down her robe at her breasts, even more mysterious to him now than when he'd touched them as a teenager late at nights in lovers' lanes in his father's car. She offered him her cheek. Then he left her and went out the door and walked the paths toward his classroom on this very first day of school, when the world was all fresh and new, a tabula rasa, swept clean of fault. He still wondered where the glitter had gone.

All nineteen faces of his ninth grade class were turned to him as he came through the door of his classroom five minutes later. They had heard from their parents and other alumnae and from the current sophomores, juniors, and seniors about Francis Plummer, also known as Clark Kent—because he was so mild and unobtrusive when he wasn't teaching—and how the very first class his freshmen experienced at Miss Oliver's School for Girls was always on "The Death of a Hired Man," by Robert Frost. Since time began. Every one of them had read it over the summer, some more than once.

None of the girls were surprised when Francis ambled toward the front of the room where he looked up and pretended to be shocked to find them sitting around the table. They'd been told over and over that's how he always started the year. He smiled and introduced himself. A stack of *Famous Little Green Books*, otherwise known as the Modern Library Collection of Robert Frost, was on his desk. He opened the one on the top, read out loud the name of the freshman girl he'd inscribed in it, and then looked up to see who raised her hand, and then he crossed the room and handed it to her. He did this nineteen times while everyone waited. Who would get to be the narrator? And who would be Mary, the farm wife who wanted to welcome Silas, the hired hand, home to die, and who would be Warren, the unwilling husband?

It wasn't until he actually started that he realized what was missing was the pain. That's what he called it—the only name he could come up with. He'd never told anyone about it, not even Peggy. That feeling that the poetry he was about to reveal to the students—or the novel, or the short story or essay—was expanding in his chest, pushing against his ribs. It would kill him if he didn't get it out. It was like being hungry as you sat down to dinner—and yet much more than that. He hid his surprise and panic and plodded on, doing all those clever things he always did, well aware no charge was coming off him, no electric passion to ignite his students' hearts.

By the time the class was almost over, the girls were exchanging looks that asked, *Why is this so famous?* And when, at last, the bell rang, they waited for a few seconds because *maybe it happens now.* But it didn't. They trooped out, avoiding his eyes.

While those mystified ninth graders were leaving Francis's classroom, Rachel took a call from Bob. "Something terrible has happened in Chicago," he said, "and I have to be there this weekend instead of with you." Rachel was so disappointed that it didn't occur to her to ask him what the terrible thing that had happened was. Their scheduled weekends together, each taking a turn at the traveling, were sacred contracts.

To make up for their disappointment, he asked her if she could accompany him to Cleveland on the following weekend where he was making a presentation at the annual conference of something or other, but she reminded him that she was to be in Greenwich at an alumnae gathering the Friday night and in New York at another on the Saturday afternoon, and there were a million reasons why she had to get right back to school that evening. Her tone of voice made it clear that he shouldn't need to be reminded. She heard a woman say something in the background, something she thought was urgent from the tone, and she knew it was his secretary. "Just a minute," he said, and now she could visualize him putting his hand over the phone. There was a moment of silence before he said, "I really have to go."

"Then go!" she said and hung up on him.

At lunch, on that first day of classes, Gregory van Buren reminded the girls at his table that one does not start to eat until the host picks up a fork. "Or," he added, precise as ever, "in the case of soup, a spoon. Today, and this evening at dinner, I will be the host." His smile was almost beatific and his voice was gentle, but there was steel behind them. "Starting tomorrow at lunch, and for the next several days, our newest arrival will be the host," he said, nodding his head toward a freshman girl across the round table from him. She looked surprised and scared, and pleased. "Thank you, Molly," he said. "The duties are few. Simply decide when we are all settled comfortably and pick up a utensil. And if our conversation ever lags, or appears to exclude anyone, you might help me rejuvenate it." He paused for an instant and then began again. "Now, we will all introduce ourselves and say a few sentences about our lives, starting with Molly, and then you will pass up your plates to my good friend Carmella," nodding to the senior girl on his right, "and she and I will fill them, and pass them back, and then I will pick up my fork and we will commence to eat." Carmella giggled, but she looked pleased too. Several other girls smiled behind their hands.

Gregory acknowledged their smiles with one of his own. "Do you know why I insist on this procedure?" he asked. "Because you are ladies and I am a gentleman and we care for each other. Therefore, we do not eat in animalistic bedlam as they do in lesser schools. This is a *dining* room, not a cafeteria."

Gregory was quite pleased with the way they reacted. It was clear to him they enjoyed telling a little bit more about themselves than their names, and he noted that the older girls, who knew each other, chose things to tell he was sure they hadn't told before. Almost everything they said, no matter how mundane, struck him as interesting and caused in him a surge of affection. It always did and it was always a surprise.

He spoke last, of course, being a gentleman. He told them he grew up in England. "No, I didn't go to Oxford. It was what they call a red brick university," he explained. And that he'd spent a summer vacation in New York City in the Seventies, taking an American history course in the daytime at NYU and going to the theater at night—and never went back to England. That part about going to the theater at night in New York City was the new part for the kids who already knew the rest. He didn't tell them why he stayed in America: that he'd fallen in love with an American woman and they got married. Nor did he tell them that they divorced.

He was quite pleased with his performance in his classes this morning—with one regret. "Oh, Loreli! Why are you telling me how you feel? The question is how does *Antigone* feel?" She was terribly hurt. Next time he'd be more careful with the tone of his voice. And this evening during study hours, he'd seek her out and explain objectivity, how first we must discern, precisely, what is actually in the text. Once we assimilate that, *then* we can discern how we feel as a result. One of these days, he would design a course in which it was against the rules to use the first-person pronoun in class or in papers.

Now that the school year had actually started, he felt even more optimistic about the school's prospects under its new young dynamic leader. Rachel Bickham was exactly the right person for exactly this moment. Nevertheless, he was feeling an itch. He despised tired metaphors, but that was the only way he could describe a new and persistent desire for more weight to carry. He wanted levers to pull to make things happen beyond the harangues he delivered in faculty meetings. Last year, Fred Kindler had helped him to understand that he'd been infantilized—such an ugly word—by Marjorie Boyd, who had made all the decisions. Fred had insisted that Gregory make the decisions in his own sphere, including the campus newspaper. If Gregory thought a story on the sexual activity of Miss Oliver's girls inappropriate, then inappropriate it was. Gregory was grateful for this. But beyond his teaching, and his co-parenting with a female teacher of a dormitory, his sphere included only advising the school newspaper and the literary magazine. It was hardly a sphere. More like a dot. He wanted to lead, but the leadership area for which he was most qualified would go to Francis Plummer for obvious political reasons—the dean of academics. So Gregory thought to satisfy his itch, he might have to find another school where there was room for him to grow. Just to think such a thought made him sad. He loved Miss Oliver's School for Girls and he wanted to work for Rachel Bickham.

EIGHT

If anyone had asked Rachel if she still thought she had all the right instincts for her job at this point or whether she was in over her head, she would have wondered why the question had even come up. Gaylord Frothingham had assured her that she was in good shape and that he'd taken care of everything. And even if she'd known about Francis Plummer's experience yesterday, she would assume that his loss of mojo was an aberration. Yes, she was disappointed in herself for hanging up on her husband without getting the details of the terrible thing that happened in his Chicago office, but she trusted him to understand how disappointed she was. She hadn't predicted that the job would be easy, only that she was the right person to get it done.

She would have felt less self-assured, though, if she had known who was waiting in her office as she as she hurried back from teaching the one course she had retained since being made head of the school. But she had no idea. The day was sunny, the sky an ethereal blue, the grass was green, still wet from dew, and she was pulsing with energy. She went through the front door of the Administration Building and down the hall toward Margaret's anteroom. She and Margaret would plan the day, including setting an appointment with Francis Plummer for that afternoon.

But Margaret wasn't at her desk. She was standing in front of the closed door to Rachel's office. Her face was flushed, her hands clenched up by her shoulders, and her normally pleasant voice a whole octave higher. "I could kill the bastard!"

"Margaret!"

"Amy Michaels's father is in your office. At least that's who he says he is. I told him please wait until you get back, but he paid no attention and barged right past."

"Wait a sec, you say Amy's father? Mitch Michaels? The radio guy?"

"Yes, him. He actually put his hand on my shoulder and pushed me aside."

"But there's a court order that he can't come on campus."

"I know. That's why I called the police."

"The police! That's the last thing we need. They'll drag him away in handcuffs. He's famous. It'll get in the paper and on TV and all over the—"

"Rachel, did you hear what I said? He put his hand on my shoulder. He pushed me aside!"

Years later, Rachel would still be amazed that Margaret had had to tell her twice. She was silent for a moment, visualizing a man shoving her friend out of his way. And then she said, "All right, Margaret, Call the *Hartford Courant.* Tell them something very interesting is about to happen."

"Really?"

"Yes, really."

Margaret gave Rachel a look of joyous exaltation. Yes, they were sisters, Margaret and Rachel, partners. "I'll go away for a few minutes to give the police and the reporter time to get here," Rachel said, as Margaret gleefully reached for her phone. "Then I'll come back."

Maybe if Mitch Michaels, sitting on the sofa, waiting for Rachel to show up, had known who painted the picture of the tree that hung above his head, he would have felt differently about Claire Nelson. Maybe he would have felt the same as he did feel, only more so. But he assumed the picture—which had drawn him to itself, right past the businesslike chairs in the center of the office—had been painted by a professional.

Sitting there waiting, Mitch thought that if he were the boss of the Department of Education, he'd give every kid who liked to do art a test. The kids in the top one percent would all be sent to art school. They'd become professionals. Like the artist who painted that tree. Not a dime would be wasted on anyone else. You just try telling him why taxpayers should pay for someone's hobby and see how far you get! But he was just being hypothetical: if Mitch Michaels were the boss of the Department of Education, the first thing he'd do was close it down.

There was nothing hypothetical about the regret he was feeling, though, for pushing that lady. Lost his cool. He was really sorry. He'd parked his car in the wrong parking lot. What, he's supposed to be a mind reader? Where were the goddamn signs? "How do I get to the principal's office?" he'd asked three kids walking side by side, arms linked. *Do they all do that?* he wondered. *Walk around clinging to each other, like fleas on a dog? Does Amy?*

They pointed the way. "*Head of school*, not *principal*," one of them corrected.

What, *principal* wasn't good enough for a private school? The very idea that he wasn't allowed on here, that he was breaking the law, couldn't visit with his own daughter—and then the secretary standing in front of the office door. Like a butler telling him to go around to the back. So he shoved her. Actually put his hands on her and pushed!

Nothing for it but to apologize. He owed her and he would. He would do it right now, before the principal arrived and he delivered his ultimatum. He started thinking up the words, but the door opened before he could think of any, and Rachel Bickham entered.

RACHEL WAS SURPRISED he was so big and so handsome in his blue suit and regimental tie, his blond hair cut short, fifties style. She told herself not to panic, she could deal with his kind, and closed the door behind herself. He didn't stand up. She waited some more, staring at him; he stared right back and didn't move. She said, "Mr. Michaels, you can't just barge in here."

"Really?" His lips made a tight little smile. "It seems I already have."

She turned her back to him and went to her desk and sat down behind it as she would if he were not there, studiously ignoring him, and glanced out through the French doors for the police to arrive. A reporter too, she prayed: *TALK SHOW HOST ARRESTED: TRESPASS AND BATTERY.* She felt his eyes on her. There was a lot of silence.

"Wow, you *are* an angry person, aren't you?" he said.

"It takes one to know one," she said, her face still toward the window.

"You're right. Birds of a feather." His voice was dark and rounded with a hint of rasp, a perfect radio voice. "I understand you have started a new program here."

She turned her face from the door and stared at him.

"I think I'll talk about it on my show."

"Mr. Michaels, it's not a program. It's just one kid."

"Really?"

"Yes, really!"

"Well then, that's what I'll say: you make exceptions for kids like her."

She'd never seen a more victorious smile than the one he shined on her then, as he watched her confusion. She didn't know what to say, so she countered with: "Mr. Michaels, you're breaking the law. I've called the police."

"Oh goody. I'll talk about that too." He stood up and stepped to the French doors and looked out over the campus. "I hope they get here soon." Then he whirled from the doors and leaned down and put his hands on the edge of her desk. He wasn't handsome anymore. Little bubbles of spit hung in the corners of his mouth. "Jesus! You let her in," he said. "A girl who does it with teachers. And in the same dorm with my daughter!"

Rachel pushed her chair back and stood up. She was tall too, and wasn't going to let anyone lean over *her.* "I decide who lives in what dorm, not you," she said, and realized right away she should have stayed in her seat so he could tower over the likes of her while she figured out a plan to cut off his balls and make him regret he'd taken her on. Besides, it wasn't even true. She didn't decide who lived in what dorm. The dorm heads' committee did.

"And I decide what to talk about," he said. There was a knock on the door. Rachel ignored it. She'd guessed what was coming next. "So you can decide," he said. "If you don't want to hear it over the radio, you can kick her out. That's a good deal for you—an easy way out. Her father's in London and there's lots to arrange. So I'll give you a month."

There was another knock. It seemed very timid. "Come on in," Mitch Michaels called as if it were his office.

The door opened. A very small policeman entered. Rachel knew who he was: a neighbor of Margaret's who had just graduated from the police academy. Theoretically, he was twenty-one years old, but he looked about fourteen to her. "Mr. Michaels?" he said.

"That's me."

"Come with me."

Michaels grinned.

"Please."

"Uh uh. My listeners would miss me." Mitch Michaels moved past the little policeman, patting him on the head as he went. "You should join a gym," he said. Then he turned around again and walked away, and the little policeman looked as if was about to cry.

Rachel told Margaret to postpone her appointment with Francis. She had an emergency to resolve.

NINE

Rachel sat very still at her desk, calming herself. Then she telephoned Amy's mother. Other than the police, she should be the first to know that her ex-husband had come on campus.

"I should have known he wasn't going to obey the order," Jenifer Michaels said when Rachel finished describing what had happened. "The only orders he obeys are the ones he gives to himself. Could I bribe you to kill him the next time he shows up on campus? Because he will, you know. How about a million dollars for financial aid if you offer him a friendly cup of coffee with cyanide in it?" And, when Rachel didn't respond, "How did Amy react?"

"He never saw her. She doesn't even know."

"You caught him trying to find her?"

"No, he came straight to the office and I called the police."

"The police? He's in jail!"

"No, he managed to leave just as the officer arrived."

"Really? They only sent one?"

"I'm afraid so. Your husband just ignored him and walked away."

"So predictable! And please don't refer to that man as my husband. He's not. He's the crazy person who is going to cause your school a lot of trouble for not giving in and letting him see Amy. Thanks for that. But why would he come to your office? Did he think you were going to give him permission?"

Rachel hesitated. "No, he didn't."

"He didn't ask? He wanted something else?"

"Yes, but it wasn't about Amy."

"About some other girl then? So you shouldn't tell me. Of course not. But it is about Amy, isn't, it? He thinks he should choose her friends. Wants them all to be innocent as five-year-olds. And what happens instead? Amy comes home with this beautiful nineteen-year-old woman who projects anything but innocence. It didn't take me a whole lot of time after Amy and I had picked up Claire at JFK for me to guess what was going to happen to poor old Mitch. She'd twist him up in knots the minute she arrived in Madison. Yes, that's what happened, I guarantee. Well, I'd come on to him too, if I had what that girl has and he was right there to torment for a whole long weekend. Too hard to resist when the prey's just asking for it. And it happened right in front of Amy. I bet he asked you to move Amy out of Claire's dorm so she wouldn't have so much time to corrupt his daughter. I bet he said that if you put them in different dorms, he wouldn't ever step foot on your campus again. But of course he will. You could put the whole United States Army on guard, and he'd keep coming back to try to see her. What you have to remember about him is he looks sane enough to be running the asylum, but he's the craziest inmate of them all. How else could he think up the things he says on the radio?"

"Mrs. Michaels, I'm not prepared to discuss your ex-husband or Claire Nelson or any other student," Rachel said, trying to sound authoritative. "I called you to inform you that your ex-husband appeared on campus against the court order and that we called the police and they came. And I assure you that we will be on guard and I'll talk with the police about—"

"Yes, yes, yes, I know, but here's what's going to happen no matter what you do. Trust me. I lived with him for almost seventeen years. You will or you will not put Amy in a different dorm, and he will sneak back on campus to see her; he'll never stop. I don't want that for Amy in the first place, and in the second I surely don't want her to be in the school when the cops do catch him and he gets revenge by making up the most horrendous stories you can imagine about your school and about Claire too—especially about her—and telling them on the radio. And even if he doesn't get caught, the idea that he's not allowed, that he has to sneak, will get to him. How would you like to be in a school when your own father is saying terrible things about your friend and your school to a huge audience over the radio? Well, that's not going to happen. Not as long as I'm alive. Amy's had her heart set on going to St. Agnes, that lovely school in England your school exchanges students with. She only postponed it until next year because Claire asked her to. You get my drift?"

Bombarded by this rush of angry words, Rachel didn't answer. The shock of Michaels's ultimatum and her concern for Claire had blinded her to the implications for Amy.

"Do you?" Amy's mother insisted.

Rachel found her voice at last. "Do we really want to give in to him?"

Amy's mother sighed. "I'll talk to Amy," she said. "And please make the arrangements with St. Agnes."

"What is it about vacations that the minute you get back it feels like you never went away?" Gaylord Frothingham asked as soon as he picked up the phone. "It's that business again, isn't it?"

"Yes, it is," Rachel answered, and went on to tell him about the predicament both schools shared. She chose not to complicate the conversation by telling him about Amy.

"Oh, poor Claire!" he said.

Rachel was taken aback. She had thought he'd be more concerned for his school than for Claire. "Why?" she asked. "Do you think he would actually name her?"

There was a silence on the line. She imagined him gazing out the window of his office across West End Avenue to Central Park, in a tweedy sports jacket with leather elbow patches and a bow tie. Then he asked, "Do you listen to his program? I do. I like to know who my enemies are. And it's fascinating, like watching car accidents. He's very smart. It's hard to dismiss all of what he says as just some more ravings of a whacko, though that's what they really are. Even liberals agree with some of the things he says. No, he won't actually name Claire. He'll just leave a lot of clues and everybody will guess. He won't talk about it on just one show. He'll stretch it out. He'll talk about your school and then, on another day, about mine, and then he'll branch out and talk about how elitist and liberal all private schools are—enclaves for the wealthy who can do anything that strikes their fancy no matter how perverse and not be punished. Claire's the perfect representative. He'll find out every salacious event that ever happened at your school, stuff you don't even know about, and broadcast it to the world. He'll go on and on, and every time he does it will also be about Claire. That's what I would do if I were he, with his agenda. It will be horrible for Claire. She'll have to leave. If you need some help in figuring out where she should go, I'd like to help."

"But how do you know that Michaels would keep to his bargain and not talk about her anyway?"

"Oh that's easy. We'll let him know we'll come after him if he doesn't. That's what alumni are for. We have a bunch in the newspaper business. They'll help me find out something he doesn't want anyone to know, and if they can't, we'll make something up. We'll make him wish he were dead, then we'll insult his mother, then we'll burn his house down, okay?"

"That's ridiculous," she said. She'd had enough male posturing this morning. "Impossible."

"Who cares? Just believe it and you'll be fine. It doesn't have to be true," Gaylord Frothingham said. "And remember if you need any help finding a school for Claire, let me know."

"We have an exchange agreement with St. Agnes School in England. We could send her there," Rachel said. The idea was delicious: foil Mitch Michaels by keeping Amy and Claire together, both out of his reach and even closer to each other, sharing the adventure of going to a foreign land. But even as she thought of this, she realized how fervently she wanted to keep Claire in the school.

"There you go! That's a wonderful school, a lot like yours, all girls, boarding, on Lake Windermere. Excellent curriculum. I happen to know the head. He's a marvelous leader, one of the kindest people I know. Plus he's a very fine artist. He'd reach out to Claire. And she'd be miles away. Think about it, okay?"

"Well, how about keeping Claire Nelson right where she is *and* making Mitch Michaels wish he were dead?" Rachel asked.

Frothingham chuckled into the phone. "That would be a lot of fun, wouldn't it?"

"It would be right too!"

"Maybe. For a philosopher. Maybe a poet. But for the school? And your job? Have you any idea how hard it is to keep a job like yours and mine? And what about Claire?" His pause had a definitive air. "Goodbye, Rachel. Let me know when you want me to talk to St. Agnes. I will put in a good word for her."

RACHEL CROSSED THE campus toward the Art Building to tell Eudora, knowing the world couldn't get more beautiful anywhere, anytime, than it was here, on this campus by the side of a river in New England in September. It was a fact for her, not mere opinion. She was surrounded by glory. What an amazement to know this in spite of the bad news she would deliver.

In the anteroom of the Art Building, more glory: three huge chairs, pieces of Kinetic Visionary Furniture designed and built by students to fulfill Eudora's assignment—*to demonstrate a sense of humor while being intensely utilitarian.* They'd been returned at the end of the summer by the Smith College Art Museum where they had been displayed for almost a year: a chair in honor of multitasking, with foot pedals for typing a novel, piano keys for simultaneously making music, a reading lamp so you can also read a book, a bracket that turned the pages, and, looming from above, a shiny cone for sticking your head into to get a permanent wave. Next to it, a Humpty Dumpty chair, disassembled into its many parts, which when you pushed a button was immediately reassembled, and next to that a chair that played "The Star-Spangled Banner" when you sat in it so that you had to stand up for it to stop. Each beautiful in shape, multicolored and shiny. A work of art that worked. To think that Claire would be separated from a teacher who could unleash such marvels!

In Eudora's kingdom, it smelled of turpentine, paint, wet clay—and silence. A dozen girls, one of whom was Claire, each at an easel, were sketching a classmate who stood on a raised dais before them. She was tall, thin, gawky, only a little self-conscious, leaning glibly on a cane, trying to look debonair in a man's tuxedo. Eudora, in a flowing yellow smock and big golden earrings, glided among her artists looking at their work, whispering, patting shoulders, sometimes nodding her head. There was nothing casual in this scene. It was dignified and formal. Learning how to see. That's a serious business. No one noticed Rachel enter. She stood in the back until the bell rang and the girls reluctantly put their easels away.

In Eudora's office, Rachel delivered the news and explained her reasons why it was imperative to send Claire and Amy away. She told Eudora that Amy's mom was going to talk to Amy about going to St. Agnes School in England on an exchange with a St. Agnes student, and that she, Rachel, would call the head of St. Agnes right away to make the arrangements.

"Wait a sec," Eudora said. "Hold on. You're not thinking straight. You're playing right into his hands, doing exactly what he wants you to do. Don't you see? Are you really that innocent? He doesn't have the slightest intention of attacking the school while Amy's a part of it. Would you do that to your daughter? Of course not. He knows that you would keep Claire here as a matter of principle. He doesn't expect us even to consider giving in to him. All he wants is Amy out of here. Away from Claire. So he makes his threat and you don't give in, and guess what Amy's mom is going to do? That's right: send Amy to some school a billion miles from here. Because she really does think he'd do that to Amy. She hates him more than we could ever. To us he's just another crazy radio jock, but she's been *married* to the guy. So she takes Amy away from us. And he has exactly what he wants."

"So keep Claire, don't do anything?"

"Right. Amy stays right here and so does Claire, and Michaels keeps his mouth shut. It's just an idle threat. You need to call Amy's mom and persuade her to change her mind."

Rachel shook her head. "I'm not going to take that chance. Besides, it's not a new idea for Amy. She'd already planned to go to St. Agnes this year. She put it off only to be with Claire."

Eudora thought for a moment. "Well, all right then. That's fine. It works both ways: we keep them both, he won't say a word because he doesn't want to hurt Amy, and if we send Amy away, that's all he wants. He'll be satisfied. We can keep Claire here and he won't say a word in that case either."

"Hmm," Rachel murmured, feeling a wisp of hope. Maybe Eudora was right. Amy was the ace in the hole. *Stay here and listen to Eudora some more*, she thought. *And I'll be convinced she's right.*

"How can you let her go?" Eudora said. "You especially. You care for her as much as I do."

Rachel's heart sunk. *You shouldn't have said that*, she wanted to say, but didn't. *Because that's why we would keep Claire—instead of sending her away like we should.* She shook her head.

Eudora looked away. It was clear how much she had at stake.

"I'm so sorry," Rachel said.

But on the way back to her office, replaying her conversation with Eudora, Rachel suddenly stopped walking and stood perfectly still in the glorious September light. "He knows that you would keep Claire here as a matter of principle," Eudora had said, looking right into her eyes. *Principle!* Why hadn't she heard that word when Eudora had actually uttered it? Even Mitch Michaels expected her to be too principled to accept his blackmail.

Rachel remembered sitting beside her father on the living room sofa years ago when she was still a girl, witnessing *60 Minutes* air an interview of the headmaster of a famous boarding school where some seniors were running a cocaine-importing enterprise. The reporter asked about a certain senior, naming him to the nation, and Rachel's father groaned and leaned forward as if doing so would comfort the headmaster. Having done his sleuthing, the reporter knew the boy was involved and he knew that the headmaster didn't. The headmaster replied, "Oh, he wouldn't do that; he's a senior prefect. I've known him for four years. He's a wonderful kid!" Then the interviewer, celebrated reporter, respected by all, had said, "But he *is* involved. You didn't know?" and laid out all the details of the boy's confession to him to prove the boy had been involved as a ringleader. If *60 Minutes* would go to this length to set up a decent man, humiliating him for the drama of it on a Sunday night, what lengths would a right-wing whacko inspired by resentment go to get his revenge on the school? Yes, Gaylord Frothingham was correct: the prudent step was to protect Claire and the school by sending her away.

Rachel started walking again. Being prudent, correct, protective, sending Claire away?

Not if she could help it.

Rachel hurried back to her office and called Milton Perkins again—this time not just to keep him abreast. The threat now being real, it had ascended to the board's domain.

Rachel told Milton about Michaels's barging in, the fact that he was violating a court order, Michaels's ultimatum, and what Gaylord Frothingham had said. She informed him too that Michaels's daughter attended the school and that her mother and she were planning to send her on an exchange to England, which she was going to do this year, or next, anyway. The only thing she left out was Claire's identity.

He let Rachel say it all without asking any questions, and then it seemed forever that he didn't speak. That long silence was a scary time for Rachel. If Milton Perkins was bowled over by this news, then things were really dark. "Milton?" she said.

"Yeah, I'm here. I was just asking myself, suppose the kid wants to finish that PG program? Why should she be pushed around? It will be her decision, won't it, Rachel? Not yours, certainly, not the school's, not even her father's, and sure as hell not Mitch Michaels's. She'll decide and then we'll stand behind her, right?"

"Oh of course!" she said—after a pause to cover her surprise. "I just assumed she'll want to leave."

"You never know," he said.

"That's right. You never do."

"Soon as you talk to her—and her dad—I'll call an executive committee meeting. I'd come to it with a plan if I were you."

"You bet I will!" Rachel said. She hadn't allowed herself to hope Claire would want to stay. Now she could.

"Good," Milton Perkins said. "And maybe you could mix in a good reason for starting a post-graduate program all by yourself."

"BUT OF COURSE that girl will have to leave," Patricia Burden, the school counsel, said over the phone. Her tone of voice suggested that a nice lady like Rachel, tucked away in an ivory tower, shouldn't get in a fight with the likes of Mitch Michaels. It was in Claire's and Miss Oliver's mutual interest to protect the reputation of both, not even to mention that of Central Park Academy, and Patricia was sure Michaels would keep quiet if Claire were expelled. "He understands the school would truthfully point out that the facts were not known when she was admitted and that as soon as they were, the separation was made. Besides," she added, "Claire was eighteen. No law has been broken."

Rachel was tempted to point out that those two arguments tended to cancel each other out, thus to show she was smarter than any lawyer could ever be, but she didn't want to talk to this woman anymore so she cut the conversation off. She had expected that the lawyer's first instinct would be to assemble weapons, not capitulate. Wasn't that what lawyers were for?

"THREE HUNDRED DOLLARS an hour for that?" Milton Perkins exclaimed when Rachel reported to him. She expected him to instruct her to pay only half the bill. She had heard the stories of his claiming he never paid lawyers more than half of the invoice.

Instead, he started talking about doctors, not lawyers. The abrupt switch caused her to wonder if old age was beginning to make its claim on his attention span, until he said, "I go to doctors so they can tell me what I have to do to be able to keep on doing what I feel like doing."

"Oh, I get your drift," Rachel said. "I'll look through our alumnae roster."

"Yup. There are some damn good lawyers on it."

"You know something?" Rachel said. "We should change the by-laws. Then you could be the chair forever."

There was a silence on the line. Then he said, "Nobody lives forever," and hung up before she could think of what to say. Coming from him, an elderly person, it struck her as an ominous remark. But she was too excited by the idea that she might be able to keep Claire in the school to let the thought linger. She dialed Margaret and asked her to get Claire's father on the line.

RACHEL REACHED CLAIRE'S father at his London bank, her fifth phone call in a row. While she waited for his secretary on the other side of an ocean to find him and bring him to the phone, she began to feel as if her body were melting. Amy's mother, Claire's father,

Patricia Burden, Gaylord Frothingham, even Milton Perkins were part of the ether and all she really needed to be the head of a school was her voice. It was an interesting sensation and she shut her eyes to intensify it by rendering the world invisible and kept them shut even after Claire's father came on the line. Then she heard her own voice telling him it was imperative that he come to the school ASAP because she and he and Claire needed to talk.

"What's she done this time?" he asked.

"It's what you both have done," Rachel said. "Or, more accurately, what you didn't."

He didn't speak for a moment. Rachel waited, enjoying his discomfort. Then he said, "I'll be there as soon as I can."

TEN

Rachel had just put the phone down when Margaret said, "Stuff is piling up. You need to pay attention."

"Stuff?"

"Yes. Like letters you need to answer. You don't want to let that radio Nazi disrupt—"

"All right, all right, I'll dictate."

They began:

Dear Mr. Hall,

We are honored that one of America's most beloved poets will read his poetry to our school, and are enormously grateful for your offer to spend the day with our student poets.

Dear Ms. Forbish,

Though we were disappointed that Miss Oliver's School for Girls was not chosen by the foundation for the grant, please rest assured that we will reapply next cycle.

Rachel dictated several more letters. "The one to the poet was fun, Margaret," she said, "but jeez, these other ones. Can't we get a robot for this?"

Margaret laughed. Behind her, Claire's picture loomed. "Bear down, dear. There are only a few more."

"Oh, you write them!" Rachel said, jumping to her feet. "I'll sign them later."

"Where're you going? Come back."

"To talk with Francis. I need his advice."

Rachel went out through the French doors and hurried across the campus. Responding to Michaels's attack had taken up the whole day;

she hadn't gotten around to appointing Francis to the new position she'd created for him, and now Milton Perkins wanted a plan about Michaels—something she wasn't about to make up all by herself. So she'd do both at this same meeting: first get Francis's advice on what to do about Michaels—how to cut off his balls and make him wish he were dead—and *then* make Francis dean of academics.

She crossed the campus at an even faster pace than her usual almost-trot. She'd been in awe of Francis since her very first days at Miss O's, when students would come to her classes still talking about what had happened in his. There were several evenings near the end of the first semester that year when the students at the dinner table over which she presided spent the whole meal arguing about whether Shakespeare was aware that he was mocking his audience for their anti-Semitism and ignorance when he wrote *The Merchant of Venice*, or whether instead he was so talented he couldn't help turning formulaic comedy on its head. Rachel had decided right then to ask Francis if she could audit the second semester of his Senior Honors Shakespeare class. He had welcomed her on the condition that she write all the papers and take the tests. In spite of her already heavy workload, which, in the second semester, included coaching varsity basketball, she agreed. She was as proud of the A she earned in that course as she was of the distinctions she'd earned in graduate school.

One morning early in the second semester that year, when Senior Honors Shakespeare was focused on *Macbeth*, Rachel had stayed in the physics lab after a class to help a student and was late. As she came through the door of Francis's classroom, he said, "Here's Rachel." He smiled at her. Then he turned to the girls sitting around the table. "Should we try it on her?" There was a chorus of yeses, and then he said, "All right, director, take it away," and before Rachel could sit down, one of the students, Linda Chaggi, tall with long black hair, stood up and took her hand and led her to the front of the room. "You're Macbeth, and you've just killed Duncan," she said. "Do you remember where you are?"

"Of course I do. The top of the stairs."

"Yes," Linda said. "Descending."

"And Lady Macbeth's at the bottom," Rachel said.

Linda nodded. "What do you need to do right now?"

Why ask her that? It was obvious. "Play it out," she said. "Read the lines."

Linda shook her head, then turned to Francis who was sitting in her chair now. "Should I tell her?"

"Give her a minute," Francis said.

But after a minute, Rachel was still mystified, on the verge of irritation. She glanced at Francis. He was obviously satisfied. The girls watched closely. It was clear they'd been through the same scenario just minutes before, with some other girl being Macbeth.

Linda broke the silence. "Why do you think it is offstage?"

"What? The murder?"

"Of course, the murder!"

"Because it's better to imagine it."

"Well?" Linda said.

"Take your time, Rachel," Francis said. "Call it up again," he said to the girls. "Get in even deeper, while Rachel does." Then he gestured to Rachel to sit down in his chair by his desk at the front of the room, and in silence for two or three minutes, everyone in that room visualized killing her king, her friend, her guest, stabbing him with a knife while he slept, and then Linda asked, "Ready?" and Rachel said she was. She climbed up on Francis's desk and no one laughed. Linda sat down on the floor, casting her eyes up at Rachel, and said, "My Husband!" And then two girls, one being Macbeth, the other Lady Macbeth, read the lines and everyone saw Macbeth descending, though Rachel didn't move, until Lady Macbeth accused him of being *infirm of purpose* and grabbed the daggers.

Francis asked, "Does anyone want to ask Rachel a question?"

Tina Carr's hand shot up, her bracelet jingling. "What line do you remember most?"

"*I couldn't say amen*," Rachel said.

"And what did you want right then?"

"Want?"

Tina looked surprised.

"Oh!" Rachel said. "For it to be five minutes ago. Maybe even only three."

"Yes, before you killed him," Tina said.

"More than anything in the world," Rachel said.

"Me too," Linda Chaggi said from what to everyone was still the bottom of the stairs. "I was him too." Her voice was full of wonder. "That's what I wanted too. For time to go backwards."

Then the part of Rachel that was just beginning not to be a man who'd just killed his guest, the king, glanced across the room at Francis. He raised his eyebrows at her, one artist to another, and nodded his head.

Ever so slightly.

EVERY ONCE IN a while Francis would catch himself feeling magnanimous to Rachel, as if, when he'd been offered the interim headship, he'd stepped aside to give youth a chance. Then he'd remind himself of the real reasons he'd turned down the position, and how surprised he'd been when Rachel refused the interim position and became the permanent head.

But it didn't surprise him when he looked up from correcting papers and saw Rachel standing in the doorway of his classroom, that she'd come to him, rather than asking him to come to her office. She was the one who needed help.

"May I come in?" she said.

"Of course." He stood up, feeling a surge of affection for her even stronger than he'd had all along—and sympathy for her youthfulness. She'd grow into her job. She was a good person—the most fundamental requirement—and smart enough to come to him, at last, to ask him to take a whole world of responsibility off her hands. It was a surprise, though, to discover he was glad for the respite from correcting papers her visit offered. He loved witnessing his students assembling their thoughts on paper, assessing their progress, and knowing exactly how to help. He'd think about this later. Right now he was too excited by the offer he was about to get.

"I love this classroom," Rachel said, sweeping her gaze as she took a seat. "The atmosphere in here makes me want to read and read and read."

He looked around the room to see what she was seeing. Nothing in the world would ever bring him to change the tables in the center of the room, arranged so they formed a three-sided square, the open side facing the front where his chair was—though he never sat down while he was teaching—any more than he would ever get rid of the Globe Theater in the back, or the framed statement above the blackboard in the front, right in the middle of the wall: *PLUMMER'S FIRST RULE OF RHETORIC: Condense, condense, condense, then condense some more, then divide the number of words by two*—but everything else he changed every week. Where last week a World War I gasmask was pinned to the wall above an enlarged printing of Wilfred Owen's "Dulce et Decorum Est," there was now a painting of a red wheelbarrow beside three white chickens strutting importantly across the foreground; in the background a red barn roof glistened in the rain. On the barn's side, like a 1930s chewing tobacco advertisement, was William Carlos William's poem:

so much depends
upon

a red wheel
barrow

glazed with rain
water

beside the white
chickens.

"Claire's?" Rachel asked, gesturing to the painting.

"Yup," Francis said.

"I thought so," Rachel said.

He watched Rachel's face as she gazed at the painting—a long time, he thought, for someone eager to get on with her business. He wondered if she were as struck as he was by the idea that a mute and stoic side of an old, weathered barn was the voice to announce an outrageous truth, and that a being so brainless as a chicken would be the first to understand. When Claire handed the painting to him, what he'd felt was more akin to grief than to mere nostalgia for an era that she and he were both too young to have experienced. The painting captured one instant, one tick of the clock. The chickens were mid-strut, about to take another. He was sure the slant of the sun's light was about to change.

"There's no explaining talent," he said, and Rachel turned her eyes from the painting to his, reluctantly he thought. "I assigned an essay about the poem, but she painted the picture instead."

"It's amazing. That someone so young could be so—"

"Wise?" he said.

Rachel shrugged. "Yes," she said, glancing at the painting again. "But not about herself."

"How could she be?" Francis said. "She hasn't had examples."

Rachel didn't answer. He wondered what she was thinking. Then she said, "Well then, shouldn't she have to write the essay too?"

Francis stared at Rachel. "Obviously," he said. "Before I even looked at the picture, I told her she owed me the paper by the next day."

A flush of embarrassment showed on Rachel's cheeks. "Of course."

Now she seemed to be gathering herself. *Here it comes*, he thought, leaning forward in expectation, his one-word answer at the ready: *Yes.* Then she said, "Well, Claire's who I want to talk to you about."

"Oh, I thought—"

"What?"

"Nothing," he murmured, leaning back in his chair. Did she expect him to *ask* for the job?

Rachel hesitated. Then she took a big breath and told him about her meeting with Clair and what she had confessed. He listened, wondering why in the world she was telling him this private stuff, and experiencing the same disbelief he always felt at such events, especially when the reports of them seemed true. If he taught another thousand years, he never would get used to them. The pain of this case was as sharp as it could ever get. He and Peggy were Claire's dorm parents. *Parents.* They'd protect her. This story would never be told to anyone else. Not ever. "Why are you telling me this? It's confidential." he said when Rachel had finished "And anyway, good for Claire for getting it off her chest."

Then Rachel told him why and he said, "Oh no!"—three

times—while she described Mitch Michaels and told what he had said to her and how he patted the little boy policeman on his head, and when she'd finished, he said, "That's terrible. Of course Claire will have to leave."

"What?"

"We've got to get her out of here."

"Francis! That's not the answer I expected from you."

He flushed. "It's the one I believe in."

"You want to go down on your knees to this guy?"

Francis looked away. "I wish you wouldn't put it that way."

"What other way is there to put it? Suppose Claire wants to stay? *Then* would you give me some ideas for keeping her?"

Francis looked back at Rachel. "In that case, I'd think of *something*," he said sarcastically. A hurt look flashed on her face. "Sorry," he said, "but if your mind is already made up, you shouldn't ask for my advice."

He watched her think about that. Then she nodded her head, and the hurt look disappeared, and in a flat, declarative tone he'd never heard her use before, she said, "You're right: if my mind's made up, I shouldn't ask."

"I'll consider it some more," he said. "But it just seems to me that it would be so much easier for Claire..." He let the sentence drift off because he could tell she wasn't listening. He thought she was figuring how to change the subject, how to segue. He leaned forward again to show her he was ready. But she ignored the gesture. He sat back in his chair, and she stood up and turned to leave. So she really had come to him to get advice about Claire. But why wouldn't she appoint him, and *then* ask?

"Yes, please do think about it some more," she murmured as she went out the door.

He couldn't read the tone of her voice, whether she was making a gentle request or a condescending prediction that with a little more thought he'd defer to her superior wisdom. With a rush of sadness, he recognized what he had given up when turning down the head of school position: *control.* It had never occurred to him that he and Rachel might disagree, that given the authority they would make different decisions. He'd been offered the helm to steer in the wise direction, but he'd stepped aside, and a person young enough to be his daughter had grabbed the wheel and yanked it hard into a frivolous and dangerous course.

He picked up the composition he'd been reading but he couldn't find where he'd left off, so he had to start all over again at the top, and soon he was irritated at the student for making the same point twice. Another surprise. "You're supposed to make mistakes," he told them. Over and over. "That's how you learn." With his red pen, he wrote in the in the margin, *Ask me about this in class and I'll show you some ways to make this point so clear you only have to write it once,* but he was irritated nevertheless. *I'm not getting stale*, he told himself. *I just need to get more sleep.*

He fought his way through the rest of the papers, and then his thoughts turned to Claire again. Surely Rachel would change her mind. It would break Eudora's heart to lose Claire's talent to another school, but if that's what it took to keep her safe, what choice did anybody have? Rachel would figure this out. Give her a little time, she's still very young. He'd help her find a school for Claire—maybe in London with her father. Then he'd take over the academic program for Rachel so she could get on with her job.

With this thought, he felt a little better.

Until he began to think about why he had refused the board's offer, and more than he ever had before, he wished he could have last year over again so he could behave in such a way as to have been worthy of the offer. Fred Kindler would still be the head, Rachel would still be chair of Science and director of Athletics, and he, Francis Plummer the dean of academics, at Fred Kindler's right hand. It was a bitter revelation. He sat in his classroom, stunned in its grip.

WALKING, MUCH MORE slowly, back to her office, Rachel was so preoccupied by what had just happened that it wasn't until she'd passed a group of girls on the path that she realized she'd said only hello to them. They'd looked surprised. She *always* stopped and chatted. There was *always* something to say to each other more than just hello.

She thought of what had just happened with Francis as happening *to* her, instead of *because* of her. It wasn't her fault that she couldn't appoint Francis dean of academics that morning right after the first faculty meeting because he'd left the campus to go to the Cape with Peggy. And it didn't really feel like her fault when she was so blindsided just now by his caution that she put off appointing him a second time. She had expected heroics, not caution. She wanted the school, with her in command and Francis at her right hand, to bury Michaels in an avalanche of righteousness, not kneel to him.

"Here they are," Margaret said a few minutes later. She put the letters down on Rachel's desk. "You said to write them."

"Already?"

Margaret smiled. "I'm much faster than any robot."

Rachel returned the smile. Margaret could always make her feel calm. She was the only person other than Milton Perkins, and now Francis, she'd told about Michaels's ultimatum. "Francis thinks Claire should leave," she said.

"He does?"

"Are you surprised?"

"A little, I suppose," Margaret said, her expression noncommittal.

"Only a little?"

Margaret shrugged.

"Well, he's wrong, don't you think?"

"I don't think he's wrong. But you aren't either. Besides, I know how much you'd miss Claire."

"That has nothing to do with it," Rachel said, a little too emphatically.

"Really?" Margaret shrugged again. "But anyway, you shouldn't be asking me. I'm your secretary, not your second in command."

"I was about to make him that, just now," Rachel said. It was a relief to talk about it.

"You didn't?"

Rachel shook her head.

"Well, you better soon. You're going to get buried if you don't," Margaret said, heading for the door. "Nobody can do your job alone."

THE NEXT MORNING, Mitch Michaels had to use the standing microphone in his dark, cluttered studio because his back hurt so much he couldn't sit. To take his mind off the pain, he imagined a traffic jam spread across all six lanes, brown smog rising from thousands of cars, and pressed his two hands against the small of his back for support, while he told the captive drivers what they needed to know: "Once a nation commits itself to freedom and liberty as we did in 1776, it commits itself to Darwinism," he rasped into the microphone. It smelled of his own breath: toothpaste and coffee and the sweet grease of doughnuts. "Yes, Darwinism, yes, evolution. Believe me, they're not swear words. That old naturalist was right: to the talented, to the hard working, go the rewards. Yes, I'm a Darwinist. And you are too, all of you, heading for work. I repeat, *work!* Not that other word that begins with W."

Dad, you're not allowed on campus. You could have been arrested!

"You wouldn't want it any other way. You just have to face the facts."

No, Rachel didn't tell me, it was Mom.

"The only way you can prop up the people . . ."

Next time you sneak on campus to see me, you're going to get a big surprise, Dad.

". . . who don't have what it takes to prop up themselves is to restrict the freedom of the rest of us. You want cream to rise to the top, you don't shake the bottle, homogenize the product."

Can't even visit my own daughter!

"Of course I'm right! Back at you right after this message."

"You all right, Mitch?" the studio manager asked. "You want me to crank the air conditioning up?"

"I'm fine, Charlie, thanks. I'd be sweating if I was sitting bare ass on an iceberg."

"Yeah?"

"Yup. Shoulda been an Eskimo."

"Or a polar bear."

"Better than being a Democrat, Charlie."

"Up yours, Mitch."

"Sorry. Where do you think I ought to go next?"

"Affirmative action, maybe, Mitch?"

"Okay, good. Affirmative action."

It was easy for Mitch Michaels to continue his attack on

affirmative action while the time he'd allotted Rachel to help Claire find another school ticked down. It would not have occurred to him to break his word, and he was well aware of the power of repetition. Even some liberals agreed that affirmative action was racist and made a mockery of justice.

Paul Nelson, Claire's father, finally arrived Monday. Because their paths never crossed during the previous year's admissions interview, Rachel had imagined a pudgy, soft body and jowly cheeks, her default picture of bankers—except, as her husband reminded her, the ones she actually knew. But he turned out to be as striking a presence as his daughter. The man in her office doorway was at least six-foot-four, lean, surely a long-distance runner or a tournament-level tennis player, maybe even a big-wave surfer. She had insisted that they meet alone before they both met with Claire, and now he was going to shine his good looks on her and charm her into forgiving him. It hadn't occurred to her yet to ask herself why she had come close to forgiving Gaylord Frothingham for the same offense and was still angry at this man looking her straight in the eye, shaking her hand, and telling her how grateful he was for "all that the school had done for my daughter."

She murmured something about "just doing our job" and gestured to the circle of chairs. He took a few steps into the office and then he noticed the picture of the copper beech above the sofa.

"That's Claire's," she said.

"Claire's? Oh my God!"

"You didn't know how talented she is?"

"Of course I did. She shows me her stuff. I'm her *father*. But it's still a shock when I first see one of her pictures. No one in our family ever showed a talent for art."

"Oh, I'm sure they had talent. They just went to the wrong schools."

"Maybe so," he said, sounding unconvinced. "She showed me the one of the two people on a beach that got her started. This one's just as good."

"Two people? She didn't tell you? It's of Claire and her mother."

"Her mother?"

"I'm sorry. I'm sure she plans to tell you sometime."

"How interesting! Do you think she thought it was her mother when she was painting it?"

"Why? You think she made it up when she showed it to her teacher?"

"Why not? It gives the picture a little extra something. She's getting graded on it, isn't she?"

"Well, *I* don't think she made it up. And neither does her art teacher."

He shrugged. "Hard to tell. It always is with Claire."

They shared one of those little moments where everyone would rather not look at each other. Then Rachel said, "I'm sure you know why we need to talk."

He winced. "Yes, Claire called me."

"She told you she told me?"

He nodded.

"She was afraid somebody might find out." Rachel said.

"Really?"

"That's what she said."

"Well, what did you tell her?"

"I assured her no one would."

"Well?"

"I was wrong. Someone has."

"Someone has?"

"Yes, someone has."

"Who? One of the students?"

"No. Not one of the students, Mr. Nelson."

"Well, then, one of the teachers?"

"No. Not one of the teachers either."

"Well, who?"

"Mitch Michaels."

"Who?"

"Mitch Michaels."

He went pale. "That guy? The radio jock?"

"That's the one. He has a daughter here. He barged into my office the other day and told me that if I didn't expel Claire, he'd go on the air and tell the world about Claire and that teacher."

"No! You're kidding me."

"Wish I were."

"Oh damn!" Paul Nelson bent over and grabbed his head with both hands. "Jesus, Claire," he murmured, as if she were in the room, "why did you have to go and do that?" Rachel was tempted to answer, *Because she could*, but she managed to keep her mouth shut. Then he let go of his head and looked up at her. "Are you sure?"

"He was right here in this office with me, and he was talking in English," she said. "And, what's more, I would have preferred to have heard about the incident from you than from him."

Paul Nelson looked at Rachel as if he'd suddenly realized she was from some other planet. "The *incident*? Is that what you call it? And I should have told you about it?"

She didn't answer. She was beginning to hear how self-righteous she was sounding.

"And what did you tell him?" he asked.

"That I decided who attended our school, not him."

"You? What about Claire? Do you actually think she'd want to stay?"

"You never know."

"Are you kidding? And the reason you wanted to meet with me without Claire in the room was to chew me out for not babbling her secret to your admissions person? You thought it would make my daughter ashamed of me? Well, let me tell you something. I thought your admissions person was very astute. She asked the questions she needed to ask and didn't pry beyond them. I appreciated that. I thought this was the kind of school that would take care of my daughter. If I thought an apology to you was called for, I'd make it in front of Claire, not you alone."

"Well, let's ask her in then," Rachel said.

Claire marched into the office with her eyes straight on Rachel and a determined look on her face and said, "I know this is about what happened between Mr. Alford and me. But we don't need to talk about it. I already know we should have told." She didn't even look at her father.

"Hold on, Claire!" Rachel said. "Is that what you called him? *Mr. Alford?*"

"Claire, that's awful!" her father said.

Claire still kept her eyes on Rachel. "Why not? That's what they call teachers there, like the opposite of why we call you Rachel here," she said, her voice going soft with approval. Rachel shook her head and frowned. Claire seemed surprised. "Oh all right, his name was Tom," she said in an exasperated tone, and Rachel had to stifle a laugh.

But then Claire started to cry. "He has a wife," she said. "He'll never teach again." And suddenly Rachel could see the young teacher as if he were right there in the office with her, a boy-man, as ashamed to have committed his profession's most heinous and banal act as he was stunned to have been the one chosen for it. She wanted to ask him, *Didn't you see this coming?*

"It was my fault, not his," Claire said between sobs. "He cried each time when we were done."

"Claire! Each time!" her father said.

She turned to her father as if she'd just noticed him, and stopped crying as suddenly as she had started. "I never said it was once. Why should he be sent away if he only did it once and then made himself stop? We never would have been caught if we only did it once. We had agreed to stop, to forget anything had ever happened, and I really was just going to tell him to have a nice weekend but—"

Rachel put her hand up. "That's enough, Claire," she said. "We don't need the details." Then she turned to Claire's father. "Do you want to tell her, or should I?" Claire was watching him closely.

"You're the headmistress," Claire's father said, then looked out through the French doors, and Claire and Rachel exchanged glances. *Oh my, with a father like this one, you really do need a boarding school.* Then Rachel told Claire about Mitch Michaels's barging in and the threat he'd made.

Claire was stunned. "Amy's father?" she asked.

"Yes, Amy's father."

Claire shook her head. "Amy wouldn't tell."

"You shouldn't blame her, Claire, if she did."

"I'm not going to say it again. Maybe I talked too loud and the window was open and her father was awake. And I know the girl who I told last year would keep her mouth shut too. Besides, she's graduated and she and Amy's father don't even know each other. Maybe somebody at the school besides old Mr. Frothingham saw us."

"How he found out isn't the point," Claire's father said.

"Yes it is!" Claire said. "Amy would never tell on me."

"Oh honey, never mind." Paul Nelson said. "Ms. Bickham here will help us find a school in London. She'll say you've decided you want to be with your dad."

"You really think that's what I should say?" Rachel said. Paul Nelson went red in the face and gave her a look that said she was the most sanctimonious person in the world. *So what if I am?* Rachel thought. She and the school would do a whole lot better job of parenting Claire than her father would. She'd ask herself later why she had to go through all this process to understand that. She turned to Claire. "Well, Claire, what is it going to be: London with your father, or here with us?"

"She has no choice," her father said. "She doesn't want her name screamed over the whole world."

"Why not?" Rachel said. "Then she'll be the victim." She watched Claire and her father pretend that was a new idea to them. "I can take care of this school, and Mr. Frothingham can take care of his, and Mr. Tom Alford will just have to take care of himself." Claire didn't speak and so Rachel added, "He's the perp and you're the victim. You don't owe him a thing."

Claire frowned. "Are you going to say that?"

"I'm not going to open my mouth. I won't have to. It's what people will think."

"But, Claire, you don't want—" Claire's father started.

"Claire?" Rachel said.

"I'll stay," Claire said. Then she paused and nodded her head, and said, "Yes, that's what I'll do. I'll stay."

"Claire!" Her father jumped from his chair.

Claire sat perfectly still, looking up at her father's eyes. It would have been obvious to anyone watching the two of them which was the stronger personality. "Dad, I said I'll stay."

Rachel watched Paul Nelson's face. She wondered how anyone so incapable of hiding his feelings could get anything done in the world and wished Claire were not there to witness him surrendering. She wanted him to want to keep Claire with him almost as ardently as she wanted to keep Claire in the school, but instead he sat down. "All right. I do have to travel a lot, and you'd be alone."

"Good, that's settled then." Rachel said. She glanced at Claire and then at the door, signaling to her: *Get him out of here before he changes his mind.*

Claire stood up slowly though, and Rachel realized she was giving her dad a chance to change his mind. He lingered in his chair just long enough to seem to be reconsidering; then he stood, maybe reluctantly. "Thank you." He put out his hand to shake Rachel's. "She'll be better off here with you."

Rachel stood and shook his hand. He was admitting the truth and apologizing for it in just one short, embarrassed sentence. "We'll take good care of her," she said. He raised his eyebrows at her, as if to say *I hope so*, then let go of her hand and crossed the office toward the door. Claire followed, glancing back at Rachel with a look that Rachel couldn't for the world decipher.

Rachel sat back down at her desk. Now she was flooded with anxiety. Milton Perkins had told her to come up with a plan for dealing with Mitch Michaels if Claire wanted to stay at the school. The special meeting with the executive committee of the board of trustees that Milton Perkins had called was scheduled for ten o'clock tomorrow morning. She could tell the members the reason for keeping Claire and taking the public beating from Mitch Michaels was that it was the right thing to do, but that was hardly a plan.

Between now and then she better think one up.

ELEVEN

Outside, Paul Nelson said, "At least come to lunch with me, Claire."

"Can't, Dad. I have classes." It was only noon. Her next class didn't start for two whole hours.

"Well, walk me to my car then."

Claire lifted her arm, making a show of looking at her watch.

"Oh, Claire, for God's sake! You can be a few minutes late. I'm your father!"

"Father?" she repeated. "Fathers are supposed to win the arguments. I'm just a girl." Claire felt tears coming, the sobs upwelling from way down in her belly. They would shake her deliciously, her resentment and sadness released, justifying her feelings, but then some students came around the corner of a building and she shut the sobs down.

Paul Nelson stared at his daughter. "Just a girl?" He grabbed her elbow, and squeezed hard, hurting her. "If you were, none of this would have happened." He started walking to his car, his big hand clasped around her elbow. She had no choice but to follow. Otherwise, the same kids would see her being dragged. When they got to the car, he opened the passenger door for her and let go her elbow. "Get in," he said.

"A BMW, Dad?" she goaded. "How long did it take you to wangle Hertz out of the one you actually paid for?"

"Get in the car, Claire," he said. "Just get in the damn car!" He pushed her in.

The leather seat felt good, luxuriant. This was exactly what she wanted from him: to be in charge of her. She realized she'd been holding her breath. "You kidnapping me?" she asked, letting it out. She wanted a father who would miss her so much he would *make* her come with him to England.

"No, I'm taking you to lunch."

"Well, I'm not hungry then."

He went around to the other side of the car, got in, and started the engine. "Name a restaurant, Claire."

"McDonalds," she said, hoping he wouldn't tolerate her behavior one more second, that he'd turn on her and chew her out, maybe even slap her in the face, but he stared straight ahead through the windshield and sighed. "The drive-through. I'll watch you eat," she added to goad him some more. He shook his head back and forth, still not looking at her, turned on the ignition, and started to drive.

A half hour passed without either of them speaking before they sat down facing each other in a booth of a seafood restaurant. There was a vague ocean smell, and on the wall next to them a fake porthole with a painting of the ocean and horizon behind it.

The girl who came to their table to take their orders was the same age as Claire, shorter, hair dyed blond, and a little pudgy. "My name is Kim," she said. "I'll be your waitperson today." Her tone made it clear she would have told them who she was in some other words if her employers allowed. She must have felt the tension between Claire and her father. She let her hand linger on Claire's as she handed her the menu. They ordered drinks: a Bloody Mary for him and, because she was legally too young to drink, a Virgin Mary for Claire.

Claire watched the sadness melt from her father's face, just a trace left behind, as he shone his good looks on Kim, like a searchlight, charming her. Claire had watched him do this a thousand times. She'd learned it from him. The difference was he did it to everybody. He was much more democratic that way than she would ever be. "Are you going to school at night, Kim?" he asked.

She looked proud and told him yes, Southern Connecticut U, night school, studying to be an accountant, and Claire said, "Good for you, I'm studying to be a painter." She didn't really say it to Kim though. She said it to her father.

"Cool!" Kim said.

"You should see her pictures," Claire's father said.

"I'd like that," Kim said. "Your salmon will be up in a bit." She left them, bouncing happily toward the kitchen with their orders.

"You have to admire that," Paul Nelson said. "Working all day and going to school at night. She'll go far."

Claire didn't answer. He was talking just to ease their tension.

"Don't you think so?" her father said.

"She didn't want to see my pictures," Claire said.

"How do you know? Maybe she would if she could. And anyway, what's wrong with being polite?"

"Dad?"

"What?"

"I really do want to be an artist, you know."

He smiled and looked happy for the first time all day. "That's great, Claire. Whatever you want to do, I'll support."

"Jeez, Dad, I'm not asking for your *permission*. I just wanted you to know."

"Claire, for God's sake! Just tell me how to talk to you, okay? Then I'll only say things that don't piss you off and maybe we can get along."

"Oh, forget it, Dad. Forget I ever said it."

"No. Let's not. I've seen your pictures. They're great. That one in the office? Of the tree? That was so good I thought it was by a professional until Ms. Bickham told me you did it." Some of the pain on his expression and the hurt in his tone melted away as he praised her. "It made me proud," he said. "When I saw your picture I recognized the tree right away. It takes a lot of talent to—"

"Dad?"

He stopped mid-sentence, frowning. "What, Claire?"

"That's exactly what I didn't want to do."

The hurt and anger blossomed on his face again. "Stop taunting me, Claire."

"I'm not. I really didn't want it to be just realistic."

"Oh? What then?" Again, some of the pain left his face. He looked expectant now, hopeful. She remembered how easy to read Amy's father's face was too. One look at their faces and you knew exactly what they were feeling. "I'm all ears, Claire," he said.

"It's hard to explain."

"Try."

She looked away. Here it was, right here, their chance for

healing. She could try to explain, and he could try to understand, how everything stopped when she was painting. She could forgive him then, for being too weak to parent her. He would know her. Or at least have tried to. That's all she needed from him. She'd get her parenting from Miss Oliver's School for Girls.

She turned back to him. He was leaning slightly forward, waiting. All she had to say was that Eudora had said to her: *You'll pay a high price for your talent. You'll pay an even higher one if you don't embrace it. So don't you dare try to get away with painting just what's already there.*

"Claire?"

But how can you say words like that about yourself to someone you hardly knew? She wasn't ready yet even to tell Rachel what Eudora had said. The only person she'd told was Amy Michaels. *I understand,* Amy had said. *You'll probably be painting that tree for the rest of your life.*

"If you can't see what I was trying to do when I painted that tree, then I failed to do it," she told her father. "You can't put it into words," she added, sounding as phony to herself as she was sure she sounded to him. "Paintings aren't words with meaning. They just are."

"I understand," he said.

"No you don't. You don't have to pretend. It's not your fault, Dad. Let's just leave it at that." She watched the disappointment on his face turn to resignation.

"All right," he said. "We'll leave it at that."

During the rest of the meal, he told her about his new job in London and about a visit he'd made last weekend with a friend to the Maritime Museum on the Thames in Greenwich. He didn't tell her anything about the friend other than her name was Deborah, and Claire didn't ask.

After he finished, she glanced meaningfully at his drink, then looked around the restaurant. No one was watching. He nodded his head and moved his drink toward her while she moved hers to him. "Why not?" he whispered. "In other countries this wouldn't be illegal." She didn't tell him she'd hoped he would say no.

She finished his drink; he finished hers. She looked at her watch.

He told Kim they didn't want dessert and put a wad of dollar bills into her hand for the tip. "Just to see your smile," he said.

In his rented BMW, he said, "You can change your mind, you know. So, if that radio jerk makes things too hard for you, let me know and we'll find another school for you in England."

It surprised her how much she didn't like Mitch Michaels being called a jerk. He was Amy's dad and he loved her. "That's not going to happen, Dad," she said. "I'll be safe where I am."

Her father nodded his head, looking straight ahead through the windshield again. But even looking at the side of his face, she could see through his sadness to the relief that he was free of the burden of parenting her. They both knew she'd disregard his curfews and his rules when they didn't suit her. She wished that wasn't so.

In the school's parking lot, a few minutes, later, she leaned across to him and kissed him on the side of his face. "So long, Dad. Thanks for lunch. I'll see you at Christmas." She bolted out of the car before he could answer and walked fast across the lawn toward her class. She heard his car start up, and she wished she hadn't been so quick. She turned and waved goodbye to the back of his car as it picked up speed.

That afternoon, Margaret came through Rachel's office door walking straight-legged, stiff and mechanical, making weird clicking noises with her tongue. She wore a skull cap from which a wire antenna stuck straight up. "Two more letters," she said.

Rachel would have laughed if she had not been imagining how, if she were on the executive committee, she would react to a brand-new head of school, chosen after the first choice refused to take the job, making a decision that guaranteed a famous talk show host's broadcasting every morning that Miss Oliver's School for Girls goes out of its way to recruit girls who have sex with their teachers.

Margaret sat down, her notebook open, ready to take dictation, just as Rachel glanced out the door and saw Gregory van Buren coming out of the library. He looked like an executive in his lightweight summer suit, and she thought, *Why not ask him? If you don't like one person's advice, try his rival.* "Later, Margaret," Rachel said, standing up, heading for the doors.

"Again?" Margaret said.

Rachel walked fast to catch up to Gregory, remembering Milton Perkins gesturing toward him and asking, "What about him?" Gregory heard her behind him, stopped, and waited.

"Can I ask you something?" she said.

He told her of course she could, any time.

"Thanks. Can we walk?" She pointed in the direction of the river.

He smiled and patted his tummy. "I could burn some calories."

She waited until they reached the trail that ran along the river where she'd walked with Milton Perkins and then she told the whole story. She watched his face closely for reactions. He winced when she told him Claire had confessed that she'd had an affair with a teacher at Central Park Academy. He showed no emotion at all when she told him about Michaels's invading her office and his ultimatum, but when she said she was going to keep Claire at the school and send Amy out of harm's way to England where she wanted to go anyway, he said, "Good for you! What's your plan?"

"I'm working on it. I thought I'd get your ideas."

"Well, here's one. You ready for it?" He stopped walking. So she stopped too. He was looking directly at her face.

"What?" she asked.

"Put your resignation in your back pocket and do anything you want."

She started to say, "That's a little vague," but then she felt her breath go out. "Oh!" she said. "Oh!"

"Once you decide to do that, the rest will be obvious," he said.

She thought for a minute, and then she said. "Tell everybody first? Before he does?"

"Go for it, girl!" Gregory said.

SO THAT'S WHAT she told Milton Perkins over the phone she wanted to do: beat Mitch Michaels to the punch; explain everything to the alumnae, the parents, and the donors before he broadcasted it to the world. "It will take the wind out of Michaels's sails before he even leaves the dock," she said. She was sure Milton would love the idea.

If she couldn't sell it to the executive committee tomorrow, he surely could.

He said nothing when she finished. She was surprised that he needed to think it over. She felt herself getting stubborn, was tempted to remind him that he was the one who had asked what if Claire didn't want to leave. Finally he said, "All right, that's a good idea." He sounded as if his mind were somewhere else.

"I hope you really think so."

There was another pause and then he said, "Sorry, I was looking at my calendar. I can't believe it. I never wrote the meeting down. I think I might have forgotten—even though I was the one who called it."

"You're just not used to not having a secretary now that you're retired," she said. She was sure that was the reason. Her father gave it when he forgot things he used to remember. He was about the same age as Milton Perkins and he was still as sharp as ever.

Now she had to rush across campus to make it in time for her honors physics class. So she said goodbye and hung up without wondering if there was another reason why he forgot. She didn't tolerate students' lateness.

So why should they tolerate hers?

That night, while thinking about the executive committee meeting tomorrow morning and what she was going to tell the members, Rachel hardly slept at all.

"You need to know some stuff about what's gone on with the board the last two years," Milton Perkins had told her very soon after her appointment. "Especially the ones on the executive committee. Managing them would make herding cats feel like an easy job." She had listened very closely. He told her the one to be most wary of was Jamie Carrington, who had just resigned in something of a huff as president of the Alumnae Association. She had been the most ardent supporter of Marjorie Boyd, one of the many who had voted against her dismissal, and when on a freezing day last year Fred Kindler, Milton, and then-board chair Alan Travelers had gone to her mansion in East Hampton to ask for her support in a plan for rescuing the school from financial disaster *without admitting boys*, she sent her chauffeur to the airport to pick them up not in her Mercedes but in an ancient open car, a beat-up Plymouth with a canvas top that couldn't be put up—and then refused to support the plan until after Fred resigned. Milton wasn't sure she was ready yet to support any head who was not Marjorie Boyd, no matter how able. "Then there's Amelia Dickenson, our famous author," Milton had gone on. "She's the new president of the Alumnae Association. You'll recognize her right away. She'll be the tall lady with the huge head of hair so blond it looks like it's on fire. She always looks like she's about to make an important announcement. She was outraged by your temerity when you refused to be the interim. I had to be my most charming self to calm her down. You're going to have to keep your eye on her. And there's the vice chair of the board, Sonja McGarvey. She's just as young as you are and makes more money every ten minutes doing something mysterious with software than I made in a lifetime, and I made a lot. You can count on her loyalty, but she has very strong opinions and can run over people who she thinks are in the way. You can also count on Alan Travelers. He was the board chair before me. He's the king of loyalty. He always does the right thing, which is why he resigned from the chair when Fred Kindler resigned. Did Fred ever tell you the story of what Alan did to Harriet Richardson?"

Before Rachel could answer that Fred Kindler had, Milton went on. It was obvious he loved to tell the story. "Harriet was one of the trustees who voted against firing Marjorie. She kept asking why did we fire her, right in front of Fred Kindler, and in a board meeting she accused Fred to his face of planning to admit boys to build the enrollment and threatened to resign, and right then and there Alan accepted it as if she actually had. When she protested that she'd only threatened, Sonja and I claimed that no, she had actually resigned, and Alan said he'd heard it too. He plucked the board papers she was holding out of her hand and pointed to the door. So at least we don't have to worry about *her* anymore."

Rachel had thought for a minute, taking all this in. Then she said, thinking about Amelia Dickenson whom they still had to worry about, "Shouldn't we change the by-laws so one person can't be the president of the Alumnae Association and on the board at the same time? Isn't that too much power in one person's hands?"

Milton had smiled tolerantly. He didn't need to be told what he'd known since before Rachel was born. He said, "There you go with your by-laws again. But you're right. It was Marjorie's doing. Our beloved dictator. Her strategy was very straightforward: make all the decisions, including the ones the board is supposed to make. Find the people who are most obedient and give them as much power as you can. Presto—someone gets to be on the executive committee of the board *and* president of the alumnae. If we tried to change that now while you're still new, we'd have a rebellion on our hands. Wait until you're established and then we'll do it."

Rachel replayed this conversation endlessly in her single bed, getting more and more nervous and more bored with it at the same time, until just before dawn she finally fell asleep.

Milton opened the meeting at precisely ten-fifteen, announcing to the executive committee that Rachel had something important to report. Everyone turned to her to listen. It was clear they were expecting something very different from what they hoped to hear: *I've found a new big donor who will help us get rid of our huge accumulated deficit. I've worked out a new budget that will actually provide a surplus the first in years.*

Rachel took a big breath and plunged in, speaking fast to get past the story of the problem Mitch Michaels presented and propose her solution to it before anyone responded. But Jamie Carrington interrupted her.

"With a teacher!" she exclaimed. "A *teacher* with a *student* doing *that!*"

The black-haired, impatient, brilliant vice chair, Sonja McGarvey, looked at Rachel and rolled her eyes. "Yes, Jamie," she mouthed, "even teachers have dicks."

"And we let her in?" Jamie persisted.

Rachel told her again that the full story of the still unnamed girl wasn't known at the time and then rushed on to finish describing the problem. Sweat ran down from her armpits as she told them about Mitch Michaels's ultimatum and watched the expressions on the members' faces: anger, disgust, resentment, glumness, and, scariest of all, caution. Then she told them how they would solve the problem, and there was a big silence and everyone stared at her, and she remembered Gregory van Buren's "*put your resignation in your back pocket and do anything you want." Back pocket? Are you kidding?* Rachel thought. *I'm practically waving it at them.*

"Tell everybody?" Jamie said. "*Everybody!* About a thing like that! You're crazy!"

Rachel waited for someone to rebut, but everyone was still watching her, waiting for their head of school to speak. "Everybody's going to hear about it from him," she said. "Wouldn't you prefer—?"

"I would prefer that no one hears about it from anybody."

"Jamie, it's a little late for that," Alan Travelers said softly.

"No, it isn't. All we have to do is ask the girl to leave." Several members nodded their heads.

"That's the one thing I won't do," Rachel said.

"Oh really? Suppose we tell you to?"

"That would be *two* reasons that I wouldn't," Rachel said. All the members looked down at their papers on the table.

Jamie's mouth opened. She stared at Rachel. Rachel stared right back. She knew she'd made a big mistake, but she wasn't about to back down. Then Jamie turned to Milton Perkins for his support. He was looking gravely at Rachel, but he was also nodding his head. Jamie's eyes opened wide. "You're *agreeing* with her?"

"She's the head," Milton said, still nodding his head. "Who stays and who leaves is her decision."

"But it's preposterous! I won't have a thing to do with this."

"Jamie, we don't want the likes of Mitch Michaels telling us what to do, do we?" Alan Travelers asked, speaking even more gently this time.

"The likes of?" Jamie asked. "Exactly what do you mean by that? You think everybody involved with this school is a *liberal*?" She pronounced the word as if naming a disease.

Sonja McGarvey laughed. "Maybe we should poll the alumnae," she said. No one looked at her. Alan Travelers was suppressing a grin. "Why not?" Sonja asked, an evil smile on her face. "We'd identify the conservatives that way and hit 'em up for more. They're the ones with the money." Jamie went red in the face and glared at her. "What, you got a better idea?" Sonja said. It was clearly time for Milton Perkins to rein them in. They all turned to him at the head of the table.

He wore a confused look on his face. It was an old trick of his, so old he didn't know he was using it. "Why are we talking about Mitch Michaels?" he asked, ignoring the fact that nobody was. He was the only one who could talk Jamie down off her high horse, but he was much too smart to try that now—or to make her say out loud what they *should* be talking about: that this was about Miss Oliver's School for Girls rising to the occasion. "Mitch Michaels is going to do what Mitch Michaels does," he said. "And we are going to do what we do. Does anybody have a better idea than Rachel's?"

Nobody answered.

Then Sonja McGarvey said she would like to help Rachel with her plan, and everybody turned to Jamie.

"Oh, all right," Jamie sighed, outnumbered.

"All right then," Milton said. "Last chance to propose a different idea."

Silence.

Rachel surveyed the room, reading expressions. Some clearly loved the idea; others seemed resigned. *If there was no other plan, then we have to go with this one.* Down at the end of the table, sitting together, three trustees were obviously not enthusiastic. They were among those who had agreed with Jamie's objection. Rachel almost hoped they would come up with an alternative. If it failed it wouldn't be hers.

"Maybe we should think some more and meet again later in the week," Amelia Dickenson said. For a celebrated author she spoke tentatively, Rachel thought.

Milton Perkins shook his head. "Amelia, we don't have the time," he said. "Mitch Michaels isn't going to wait."

Amelia thought for a second. "Well," she said, hesitating once again, "if that's the case, I agree. We shouldn't wait."

"So?" Milton said. "No other suggestions?" No one spoke. "Good, we have a decision."

"As long as I get to approve how we word the message," Jamie added, and everybody agreed, emphatically, in unison, that yes, she should, she would know exactly how to put it.

And then Alan Travelers, speaking as the chair emeritus, pointed out that Rachel hadn't really started a post-graduate program.

No, all agreed, it was just one kid—all except the three members at the end of the table. Rachel sensed their frustration in her bones. But she knew it didn't make any difference. The most loyal board of trustees in the world couldn't keep her in office if her strategy didn't work. Her name was on it. She wouldn't last any longer than Fred Kindler had, and her failure would be even more ignominious.

For as long as she lived, Rachel would remember the sadness she'd felt last spring when Fred stood on the auditorium stage and announced his resignation. For that's what it was: a resignation in both senses of the word. That he was resigned to his decision to resign for the sake of the school brought him the dignity that such a man deserves. But then Karen Benjamin, the editor of the *Clarion*, acting more like a grown-up than the grown-ups did, took the stage and demanded the school thank him for his service by applauding, and more people didn't clap their hands than did. The look on Fred's face in that too-silent auditorium was shattering for Rachel. And as soon as the school knew Fred wasn't going to be their head anymore, when the alumnae went to work and did what he had asked them to do to save the school, it was then that Rachel wasn't sure that she could ever act as gracefully as Fred Kindler had. He had retained every ounce of his self-worth.

Now maybe she would find out.

AFTER EVERYONE HAD left, Rachel stayed to thank Milton for his support. He wouldn't let her finish. "That's not the way we handle Jamie," he said. He wore the same grave look he'd sent Rachel in the meeting.

"I know," Rachel said. "It was dumb."

Milton nodded, satisfied that Rachel had learned a lesson. "I was dumb too, as a matter of fact. I must be getting old," he said. "I can't believe I didn't think to call Jamie and tell her ahead of time what was coming up. She likes to be conferred with. Who doesn't? Besides, she gives almost as much money to the school as Alan Travelers and I do, so I think she deserves it, don't you?"

Rachel agreed and as soon as she got back to her office, she called Jamie.

"Oh!" Jamie said. "Two in a row! Milton Perkins just hangs up and then the phone rings again and it's you. He called to thank me for offering to write the message. Isn't he a doll?"

Rachel agreed that he was—though *doll* was not quite how she thought of Milton Perkins. She couldn't tell whether or not Jamie was being sarcastic, and regretted all the more the way she'd handled her. She hastened to apologize. "It's just that I felt so strongly," she said. "I should have explained."

"Well, I have to admit, I'm not used to being talked to like that."

"It was discourteous. I hope you'll forgive me."

"Oh you're forgiven," Jamie said offhandedly. And then, after a pause: "Rachel? You don't mind me calling you Rachel, do you?"

Rachel didn't doubt Jamie's sarcasm anymore. "Of course I don't mind," she said, "Everybody calls me Rachel."

"Well then, call me Jamie."

"All right."

"All right what?"

"All right, Jamie."

"There you go! How'd that feel?"

"Fine—Jamie."

"Good. Now bygones are—whatever they are."

Rachel couldn't resist: "Bygones?"

There was a long silence, and then Jaimie said, "Right, and tell you what—I think your idea is marvelous." She pronounced the word slowly, with an obvious irony: *mar-vel-ous.* "I wish I'd thought of it myself."

"Thank you," Rachel said, still pretending not to catch on. "We are going to make it work."

"You bet we are, young lady. And I'll tell you another thing. I'm so glad we have a *woman* head again! After we had a *man* in here. For a whole year!" Jamie spoke in the same ironic, and very upper-class, tone, mocking the school now, not just Rachel. It was rather refreshing to Rachel, after hearing so much universal, unquestioning adulation of the school. "Can you imagine?" Jamie went on. "This is Miss Oliver's School for *Girls*!" Then she hung up.

Rachel sat perfectly still, so uneasy she forgot to put the receiver down until the insistent buzz on the line penetrated her consciousness. *I did it again*, she thought. Bygones. As if Jamie were too dumb to know. Twice in one day! She picked up the phone again to tell Milton Perkins that maybe they had an enemy now in Jamie Carrington. She would also have to confess her sin. But Jamie Carrington? The lady who gave almost as much money as Alan Travelers and Milton Perkins? Who served the school still as president of the Parent Association? *No, she's just like me*, Rachel told herself. *Anybody messes with us, we pay them back —with interest. But traitor? No way.* Rachel put the phone down. Still, the worry lingered. She'd keep her eye on Jamie Carrington.

"Oh, don't worry about Claire," Sonja said that evening at the Head's House on campus. She'd come to help make the plan and Rachel had started to have second thoughts. She told Sonja that she thought being the blameless victim could become a persona not easy to abandon for an adult, let alone a teenage girl. "But we'll cook up a way to protect the girl," Sonja promised. Rachel wasn't convinced. She remembered Milton's remark about Sonja's running over people who got in the way.

Nevertheless, it was pleasant for Rachel to have her company in the house. They had tacitly agreed to work there instead of in Rachel's office. Sonja lived alone. Rachel suspected she had ways of getting doses of romance when she needed them from people just as busy, and then putting everything back in its box. She was a beautiful woman, shiny black hair framing a face she projected knowingly on the world, and a body to die for.

She took the jacket of her business suit off that evening, throwing it over the back of the sofa, and walked around Rachel's cavernous, husbandless living room that was meant for fundraising, too restless to sit, while they made the plan together. They would use the publicity Mitch Michaels provided to show Miss O's at its best. They made a list of the alumnae who would be asked in each city to host a meeting.

Rachel finally persuaded Sonja to sit down on the sofa and went to the kitchen and came back with an open bottle of very good red and two glasses and asked her if she'd like to spend the night. It was eleven o'clock. They could finish the wine. Sonja gazed at Rachel for a second or two and then said no, she should get home pretty soon, and Rachel wondered if tonight was one of the nights she might have someone waiting. Sonja did linger long enough though to have a glass, while all of a sudden it occurred to Rachel that they could ask all the current and past parents, every alumna, and all the students to never listen to Michaels's program. "He can rant all he wants," she told Sonja. "Nobody who has anything to do with this school will ever hear a word."

Sonja's face lighted up. "He won't exist!" she said. "See, I told you we'd cook up a way." Rachel laughed and picked up the bottle to pour her another. But Sonja put her hand over the glass. "Tell you what," she said. Rachel's heart lifted. She knew what was coming next. She could see it on people's faces when they wanted to give. "I'll buy every radio in the school," Sonja said. "How about that?"

"I think that would be just fine," Rachel said. "You can give them to the Salvation Army."

"How much do you think?"

"How about one million two hundred thou?" Rachel ventured. *Might as well go for the whole bundle at once.*

Sonja smiled. "That's a bit stiff. And it lets the board off the hook. How about three hundred K over three years?"

"All right then. We'll put it toward paying down the accumulated deficit."

"Obviously. What else would you do with it?" Sonja said. She stood up to go and Rachel walked with her out the door to the driveway. "This is going to be fun." Sonja said and gave Rachel a hug. Then she got in her Mercedes and drove away.

TWELVE

The phone was ringing when Rachel went back inside. She rushed across the living room toward it, elated. First the board accepts her plan, then Sonja steps in with a huge gift, and then Bob calls. All in one day! "Hi, Bob, guess what. Sonja's going to buy all the radios," she exclaimed, forgetting that Bob wouldn't have the foggiest idea what she was talking about. "Isn't that amazing? For three hundred thousand . . ."

"I'm sorry, Rachel, but this is Jenifer Michaels."

"Who?" Rachel said, her disappointment surging.

"Amy's mom."

"Oh! Of course. What's wrong?"

"Amy just called me. She's changed her mind."

"Changed her mind. You mean she's not . . ."

"That's right. She says she's going to stick to her original plan and stay right where she is and go to St. Agnes next year. She doesn't mind seeing her father once in a while for just a little bit. She says if he wants to get caught and put in jail, that's his problem, but I suppose what she's really saying is she's glad he cares that much. I guess I should be happy about that. I don't know what to do. I think there's something going on you haven't told me."

"I'll talk to her."

"Tonight?"

"Yes."

"Oh good! And I'm sorry that I wasn't the person you . . ."

"I better get going before Amy goes to bed."

"All right then, good night—and Rachel?"

"Yes."

"I do hope you can persuade her."

"I do too," Rachel said. She wanted to add, *You don't know how much*, but of course she didn't.

She hurried across the campus toward Amy's and Claire's dorms. She had already guessed what had transpired between them. In spite of her worry that the strategy for keeping Claire and demolishing Mitch Michaels was falling apart before the first step was taken, it made her glad that kids could care so much about each other. She was sure they'd both be in Claire's room.

She was right.

"I know what this is about," Amy said before Rachel was all the way through the door. She was sitting at the foot of Claire's bed. Claire was sitting up against the headboard at the other end, next to an array of teddy bears. *She's nineteen*, Rachel thought. The teddy bears were substitutes for a family. She felt a rush of sadness.

"I told my mom not to bother calling you. It wouldn't do any good," Amy said.

"Well, she did anyway, Amy," Rachel said. "Aren't you glad she cares?"

Claire started to scramble up out of bed so Rachel could sit down on it. She looked relieved that Rachel had appeared. Rachel gestured for her to stay on the bed and sat on the edge of Claire's desk. She felt more persuasive looking down on them than looking across. But seeing the two friends side by side on the bed, it was tempting to agree with Eudora: if Amy stayed, her father's threat was nil.

"I told her what her dad was going to do if I stayed," Claire said.

"Not *if. Because*," Amy said, turning to Claire. "What about your art? What about the Rhode Island School of Design? Eudora would die. You're not going anywhere." She turned to Rachel. "And I'm not either. Would you run off to England and leave your friend all alone when she's being attacked?"

"I tried to explain that if she stays I have to go," Claire said. She put her arm around Amy. "So please explain why it's best for her to go because she won't be here when her father says things about the school, and maybe if she goes, her father won't do it, and besides she wanted to go there anyway. And anyway, we can write . . ."

"Next year. That's what we decided. That's when I would go." Amy's voice was rising and her face was getting red. "When you're not here anymore. Then when my mom called and said let's go this year to hide from my dad, I said, sure, why not. But then you told me what's going to happen. So of course I changed my mind—just like you would if it was the other way around."

"All right then," Claire said. She glanced at Rachel as if to say, *Watch this.*

"Oh, I just wish he wasn't so crazy!" Amy said through her sobs.

Claire took her arm from around Amy shoulder and turned to her and took her face in her hands and leaned in, their two foreheads almost touching. "We'll both go," she said. "How about that, Amy? You and me together. We'll both go to St. Agnes."

"But your art. And Eudora."

"Never mind," Claire murmured. "I can paint over there."

Amy shook her head, still in Claire's hands.

"Yes, I can, and I will." Claire let her hands drop. She gazed at Amy.

Amy's sobs subsided. "You'd do that for me?"

"You would for me, wouldn't you?"

Amy nodded. Her crying stopped. "Of course I'd do it for you!" A pause. "I'll go to St. Agnes this year. That way you can stay here with Eudora."

"Really, Amy? Are you sure?"

"I'm sure—as long as you promise to write."

"Oh, I'll write," Claire exclaimed. "I'll send pictures too." It was she who was crying now. Just a few small tears, but they were sufficient.

And Rachel had to turn away to hide her own. She was thirty-five years old and had never seen sincerity and performance become one and the same. She wondered which had come first. "Well, that's settled then, Amy. Shall I call your mother, or will you?"

"I'll call her. I want to hear her be happy."

Rachel nodded. "You've made a good decision." She stepped forward and hugged Amy. Then she turned to Claire. "You have too." Claire returned her hug, squeezing hard.

Rachel left, crossing the campus in the dark. All the stars were out. What a relief to have the problem solved! But now that no one could see them, her tears were streaming down her face.

NOW IT WAS imperative to get Claire off campus so Michaels would think she'd been expelled. While she was gone, Rachel and the board would build a fortress around Claire and the school by getting the school's version of the story out first, and then persuading the school community not to listen to his. When all those ducks were lined up in a row, they'd bring Claire back and send Amy to England.

Eudora cooked up the Miss Oliver's School for Girls Program of Off-Campus Experience for Emerging Artists, and named Claire Nelson the inaugural recipient, which, with the help of well-placed alumnae, became news broadcasted on radio and TV in Hartford and New Haven and printed in the teen sections of the *New Haven Advocate*, *Hartford Courant*, and in *Madison Shoreline Times*—all for the benefit of Mitch Michaels, who, it was assumed, would think that this was a cover-up and that the lucky recipient would decide not to return to Miss Oliver's School for Girls. Amy said she wouldn't take any calls from her father so she wouldn't have to lie about the reason Claire was not on campus. It was an easy promise to make, given her anger over her father's desire to separate her from her best friend. And, as Rachel and Eudora gleefully agreed, the various public announcements weren't lies either: Claire was an emerging artist, and she would be off campus, and she would be having an experience.

By the time Michaels discovered that Claire hadn't been expelled and was telling the world his version, no one who counted would be listening. And an even better outcome, now a strong possibility, was that Michaels would be so happy when he learned that Amy was on an exchange miles away from Claire in England, he wouldn't attack the school. He'd have less incentive. He'd keep his mouth shut.

Claire and Rachel agreed that Claire wouldn't go home to her father. The reason, they said, was it didn't make sense to fly all the way across the Atlantic and back for so short a time. So Rachel called her husband Bob in New York City and explained the situation to him. Would he host a visit from Claire for a few days? She was ready for his being disturbed that her plan amounted to telling Mitch Michaels a lie. She already planned a response: *you'd lie to Hitler, wouldn't you?*

But Bob didn't even seem to hear Rachel's plan. It was Claire, and what she'd done, that he focused on. "Claire!" he exclaimed. "She did that?"

"No," Rachel countered when she'd recovered. "The teacher did it."

"Rachel, that's baloney. It takes two to tangle."

"*Tango*," she said. "It's *tango*, Bob. Will you help us or not?"

"Yeah? Well, it could be a polka for all I care. Having her stay here, it's just not a good idea."

"Oh come on, Robert. You'll be safe. You can lock your bedroom door."

"That's not funny, Rachel."

She agreed that it wasn't, but she didn't apologize. It had actually crossed her mind that he was worried Claire would try to seduce him.

"What are you thinking, Rachel? How do you think it would look? If you were going to be here too, I'd say yes in a heartbeat. Call your sister."

Rachel didn't answer. Of course Michaels would jump all over this. Claire and Bob living together. Arranged by his wife. What *was* she thinking?

"It's not like you not to think through everything," Bob said. "Slow down, stop panicking. You're going too fast." He paused while she thought about that. Then he said, "You'll beat this guy, Rach. He's a storm that will pass."

"I'm sorry. It was a dumb idea. I guess I just wanted you to be my partner in this. It would be like—"

"What?"

"You know—like we were her mom and dad."

"Oh, Rach!"

"Yeah. Pretty dumb, wasn't it?"

There was a silence on the line. Then he said, "Say hello to your sister for me, okay?"

"Yeah, I'll give her your love—and Bob?"

"Yes?"

"Thanks."

"Hey, anytime," he said. Rachel wanted him to say he'd call her sometime when he was confused and panicking and going too fast. But he was much more experienced at weathering storms. So why should he? Besides, she didn't have time to talk—not right then with everything she had on her plate. She blew him a kiss over the phone.

"That's a nice sound," he said as she was hanging up.

She didn't call her sister. She called Sonja, amazed at herself for not thinking of her first. Sonja came out of a meeting to take her call. "Of course!" she said before Rachel finished asking. "Tell Claire to be ready in an hour. I'll send a car."

Rachel walked across campus to the Art Building and interrupted Eudora's studio class to get Claire, and they walked to Claire's room together, where Rachel found herself fussily refolding the clothes Claire already put into her suitcase. Claire didn't seem to mind. Then, while Claire packed a sketchpad, charcoal pencils, and a watercolor kit into a canvas satchel, Rachel gathered up the books Claire would need to keep up with her assignments and put them into her backpack. She had a strong desire to sit on the edge of Claire's bed and talk. On the wall above Claire's desk were watercolor scenes of the river. The one of Francis Plummer and his son Sidney standing in snow in bright red life jackets drew Rachel's attention first. Francis spent every Saturday and Sunday afternoon he could get away running rapids with his son in the springtime when melting snow made the water high. Rachel knew this was a point of contention with Peggy, who didn't approve of their taking risks—not when the reward was merely fun. "When did you do these?" Rachel asked.

"I didn't. They're Eudora's."

"Eudora's?" Rachel said, still looking at the painting of Francis and Sidney. The resemblance of the two in the painting to the real Francis and Sidney was remarkable. Yet Rachel was already wanting something that wasn't in there: something about the someday when Francis couldn't run rapids anymore and Sidney still could, she guessed. She didn't want to recognize the two people in the painting anymore, their bright red life jackets against the snow, their paddles upright by their sides, like warriors' spears. She wanted them to be Everyone.

"See the way Eudora's emphasized the red in the life jackets?" Claire asked. "It's not just two guys out for a Sunday paddle. They wouldn't be wearing life jackets if it was. It's about danger, testing yourself, having *real* fun."

"Now I do."

"And the way she's composed so your eyes go right to Francis and his son?"

"Yes, I do. Claire?"

Claire shook her head for Rachel not to interrupt. Rachel guessed she didn't want to be asked if she missed something too, if she understood that Eudora was passionately nurturing a talent greater than her own. "Eudora didn't want to give the paintings to me," Claire said, "but I kept asking. She's the best teacher in the world."

Yes, Rachel thought, *Eudora and Francis Plummer—and Gregory van Buren. They don't come any better.* "Tell me something, Claire. That picture you painted of two girls on a beach: was one of them really your mother?"

Claire didn't answer right away. Rachel guessed the question was a surprise. "Maybe not exactly," Claire said at last.

"You said it was," Rachel accused.

"Yes, I did—because it's kind of hard to tell someone what you were really painting was how it feels not have a mother."

"Oh, I understand," Rachel said. She really did. It couldn't be different from how it feels not to have a daughter. That she didn't know whether Claire was telling the truth or not didn't make her hunger to be a mother any less intense. She looked at her watch. "It's time to go."

The car was already in the driveway. The driver was not a stranger Sonja had sent. It was Sonja herself who got out of the car to greet them. "I changed my mind about sending a car," she said sotto voce to Rachel. Rachel squeezed her arm in thanks and introduced Claire. They loaded Claire's stuff into the trunk and then Claire got in the front beside Sonja, and Rachel heard her say, "Thanks for coming yourself."

THIRTEEN

No one at Miss Oliver's School for Girls was surprised at how easily their school was galvanized to action, passionately dedicated to Mitch Michaels's defeat. A cautious, defensive strategy, even if it included a refusal to let Claire go, would have been nowhere near as inspiring.

For almost everyone this wasn't a crisis. It was an opportunity to show the world what kind of a school Miss Oliver's was. It was a feminist cause. And it was emphatically—it was hard even to begin to express how emphatically—a chance to humiliate the enemy. Mitch Michaels, proxy for every insult, real or imagined, to women's potential since time began, was doing the school a favor.

What was surprising was how smoothly the team of Alan Travelers, Milton Perkins, Sonja McGarvey, Rachel Bickham, and, yes, Jamie Carrington, too, pulled off the logistics. In just three weeks, they held meetings in Los Angeles, San Francisco, Denver, Portland, Seattle, Chicago, Cleveland, Atlanta, Miami, Washington, Philadelphia, New York City, Greenwich, Scarsdale, Boston, and Portland. Fifteen cities in twenty-one days. Margaret was the hero. She served as command center for all the arrangements, working with a fervor extraordinary even for her. Coming back to her office late one evening, Rachel caught her doing a solitary jig, waving her hands above her head, snapping her fingers, a big smile on her face. "Seattle's all set," she announced. Behind her on the wall she'd taped a roll of butcher paper where she'd charted every detail.

Nevertheless, it was a little scary, even for a person like Milton Perkins, to stand up in a living room in front of the alumnae and parents of girls now at the school and, after thanking the hostess, say the scripted words Jamie Carrington had composed:

"We are gathered here tonight so that I can tell you our school is about to be attacked. Mr. Mitch Michaels, whose name some of you might recognize to be the same as the host's of the popular radio program, will soon broadcast information whose only purpose is to damage our school. That information, obtained inappropriately, if not illegally, has to do with one of our students, whom we treasure and hold dear as we do every girl at Miss Oliver's School for Girls. This information, which should be confidential even within our school, has to do with her being sexually abused by a faculty member at her former school. Mr. Michaels will say that he knows that our student was not the victim but the initiator, a statement that is preposterous since the teacher was an adult with authority over students, but nevertheless credible to Mr. Michaels's audience, given their allegiance to him. He will also assert that such behavior is typical of the values of the elitist Miss Oliver's School for Girls in particular and all independent schools in general. Mr. Michaels offered to keep silence if we expelled the student—which of course we refused. We will nurture her, protect her, supply her with the education she is due, and send her out into the world an empowered young woman, a proud alumna of Miss Oliver's School for Girls."

Then silence. Then everybody talking at once. Then some inevitable questions and the response which was that no more could be said, and then the audience's understanding: of course, *no details.* The whole point was not to know. If you were smart enough to graduate from or send your kid to Miss Oliver's School for Girls, you were smart enough always to know how to behave. It was no different for the thoroughly indoctrinated husbands who accompanied their wives to the meetings. They were also quick to say they'd never to listen to Mitch Michaels. Ever. And not to breathe a word of this to anybody, especially not the students or anybody else at school, until Rachel had brought the school together and told them. They would know when that was because they'd get the letter Milton Perkins and Rachel would send to the whole school community.

They were delighted with the notion that every girl in the school was about to give her radio to the Salvation Army. It was always at that point that the hostess, who had been coached ahead of time, of course, announced that Sonja McGarvey was "buying" the radios with a small gift of three hundred thousand dollars over three years and waited for another plant in the audience to suggest that the alumnae match Sonja's gift. Dollar for dollar.

Rachel explained the plan in the nearest cities: New York, Greenwich, Scarsdale, and Boston, thus limiting her time away from school, while the others on the team did the rest. Each meeting went late into the evening because people wanted to express outrage, declare loyalty, sympathize with the unnamed victim, and suggest ideas. It disturbed Rachel's sense of justice that she couldn't advise them to be as angry at the teacher who violated Claire as they were at Mitch Michaels. She couldn't erase the image of Claire's paramour crying after "every time we did it," but of course she kept that to herself. She did notice, though, blank expressions on the faces of some of the younger alumnae, but they kept as silent as she on the subject.

"You and I know not everyone's going to keep that pledge," Milton Perkins told Rachel during their weekly meeting near the end of this process.

"Of course not. But they won't dare admit it."

"Which makes it as good as if they were keeping it," Milton Perkins said. "Almost, anyway."

Rachel frowned. "*Almost* is what we should worry about though, don't you think?"

"I don't believe in being worried," Milton said, shrugging his shoulders.

"Wary then?"

Milton smiled. "Wary's good."

Rachel nodded. "I've been so busy I haven't thought about all the ways this thing could backfire."

"Not busy, Rachel," Milton said, shaking his head. "Exhilarated. This was too good a fight for you to pass up. That's why, not because you were busy. If you'd stopped to worry about all the things that could go wrong, where do you think we'd be now?" He hesitated, and then he added, as if he'd just remembered, "But there is one person I know we *should* worry about."

Rachel leaned forward. "Who?" It crossed her mind that Milton would say Jamie Carrington, but she tossed the thought away. She'd been keeping an eye on Jamie. Nobody could have been more enthusiastic or worked harder, not even Milton Perkins.

"Harriet Richardson," Milton said. The lady who had threatened to resign, a course of action to which Alan had accepted. "I was wrong to think we don't need to worry about her. You should have seen her face. She's not going to pass up any chance to get revenge."

"Well, maybe I could talk to her," Rachel said. "After all, I'm not Alan Travelers and I'm not Fred Kindler."

Milton shook his head. "No, you're not, but I don't think she approves of your tan."

"Really!"

"Yes, Rachel, really."

"A Miss O's person?"

Milton shrugged. "And if you think getting fired from the board charged her batteries, wait until she hears Mitch Michaels on the radio talking to the whole world about sex at Miss Oliver's School for Girls. I think she must have been a hundred and ten before she learned the facts of life. We can only hope she'll have a heart attack and die. But she's so pickled in sherry, she'll probably live forever."

"Milton! I've never heard you talk about anyone this way."

"Yeah, well, you've never heard me talking about Harriet Richardson before," Milton Perkins said.

FOURTEEN

More and more these days, a sentence would get stuck in Francis Plummer's head, some point he wanted to make in an imagined argument, or the punch line of a joke repeating itself over and over, boring him to insanity. This morning, when the usher at Peggy's church—because that's how he thought of it: Peggy's church, because it certainly wasn't his—had gestured to the pew where Peggy always sat, *Mardon me, Pam, but you're occupuuying the wrong pie. May I sew you to another sheet?* arrived unbidden. The sentence had clanked in his brain since the service had begun. He'd tried to drown it out by reminding himself that there really had been an Oxford don named Spooner who'd really been an usher in church. But telling himself what he already knew didn't work; so now he was reciting the Nicene Creed. Maybe the thought of Peggy's astonishment would silence his brain. *The resurrection of the body*? he'd asked her more than once. *Are you kidding*? *There isn't room.*

Peggy glanced sideways at him, her eyes widening in surprise. He returned the glance, shrugging his shoulders, and he let out a breath, freed from the din at last, and thought she smiled, but he wasn't sure—until she took his hand, grateful that he was, at last, accompanying her at church. He clung to her hand until the Creed was done and they sat down, their hips touching. His right thigh pressed all along its length against her left.

Last night she'd moved into the barren bed space, grown habitual between them since before he'd moved back in with her, and they pressed against each other as they were now in the pew. He understood. She was offering her still beautiful, full-breasted fifty-five-year-old body to him as part of their marriage renewal plan: Step One—resume mutual residency. Step Two—resume sincere conversations. Step Three—resume sex.

Which was why he had just lain there. Sex on demand was not their cup of tea. He knew she was grateful, and after a while, he heard the steady breathing of her sleep.

"Nobody can get it up every time," he joked to Peggy in the morning. She smiled and kissed him lightly on the cheek. It occurred to him then that *Nobody can get it up every time* explained his classes lately too. It wasn't a question of design, nor of delivery. Both were tried and true. No, for too many of the classes the question was: *Where has all the passion gone, the spontaneity?* The answer: *Nobody can get it up every time. Nobody can get it up every time. Nobody.* Over and over relentlessly, until it was time to get in the car and drive to church with Peggy.

"Come on, man, you've been talking about black folks," a caller named Tom said a few days later, his voice going out to millions all the way from Spokane.

"No, I wasn't."

The caller laughed.

I'm sorry, sir, but I don't know where Amy is.

"Really, it's not about black or purple or yellow or green, it's about what's right and what's wrong," Mitch Michaels said, his voice rising just the right amount, and the caller laughed again.

Sure, I'll ask her to call you when she gets back.

"Yeah? Well how come it's always them who get in with the lousy grades?"

No, she still isn't here. Maybe she's in the library.

"Libraries? Why we talking about libraries? It's colleges where the problem's at."

"Well, it happens in libraries too," Mitch Michaels said, thinking fast. "That's why I said it."

The next day, Claire returned to the school.

Delivered by Sonja a few minutes before Morning Meeting, she came into Rachel's office, hesitating just long enough in the frame of sunshine flooding through the French doors to be seen as a stunning woman in a painting. It was an unconscious, instinctive act. Rachel wanted to tell her to turn around and come back wearing a repentant look, but she settled on a blank look on her own face—and not speaking.

Claire pretended not to notice. She and Sonja walked past the circle of chairs and sat down next to each other on the sofa, as they would for a casual chat, irritating Rachel all over again. The painting above the sofa loomed over the scene. Rachel gave Sonja a significant glance, expecting an acknowledgement of her feelings, but Sonja pointed her chin at the paper Rachel held in her hand, as if to say, *Go ahead, read it, like we planned.* It was the same script, word for word, that had been read in all the meetings and that Rachel was about to read to the whole school. Rachel composed herself and read it to Claire so Claire would know what would happen next. When she finished and looked up, Sonja was patting Claire's hand.

"Everybody's going to guess it's me before you even finish," Claire said.

"You're right," Rachel said. "You're absolutely right. Why, do you think?" She wanted to hear Claire admit that she didn't always try to retreat out of sight, that sometimes she couldn't help using the power of her beauty on the girls—especially the young ones, her paparazzi—as she had on her Mr. Alford.

"I just know they'll know, that's all," Claire said. "Who cares why? So why not just come right out and tell them it's me?"

"Because that's what *he* wants," Sonja said.

"Which is why *we* won't," Rachel said. "Yes, everybody's going to know it's you. But almost everybody is going to understand that it's us against him. Almost everybody will talk about this inside the school and some will talk about it with you—at least I hope so for your sake—but almost everybody really will not keep a secret radio, and almost everybody really will not talk about it outside of school."

"And the ones who do won't admit it," Sonja said.

"Oh, I understand that part," Claire said.

"Good," Sonja said.

"But not the other part, Claire? Your part?" Rachel said.

Claire looked hard at Rachel, as if now maybe she would try to answer the question, but Sonja murmured, "Not now," and nodded her head toward the French doors. Claire and Rachel turned to look. The girls and the faculty were trooping across the campus to the auditorium. Rachel turned back to Claire. She was calmly watching the procession as if it had nothing to do with her, and Rachel felt a rush of resentment. Claire was going to get away with it, not pay the piper at all, not one red cent. "You better be ready, Claire," Rachel said.

"Claire will be fine," Sonja said. She squeezed Claire's hand, the red of her nails shiny against Claire's unpainted ones.

RACHEL WAS SURE some of the girls knew what she was going to tell them. At least a few of the alumnae in all those audiences must have broken their promise. The news was just too exciting not to share. Rachel had no desire to find out who they were, but it was clear to her that if she had to wait one more day, everyone would have known before she told them.

The auditorium was quiet when she finished reading the script. She looked up from it, out at the faces. Some of the girls looked straight back at her, hoping to catch her glancing at Claire. They were still in the process of guessing and wanted to be sure. Rachel supposed that Claire was looking straight ahead, but she didn't know because if she looked to find out, she'd give the secret that wasn't a secret away. Then Rachel explained how everybody was not going to listen to the radio for the rest of the year, and the clapping started.

Sonja came forward and stood next to Rachel at the podium and everyone stopped clapping because she was so stunning. Then Sonja offered to buy every radio in the school for three hundred thousand dollars and the pledge that there would be no radio remaining in the school, not even one, and explained how the alumnae were sure to raise another three hundred thousand to match hers. Six hundred thousand dollars! There was another silence for a second or two, and then applause broke out and laughter and everyone babbling at once. No other school in the whole wide world would ever come up with such a crazy, wonderful, inspiring idea. *Thank you, Mitch Michaels!*

Just as the noise subsided, a girl in the back stood up. "What about TV?" she asked. "Won't it get on TV?"

"That's a great question," Sonja announced. "I bet some of

you can answer it." Several hands flew up. Sonja pointed to Bridget Younger, a sophomore who a year ago wouldn't have dared to venture an answer that might not be right.

"Michaels doesn't talk on TV," Bridget said, standing up. She'd dyed her blond hair an attention-getting red. "Not even on Fox Propaganda. We'll be on TV, not him. It's called secondary news."

"Oh!" Sonja said, "I've never heard either of those terms."

"I know, I just made them up."

That night, right after study hours were over, there was a party for Amy Michaels in Francis and Peggy's dorm. Rachel attended, of course, and so did Gregory van Buren, who was Amy's advisor, and all the girls in the dorm, including Claire, and the whole volleyball team on which Amy was a star. There was pizza and ice cream and a great big cake with *GOODBYE, AMY, WE LOVE YOU!* in pink icing across the top. Everybody knew why Amy was going away, but no one said anything.

Tomorrow, Amy's mom would come to school and get her and fly with her across the Atlantic to enroll her in St. Agnes School on the shores of Lake Windermere in England, as Gaylord Frothingham had urged for Claire. Because Rachel was so busy, Gregory van Buren had arranged for a year's exchange with Suzi Reynolds, who was also a sophomore and an even better volleyball player than Amy. She would arrive at Miss O's as Amy would arrive at St. Agnes. Gregory had reported to Amy and her mom and Rachel that St. Agnes's headmaster, Larry Jenkins, seemed to be exactly the man Gaylord Frothingham had said he was: a brilliant school man, extraordinarily kind, and, as a talented artist and on-the-side farmer, an example for his students of the well-rounded life. As the party ended, Claire gave Amy a very long hug and a kiss on the cheek and a promise to stay friends forever, and Gregory gave Amy a book of Wordsworth's poems and a hiker's guide to the Lake Country.

On the way home, Rachel felt as she thought eighteenth-century naval ship captains must have felt before their battles began, when they cleared away everything before the onslaught. She'd been reading Patrick O'Brien. Claire was as prepared as she could be and

Amy was out of harm's way. Rachel was exhilarated.

"THAT AWFUL RADIO man is on the phone," Margaret told Rachel the next morning. Rachel's neck was immediately stiff with tension, and her temples started to throb. "Shall I tell him you're in Australia?"

"No, I better hear what he has to say."

"I suppose it can't do any harm. It's just a phone. Do you mind if I listen in? It's not like we need to play fair with him." And when Rachel didn't answer right away, Margaret said, "Okay, I'll listen in." She pointed to the phone on Rachel's desk. The red light was blinking. "You ready?"

Rachel nodded. She picked up the receiver and held it to her ear for several seconds, and then: "Yes?"

"Good morning."

She didn't answer.

"Good morning to your secretary too. I wish I knew her name. I would tell her that her breathing's rather loud. Allergies, I suppose." Then there was the clicking sound of Margaret hanging up, and the sound of Mitch Michaels chuckling. "Oh, please, tell her to get back on the line. I want to apologize for pushing her aside that day."

"Mr. Michaels. What do you want?"

"Actually, I really would like to apologize," he said, his ironic tone disappearing. "Seriously. If you put her back on, I will."

"Mr. Michaels, I'm going to hang up now."

"But I have news for you. I would prefer to tell it directly to you than on the radio."

"I don't listen to the radio, Mr. Michaels."

"Of course not. I wouldn't either if I were you. But I do want to be sure you understand how easy it was to snooker you. I knew you wouldn't kick that girl out. You'd have to keep her as a matter of principle, right? So you would have to send Amy away. And that's all I really wanted. It was just a shot in the dark. I was sure you'd see right through it and keep both of them. But you fell for it. Hook, line, and sinker! I couldn't believe my luck. Now I not only have Amy out of your clutches, I'm free to attack your school. Did you really think I would say those things about your school if Amy was there? Even though they're true. Oh my God! Didn't you get any advice? Or did you just not listen? Anyway, here's some, and I hope you'll take it: find another job. One that doesn't take a lot brains."

Then he hung up.

FIFTEEN

That afternoon, the letter went out to every alumna, every parent, past and present, every trustee emerita, every donor and foundation that had ever funded the school, and every school in the National Association of Independent Schools, every public school that had ever sent a girl, all the admission directors of every university or college Miss O's graduates had attended, and every firm the school did business with. Co-signed by Milton Perkins and Rachel Bickham, it contained the same scripted words that had been read all over the country and Rachel had read yesterday afternoon to the school.

The very next day, Mitch Michaels informed his listeners, eager for scandal to enliven their early mornings, about sex with teachers at a certain all-girls boarding school, a nest of feminist intransigence, on the Connecticut River just south of Hartford, and assured them there would be more of such news each morning for at least the next six months or so—because that's how long it would take to tell it all.

Two days later, in a heavy rain, a Salvation Army truck arrived on campus during the lunch hour as Rachel had requested, so classes wouldn't be missed. The girls trooped across the campus in their slickers carrying their radios and helped the driver load them, and then they invited him to lunch while a reporter for the *Hartford Courant* took notes. She was the daughter of a business colleague of Alan Travelers and had been properly instructed. The resultant piece, which included an interview with Rachel and appeared the following day on the front page, was all about service learning at Miss Oliver's School for Girls. The lesson to be learned: radios distract students from their studies, so the girls decided they would be better placed in Salvation Army shelters.

The next morning Rachel's best candidate for the business manager position called to accept the offer made to her a week before.

Rachel had begun to fear she would turn it down. Mabel Walters was fifty years old, formerly the CFO of a hospital, perfect for the job. "I read the article in the *Courant*," she told Rachel. "That's all I needed to convince me." So Mabel would join Director of Admissions Nan White, for whom Claire Nelson had painted the picture of the gates to the school, and Director of Development Dorothy Strang. All that was left to fill the administrative team was a dean of academics.

In mid-October, Sonja's check for fifty thousand dollars arrived in the mail, the first installment, with a note saying another would show up in March. By the end of October, fifty thousand dollars of the matching gifts had also arrived. Though Mabel Walters was pleased to get this news in the very first week of her new job, her celebration was appropriately restrained. "A hundred thousand is a nice chunk of cash," she acknowledged to Rachel, "but it's a long way from the four hundred thousand we need to meet the pay-down schedule on our loan."

By this time, Rachel and the board members were getting calls from newspaper reporters asking for a comment on what Mitch Michaels was saying on the radio. Rachel told them she couldn't possibly have a reaction to what she hadn't heard, and when they tried to quote him to her, she told them she really had an awful lot of work to do. Could they call back some other time? Milton Perkins just said, "Mitch who?" and hung up. Sonja McGarvey and Alan Travelers never took calls directly; their secretaries said they would call back—if they had the time. Once though, while Sonja was conducting a Q and A session after making a speech at an industrial conference in Boston, a reporter asked her was it true she was "a trustee of that school in Connecticut." She answered that she was and proceeded to convince the audience that "we damn well better start educating all our students as well as we do at Miss Oliver's School for Girls if we didn't want to get our lunch eaten by China, and probably India too. Maybe even Bangladesh."

Yes, this was a time of elation at Miss Oliver's School for Girls, despite Mabel Walters's worry.

Especially for Rachel. She was getting dozens of phone calls every day from alumnae, most of whom told her how proud of the school they were. Even of her. Who could blame her for enjoying these calls?

She and Milton Perkins agreed it was imperative to linger on the phone as long as the caller wanted, especially with those few who called to express concern, many of whom swore they were keeping the pledge not to listen to Michaels's program but then would say something to reveal that they were. Rachel pretended she didn't catch on. "Engaging with these people is how you build community, how you earn support," Milton said, as if she didn't already know. If that took up all her time, so be it.

But, after maybe a week or so, the calls slowed down and she turned her attention to the inside of the school, its machinery. She was still sure Francis Plummer should be her dean of academics, but she had to admit, she wasn't quite as enthusiastic now as she was before he had advised her to give in to Mitch Michaels and send Claire away. Had he changed his mind? It was a surprise to have any questions at all about Francis Plummer. And surprising, too, that she was thinking about Gregory van Buren. *Go for it, girl!* he'd said. Where did he learn to talk that way? He was from *England* for goodness sake!

As soon as she could focus on something other than the incessant phone calls and all the other ramifications and excitements of Mitch Michaels's nationally publicized attack, she'd bring Francis in, and the good long talk she was sure they'd have would answer the questions that kept coming up into her mind, even though she was so busy. They seemed sacrilegious to her. Like why wasn't she hearing stories about his exploits in class anymore? Always before, it had seemed to her new chapters were being added to the Francis Plummer Legend almost every day. And it had occurred to her once in the middle of a sleepless night that she hadn't heard any arguments at her dinner table like the ones about the *Merchant of Venice* that had seduced her into taking his Shakespeare course three years before.

Meanwhile, Claire Nelson, the unacknowledged focus of thousands of words streaming over the radio on Mitch Michaels's dark sarcastic voice, seemed fine to Rachel, not unduly stressed. The only visible change was an increased quietness and an even more intense focus on her art. Rachel wondered whether Claire was a healthy soul who had committed to her art, as some other girl in times past, repenting of her sins, might have joined a convent.

Or was she simply impervious? What did grow clear to Rachel, as November came and went and winter vacation loomed, was that Sonja was the one affected. Her personality had softened. There was a new wistfulness in her expression, as if she missed the days before she and Claire had bonded, when all she had to worry about was her business career.

One evening, a few weeks back, Rachel had had to ask Claire to leave her office where Claire had come to study because there were confidential phone calls Rachel needed to make. Since then, Claire had not spent any evenings studying in Rachel's office. Recently, though, other girls had. Studying with the head in her office in the evenings had become the cool thing to do. Rachel enjoyed their company. The atmosphere was warm and cozy and felt like family, causing her to feel the absence of Claire even more sharply, and she remembered Sonja's protectiveness of Claire in the head's office when she had brought Claire back to school. Someone needed to make Claire address her issues. She worried that Sonja wasn't the person for that job. Eudora would have to help.

But mothers are protective, and art is risk and danger. So Rachel shouldn't have been surprised when she worried aloud to Eudora about Claire's guidance and Eudora told her, "I'm not interested in Claire's happiness. In fact, I don't want her ever to be content. What I care about is that she realizes her potential."

"Oh, come on!" Rachel exclaimed. "You're not a sophomore anymore. You don't have to believe that old canard that you have to be a drunk or crazy or suicidal to be an artist."

"Of course I don't. Some paintings hang on walls and I can look at them and see the world in a way I've never seen it before. That doesn't change when I learn the painter was feeling depressed and cut off his ear. That's just biography. The painter had a talent, that's what counts. And this kid Claire Nelson has talent. A whole lot more than any student I've ever had. It's as if she dropped out of the sky into my studio. If it is wrong for a school person to think of a child as a vessel for a talent, then maybe you should fire me. But she's the only one out of all the kids I've taught, and probably ever will be.

Claire understands this in some subliminal way. Maybe later she'll understand it enough to put it into words, or maybe not, I don't really care. Right now what she knows she needs is that I be fierce and severe and demanding, and focus on her talent. With that level of talent, I'd sacrifice the person to the potential product every time. I couldn't do that if I were her mother."

Claire didn't fully recognize that she was avoiding Rachel until one cold December afternoon, while walking on the path from the Science Building to Eudora's studio, when she saw Rachel coming toward her and wished there were a divergent path she could take. It was a shock. She loved Rachel Bickham.

Claire didn't think she was so much avoiding Rachel's company though as preferring Sonja McGarvey's. Sonja was easier to be around. She didn't try to make Claire think about stuff she didn't want to think about. Maybe she assumed Claire would figure things out for herself. And Claire and Sonja were akin in their precocity—though Claire would not have used that word. As far back as she could remember, Sonja had been "getting to the verb," as she put it, so much faster than all her peers that she felt lonely most of the time, and Claire understood already that she'd been born with artistic abilities that her classmates couldn't fathom and even Eudora Easter couldn't match.

Rachel slowed her walk and stopped. Claire stopped too.

"I haven't seen much of you lately," Rachel said.

Claire met Rachel's gaze straight on. "You've been busy. I didn't want to bother you."

"I'm never that busy, Claire."

Claire nodded. "Okay."

"How are you holding up?"

Claire pretended she didn't understand. "Holding up?"

"Are you talking to anyone?"

Claire managed a blank look.

"You know who I mean, Claire. Kevina Rugoff, our school counselor."

"No. Why should I?" Claire said, and before Rachel could

respond, "I've really got to go now, Rachel. I don't want to be late for class."

"Go then," Rachel said, trying to sound matter of fact, and sounding as hurt as she really was.

"Okay. See you later, Rachel." Claire moved past Rachel heading for the studio, and for a few seconds Rachel watched her walk away.

Then she turned and hurried to her office. She would put Claire out of her mind and focus on the meeting that was about to start with Mabel Walters. Mabel had spent the majority of her time since her appointment learning everything she could about the finances of Miss Oliver's School for Girls. "There are some pressing issues you need to understand," she told Rachel. "I'll need a whole afternoon with you for starters."

Like Eudora Easter and Gregory van Buren and Francis Plummer, Mabel was almost twenty years older than Rachel. She had long gray hair and was so small that when she sat in a chair, her feet didn't touch the floor, and she leaned forward when she had a point to make.

That afternoon session, under Mabel's tutelage, Rachel learned how far the school was from financial sustainability despite the politically expensive steps Fred Kindler had taken to begin that journey, such as firing the beloved, incompetent, overpaid former business manager. She hadn't understood how alien to the culture of the school financial discipline was until she saw how shocked Mabel was to have discovered its absence in every layer of the operation: the kitchen and dining room, the use of energy, the years of deferred maintenance, with no plan for catching up. It went on and on.

"I'll chip away at these, but somebody's got to bring the money in," Mabel said. "And the most important of those somebodies is you. You need to turn more of the operation over to someone else—like the academic program, for instance. Why are you running that? You should be out *there*." She pointed out the window of her office, presumably at the larger world where the alumnae lived. "Raising money." She held up her thumb and forefinger only a quarter of an inch apart. "This school's been operating since 1928 and it still has an endowment that is only this big."

THAT THE NIGHT Rachel dreamed she and Sonja were standing in Rachel's bedroom—the one with the single bed where Rachel was sleeping—on opposite sides of a baby's crib, looking down in it at a strangely tiny baby staring back up at them. He—or she, there was no way to tell—was the size of a fifty-cent piece on the middle of the mattress. "Don't worry, it will grow," a voice behind them said. Rachel and Sonja turned around. Claire was standing there in the doorway, an elegant, almost elderly woman, her raven hair turned white. She was still tall and thin—and even more magnetic.

SIXTEEN

One morning in early January, Mitch Michaels awoke, relieved that at last the lonely Christmas holiday season was over, and realized he was bored talking about that school. Yes, he'd been hoodwinked by that Bickham woman. And yes, it was an outrage. For weeks now he'd been telling his audience what really went on at the nation's most prestigious institutions, "where you and I can't send our children because we aren't PC enough and don't have a trust fund," using a certain all-girls boarding school just south of Hartford on the Connecticut River named after a spinster whose name began with O and couldn't think of anything better to do with her money as the emblem of the hidden sickness of liberal America. He'd listed at first certain low-level sins—pot smoking, for instance, and reading the *New York Times*—to build conviction in his audience, for which he held an unacknowledged contempt equal to that for the school he was traducing, for actually believing this enraged drivel that he issued every early morning to avenge himself for the lost family, his addictions, and the waste of his time and talent—and, not at all incidentally, to make a very good living. He'd moved quickly up the scale to cocaine and then LSD and Ecstasy consumed in huge amounts and the huge unsupervised allowances that afforded them, and then to hints of incest, abortions in the school infirmary, and always, without fail, an extended riff on the student who'd had sex with a teacher in her fancy New York City school and so had to escape to the all-girls boarding school *whose headmistress was so eager to get her hands on the millionaire father's promised gift, also known as bribe, she'd created a post-graduate program just for her.*

Morning after morning of this, and it had begun to pall.

But the most powerful reason for his dwindling motivation to continue besmearing Miss Oliver's School for Girls was that his daughter Amy was miles and miles away from it now, across a whole ocean. So stop, forget about it, just let it go. Why should he care, now that Amy wasn't there?

So, back to affirmative action. He wouldn't know what he was going to say about it until he leaned into the mike, but whatever it would be, it would be his last rant on the subject because that one was getting boring too. Lately he'd caught himself wishing he could do sports again—so much easier on the nerves. Because, really, who cares which team wins and which team doesn't? "How would you like it if you got all As and were turned down and then heard about some woman who got in with only Bs," he asked his listeners that morning, but he sounded hollow to himself and didn't care, and for the rest of the hour he was on auto-pilot. This happened more and more these days. His loneliness for his daughter would erupt in him in the middle of the program, filling him with a sadness that expanded in his gut and pushed against his ribs and caused him to shake his head back and forth. When he signed off, he wouldn't remember what he or any of the callers-in had said.

But this time, he wasn't on auto-pilot because of grief. Somewhere between the subject and the verb of the sentence he'd just shoved out onto the airwaves, it had occurred to him that his ex-wife wouldn't have thought of getting a court order to keep him off the St. Agnes campus. Why would she, it being so far away? And even if she tried, she probably couldn't. It was a different system; she wouldn't know how.

Later that day, Rachel returned from lunch to find two ninth graders standing in the middle of her office. Sally Brinton was tall and wore her blond hair in a braid, and Michelle Raney, almost as tall, had red hair down to her shoulders. They both looked scared.

"I hope it's okay," Sally said. "Margaret wasn't here."

"And your door was open," Michelle said.

"Of course it's all right."

They looked at the chairs in the center of the office, then at each other, then back at Rachel.

"It's going to be okay," Rachel said, "whatever it is. I won't bite."

They smiled sheepishly, and sat down and looked at each other again.

"Go ahead, Sally," Michelle said.

Sally shook her head.

Michelle shrugged, then turned to Rachel. "It's about Mr. Plummer. He—"

"Screamed at us," Sally said.

"Screamed?"

Both girls nodded their heads.

"Today? In class?"

They nodded their heads again.

"My goodness! Was this the first time?"

"Well, the first time he actually screamed," Michelle said. "All the other times he almost did. We weren't listening, I guess."

"Listening? But most of the time he gets *you* to talk."

They looked at each other. Michelle shook her head.

"Uh uh," Sally said. "He just talks and talks and talks."

"It's boring," Michelle said.

Rachel and the two girls were silent then, sharing their astonishment. Rachel tried to picture Francis screaming—actually screaming in class! Was he standing up? Or sitting down? "Thanks for telling me, ladies," she said at last. "I'll talk to him."

They stood up abruptly. There was nothing they wanted more than to get out of there. So Rachel stood up too, and the two girls fled.

Rachel was self-aware enough to understand that a more experienced leader would put the situation at a distance, and then, unhindered by her own emotions, proceed to find its best solution, whatever that was. She might've even been able to enjoy thinking about it as an interesting small-scale replica of how the world actually worked. She knew perfectly well that apostasy tends to reside with the young. Sally and Michelle, mere ninth graders (whom Rachel thought of as "freshwomen"), had heard the creed and discovered it wasn't true anymore. Like Galileo and his telescope, they were the first to tell. But knowing how she should behave only doubled

Rachel's pain. She knew what she had learned was truth, but it still felt like blasphemy to her.

She asked Margaret to make an appointment with Francis as soon as possible. Margaret looked worried. "I just want to talk to him," Rachel said.

"Okay," Margaret said, reaching for the phone to call Francis. She still looked worried. Rachel fought off the urge to ask her what she'd been hearing and returned to her office to ready herself.

She sat down behind her desk and forced herself to imagine the Francis Plummer Legend as a material object that she enclosed in a box. She picked up the box, acknowledged its heaviness, and carried it across a field of tall grass, browned by the sun, into a tall gothic house whose once white paint was now dark with age, and climbed narrow stairs to the attic where she put the box inside an ancient cedar storage chest. She'd retrieve it later, when and if she wanted to. Calmer now, more resolute, she reminded herself that this was the kind of challenge she had signed up for. *So embrace it.* Then, pushing out of her mind the ironic fact that Francis Plummer was the person she had chosen to solve exactly the kind of problem Francis Plummer was causing, she visualized staying behind her desk to keep the meeting formal and matter of fact. She would start by asking him what he thought about his ninth grade class.

She began to take deep intentional breaths to empty her mind and center herself. She figured she had at least five minutes to spend this way. And then she would be ready. But before she had taken ten of those deep breaths, she heard Francis say hello to Margaret in her anteroom, as if, knowing she would need time to gird her loins to deal with him, he'd sprinted across the campus after getting Margaret's call.

"Good afternoon," he said, briskly entering her office a moment later. He took one of the central chairs before being invited. "What can I do for you?"

The implication he was there to do her a favor threw Rachel off course. She hesitated.

"Sally and Michelle," he said. "Right?"

"Yes. They said you yelled at them."

"They're right, I did. It seemed like the thing to do at the moment. They got the point. I won't have to raise my voice again."

"But if they got the point, why—?"

"Did they come to your office? Is that the question? Why they complained? They aren't used to being held to a high standard so they went to *you* to complain, that's why. I'm sorry you had to be involved. I wish you had simply told them to speak to me about it."

"I didn't tell you to come to my office to tell me what I should have done. It's the other way around," Rachel said. She was angry now, and in control of the meeting at last. "They're just ninth graders. You're a famous man. They were intimidated."

"Well, I hope you don't think I got to be famous, as you put it, by being intimidating."

"No, but—"

"Good. Here's what we are going to do then," he said. His tone of voice brooked no discussion. "I will talk to Sally and Michelle. I'll say I'm sorry for having raised my voice. I'll tell them that when they have a problem they need to talk to me about it directly, and then I will talk with the whole class. I'll admit we've gotten off on the wrong foot, but we have a lot of the year left. We will figure out how they and I can make this the best English course they've ever had."

"That's a good idea, Francis."

"I'm glad you like it," he said, before she could think of what to say next. He sounded sarcastic and paternalistic at the same time. Then he stood up. "Now I have to go, or I'll be late for my seniors." He left through Margaret's anteroom before she could answer.

Rachel sat very still, staring out the French doors at the campus. It had started to snow. Watching the whiteness slowly gathering on the dark, bare branches of the copper beech did nothing to soften her embarrassment.

She visualized a different meeting in which she told him to sit back down when he had said, "Now I have to go." That he would go when she excused him, not a minute before, and that she intended to observe his ninth grade class at least once a week to check up on him.

That's what the person who had told Milton Perkins, "*You've got to want me enough now to want me permanently,*" and who had come up with the way to silence Mitch Michaels would have said. She remembered the first faculty meeting when she stared at the teachers who had arrived late. It was frightening to understand that if one of them had been Francis Plummer, she wouldn't have dared.

Francis walked fast toward his classroom—not to get there soon so much as to get as far away as fast as he could from Rachel's office. He'd always loved the silence that came over the campus when snow was falling on it, the girls huddled, warm and secure, inside the buildings, and when the sun came out again and the new snow lay like sugar on the lawns, he would shiver with his happiness to be who he was, doing what he was born to do at this school he loved. But today, all the snow did for him was land on his glasses and make it hard to see.

Why did he run over Rachel like that? She'd despise him for the rest of her life. Why didn't he just admit that he'd lost it in class? He'd been trying to get his freshmen to love Richard Wilbur's "Ballade for the Duke of Orleans," a poem he loved for all the reasons that there were to love a poem. "Pay attention," he'd yelled. "Pay attention! I'm talking to you!" And then the embarrassment, theirs as much as his. All nineteen of them found some other direction to aim their eyes. Michelle and Sally aimed theirs at each other. And then all he could think of to do was talk—which was what he had already been doing. Explain. Explain. Explain. He should have stopped and grinned and said, *Have I quelled your interest yet? Do you think you might ever read a book that's not an exam? If so, I'll keep on talking.* Clark Kent had always been able to pull the rabbit out of the hat. But he was just Francis Plummer today.

He stopped walking. Snowflakes were melting on the back of his neck and dripping down below his collar. He entertained a vague feeling that if he returned to Rachel and they talked, really talked, some disaster would be avoided. But no, he'd do what he had told her he would do: first talk to Michelle and Sally, and then the class.

"You go on ahead," he said to Peggy that evening in the foyer of the dining room. "I need to talk to someone." She moved on, without comment, toward the table where they'd played the role of mother and father for nearly thirty-five years. Peggy would be the last person to hear the whispers of what had happened this morning.

He waited nervously for Michelle and Sally to appear. He'd decided to meet them this way, as if casually, instead of calling them to his classroom, which would have been more threatening.

He watched his world assemble as the school trooped out of the dark into the bright warm light, everybody stamping snow off their feet. It didn't occur to him how idiosyncratic the scene was. Four hundred students and forty teachers, single ones like Eudora Easter, and families, toddlers, holding parents' hands, the students, except for an independent few, without coats or jackets. It was a Miss O's quirk not to put on coats or jackets to go to class, or the gym, or meals, thus to show how much tougher girls were than boys. Watching girls stand on one leg and bend down to take their wet shoes off, Francis was reminded that it was getting hard for him to stand on one leg. He'd started to sit down in the mornings when he put on his pants. The girls chucked the shoes into corners, making an unsightly mess guaranteed to inspire a diatribe by Gregory van Buren that they would admire and enjoy, and completely disregard.

At last, Sally and Michelle came through the door together, as he had guessed they would. They saw him and quickly looked away. They were both wearing heavy sweaters and Sally had a scarf around her neck. In a different situation, he might have kidded them for being so sissified. "Ladies, do you have a minute?" he said, walking beside them. He had planned to add, *Don't worry*, but he didn't. Why shouldn't they be worried? He certainly was. "Let's meet here right after dinner," he said. He didn't wait for an answer.

He was as nervous during the dinner, which lasted forever and ever, as he was sure they were. But, he told himself, he knew how to pretend he wasn't. And they didn't.

"Where would you like to talk?" he asked out in the foyer after dinner, letting them know they had some control, that they were peers working together to solve a problem that they had caused as much as he. They looked at each other, then back to him and shrugged. Their faces wore a stubborn and sullen look. "How about there?" He pointed to the lounge, a big room on the other side of the dining hall, where there was a sofa and a cluster of big stuffed chairs and a grand piano. He started that way and they followed him into the lounge and across it toward a far corner where they wouldn't be interrupted. Halfway there he realized it was a mistake to talk here where everybody in the room would see them. Every girl Sally or Michelle had told would know what they were talking about. Humiliation flooded him, amazement and hurt pride.

He sat down on a stuffed chair. Sally and Michelle sat down on a facing sofa. They wouldn't look at him. On the wall behind them was a portrait, in mild pastels, of a teenage Miss Edith Oliver in a blue summer dress. It was the first time he realized how pretty she was. She held a pair of white gloves in one hand and a big yellow sun hat in the other, and her hair was tied in a bow at the back. She didn't look at all like the spinster she would become, smiling down at the three of them.

"I told Rachel I would talk with you," he said. He heard a quaver in his voice. Sally and Michelle said nothing. "So, what do you think we should do?" he asked, and the girls still didn't speak. So he said, "You were right to tell Rachel. I'm not angry at all, and I need your help." He watched their surprise.

"Help?" Sally said

Francis nodded. "To make it all better," he said. "To get us back on track. We're going to do the 'Ballade' again tomorrow. So here's what I need: Sally to tell the story of Adam and Eve at the beginning of the class. And right after that, Michelle, you read the first two verses of Keats' 'Ode on a Grecian Urn' in our anthology." He stopped and watched them thinking. "You see where we're going?" They nodded their heads. The class had read and discussed the poem early in the year. The girls knew about the maidens loth and the mad, forever unrequited pursuit of them by men or gods while pipes and timbrels played, but they still looked suspicious. "Well, I'm glad I wasn't *that* boring," he said. He stood up. "And—just one thing more—"

They looked up at him, waiting.

"Don't be embarrassed when I thank you for telling Rachel."

While Francis was talking with Sally and Michelle, Rachel was hurrying to her office. If she focused on composing her monthly letter to the parents and alumnae on the state of the school, not letting other concerns weaken her concentration, she'd be able to finish by ten p.m. so she and Bob could talk on the phone before he went to bed. That morning, she had written *CALL BOB* on her calendar next to the ten o'clock line.

Whether in letters, her frequent speeches, or interviews, ideas for what to say and how to say them usually came easily to Rachel. Not tonight. Instead, what came to her, as it had all day, was yet another replay of her meeting with Francis. She told herself she wouldn't ever relinquish her power to him again. And then she told herself the truth: she could hang on to all the power she had, and he would still have more. About three thousand and six hundred alumnae revered him. He was the face of the school, not she.

She started the parents letter by reporting on the Michaels affair. By nine-thirty, she had a draft. By nine-forty-five, she had decided to delete the paragraphs about the Michaels affair. The whole point was to ignore Mitch Michaels. Now the letter seemed too short. By the time she had a new draft, it was eleven p.m. When he was alone in New York, Bob was sound asleep by ten-thirty and awake at five-thirty, in his office before seven. She went to the Head's House and straight to her single bed. She'd call him in the morning.

When the alarm went off at five-thirty, Rachel had to force herself to get out of bed and get ready for the day. She could call Bob while she was still in her PJs, of course, but she wanted to be up, showered and dressed. She wanted to treat the call just as importantly as an appointment in her office. As a matter of fact, it *was* an appointment. She'd written it in her calendar, hadn't she?

"Hi," she said, when he picked up the phone. "Surprise. Surprise."

"Rachel! Are you all right?"

"I'm fine."

"It's so early."

"I just wanted to talk."

"Yeah, I did too."

"So, why didn't you call me?"

"I don't know. I guess I thought you should."

"Well, I just did."

He didn't answer.

"Bob, what's wrong?"

"Nothing that can't wait."

"Wait for what?"

"For you to ask."

"Bob! I just did."

There was a long silence.

"Come on. What's up?"

"All right, here's what," Bob said. She heard him take a big breath, and then he said, "Remember, I told you something terrible happened?"

"Yes, I do—oh my goodness!"

"That's right. You never asked."

"Damn. What's wrong with me? I'm so—"

"Rachel, don't. I've waited so long already to tell you! I don't want to wait some more while you apologize. George Boem hung himself. Our Chicago guy. I still don't know why."

"Killed himself!"

"I liked him a lot."

"Oh I'm sorry, Bob."

"Yeah, me too."

"I thought when you said something bad had happened, it was about the business. I didn't think it was about—"

"A person? A real, live human being?"

"I didn't mean to hurt you. I should have asked. I—"

"You didn't know him," he said. "You never met him."

"Are you excusing or chastising me with that?" She waited and waited for his answer. She could almost hear him think.

"Neither," he said at last. "It's just the way it is."

"No!" she said.

"I'll see you in three weeks, Rachel. Right now I have a breakfast appointment at seven. It's all the way downtown."

"I'm sorry, Bob."

"Don't worry about it," he said brusquely. "I have to go. I really do. I'm late already."

"Well, goodbye, then," Rachel said. She put the receiver back in its cradle. Now she understood the source of the tension she'd felt between Bob and herself when she and Bob and her father and brother and sister had been together at the school for a few days at Christmas. It had been there just under the surface all that time and she realized now he'd been waiting for her to ask the question, but she had been too concerned for her father to catch the hint. Rachel and her siblings, and Bob too, always focused their attention on the elder Bickham at Christmas. That was when his loneliness for his wife would arrive again with all its original force. Sometimes it seemed to them he was waiting for her to appear in the living room from the dining room to announce that dinner was ready, or on the landing on the stairs to wish them a good morning.

Rachel walked across the campus to the dining room for breakfast. She had told a student she would meet her there to help her with her physics homework. She moved fast. It was still dark and she wasn't wearing a coat, of course, and it was much too cold to tarry.

Did Bob cry at the memorial service for George Boem, she wondered, as she hurried along, *the man I didn't know? Or alone in his New York apartment?*

Or is he crying now?

At eight-fifteen that same morning, Francis stayed in the teachers' lounge, as he had on the first day of classes, until after all his ninth graders had entered his classroom and taken seats around the three-sided square of tables. Last night, he'd planned this to emphasize to the students that he and they were starting all over again, but he hadn't thought about the several teachers who didn't have a first period class. They were sneaking glances at him over their coffee cups, wondering why he wasn't in his classroom. He glanced at his watch, faking amazement to discover it was late. "I didn't hear the bell," he lied, and hurried out into the hall, wishing he'd hid in one of the stalls in the men's room.

A moment later, he sauntered into his classroom and pretended to be surprised to find students sitting there. Then he forced a smile and said, "It's clean-slate time. Let's begin all over again. We'll get it right this time, I promise."

Silence. Nineteen pairs of eyes full of surprise, suspicion, and curiosity felt like an actual weight on his face. He shrugged. "We'll start with a story Sally has agreed to tell," he said. "Sally?"

So Sally, clearly embarrassed to be telling a story everybody already knew, talked about how God told Adam not to eat the apple of knowledge but he did anyway and so got kicked out of the Garden of Eden and was very sad. "Which is pure BS," she added. "There's no such place."

"Thanks, Sally," Francis said; then, turning to the class, "Just hold that story in your head, all right? Just the story, without Sally's editorializing. And now Michelle's going to read the first two verses of a poem you already know." There was nothing in his demeanor to reveal how nervous he was.

Unlike Sally, who'd stayed in her seat, Michelle came up to the front of the room, taking her time. She paused dramatically before announcing: "Ode on a Grecian Urn, by John Keats, 1795 to 1821." Several students giggled. Michelle ignored them and proceeded to recite the lines by heart, looking straight at her classmates, not once glancing down at the poetry anthology in her hand. The girls sat still, listening. Michelle had practiced last night and had come to love the poem. Gregory van Buren, who required students in his class to memorize at least five poems every semester, had coached her.

When Michelle had finished, there was a silence, which Francis allowed to linger. Then he asked her to repeat the last four lines of the second verse. She was delighted to.

Bold Lover, never, never canst thou kiss,
Though winning near the goal—yet, do not grieve;
She cannot fade, though thou hast not thy bliss,
For ever wilt thou love, and she be fair!

"Michelle, you're a great reader," Francis said. Then to the class. "Hold that too."

He had planned to ask one of the students to read the "Ballade" now, but he changed his mind. It wouldn't be fair to ask a student to measure up to Michelle's performance. Besides, everything depended on their being moved by the poem, and he really had never met anybody who read aloud better than he, not even professional actors—except maybe Richard Wilbur himself, who chanted all his poems. Francis would read the first verse and let the students read the others. He started to read, discovering that he was chanting too. It was a surprise.

Ballade for the Duke of Orleans
who offered a prize at Blois, circa 1457, for the best ballade employing the line "Je meurs de soif auprès de la fontaine."

Flailed from the heart of water in a bow,
He took the falling fly; my line went taut;
Foam was in an uproar where he drove below;
In spangling air I fought him and was fought.
Then, wearied to the shallows, he was caught,
Gasped in the net, lay still and stony-eyed.
It was no fading iris I had sought.
I die of thirst, here at the fountain-side.

He looked up at the girls. "*No fading iris?* What's that about?"

No one raised her hand. He waited. Still, they were silent, eyeing him warily. Yes, they had listened to Sally and Michelle, but here he was trying to shove this poem down their throats again. He would have to tell them the answer, do the talking. That had been the problem all along. "No one knows?" he challenged, looking straight at Alice Boorman, sitting to his right at the front of the table where he stood. She was very small, had black hair and great big earrings, and was always the first to raise her hand. "Alice?"

Alice looked around the room at her classmates, ignoring him. "It's like you want something and then you get it and then you don't want it anymore." Her tone suggested the answer was so obvious he shouldn't have asked the question.

"Is that good or bad, you think?"

Alice shrugged. "I don't know. It's just the way it is, that's all."

"Yes. Whether good or bad," he agreed, taking the little she had given him. Then, throwing out the bait for more, "What does *spangling* mean?"

Alice thought for a moment. "Glittery?" she said.

"Ah!"

Alice's expression brightened in spite of herself. "It means the sky is blue and the sun is out and it is beautiful."

"Yes, a great day to be alive," he said, confidence rising. "What is he fishing for, you think?"

"He?" Molly Rintoul said. A thin girl with red hair. Her sister was a senior. "How do you know it isn't a she?"

He smiled, not surprised by this agenda. This was Miss Oliver's School for *Girls*. "The person then."

"Trout," Molly said. "What else?"

"Right. Or salmon maybe. Certainly not catfish."

"Or suckers, not even perch," Molly said. "They're ugly."

"That's right, and trout are beautiful, aren't they?" He spoke to Molly as if she and he were the only people in the room—which guaranteed that everyone else would listen in. It was his good luck to have a girl in the class who loved to fly fish as much as any man. "Iridescent sides and lovely shape," he added, and then was silent for a few seconds while he hoped they all visualized live trout swimming. Then, rounding first, heading for second: "Anybody ever see one die?"

"I have," Molly said. "They lie on their sides opening and closing their mouths, trying to breath. They look so surprised they can't, and every once in a while they shake all over. You can see how much they don't want to die. I keep telling my father to put them back. You don't even have to take them out of the water. You just grab the fly between your index finger and thumb and twist the fly out of its lip and the fish swims away."

"Still alive!" Francis said.

"But my father just keeps on bringing the ones he catches home to my mother. She makes him cut their heads off."

"Oh dear! Maybe you should read them this poem."

Molly shook her head. "They wouldn't like it."

"Do you like it, Molly?"

"So far? Yes."

"Okay, let's do the next verse and see how we like that," he said. "Who wants to read it?" He knew Donna Ford would raise her hand. Otherwise he wouldn't have asked. The last thing he needed right now was to have someone butcher the poem. Donna loved to read aloud and was good at it. She wanted to be an actress when she grew up. When Gregory van Buren told her she wouldn't ever get an audition if she didn't take the ring out of her nose, she had another put in and now she had two. She was too smart to try to chant:

Down in the harbor's flow and counter-flow
I left my ships with hopes and heroes fraught.
Ten times more golden than the sun could show,
Calypso gave the darkness I besought.
Oh, but her fleecy touch was dearly bought:
All spent, I wakened by my only bride,
Beside whom every vision is but nought,
And die of thirst, here by the fountain-side.

"We read the *Odyssey* in October, and you know who Calypso was, so who wants to talk about her?" Francis asked.

"You," Angela Bickford said, before anybody could raise her hand. "You're the only guy in the room."

"Angela!"

"Calypso's going to be in a guy's head, not a girl's—unless she's a lesbian," Angela said. She always kept her dark glasses on when she came inside.

"Well! I must have read this poem a hundred times and I never thought about that," Francis said. "Go on. Let's hear more."

"So, when he finally gets home to his wife—"

"Wait, wait, stop right there, Angela. How long has he been trying to get home to her?"

"I don't know. Ten years?"

"A long time," Francis said. "A long, long time."

Angela looked irritated. "That's why I said *finally*."

"Sorry, Angela, I wanted everybody to remember he didn't exactly zip straight home. We talked about that, remember? Or, rather, I did," he added, sheepishly. "And not only because of the things that happened to him, right, Christie?" he said, turning to a girl who was nodding her head at his admission that he'd talked too much and bored them to death. She didn't answer. "Christie?"

"What?" Christie challenged.

"The other reasons he took so long."

Christie looked around her at her classmates, as if asking permission to answer. Then she looked back to him, apparently satisfied. "He kept stopping to check things out."

"Right, like who else?"

"Adam, of course."

"Yup," Angela said. "First he checked out the apple, and then he checked out Eve." Everyone giggled, except Francis, who laughed out loud. "And Odysseus checked out Calypso," Angela said. "I knew we'd get back to that."

"So did I," Francis said, still grinning. He turned to the class. "Where were we on that subject?"

"Angie said Calypso only exists for men," Danielle Orth said. "Which I think is crazy."

"Not to me, it isn't," Angela said. "She's what only a man would dream up."

"Nobody dreamed her up. He spent a whole year with her," Danielle said.

"Checking her out," someone murmured, and everybody giggled again.

"It's just a story," Angela said, and Francis thought: *Here it is, right here. What I have to work with.* He didn't need to look at his watch to know how fast time was running out.

"We'll talk another time about what's more real: what happens in your everyday life or what happens in the story you would write about it," he said. "Right now I assume all agree that when Odysseus finally gets home to his wife, beside whom every vision is but nought, he feels like he's dying of thirst right beside a fountain."

Nancy Grey frowned. "In the poem or real life?"

Francis laughed out loud again. "Nancy, what did I just say?"

Nancy blushed. "Oh that's right. We'll talk about it later."

"You bet we will, Nancy. Don't let me forget, okay?" he said, and then he announced the homework: "For tomorrow, write one side of a page, no more, no less, explaining why Odysseus feels the way he does when he gets home."

"Isn't that obvious?" Molly said.

"You'll find out when you write it," he said. "Now let's listen to the rest." He recited the rest of the poem from memory, chanting again:

Where does that Plenty dwell, I'd like to know,
Which fathered poor Desire, as Plato taught?
Out on the real and endless waters go
Conquistador and stubborn Argonaut.
Where Buddha bathed, the golden bowl he brought
Gilded the stream, but stalled its living tide.
The sunlight withers as the verse is wrought.
I die of thirst, here by the fountain-side.

ENVOI

Duke, keep your coin. All men are born distraught,
And will not for the world be satisfied.
Whether we live in fact, or but in thought,
We die of thirst, here at the fountain-side.

Now it was time for him to talk and for them to listen. So he explained *Where does that Plenty dwell, I'd like to know, That fathered poor Desire,* riffing on the notion that this very class was a mere imitation of the real one in his head, and speculating, along with Tennyson—whose poem "Ulysses" he admitted he'd also bored them to death with earlier—that as soon as Odysseus arrived home, he wanted to leave again.

Francis did that in only five minutes and then he said, "Oh, by the way, did you notice that Richard Wilbur has used almost very *aught* sound in the English language?"

"He did?" Nancy Grey said.

"Yes, Nancy he did. Read them."

Nancy read: *taught, fought, caught, sought, fraught, besought, bought, nought, brought, wrought, distraught, thought.* She looked up at him.

"Yes, isn't that a wonder?" Francis said.

Then the bell rang and no one moved. He smiled. "Was that the bell I heard?" They sat still for another few seconds. Then they stood up and picked up their stuff. "Michelle and Sally, thanks for straightening me out," he said. The girls stared at him for a second and then at Sally and Michelle, and then they filed out of his classroom. He heard them talking out in the hall. He hoped it was about the "Ballade."

"I'm almost back on track again," he murmured to the Globe Theater in the back of the room. He was right. It wasn't the best class he'd ever taught. But it wasn't the worst either. One thing was clear though: he was exhausted.

SEVENTEEN

On an evening late in January, Francis and Peggy Plummer returned from the evening meal in the dining room to find a fat yellow manila envelope had been pushed through the mail slot in the door. Levi had come to the door to greet them. He was standing with his front paws on it, wagging his tail. Peggy pushed him aside and picked the package up quickly. "What is it?" he said. She didn't answer. He shrugged and moved past her into the living room. It was a catalogue, what else? Nobody needed to write them letters. Their entire lives were contained in the school.

Peggy stayed behind in the foyer—to read it, he assumed. He was mildly surprised. He'd never known her even to glance through a catalogue. He sat down on the sofa and picked up the *New York Times.* It was open at the Op-Ed page, which Peggy always read last before she left for the library.

But did he really want to find out how many books David Brooks had read since yesterday? No, he didn't think so. He picked up the Arts section, looking for the book reviews.

Then Peggy came into the living room and, bending down to where he sat on the sofa, handed him a letter. The expression on her face was so strange a mixture of surprise, excitement, and worry that he didn't even glance at the letter in his hand. "I'm sorry. I should have told you," she said, looking down at him.

"Tell me what?"

"That I applied."

"Applied?"

"Read the letter, dear."

He bent his head down to read.

The letter, from Columbia University, informed Peggy that she had been selected to participate in a year-long combination of academic study at Columbia University and life in a reconstructed Blackfoot village. The program would start in April and continue to June of the following year. The grant would pay her salary and benefits and cover essential living expenses for the entire time of her leave of absence from the school. *You will experience the life view and spirituality of the Blackfoot people who, living close to nature, believe in nativist deities, animating the universe.*

Why were they giving this to her? He didn't dare look at Peggy, so he kept his head down and read on and learned that Peggy had been selected *over other worthy candidates, because of her outstanding performance in curating the Collection of Pequot Artifacts in the library, making the Collection central to the humanistic curriculum of the school, and because of the brilliant, strategic work she had done to help the school establish a partnership with the Pequot Nation so that the Collection and the room in the library where it was housed, now belonged to the Pequot Nation, and attracted hundreds of visitors each month, many of whom would otherwise never have set foot on the campus.*

Francis read the letter twice while Peggy watched his face. He had never confessed to her that the archaeological dig he'd gone on last summer instead of staying home to orient Fred Kindler wasn't just a failed vision quest; it was a failed archaeological dig. If Peggy knew how farcical the whole adventure had been, she'd make an even stronger claim that he'd been having a crack-up. The students, Francis, and the dig's leader, a dreamily incompetent man named Livingstone Mendoza, did manage to construct an authentic Ohlone village on the shoulder of Mount Alma, near San Francisco, where a gigantic housing tract was already metastasizing, but then the president of the Mount Alma Improvement Company gleefully insisted it be ringed round with large green, plastic, and astonishingly odiferous Porta Potties. They never did find any artifacts, and, to Francis's relief, no bones either, and they never got the Ohlone rituals right—not even on the last night in the sweat house, where Francis, sure he was about to expire in the heat, discovered he was telling jokes instead of chanting: "What's the difference between a BMW and a porcupine?" Nobody answered of course, and so he informed them, "With a porcupine, the pricks are on the outside." He had wondered why no one laughed.

At last he looked up from the letter at Peggy. The bitter paradox that she, not he, had been chosen to explore his spiritual territory wasn't the only news hanging in the space between them: she had taken a purposeful, decisive step forward in her profession when she applied for this grant last May, and now she had won it, leaving him behind. It was as frightening a revelation to her as it was to him. She wasn't going to turn around and come back to him. He would have to follow.

He was the first to speak. "We just got back together and now you're going away?"

"Not until April," she said, managing, somehow, to find a tone as reassuring and calm as his had been plaintive. "That's plenty of time."

"Oh, we're on a schedule?"

She shook her head. "That's not fair, Francis."

"Goal Number One," he said bitterly. "Heal marriage by April."

"We could heal it right now if you congratulated me," she said. Then, after a pause, exaggerating, "I won it over thousands and thousands of applicants. Maybe that's why it took them so long to decide."

"You didn't even tell me you were applying."

"You weren't here to tell, remember?"

"How could I forget? You kicked me out."

"Are we going to go over that again? Just let me know, okay? So I can put my fingers in my ears."

"And when I came back, you still didn't tell me."

"That's because I didn't think I was going to get it," Peggy said. "I said to myself, why stir the poor little man up if I'm not going to get it?" Peggy's voice was trembling now. "And you know what Goal Number Two should be? That you grow up. Francis Plummer stops being a baby. He actually thinks that things should change every seven hundred years or so. How's that for a plan?" She turned from the living room toward the kitchen.

"Come back, Peggy. Damn it, come back." She was in the kitchen now, out of his sight. There was the sound of the backdoor opening. "Where're you going?"

An instant later, she was back in the living room doorway.

"I'm going to tell Rachel. She'll be glad that people on her faculty get awards. I'll go there and get congratulated while you sit here and wallow in your jealousy and resentment." She turned away, disappearing again. A few seconds later the backdoor slammed.

"THIS IS BRILLIANT!" Rachel said before she'd even finished reading the letter. She continued reading to the end, wondering all the while what this news meant for Francis. Finished, she looked up at Peggy. "It's in absolute alignment with everything we're trying to do with our anthropology courses and our partnership with the Pequots. It couldn't be more perfect. Hooray for you! It is great for your career and great for the school. I can't wait to tell the board and the alumnae and get it into the newspapers."

"Thanks. It was easy to think up the idea—for all the reasons you just said. I applied last spring, before you were the head. I'm sorry, I should have told you, but I didn't hear from them and I assumed I was turned down, so there was no point. And besides, I had other things on my mind. Francis and I were still living apart."

Rachel waved the apology away. "I bet he's happy for you now."

"He is. He's delighted for me." Peggy looked Rachel straight in the eye and her voice was firm. "He said the same things you just did."

"Of course he did. Why wouldn't he?"

Peggy lowered her voice. "Well, we did just get back together, you know."

"Hmm," Rachel murmured. "I almost forgot about that. But you can visit each other on weekends. As a matter of fact," she said, her heartbeat rising, "I could arrange some time off for Francis so he could visit you. That would be really interesting for Francis."

"Yes, it would solve the whole problem," Peggy agreed.

Rachel nodded. "You and Francis will put everything into those visits."

Peggy leaned forward. "That works for you and Bob?"

Rachel shrugged. "Sort of."

"I'm sorry. I didn't mean to pry," Peggy said, leaning back again in her chair.

"It's fine. You're not prying," Rachel said. There was no subterfuge in what she was saying now. "You get lonely, that's what happens. You want him to be there, and he isn't. But it's not the end of the world."

"Of course not."

"I couldn't stand it, though, if I weren't so busy. But, you know—sometimes I'm almost glad he isn't there, because if he were I'd have to stop working and talk to him."

"Me too," Peggy said. "There're lots of time when I'm glad I have just got to get something done in the library, or a girl in the dorm gets sick."

Rachel smiled. "Or the head of school calls another faculty meeting. Have you ever thought of setting aside time, making an appointment with Francis, putting it on your calendar so you have to keep it?"

Peggy shook her head. "Never even thought of it."

"I have. You know, such and such a time: call Bob."

"Does it work?"

"Not sure yet. I've only done it once."

"Well, you just keep right on doing it!"

"He told me something I should have known already."

"See? That's what I mean."

"But he wouldn't let me apologize. I tried, but he hung up."

"Oh," Peggy said, deflated. "I'm sorry." Then, her voice brightening again, "But it's a beginning."

Rachel's expression brightened too. "I hope so."

"Anyway, you're ahead of Francis and me," Peggy said. "He would just mock the idea." She looked at her watch. "Oh dear, I'm on study hour supervision in the dorm tonight. I'm already late."

"Don't go. Let Francis take it."

Peggy stood up, shaking her head. "He meets with the Poetry Club on Tuesday nights."

Rachel stayed in her chair. "How long has he been doing that?"

"Forever."

There was a moment of silence while the two women looked at each other, and then Rachel said, "He's done everything forever, hasn't he?"

Peggy glanced at the door.

Rachel pretended not to notice. She let the silence linger. Then she stood up too.

"Good night, Rachel," Peggy said.

"Good night. And Peg?"

"Yes?"

"It's been good to talk."

Peggy smiled and left, hurrying across the campus to her supervision duty in the dorm.

LIKE FOR A lot of couples, the Plummers' way of apologizing after a quarrel was to wait for an appropriate moment an hour or two later and start talking again as if there hadn't been a quarrel. It was less embarrassing than saying, *I'm sorry*, and it saved them from actually having to forgive each other. It was for this purpose that Francis hurried back to the apartment after the Poetry Club meeting and was standing at the door that led to the dorm when Peggy returned from her supervision duty. He knew she wouldn't be surprised. "Hi," he said.

"Hello," she murmured without looking at him, and moved past him into the living room.

"How's everybody in the dorm?" he asked, following her out of the living room and down the hall toward their bedroom.

"Fine."

"Good. Nobody sick?"

She shook her head.

"Good. Want some tea?"

"Francis, stop it. If I wanted tea, I'd be in the kitchen."

"Yeah, you must be tired."

"How perceptive you are. What was your first clue? That I'm headed for bed?"

"That must have been the one," he said, following her into their bedroom. She sat down on the side of the bed, bending over to take off her shoes. He took off his sport coat and, though—or maybe even because—she'd made it clear to him that she had got used to a tidy bedroom while he'd been gone, he chucked it over the back of a chair, following it with his shirt and tie. With a satisfying predictability, she glowered at the mess. "Sorry," he said, his cheerful tone making it clear that he wasn't. He picked up the clothes and made a show of hanging them up on his side of the closet. With his back to her, he said, "And how did your meeting with Rachel go?" He didn't expect an answer and he didn't get one.

He took off his shoes and placed them precisely side by side on the floor of the closet. Then he stripped off his trousers and hung them up, and then he crossed the room in his T-shirt and boxers and sat down on the bed beside Peggy and waited. She didn't speak. He put his hand on her knee, resting it lightly. She looked down at it as if deciding whether or not to shove it away.

"I bet she was happy," he said.

Peggy turned her head and looked at him. "Who?"

He grinned.

She grinned back in spite of herself. "Yes, she was."

"She congratulated you?"

"She did. I told her you did too."

"Really? You lied to the head?"

"Well, what would you have done? You think she would have believed me if I told her the truth?"

He looked chagrinned. "No, I don't suppose she would."

"I told her you fell all over yourself congratulating me."

"That I jumped up and down with happiness?"

"Those very words."

"Well, I am happy for you, Peg,"

"You sound like you mean it," she said, miming astonishment.

"I do, Peg. I really do."

Peggy thought for a moment. Then she put her hand on his, still resting on her knee. "We'll be fine, Francis. I'll be in New York much of the time. I can come here on weekends and you can come to New York."

"Much of the time? Where else?"

"Montana."

"Montana!"

"Yes, Francis, Montana," she said, exasperated again. "It's not the moon."

"You're right," he said, retreating fast. "It's not the moon."

She squeezed his hand. "Francis?"

"What?"

"Say it again."

"Congratulations."

"Yes. And like you mean it."

"All right, Peg. Congratulations."

"Thank you, Francis."

He leaned to kiss her on the cheek, but she put her hand on his chest and held him off. "You'll visit me in Montana?"

"I will."

"Promise?"

"I promise."

She took her hand off his chest. "I can't wait to see you in a loincloth," she said, and he leaned the rest of the way in and she kissed him on the lips.

MS. HARRIET RICHARDSON, retired educator, widely respected for her stellar career as dean of students in not one but two of the nation's most prestigious women's colleges, normally listened to the radio in the evening when she was having her sherry and making her dinner, but this morning she was listening to Mitch Michaels's program, so it felt enough like evening for her to have a few glasses while she was making her breakfast.

Listening to that awful man was her way of getting revenge for the humiliation she'd received from Alan Travelers for his instantaneous acceptance of her offer to resign from the board a year ago. She had always been able to get the last word, the coup to render her victorious, once silencing William F. Buckley, for instance, with: *Young man, you have succeeded in proving to this audience only that a very silly man can own a very large vocabulary.* But she'd had no words for Alan Travelers when he said, "I accept," and gently pulled the board papers out of her hand, and everybody watched her get up from her chair and walk to the door that was almost too big for her to push open. So, of course she didn't owe the school the pledge not to listen to the deranged rants of Mitch Michaels. In fact, she listened every morning.

And every morning, she grew angrier and angrier—but not at Mitch Michaels. He was beneath her anger. Her fury was directed at the new administration of her beloved Miss Oliver's School and its oh-so-up-to-date board of trustees. To go out of their way to choose that woman, right past Francis Plummer, or even Gregory van Buren, both twice as experienced, her betters by far, just because she's a person of color! That ridiculous term. *If I put rouge on my cheeks, am* I *a person of color*?

She figured Mitch Michaels had switched to other subjects so that listeners wouldn't get tired of hearing about Miss Oliver's School. He'd start up again soon after giving it a little rest. But if Francis Plummer had been in charge, that girl wouldn't have been admitted in the first place and none of this would have ever happened.

Every morning, Ms. Harriet Richardson tried to guess who among the Oliver community might also be listening. That morning, fueled by remembered humiliation and her breakfast sherry, she started making a list of their names. She thought they might respond favorably to an invitation from her to come to a meeting.

ON THAT SAME morning, Rachel received a call from her father. She was surprised. She usually called him on Sundays when she had more time, but here he was calling her at ten o'clock on a weekday morning to tell her about the weather and some repairs he might make to their cottage on the Vineyard, and she knew he was getting up the nerve to bring up the subject that had been on both their minds since last June when she had accepted her position as head of school and postponed having a child. She didn't help him out one bit getting to that subject, and so he finally blurted, "Your time's running out, you know."

Rachel was already a year older than her mother was when she was conceived. She couldn't count the times her father had told her in his gruff way what a gift she was. Now, from miles away over the phone, he said, "So shouldn't you be in a hurry?" and, when she didn't answer right away, "I take your silence for a yes."

"Yes," she said. "Yes, yes, yes."

"Well, then?" he asked, getting the last word, as usual. He put his phone down, but Rachel held on to hers and dialed Bob.

"It's me," she said the instant he answered his phone.

"Rachel! What's this about?"

"I'm lonely, that's what."

"You are?"

"Aren't you?"

"What do you think?"

"I think you better be."

"Well, I am."

"All right then," she said, and went on to tell him she was going to postpone the all-day planning session with the business manager scheduled for the coming Saturday in which they'd project the budgets forward over the next three years—and he better free up his weekend too. She promised to leave for New York no later than three on Friday afternoon. If the traffic wasn't too bad, she might get there by seven.

And he said he'd make dinner.

WHILE RACHEL WAS on the phone with her father and then her husband, Claire was alone in her room, drawing pictures she would send to Amy in England. She worked in her room in the dorm rather than the studio because she didn't want anyone other than Amy to see them, not even Eudora Easter. Each picture filled a letter-size sheet. In one of these, two girls sat close together on a beach. In another, Amy sat at the tiller of *Amy's Delight*. And in another, two girls lay on their backs, looking up at the sky, their arms outspread as if they were making angels' wings in snow. Their fingers were touching. Above one girl's head the words *You are the only one I'd ever tell* floated.

Claire wrote on the accompanying letter:

These are just for you. At first I thought I told you because I like to take chances. Then I thought I told you because I don't like doing what I'm told to do and Mr. Frothingham and my father told me over and over not to tell anyone. That's not why I told a person last year. I told her because she was naive and needed to know, and I always knew that's not why I told you.

Now I know I told you because I wanted you to know. I want us to be friends forever and ever and ever. The next time we are together, we are going to prick our fingers and press them together and mix our blood.

I have a new friend, a woman named Sonja McGarvey. She's ten years older than me and already a millionaire, maybe even a billionaire, for all I know, but that's not why I like her. I spent a couple of weeks at her house. I'll explain why when you come home, but you probably have already figured that one out. And I spend school breaks there too instead of flying all the way to London and back. I like being there. We go to museums together. I tell her what I see in the art we look at, and she really listens. She calls me up every once in a while just to see how I'm doing. She's a venture capitalist. I didn't know what that was until she explained to me. It is interesting. Very complicated. She loves to take risks. She's also very funny. She says things that other people only think.

I love writing to you. The only thing I'd like better is actually talking. I think of you as a sister.

Love, Claire.

P.S. I almost forgot to tell you: you don't have to worry about what your dad is saying on the radio anymore about Miss O's and you-know-what. He's stopped. It was in the TV news, that's how we found out. Maybe he got bored. Maybe he figured out that nobody around here listens to him. I know you think he's pretty weird and you hate the things he says on the radio, but just remember he loves you. I could feel it pouring out of him all over you that whole weekend. If he was my dad, I wouldn't give a damn what he says on the radio. Maybe he's just doing that for money.

Love again.

C

The person who opened the door for Rachel at the River Club two days later, when she appeared for her monthly Friday lunch with

Milton Perkins, was a geriatric version of every butler who has ever appeared on Masterpiece Theater. He looked even more surprised to see the likes of her at the front door than he had the month before. "It's me again," she said brightly, hoping for a rise, but, poor man, he didn't seem to hear her. He commanded her to wait in the lobby while via some invisible semaphore apparently available only to Anglo-Saxons he informed some other vassal that she was at the front door, and that second vassal in turn informed Mr. Perkins, and then: "Mr. Perkins will come downstairs and speak to you here."

"Why? That would just interrupt his martini," Rachel said and handed him her coat. She wanted very much to brush the crumbs off his lapels and the vest that covered his rounded tummy, but she kept her hands to herself and climbed the stairs. The eyes of the gray-haired Yankees, each in his golden frame, followed her as she ascended. She decided they approved.

In that capacious dining room, Milton Perkins was already at his table. He saw her coming, and his eyes lighted up and he stood to greet her. "I knew you'd be on time," he said, his voice full of approval. Gray suit and vest, a crisp triangle of a handkerchief in his chest pocket, blue eyes, gray hair, parted exactly in the middle. The person who had forgotten a critical executive committee meeting was nowhere in sight. Milton Perkins was still a very handsome man.

He pulled out her chair for her, then pushed her in, just as her father had done for her mother at dinner every night of their lives. The table was covered in thick white cloth, the silver gleamed, the glassware sparkled, the napkin Rachel placed on her lap had an actual weight, and a tall, gorgeous Latin American waiter handed them the menus bound in red leather. Milton Perkins ordered a dozen oysters for each of them and asked Rachel what she wanted to drink. "Water, I guess," she said offhandedly, and pulled the list of things she wanted to talk about out of her suit jacket pocket, placing it on the table, as the waiter lingered.

Milton Perkins didn't even glance at the list. "Water?" he said. "It's Friday afternoon."

"But I always come here on Friday and I always—"

Perkins grinned. "What do you think, Carlos?" he asked the waiter. "Would a martini do?"

Carlos looked down at Rachel and raised his eyebrows. He wasn't about to persuade a fellow dark-skinned person to obey the boss.

"Well, it *is* Friday afternoon," she murmured looking up apologetically at Carlos's heartbreaking eyes, "and *I am* taking the weekend off."

"Yes, ma'am," Carlos said. He kept his face toward her so Milton Perkins couldn't see the skepticism in his eyes. Then he picked up the two menus and marched regally off. She let her gaze follow him, imagining him without any clothes: the broad muscles of his back, tapering to the waist, the long, sinewy legs in their chocolate skin, the—she realized Milton was watching her watch. The man didn't miss a thing! "Well, about this list," she said.

"Give it to me." She handed it over to him. He put it in his pocket without a glance. "It'll wait till Monday."

"But there are important things on it!"

"Are they going to stop being important on Monday?"

"No, but—"

"You expected to get them done today. Off your to-do list." He reached and patted her hand—the kind of affectionate, fatherly gesture her dad always wanted to make but never managed. "But let's talk about you instead. How are you holding up?"

"Me? I'm fine."

"Good." He studied her face.

"Really."

He smiled and cocked his head to one side.

"Milton, you'd be the first to know."

"Really? You'd tell your friend Eudora Easter first, wouldn't you? I hope so anyway. And Francis Plummer. Who else?"

"Gregory van Buren."

"Van Buren? Well, I guess I'm not surprised."

"He told me to put my resignation in my back pocket and do anything I want about Michaels," Rachel said. "He was like an uncle."

"An uncle?" Milton let that roll around in his mouth. "Maybe that's what he's for now, at this stage of his life and yours."

"Oh!" she said. "You think?" Carlos was coming toward them, now bearing their martinis on a silver tray, and Rachel told Milton Perkins how powerful she'd felt when Gregory said, "Go for it, girl!"

She wanted Carlos to hear—which was absurd, of course. Why would he care? And anyway, Carlos put the martinis down on the table and skedaddled, as if his new mission in life was to see if he could be unobtrusive and still be six-foot-five.

Milton sipped his martini, savoring it, like an old man who knew there were only so many in a lifetime. But Rachel ignored hers. Her mind was too full of the idea of people entering new stages in their lives to think about martinis. People like Gregory van Buren. Her heart too, maybe, more than her mind. Yes, way more, she thought: new rooms, new furniture, new goals, new hope, new energy. Sunlight flooding in.

Milton put his glass down and nodded at her, commanding her to partake, breaking her reverie. She already knew what he was going to say. "I hope you're leaving campus on your weekend off."

"I am. I'm going to New York to be with my husband." She took a sip of her martini. The weekend had begun.

"Don't drive. Take the train," Milton Perkins said. "So you can have two of those."

"Maybe three," she said.

"I'll drive you to the station then," Milton said as Carlos came back with the oysters. Milton ordered another martini for each of them and told the story of his first oyster, how his godfather took him to the Oyster Bar at Grand Central Station and begged him to try at least one, how horrible they looked: big gobs of mucous and alive to boot, and finally how his godfather said, "I'll take you to a Dodgers game if you do," and so he did and since then he'd eaten at least a million. Milton downed his martini and all his oysters as he talked and Rachel matched him sip for sip and slider for slider.

"You know what I really love about raw oysters?" she said. "The way the sauce stings the inside of my nose."

Halfway through their second round of oysters and martinis, Milton asked who was going to be in charge over the weekend when she would be in New York. She told him Gregory van Buren.

"Van Buren again," he said.

"That's right. He'll call me if something comes up."

"How big a something?"

"He'll know how big."

"Well then?"

An oyster was halfway to her mouth. She stopped its journey, suspended it in air.

"Gotcha," said Milton Perkins.

She felt a jolt in her brain. He watched her eyes. She restarted the oyster's journey, put it in her mouth and chewed, waiting for him to say the rest.

"Seems to me if van Buren can run the whole show while you're absent, he can run part of it when you're present," Milton said. "Pretty darn well too." He paused to let her think about that, and then he said, "The board expected you to delegate stuff right off the bat. You and I talked about that. But it's January already."

She started to say she just needed a little more time to think, but instead she blurted, "I'll put Gregory van Buren in charge of academics." Immediately, she felt sad for Francis. Then frightened because she would have to tell him first, before she told Gregory, then she realized she'd been heading this way ever since Francis told her Claire should leave. Then she felt an enormous relief.

"Good!" Milton said. "The board will be relieved."

They finished the oysters and drained the martinis, and she told Milton how she'd always wanted to go to a fancy restaurant and order martinis and oysters, then just skip the main course and go straight to dessert—especially when the dessert was apple pie à la mode. "Yes, with ice cream on it," Milton agreed.

So that's what they did.

Milton drove her straight to the station. She was delighted not to have to go back to the school because she kept a supply of everything she needed at the New York apartment. It was a dreary winter afternoon. Patches of dirty snow lay along the curbs of Fieldington's streets. Ahead, the squat railroad station was covered in tired yellow paint, like stale mustard. But it was all beautiful to her.

"You've made a good decision," Milton Perkins said as they came into the parking lot. "You'll know how good when you can leave the school for longer than just a weekend."

"Like for a maternity leave?" she asked. She didn't suppose she would have if she hadn't had three martinis. His face lighted up. "I was just using that as an example," she said.

He smiled as if he knew something she didn't and jumped out of the car to open her door, and once again she was reminded of her father. He put his hand on her elbow and walked her to the platform. "Say hello to your husband," he said, patting her shoulder, and went back to his car. She waved goodbye. And he drove away.

At the ticket window, she waited behind a couple who were arguing with the station master about the price of tickets for people over sixty-five. Those same three martinis let her laugh out loud when the woman, who had been talking in a low voice so as to pretend she was being polite, turned on her husband as he was about to attempt to speak and bellowed at him to stop interrupting.

The man turned on Rachel. "Who the hell are you laughing at?"

"Whom," she corrected.

He froze right there in his shoes, his face first contorted with affront, then, when her business suit registered, with confusion. If she wasn't a maid, who was she? "It's the objective case," she said. "Didn't you learn that in school?"

"Wha?" he said.

She turned her back on him and his vociferous wife and sashayed out to the platform. She was having a wonderful time! She'd buy her ticket on the train.

She got to the apartment long before Bob did. No surprise. Why would he leave the office sooner than usual? She got out of her business suit and into the shower, and then she put on a dress that would make him to look at her the way she liked to be looked at, especially by him.

She felt sleepy and a little headachy from the martinis, so she went into the kitchen to make herself some coffee. It was the smallest room in a very small apartment, and she looked and looked but she couldn't find the coffee, and her head hurt a little more. "Where the hell do you keep it, Bob?" she murmured aloud. "And just when are you coming home?" She rinsed the encrusted eggs off a plate and the glued-on cold cereal from a bowl he had left in the sink and opened the dishwasher to put them in, but it was full. There was a half-full beer bottle on the counter. It smelled awful, and he'd spilled some raisins on the floor that she kept stepping on, and every cabinet door was open. "Bob!" she said aloud, not murmuring now. "Is this how you run your business?" There was no answer, of course, so she cleaned up the mess and ran the dishwasher, careful not to spill anything on her dress. He could have told her there was a mess in the kitchen. She would have cleaned it up before she changed!

Like so many New York apartments it was hot in there, so by the time she had his kitchen tidied, her armpits were sweating, threatening her dress. She was in the process of wiping her armpits with a paper towel when the door popped open, and there he was. Her husband! Not ten feet away. "Where the hell do you keep your coffee?"

Then her heart turned over. He was frozen in his shoes like the old man in the station. But that round face of his! Those blue, blue eyes! Such joy in them! To see *her*. They crossed the room toward each other and put their arms around each other. She was still holding the paper towel. Then they kissed. Then they let each other go and stepped back from each other and she dropped the paper towel and unbuttoned his overcoat while he unbuttoned her dress. "Oh my goodness, I left my diaphragm home!" she said.

He paid no attention, reaching his hands behind her and unclasping her bra. "Did you hear me?" she said.

"I think so," he murmured. "Something about a diaphragm." Then he took her hand and they walked together into the bedroom and got up on his unmade bed and made the most delicious love she could remember.

Oh my God! How she loved that man! And how glad they hadn't waited three whole weeks!

EIGHTEEN

Rachel decided to wait until the February break, an extended weekend that started on a Wednesday, to inform Francis that he was not going to be the dean of academics, and then appoint Gregory to the position. She didn't want Francis to have to teach his classes having just received such devastating, humiliating news. But she awoke one morning a week after her meeting with Milton Perkins, and with still two weeks before the February break, so overwhelmed with yearning to get the dreaded moment behind her, she told Margaret to make an appointment with Francis.

Margaret nodded her head up and down vigorously in a tone of resigned approval: at last her boss was going to do something about Francis Plummer, whom she'd known for years and loved. Like all the best administrative assistants, Margaret knew a whole lot more about what was going on than she let on, but even Margaret didn't know Rachel had decided to put Gregory van Buren in charge of academics. She told Rachel she'd call Francis in thirty minutes when second period was over because Francis didn't have a third period class, but, before those thirty minutes were anywhere near past, Rachel began to worry that she'd lose her nerve and use the appointment to make Francis the dean of academics "Never mind," she told Margaret. "I don't need to talk with Francis."

"Really?" Margaret frowned.

"Yes, really," Rachel snapped and went back into her office and closed the door, wondering if she's made the right decision after all. Why surprise, confuse, and disappoint everybody? And yet Milton Perkins had said, "What about him?" when Gregory van Buren had walked by, and no one wanted her to succeed more than Milton Perkins did. Yes, Francis was the one with more charisma. But she didn't need charisma at her right hand. She could turn her own on whenever it was needed. She needed pragmatism, order, efficiency, a clear understanding of how things really worked, a distance from one's own feelings, and the insight to understand that the way to inspire *her* was to tell her to put her resignation in her back pocket and do anything she wanted.

And no hour went by since her weekend with Bob in NYC that she didn't wonder if she were pregnant. Torn between the hope that she was and the fear that she couldn't bear a child and be a brand-new mother and the new head of school at the same time, she chose not to find out. She'd just wait and see.

If she hadn't been so busy and so new in her job, she might have stepped back and thought about how uncharacteristically she was behaving to be so indecisive. She would have asked herself where had the woman gone who'd told Milton Perkins, "You've got to want me enough now to want me permanently."

Instead, she worked harder and harder. She was handling all the issues she had planned to assign to Francis. She had a board to manage, alumnae all over the country she needed to get to know, and four hundred girls who expected her interested presence in the dorms during the evening, in the dining room at meals, at their athletic games, their drama and music performances, and most of the important discipline problems came to Rachel, along with a host of issues that, in a less primitive system than the one she had inherited, would have been handled by someone else.

The huge load of work was another reason, or maybe an excuse, for postponing telling Francis until the February break. And also there would be less uproar if it happened then, when the girls and many of the faculty would be away. In the meantime, she needed to know how Francis was performing in his classes.

On one of her evening tours of the dormitories, Rachel walked the path toward the dormitory where the school's first apostates, Sally Brinton and Michelle Raney, lived. She would drop in on them and casually glean information about whether or not Francis had righted the ship in his freshman class. She felt like a spy, but what else could she do? There was a fierce culture of teacher autonomy at Miss Oliver's School for Girls—one would require the skill of a dean of academics to overcome. Teachers closed the doors to their classrooms at the beginning of every period and proceeded to teach as they alone saw fit. Now that Sally and Michelle had squealed on Francis, there was no way Rachel could pretend to visit his class to learn from the master. To visit his class for the purpose of checking up on him would be a horrific insult and a blasphemous act.

It had turned warm. Rain was falling on tired snow. Fog rose around Rachel's legs, and the lighted windows of the dorms were a yellow blur in the dark as she neared the building. Once inside, she was glad for the warm bright light of the common room where she sat down on the sofa to chat with several girls who had gathered there to study. But she was distracted. The conversation went nowhere and she called one of the girls by the wrong name. The girl was surprised and hurt, and Rachel felt her own cheeks get hot. She apologized, maybe a bit too profusely, and excused herself, and then she made a show of popping in to several rooms so she wouldn't be seen as singling Sally and Michelle out.

She found Sally sitting up in her bed next to a fat teddy bear, holding the end of her long blond braid in the fingers of one hand, a book in the other, and looking even younger than her fourteen years. Rachel guessed she'd graduated from sucking her thumb to fingering her braid only a little while before and felt a pulse of sadness wondering who had sat on the edge of Sally's bed braiding her hair. Wouldn't her mom want to be the one, instead of sending her away for most of the year?

"Hi, Rachel," Sally said, glancing guiltily at the desk where she should have been studying.

Rachel pretended she didn't notice. "Hello, Sally. How are things for you these days?"

A guarded look appeared on Sally's face. "Fine. Everything's fine."

"Good. What are you reading?"

Sally held up a sheaf of copied pages for Rachel to see. "Countee Cullen."

"How is it, Sally? Do you like it?"

"It's okay."

"Only okay?" Rachel said, disappointed. She had been thrilled by the poetry of Countee Cullen and Langston Hughes and W.E.B.

Du Bois during her freshman year at Smith.

"I like Lawrence Dunbar better. We are doing a whole week of American Negro poetry."

"I'm glad you are, Sally. I wrote a term paper about James Baldwin my sophomore year at Smith. Of all the stuff I studied that year, that's what I remember the most."

"No kidding."

"Yes, but we said *African American*, not *Negro*."

"Oh, we do too," Sally said. "But sometimes we say *black*." She held up the pages again. "But that's the title of the book Francis copied this section from. It's really old!"

Well, tell him to find a new one, Rachel thought, but she bit her tongue.

"Is that what you came to ask me about?" Sally asked, watching Rachel closely. "What we're reading?"

"No. But I saw that you were reading and it made me want to know," Rachel said, comforted just a little that this was partially true.

"Well, just in case you also want to know: it's going okay in class now." Sally's tone was just ironic enough to show she understood Rachel hadn't stopped by just to say hello. "The first class after we told you was actually great. Then they kind of slipped a little. But like I said, it's okay. He doesn't scream at us. You must've said the right thing to him, or something."

Yes, or something, Rachel thought, remembering her meeting with Francis. Now she was even more ashamed of it. "I think it must have been just a little slump he was in to make him scream," she lied.

"Yeah, I guess. Anyway, it's over."

Rachel put her hand on the door knob, her mission completed, and turned her face away. She didn't want Sally to see how crestfallen she was. "Well now, I'll let you get back to Countee Cullen."

"All right, thanks for coming by," Sally said. Then, her voice brightening, "Can I read your James Baldwin paper?"

Rachel turned back. "Oh, Sally, that was years ago. I haven't the foggiest idea where it is."

"Okay, but I bet it was interesting."

"I hope so, Sally."

"I mean, you know, coming from you."

Rachel understood Sally was saying, *I'm white and you're black, so stay, there's so much we need to talk about*, but she couldn't tolerate any more pretense. "Good night, Sally," she said.

"Anyway, thanks for talking to Francis," Sally said to Rachel's back as Rachel fled. She didn't need to drop by Michelle's room. She'd learned enough from Sally.

Rachel walked back through the fog to her empty house feeling that hollowness people feel when they've been weak. Two girls returning from the library approached her on the path. She was relieved when they left it for another, heading for their dorm. She didn't like herself well enough to present herself to anyone right then, let alone kids she was supposed to inspire. She'd already taken advantage of a fourteen-year-old kid and disillusioned her twice: first by showing her how sneaky adults in power can be; second by refusing to accept her invitation to talk with her about race. She carried this shame and the bad news about Francis Plummer into her house. Yes, Francis had improved, according to Sally, from the low point that she and Michelle had reported. He was doing okay, in Sally's parlance. But Rachel knew that once one reached a certain level of excellence, one can't descend from it and not be a failure.

The house, which she had left that morning at a quarter to seven, felt almost as cold as it was outside, but Rachel didn't turn up the heat. She put a shawl over her shoulders, turned on the TV, and watched mindlessly program after program in which she had no interest, until at last, in the early morning, she went upstairs to try to sleep. The sheets in her single bed felt as cold as the air. It took forever before her body warmed them. When they did, she fantasized a new conversation with Sally about James Baldwin, and finally drifted into sleep.

NINETEEN

It was early February by the time Mitch Michaels had managed to arrange for a substitute to fill his daily radio hour so he could go to England to be with his daughter. He was proud to have selected a woman, over the advice of his bosses. Abigail Winters had been the only one politic enough to ask for his advice: *the faster you sling the numbers, the more convincing you sound.*

If she would do as well as he predicted, maybe he'd let her stand in for him on a regular basis. Maybe if he took more time off he wouldn't need so many pills. And he had projects in mind for the freed-up time: learning Spanish for starters, reading all of Shakespeare again, every play, every sonnet, and just the other night he'd dreamed he was in a classroom studying advanced economics. He didn't know whether it was the New School, NYU, or Columbia, but wherever, he was there under an assumed name, a *different identity*, and everybody in the class was younger than he was, even the professor.

The best dream of all, though, was two weeks on *Amy's Delight* with his daughter. Just the two of them. They cruised to Gloucester and he told her the stories he'd saved up for her about the summers he'd spent working on a fishing boat out there when he was in high school. Then they sailed through the Stellwagon Bank where the whales gathered by the thousands in the summer to feed for their long journey south, and he watched the wonder on Amy's face and heard her say, "Look Dad, you can almost touch them!" After that, when she knew who he really was and forgave him, they sailed home.

He was afraid to call her beforehand to tell her he was coming. She might tell him not to come. But once he was there, there was no way she would refuse him.

Two Ambiens, one Vicodin, plus a Chinese concoction against jet lag, pressed on him by his Democratic friend Charlie, his studio manager, and *zero vodka* got him to Heathrow at dawn in very good shape. Then he rented a car and arrived at St Agnes School, high on a bluff above Lake Windermere, in the early afternoon of a sunny winter day, surprised at the beauty of the countryside. He'd hated all that smarmy crap about daffodils and wandering lonely as a cloud he'd been forced to read in high school. *A cloud?* he'd said to the teacher. She practically drooled over every line Wordsworth ever wrote. *A fucking cloud!* She'd sent him to the principal.

But now, stepping out of his rented car, he almost said out loud, "Oh my God, just look at this!" The snowless lawns, still deep green, sloped down toward the lake where the slanted sun sparkled on blue water. Tall, forested hills lined the farther shore. Above, two round white clouds flew from west to east. He turned around to face the school buildings across more lawn whose widely spaced trees were centuries old, their leafless branches like lace against the sky, and started to walk on the path toward the buildings. Amy was in one of them!

The central building whose front steps he climbed a minute later didn't look like any school building he'd ever seen. It was brown stucco with big square chimneys at both ends, and a wide porch along the front, strewn with backpacks, hockey sticks, soccer shoes, kayak paddles. Fat pillars held up the roof above. Several bicycles leaned against them. As he crossed the porch, a huge brown dog awoke just enough to raise his head and thump his tail to say hello.

He pulled the big front door open and almost bumped into two girls on their way out. They retreated back into a high-ceilinged anteroom and held the door open for him. They were dressed exactly the same, in green blazers, white piping at the cuffs and lapels, gray flannel skirts down to just above the knees, high green stockings, sensible shoes. Uniforms! He was delighted. "Thank you!" he said. "Are English girls all this polite?" The girls smiled tolerantly at him and shrugged. "Can you tell me where I can find Amy Michaels?" he asked. "I'm her father."

"We're sorry, but there's a rule," the shorter of the two girls said. Her red hair came down to her shoulders. She looked apologetic and pointed to a placard mounted on a stand to the right of the door: *Visitors will please check in at the Office of the Assistant Head of School.*

"Oh, of course. I should have known," he said to cover his sudden worry that he wouldn't be allowed to see Amy in this school either.

Both girls smiled. "Please follow us," the redhead said. He hesitated for a second, imagining turning around and searching through all the buildings until he found Amy, then he followed them across the anteroom into a large square office whose tall windows let in the sun. A short woman in a business suit and gray hair stood up from her desk. "Hi, Ms. Bromley," the redhead said. "This is Amy's father. He's come to see her."

"Thank you, ladies," Ms. Bromley said, smiling at the girls. Her blue eyes were magnified by rimless glasses.

Then, as the girls left, Ms. Bromley turned her smile on him and put out her hand. It was surprisingly firm. "Welcome, Mr. Richardson. What a nice surprise. Amy will be delighted."

"No," he said. "Michaels. I'm Amy Michaels's father."

She let go of his hand, and moved back a step. "Oh, from America! I'm sorry, I thought—" She paused. "Please wait here." She took another step back as if guarding the door so he couldn't get out. "You'll have to talk to the headmaster."

"But all I want to do is visit my daughter."

"Please, sit down, Mr. Michaels." She pointed to a chair. "I will bring the headmaster right away. He'll explain."

He looked at the chair, shaking his head, too tense to sit. Ms. Bromley left the office. He heard her footsteps moving fast in the hall.

MS. BROMLEY DIDN'T even look in the headmaster's office to find Larry Jenkins. He'd be somewhere on campus, leading by walking around. She found him in Senior History where they were studying World War Two. The teacher had asked him to tell the girls what it was like to be a little boy in London during that time. He was talking about a relative who'd survived the trenches of World War Number One, who actually thought the Nazis were going to win World War Number Two, when she stepped into the classroom and, with an urgent gesture, motioned to him to come.

"But surely we can let the poor man see his daughter for a few minutes," Larry Jenkins said out in the hall after she told him. He'd chosen her to be his assistant because she'd enforce the rules, while he pretended he only knew of two: One, work hard. Two, be nice.

"No. Absolutely not," she said.

"But he's not a dangerous man. He's just a man who has strange ideas and says them on the radio. Hell, so does Margaret Thatcher. We'd let her see her kid if she wanted to, wouldn't we?"

In spite of herself, Ms. Bromley smiled. "Yes, but the mother has custody," she reminded him. "Complete control, and she won't let it happen. She's the one who enrolled Amy here. And she pays the tuition."

"Well, suppose we called her up?"

Ms. Bromley shook her head. "That won't work. You'll never convince her."

"I think I'll give it a try," he said.

He started walking so fast across the campus toward his office that for each stride of his long legs, she had to take two. "Don't you think you should—"

"Talk to him first? You're right, I should. I'll see what he has to say for himself. Then, if I think he's not up to mischief, I'll persuade Amy's mom."

"Or try to," she corrected. She was almost running now to keep beside him.

MITCH HAD PULLED himself together by the time Ms. Bromley returned to usher him into Larry Jenkins's office. He was going to be reasonable, calm, conversational. All he wanted to do was visit his own daughter.

He noticed right away that Larry Jenkins's office was even bigger than Ms. Bromley's, just as sunny, but nowhere near as tidy. Some of the books on the bookshelves that lined two walls were upright, some on their sides. Paintings, some professional, others obviously by kids, covered the other two walls, and the headmaster, looking just like a headmaster should in a blue blazer and flannel trousers, crossed the room to him with his hand out, accompanied by the huge brown dog that had been on the front porch.

The dog shoved his nose into Mitch's crotch, wagging his tail. Mitch leaned down to pat him on his head between his ears. He really did like dogs. "Careful," the head warned, "he's pretty slobbery." Then the dog lifted his head and shoved his wet snout into Mitch's right hand, and Larry Jenkins shrugged. "See what I mean?" he said, and grinned and shook Mitch's left hand, and kept holding it while he turned and said thank you to Ms. Bromley.

"Yes, thank you so much, ma'am," Mitch said.

"Have a seat, Mr. Michaels," Larry said, gesturing to one of the stuffed chairs at the table as Ms. Bromley left, closing the door behind her. "Can I get you some tea?"

"No thanks," Mitch said. He hated tea.

"Really? I'm going to have some. It's right here." Larry crossed the room to a table in a corner behind his desk and began to brew the tea.

"Well then, all right. I guess I will," Mitch said. If it made this guy happy, he'd drink an ocean of it. "I flew all night and am fading a bit, I have to admit."

"Good, I'll make it strong then," Larry said, and the big brown dog thumped his tail on the floor.

There was a silence then, except for the sound of the water beginning to boil. Mitch said, "Is this your dog?"

"He is," Larry said. "When one of the dorms isn't borrowing him. Sometimes he stays away a week. My wife goes and gets him and brings him back. He passes a whole lot of gas after all the food the girls give him. We don't mind though. We just open the windows. Do you have a dog?"

"I used to," Mitch said. "I mean, we used to."

"Before you and your wife divorced?"

"Yes."

"And Amy left?"

"Yes."

"Well, that's got to be tough," Larry said. His back was still to Mitch as he finished pouring the tea. "I would surely want my dog for company at a time like that."

"Thanks," Mitch said, feeling a rush of gratitude.

Larry turned toward Mitch, carrying a tray with two cups of tea and a plate of cookies. He put it down on the table. "Eat," he said, pointing to the cookies. "There's a rule in here: nobody gets out without at least one cookie."

Mitch sipped his tea. It tasted surprisingly good, pungent and hot, and he took a cookie.

"Take two," Larry said. "They're small. And you can give one to Big Dog if you want. He'll be your friend forever."

Mitch held a cookie over the dog's open mouth and dropped it in. "Is that his name, Big Dog?"

"Yes. He started life as Count. He was actually a little dog when he came to us, but now whenever a new girl meets him for the first time, she says, *What a big dog!*"

"That makes a lot of sense," Mitch said. "Our dog was a girl. Tiny."

"She was small?"

"Oh no, she was big and fat."

Larry nodded. "Of course. Why in the world wouldn't you call a big, fat dog Tiny?"

Mitch nodded again. Both men sipped their tea. Mitch took another cookie. Big Dog thumped his tail and looked longingly at the plate.

"So you want to see Amy?" Larry said.

"I do."

"Of course you do. I would too. Let me call her mom and see if I can persuade her."

"Oh thank you!" Mitch said.

"She'll want to know you don't plan to take her away from here."

"Take her away? I love it here!"

Larry smiled. "As a matter of fact, so does Amy."

"I bet everybody does. Why wouldn't they? And I know why: you!"

Larry laughed and stood up. "Don't be silly. Half the time I don't have the foggiest idea what I'm doing. I'll call from Ms. Bromley's office. You stay here and keep Big Dog company." He headed for the door.

"How are you going to persuade her?" Mitch asked.

Larry took another step toward the door; then he turned back to face Mitch. "I'll just tell her you love Amy," he said. He went out of the office and left Mitch waiting.

"No, he didn't. He couldn't have! Even he's not that out of his mind!" Jenifer Michaels shouted. Larry winced and moved the phone well away from his ear, raising his eyebrows at Ms. Bromley who sat behind her desk and heard every word. "Why should I let a crazy person see my daughter?" Jenifer asked. "Just tell him no."

"Actually, Amy's his daughter too," he said as gently as he could. There was a long silence on the line. "Mrs. Michaels, you there?" Larry said.

"Suppose you just don't tell Amy that her father's on campus?" Jenifer's voice sounded doubtful. He didn't answer. "Oh, of course she has to know!" Jenifer said. "It's exasperating. He pulls this stuff all the time. She'd find out anyway, wouldn't she? He's cunning, that's what he is. Why couldn't he just stay away?"

"Aren't you glad for Amy's sake he loves her so much he couldn't?" Larry asked, raising his eyebrows at Ms. Bromley.

"Yes, I'm glad," Jenifer said in the same exasperated tone. "I'm her mother, what would you expect? How long would he stay?"

"If Amy agrees? Not for long. I'll suggest he take her out to dinner tonight. Amy could bring a friend with her. That would make it easier for her and her father," he said, and now Ms. Bromley was nodding her head.

"All right, then. I guess I'm resigned to it. I just wish he'd asked me first."

He was about to remind her that she would have said no and her ex-husband would have come anyway, but Ms. Bromley was shaking her head vigorously and making slicing motions at her throat. So he said, "I understand, Mrs. Michaels."

"Well, I don't think anybody who is still happily married understands. People who don't have to fight over their kids," Jenifer said, and then the line went dead.

He put the phone back in its cradle. Ms. Bromley was staring blankly out the window. "You look downcast," he said.

She shrugged. "I wish parents were like geese. Then, once they find a mate, they'd stick together for life. It would be so much easier on the kids."

"Will you tell Mr. Michaels his wife gives permission?" Larry asked Ms. Bromley. "I don't think I could stand watching him be grateful. I'll go get Amy and bring her over."

"If she agrees to come," Ms. Bromley said.

"I know. *If.*"

"Would you come?" she asked.

"At her age? After what he's done? Probably not. But I'm going to promise her that he'll ask her to forgive him."

"Do you think he will?"

"Well, wouldn't you want forgiveness for something like that?" He was out the door before she could answer.

AMY'S ROOMMATE, SARAH Lavade, a short black fifteen-year-old, opened the door to Larry's knock. Amy was sitting on her bed. Before he could say hello, she said, "I already know he's here, Mr. Jenkins. Adrienne and Gemma told me. Please tell him to leave."

"Yes, tell him," Sarah said.

"Sarah, would you leave us alone for a few minutes? I need to speak with Amy."

"She can stay," Amy said. "She knows everything."

"Please," Sarah said, plunking herself down beside Amy on the bed and crossing her arms. "Amy's my friend."

He hesitated for only an instant before he decided Sarah was right. What chance would Amy have arguing with a headmaster all by herself? He'd always said if you can't tell the difference between flexibility and indecisiveness, you've got no business working in schools. "All right then, Sarah, that's what friends are for." He sat down on the edge of Sarah's bed, facing them. "Well, here's the situation—"

"But she already knows the situation." Sarah had a soft, lyrical Caribbean accent that always surprised. "Why go over it again?"

"Well, Sarah, just in case there's a part of the situation Amy doesn't know. And if you'll let me go over it, then maybe I'll understand the situation better myself." He turned his gaze from Sarah to Amy. "Because it's actually a rather complicated situation, isn't it, Amy?"

"No," Amy said.

"I think it is."

"I think it isn't."

"See?" Sarah said. "And it's what Amy thinks that counts, isn't it? Since it's her father and you can't make her talk with him."

He smiled at Sarah. "Oh I wouldn't dream of making Amy do anything." He turned to Amy. Her face was blank. He wished he knew what she was holding back. "But he's stopped, Amy," he said, focusing on her exclusively now. "He hasn't said hurtful things about your friend or Miss Oliver's for several weeks."

"I know," Amy said.

"He has?" Sarah said.

He nodded, holding up three fingers. "Three weeks, at least."

Sarah turned to Amy. "Why didn't you tell me?"

Amy shrugged.

"Three whole weeks," Larry said. "Not one bad word. And you know why he's here, don't you, Amy?"

Amy nodded.

"Of course you do. To ask for your forgiveness."

"Really?" Sarah said. "How do you know?"

"He told me, Sarah," he said, still looking at Amy.

Sarah turned to Amy. "You think that's true?"

"Of course," Amy said. "That's what he would do."

"Well, that's pretty cool," Sarah said. "My dad would never do that. Maybe you should see him, after all. You'd feel better. He'd feel better."

"Mr. Jenkins?" Amy said.

"Yes, Amy?"

"Can we just stop talking?"

"Stop talking?" Sarah said.

"Please," Amy said. She looked at Sarah and then at him. "I'd like to be alone now. Can I just be alone?"

"Of course, Amy. Does that mean—?"

Amy nodded her head.

"Are you sure?"

"I just don't want to see him. Please don't ask me again."

He wanted to ask once more if she was sure. He wanted to just sit there until Amy changed her mind. But he knew better. "All right then, that's what I'll tell your father," he said. "Come on, Sarah, let's you and I do what Amy asks."

WHEN LARRY ENTERED his office, Big Dog rose up from where he'd been lying next to Mitch's chair and gamboled across the room to say hello. Larry pushed him aside. Mitch stayed in his chair, waiting, his expression as blank as Amy's had been.

"Amy refuses to see you," Larry said.

Mitch stood up. "Thanks for telling me," he said—as if Larry had told him what the weather was going to be tomorrow.

"But I told her you came to ask her for forgiveness," Larry added.

"You did!"

"Yes."

"What did she say?"

"We didn't quite get there," Larry admitted.

"I see," Mitch said.

Mitch's reaction—or rather the lack of it—frightened Larry. Emotions so unnaturally compressed must explode later to someone's harm. Maybe Amy's.

"Thanks for your efforts." Mitch put out his hand to say goodbye. His face was still expressionless, an absolute mask.

"I'll walk you to your car," Larry said. He had planned to do so out of sympathy; now he would do it to make sure that Mitch Michaels got in his car and drove away.

"That would be nice," Mitch said.

MEANWHILE, AMY WAS immersed in the letter and pictures Claire had sent to her. The instant her headmaster and roommate had gone out the door, she had pulled them out from under her mattress. Amy had learned the letter by heart, but she read it again anyway, and then she lost herself in the drawings—especially the one of two girls side by side on the beach. It was drawn from the back. The younger girl's face was therefore invisible: she was gazing out to sea. But the older one's head was turned, her face seen from the side, whispering in her friend's ear. Words meant for no one else to hear. Claire had remembered that moment, utterly apprehended it in her drawing, embodied it with all the intensity it had had when it was happening—maybe even more—and made it last forever. Before she had met Claire, Amy didn't know that such a thing could be.

After a while, she slipped the letter and the drawings back under her mattress. It was time to go to her next class. She looked out the window to check the weather. Would she need a coat? There was her father and the headmaster crossing the lawn to the parking lot, and she felt a panic of loneliness. It would go away if she rushed across that lawn to be with her father. But she stayed right where she was—not because he'd said all those bad things about Claire and her old school on the radio. There was no harm in that: nobody they cared about paid any attention. It was because he thought Claire was bad for her. A corrupting influence. For that, she couldn't forgive him.

"Hurry up," she whispered as her father and her headmaster crossed the lawn. "Keep going, before I change my mind." Her loneliness erupted still more as the two men went around the corner of a building and out of sight. She refused to let herself cry, though—not with a class to go to. It started in just five minutes. She'd let herself cry tonight. Stifling her sobs in her pillow so she wouldn't wake Sarah up.

"Take care of yourself," Larry Jenkins said to Mitch Michaels as Mitch opened the door of his rental car. "I bet after a while she'll come around." He was a little ashamed of himself for thinking Mitch might do something crazy, now that he was about to drive away.

"I hope so," Mitch said and shook Larry's hand again and got in his car. His back was killing him. A few miles from the school, he pulled into a space meant for enjoying the view of Lake Windermere. He turned off the engine and, for some reason he didn't understand, locked the doors. He swallowed two Vicodins. Then he put his forehead on the steering wheel and wept. Sobs of pent-up sadness exploded up and out of him from down in his chest. He was strangely aware of relief, and when the convulsions finally stopped, he tried to start them again, but he couldn't. So instead, he kept his forehead on the steering wheel and went to sleep. When he awoke it was dark. He turned the engine and the headlights on and headed back to the school.

A half a mile from the school, he saw a place where he could hide his car among some trees beside the road, and he parked the car there and started to walk, telling himself, *Turn around, get back in your car, this is crazy.* He crossed the parking lot where he'd got out of his car this morning and then he crossed the lawn and hid behind a tree next to a path. Maybe Amy would walk by on her way from the dining hall to the library or her dorm. It was cold; some branches above him squeaked as they rubbed together, moved by a wind that smelled like snow.

A car appeared on the path. It had a rack of lights on its roof. Mitch moved to the opposite side of the tree, making himself thin. A searchlight on the car flashed on and swept its gleam, catching him full on his face, blinding him. He stood still, unable to move. He was actually surprised that this gentle place would need to hire a security firm. Then he ran. Behind him, he heard the car door open and slam shut and footsteps pounding after him. Mitch ran and ran, finally reaching the road. The footsteps stopped. He hid in some bushes by the side of the road. He was gasping, out of breath, making too much noise. He tried to stifle his breathing, but that only made the gasps louder and he grew dizzy.

The car came down the school's driveway sweeping its bright yellow gleam of the searchlight right and left and turned up the road, toward where Mitch was hiding, but away from his hidden car. Mitch lay flat down, his face in the dirt, and the bright gleam swept above him. He watched the car continue up the road around a corner then reappear a minute later, coming back down the road toward him again. He was sure this time he would be spotted. He saw himself led in handcuffs by a large man with *SECURITY* on the back of his jacket and a self-satisfied look on his face into Ms. Bromley's office, where Larry Jenkins greeted him sadly, shaking his head. But this time, the searchlight swept along the other side of the road, and then the car turned back up into the school's driveway and disappeared. Mitch was sure it was a trick. He stayed, unmoving in the bushes, shivering with cold for another thirty minutes, before he snuck back to his car, where he had another panic because he couldn't find the keys right away. He got in and drove away, leaving the headlights off for at least a mile. Then he drove as fast as he could, full of shame and embarrassment, guilt and sadness, all the way to Heathrow, stopping only once for a bowl of soup, because he hadn't eaten since the tea and cookies, and one more Vicodin.

TWENTY

A few days after Mitch Michaels had returned from his abortive trip to England, Patience Sommers, who had partnered with Peggy as Francis's substitute dorm parent when he and Peggy were separated, appeared in Rachel's office. Rachel had already asked her to be Peggy's substitute in the dorm when her sabbatical would start later in the year. "Have you got a minute?" Patience asked. She was tall, thin, with glasses, and red hair cropped short to just below her ears.

"Of course I do," Rachel said. She was lucky to have a person as gifted as Patience available as a substitute teacher who could coach sports and teach English, Latin, and history, including the history of art. Patience was forty-six years old. She'd been the successful head of a school in California for ten years until two Julys ago. Now divorced, her children flown from the nest, she'd come to the Hartford area to be near her elderly parents, bringing a reputation as a superb teacher and an eagerness to get back to the classroom. Rachel would have hired her in a heartbeat for a full-time position, if there had been an opening.

Rachel gestured to one of the chairs, but Patience remained standing. "This won't take a minute. You probably know, but just in case no one's told you yet, your radio friend started talking about us again this morning."

"Oh no!" Rachel slumped back in her chair. So her strategy against Michaels hadn't worked. *How could I have been so sure it already had?* she wondered, staring at Patience's calm face.

"Yes, I'm afraid he has," Patience said. "He talked relentlessly about what a wonderful school St. Agnes is and how much better off his daughter is over there in St. Agnes's solid, conservative, old-fashioned regime than in our permissive one. He never mentioned his daughter before. It's a new way of attacking us. Which is crazy, of course, St. Agnes is just as progressive as we are. And, by the way, he's learned that word, *progressive*. You have to admire the way he makes it sound—like something rotten that people like us love to eat." She paused in wonderment. "How do people like him get this way? What happens to them?"

"I don't know. I've been trying to convince myself he wouldn't start up again. Now you tell me that I've been right to worry."

Patience shrugged. "There's not much point in worrying about Michaels. He will do what he wants to do, and we have no idea what that will be. I bet he doesn't either. He's crazy, remember?"

"Thanks. That's good advice."

"I hope you don't mind my advice. It's just that I've been through stuff like this and sometimes—"

"I understand," Rachel interrupted, discovering she didn't want to hear about the *sometimes* when presumably she'd been deficient. She just wanted the advice. "Please don't ever hesitate," she said.

"Well, I might hesitate," Patience said, "except when you ask. Anyway, I'll let you get on with your work." She turned to leave.

"Wait. I have one more question," Rachel said.

Patience turned back.

"Who told you Michaels was starting up again?"

"Nobody."

"Nobody! *You* listened?"

"Of course. I never took the pledge. Why should I have? I didn't work here when Michaels started because Francis had come back, and I'm only half-time now."

"Oh, I see," Rachel said. "I guess that makes it all right then?"

Patience ignored Rachel's sarcasm. "Don't you think *somebody* should tell you what he says?"

"No."

"Don't you think it's dangerous not to know?"

Rachel shook her head. "Not as dangerous as knowing."

"That's amazing!"

"Actually, I'm amazed too, now that I think about it," Rachel said. She sneaked a look at her wristwatch.

Patience headed for the door. There she stopped. "You want to know what the hardest thing for me was when I was the head?"

"What?"

"Not to be too grateful for what people have done in the past."

Rachel didn't answer. She felt as if she'd been caught committing a crime. Patience could see right through her.

"It's hard," Patience said. "But it's what's happening now that counts." She left before Rachel could respond.

TWENTY-ONE

"You wanted to see me?" Francis stopped only a few feet into Rachel's office on the first morning of the February break, his look guarded.

Margaret had set up the appointment the day before. Rachel had not been able to sleep that night, and now her heart was pounding.

"Yes, I wanted to talk," Rachel said, moving around her desk to the door. "Let's take a walk. It's nice outside." She slid the doors open. Outside it smelled like spring. Bob had mentioned once that it was easier to deliver bad news on a walk than in an office.

Behind her, Francis didn't budge. "No, let's not drag it out. You can tell me here," he said in a monotone she'd never heard from him before. She slid the doors shut again and steeled herself before turning around. He still hadn't moved. He said, "I kind of knew what you were going to tell me when Margaret said you wanted to talk, but as soon as you said, *Let's walk*, I knew for sure."

"Let's talk in here then." She motioned to a chair.

He shook his head and stayed right where he was. "When did you decide?"

She shrugged. "Three weeks ago."

"Three weeks? You thought it would be easier if you waited till the break?"

"Yes, I did."

"For you, or for me?"

The question was an arrow in her heart. She didn't know the answer.

"Never mind, I understand," he said. His voice was gentle, forgiving her. Then, after a pause, "It's van Buren, isn't it?"

"Yes."

"Well, now I know," he murmured, looking away, hiding his face, and he turned to leave. Then he seemed to change his mind, turning again, moving toward her where she was still standing by the French doors, and she realized he didn't want to go back through Margaret's anteroom and have his old friend see the humiliation on his face. She slid the doors open for him, and stepped aside. He stopped in the doorway. "Tell me something: would you have appointed me just before Labor Day weekend if Peggy and I hadn't left early?"

She nodded her head.

"It's so strange to think about," he said. Then he went the rest of the way through the doors, and she felt an enormous relief as she watched him walk across the campus toward his apartment.

EVEN BEFORE HE opened the door, Francis smelled the freshly baked bread.

"Want some?" Peggy said, standing by the oven. She hadn't pinned up her hair yet. It was cascading down to her shoulders. "I'll bring you some," she said, before he could answer, and pointed to the living room because the kitchen was her arena, not his, and he went into the living room and sat down on the sofa and heard her cutting the bread and pouring the coffee—and the silence on the other side of the wall where, because it was the February break, the dorm was empty.

"Let's go someplace together today," she said, still out of his sight in the kitchen. "Let's not work." He knew she was squinting her eyes the way she did when she was deciding things. "What do you think? Barkhamsted Reservoir, a picnic lunch? It's so nice outside, like spring already."

"Okay," he said. "Sure. Why not?"

"Good. Just you and me. And we won't talk about school, will we, Francis?"

"No, we won't." He stared at the coffee table. "But first I have something to tell you."

"Of course," she said. "You had an appointment with Rachel." And then she carried a tray bearing the coffee and the bread, slathered with butter and marmalade, into the living room and set it down on a low table in front of the sofa. She poured the coffee into the two cups from the thermos pitcher with a dent, which Siddy had made when he was five years old by dropping it on the hard kitchen tiles to see if it would break. Peggy sat down in a chair facing him. He'd hoped she would sit down on the sofa next to him where she couldn't look directly at his face.

"She's appointing Gregory instead," he said.

Peggy's face was blank.

"You didn't hear me?"

Peggy nodded. "I heard, Fran."

"Well, I guess that's that." He started to stand up.

"But you haven't eaten your bread yet and I made it just for you."

He sat down again.

"How disappointed are you, really?" Peggy asked.

"What?" he said. His voice rising. "What kind of a question is that?"

Peggy raised her eyebrows. "I wish I'd asked it earlier. You were asked to be the head and you turned it down. So maybe you don't want to be an administrator. Maybe you don't really want to be dean of academics. But if you do, I'll be disappointed too."

"Peggy! Everybody was expecting that I would be the one."

"Including you."

"Yes, of course including me."

"So maybe you're just embarrassed then." She leaned forward, picked up a slice of bread, offering it to him. "Eat," she said, "it's the kind you like. Did Rachel say why?"

"She didn't need to," he said, still holding the slice of bread.

"Well then, maybe you'd tell me."

"I think you know."

"How would I, know, dear? Nobody's going to tell me. I'm your wife."

He took a bite of the bread. It was delicious. So he took another. And then a sip of coffee. It was black and strong and rich. Then he put the cup down on its saucer and said, "Nothing's happening in my classes, Peg. Nothing. You know why?"

She shook her head.

"I'm bored."

"Bored? With *Macbeth*? With Robert Frost? Faulkner? With

teaching kids how to write?"

"No, Peg, with *me*."

She sat back in her chair. He heard the silence again. She looked so sad that he wished he hadn't told her. "Well, now," she said at last, "that *is* something to worry about."

AS SOON AS Francis was out of sight, Rachel telephoned her husband. She had bad news to give him: this morning she had awakened to menstrual cramps. Their lovemaking in New York three weekends ago had not made her pregnant after all.

"Oh, Rach!" he said. "I'm so sorry."

"Were you really hoping too?"

"Of course I was. It must have been the stress."

"Oh? Yours or mine?"

He didn't answer.

"Sorry."

"Rachel, please—"

"I have to go," she said. "I have an appointment with Gregory van Buren to ask him to be the dean of academics."

"Can't we talk a little? You can be a few minutes late."

"Are you kidding?" she said. "With Gregory van Buren?" And then she hung up. And then of course she was ashamed of herself and dialed right back, but his secretary told her he'd just left the office. "Really?" she said. "How did he seem?" The secretary didn't answer. "Pissed off?" she suggested and the secretary still didn't answer. So she hung up again and waited some more and called again, and this time the line was busy. And now, if she didn't run, she really would be late.

SHE MET GREGORY under the copper beech. They had agreed to walk while they talked rather than sit in her office. After all, this was the February break and the sun was out. He had allowed himself not to wear a tie for the appointment; instead, a deep-blue turtleneck shirt, white Brooks Brothers button-down shirt over it, and over that a blue blazer. No overcoat. It would have ruined the look. "My! My!"

Rachel said. "All you need to be the earl of something or other is a riding crop."

Gregory van Buren was the only man she knew who could keep a straight face and smile at the same time. "I dress for the company I keep," he said. "The river I presume?"

"The river," she replied.

They walked beside each other through the fecund smell of the river under a blue sky and little white clouds, until they came to a granite ledge the sun had warmed. They sat down there and she popped the question. "How would you like to be in charge of academics at Miss Oliver's School for Girls?"

"I can't think of anything I'd rather be," he said without an instant's hesitation.

"Well, you are then. As of now. You'll have lots to do."

"Yes, pruning mediocrity for one. But bypassing Francis? Is that fair?"

Rachel looked down at her hands.

"Oh, of course. You've spoken to him already." Gregory sounded chastened. "That was dumb of me."

She didn't answer, still looking down at her hands.

"That must have been hard," Gregory said.

She nodded, turned her head up and saw an osprey soaring. It melted her sadness about Francis a little to see such grace. "Very hard." It was enough. She'd heard admiration for her in Gregory's tone, and sorrow for Francis in equal measure, and now she wanted to work with him even more. She turned to him and said, "Yes, pruning mediocrity. If you can find the courage to identify the people who shouldn't be here anymore, I'll find the courage to get rid of them—whether it's fair or not."

He thought about that while she watched the osprey again. She knew he was going to say yes.

"I chair the curriculum committee, not you," he said a moment later. "I lead the discussion that defines excellence in teaching and the way we supervise and evaluate."

"That's right," she said.

"And if we disagree about hiring, you'll support me."

"Probably."

"Probably?"

"*Probably*'s good enough," she said.

He thought about that for a while too, and then he said, "I accept. You have a job description, I assume."

She turned to him and smiled. "I do now," she said.

They sat, their bottoms warmed by the granite slab, while a doe appeared out of the woods not far away. The sound of her hooves on the rocks at the river's edge drifted to them. The doe dipped her head daintily to the river and drank. Then she lifted her head between sips and stared toward them. Sensing them, not seeing. Then the sound of her hooves on the rocks again as she melted back into the trees. They left soon after.

Gregory walked with Rachel right to the French doors. Just before she went in, he said, "How strange. When you called to tell me you wanted to talk, I was about to ask you for an appointment. I was going to tell you that next year would be my last here. I was going to look for a job like the one you just gave me. I was getting restless."

"Oh my goodness!" Rachel said.

"Now I don't have to."

He turned from her then and she watched him walk away toward his apartment. Years ago, soon after his wife left him, he'd come to Miss Oliver's School and lived like a monk ever since. "Gregory van Buren," she murmured aloud. "You and I. We are going to be a wonderful team."

"I HAVE SOMETHING to tell you," Rachel announced to the faculty the following Monday when the school had reconvened. She stood up feeling weak in her legs for what she was about to say. All the other items on the agenda had just been concluded. Later, she wouldn't remember even one of them.

She drew a big breath and said, "I have created a new position, dean of academics. The person holding that position will chair the curriculum—" and the room burst in applause, drowning her out, and everyone, turned and smiled their congratulations at Francis, sitting next to Peggy in the back row, looking very pale. The one exception was Gregory van Buren. "It's about time!" someone yelled.

Apparently, those who had heard the whispers that Francis might be floundering in his classes either didn't believe them or assumed that he'd get back on track as soon as he got the appointment he'd deserved for so long. So Rachel raised her voice and repeated what hadn't been heard. "I'm proud and happy to tell you that person is Gregory van Buren."

Then came the sound of twenty people gasping. Then silence.

Heads turned to Gregory several heartbeats later, and a few brave souls clapped for him. Gregory bowed his head, acknowledging the applause. "Thank you very much," he said, as if he really believed they really meant it.

Then Rachel said, "The meeting is adjourned," and everybody except Gregory and Rachel fled. Francis and Peggy went first.

"I'm so sorry, Gregory," Rachel said. "I should have named you before I named the position."

"Don't worry, they'll get over it," Gregory said, smiling at Rachel in the empty room.

That night, sleep failed Rachel again. With the dread of telling Francis that he wasn't going to be the dean of academics behind her, and full of confidence that she would succeed with Gregory at her right hand, she'd gone to bed free of tension, expecting a full night's sleep. Instead she lay for hours and hours and hours in the dark grieving that she wasn't pregnant.

It was as if she finally had the time.

TWENTY-TWO

It was on the Monday morning of the second week of March that, somewhere between the subject and the verb of a long, convoluted sentence, Mitch Michaels first lost track of what he was telling his listeners. He stopped talking for three whole breaths while he tried to remember what he'd been talking about, and Charlie, his studio manager, stared at him through the glass wall that separated their lairs. On the fourth breath, still lost, Mitch launched another topic, though for all he knew it was the same one. He hoped his listeners wouldn't notice, but just in case they did, he managed to insert a sly confession that maybe he'd drunk a little too much over the weekend and asked them to remember at least one Monday dawn when they weren't at their best either. When the hour was up, Charlie congratulated him on *one of the best shows ever.* "For a second or two, you had me scared," he said.

Mitch was still scared. He thought this might keep on happening. And it was March, the gloomiest month when he always expected it to be spring by then and it never was, and it seemed like forever before it would be warm enough to go sailing, and he hadn't had even one good night's sleep since he'd returned from England, and his back hurt more than it ever hurt before, and so he said goodbye to Charlie and jumped in a taxi and went to his New York doctor's office.

In the waiting room of the doctor's office on Park Avenue and 83rd Street, where he was admitted without an appointment because, after all, he was Mitch Michaels, there was a *New Yorker* cartoon from the 1930s, much enlarged and framed on the wall: a stout middle-aged couple, the husband in a tuxedo, the wife in long evening gown, was being addressed through the window of their first-floor luxurious Manhattan apartment by another couple outside on the sidewalk dressed exactly the same. "Come along. We're going to the Trans-Lux to hiss Roosevelt," the couple on the outside says. Pleased to be part of a clientele who knew enough history to understand this joke, Mitch admired the doctor for being self-aware enough to make fun of his own tribal culture in which he was as famous for his extortionist prices as for his skills, and whose office was even more elegant than the apartment in the cartoon.

And so was the handsome brunette nurse in her tailored, crisp white uniform dress, who commanded him to roll up a sleeve in the examining room before the doctor entered it. He guessed she was about the same age as his ex-wife, somewhere in her forties, and imagined her body containing that mixture of mature sexual knowingness and retained youth that he'd been longing for since his ex had left him, taking their daughter with her. The nurse's long, manicured fingers, on one of which was a wedding ring, pressing on his bare skin as she wrapped the cuff of the blood pressure machine around his arm was all that was required to stir lust in him after so much celibate time. He kept that celibacy secret as if it were a crime, and yet he was proud of it. The nurse's manner was impersonal, professional, efficient, like how he imagined a busy call girl on a tight schedule might be. She leaned over to insert the thermometer in his mouth to discern his temperature, and while the cuff on his arm squeezed tighter and tighter like some lurid bondage device he could only imagine, he looked down between her breasts, amazed at her nonchalance.

"And what are we seeing the doctor today about?" she asked—as if she didn't know, pulling the instrument out of his mouth and squinting at it to read. He wanted to answer that he thought he was going crazy, but he told her his back was hurting him again, which was also true. "I'm sure that's why your blood pressure is elevated today," she answered, shaking the thin red line down, her tone contemptuous to let him know that she listened to his show and disagreed with every word, and then she told him the doctor would be with him in just a minute.

"No, he won't. People like him never keep anybody waiting for only a minute," he said. She didn't deny it, just turned briskly around so that the bottom of her skirt flared up above her knees and left him there waiting.

The doctor, arriving forty-five minutes later, was also brisk. He was short and stocky, totally bald, and wore a white coat and big, round glasses. He didn't even ask what Mitch was there for before he wrote an illegible prescription for twenty more pills and then delivered a lecture about the perils of Vicodin: loss of attention, extreme irritability, mood swings, insomnia, the constant need to increase the dose for the same amount of pain, addiction, and ultimately—he paused here and nodded his head and left the word unsaid.

"Thank you," Mitch said, taking the slip of paper from the doctor and slipping it into his wallet. He'd heard a similar lecture from his doctor in Madison last weekend.

"I won't give you any more," the doctor announced. "This is absolutely the last."

Mitch just grinned at him.

The doctor, accustomed to subservience from his patients, flushed and frowned and waved his finger. "I mean it. I don't want you to die on me, and even more than that, I don't want to go to jail." He turned and plucked a brochure off his desk. Mitch knew what it was. The doctor had hinted about it before. On its cover: a photograph taken from a low-flying airplane of an island coast, a blue ocean landing on a sunstruck beach, and just inland of this a mountain rising, at the foot of which there was a large, handsome, white-sided building next to tennis courts, a swimming pool, and palm trees on a lawn. "This is the Hawaii site," the doctor said. "You'll love it. Very luxurious. Much richer process than your normal everyday twelve steps." The doctor stuffed it firmly in the side pocket of Mitch's suit jacket. "Commit to it," he said. "Otherwise you'll be dead in a year."

TWENTY-THREE

There were some faculty members who would always believe the decline of Francis Plummer's ability to work magic in his classroom began when the new head of school showed her preference for his rival. It was an insult, they still say, a disregarding of thirty-five years of extraordinary performance that took the heart right out of him. Others, once they got over the embarrassment at the public shaming of their colleague, began to admit to themselves, if not to each other, that Francis had begun to falter much earlier in the year—and possibly even the year before, when he and Peggy separated.

Some of these same people began to think that maybe Gregory van Buren was the right person for the job after all. It was a comfort to know there was nothing magical about the man who would lead them, that instead he was a linear thinker, logical, organized, discreet, businesslike, obsessively punctual, and strict about rules. They also discovered respect for their youthful head of school for having the nerve to appoint him instead of Francis, and wondered why they hadn't seen before what she had seen in Gregory van Buren.

The truth of the matter was that Francis's decline had manifested itself at first only in the political, interpersonal arena: his trumped-up vision quest, his rebellion against the new head, his resistance to change, the turmoil in his marriage. News of these falterings came to the students only in vague, discounted rumors last year while he'd still been a star in the classroom. So from the students' perspective, there was no doubt when Francis's decline had started. They were the ones who had experienced the letdown, starting on the very first day of classes this year. They wondered what had happened over the summer because it never had crossed their minds that somebody would make him into an administrator. He was a *teacher.* Why waste his time in an office?

But who wanted to believe her hero had fallen—much less tell his boss? Except for Sally Brinton, who had revealed to Rachel that Francis's performance had climbed from terrible to satisfactory at best, no student or teacher would tell Rachel that Francis Plummer's teaching was anything but heroic. They knew she knew. Everybody always knows such secrets. That's why news of them always travels in whispers. Inadequate teaching was a corruption at the heart of the enterprise, a festering that must not be allowed to continue. Everyone was waiting for Rachel to perform the healing. She was the only one who could.

Not long after he'd been appointed dean of academics, Gregory van Buren appeared in Rachel's office with a worried look on his face. "I have a concern," he said.

Rachel smiled. "Only one?"

Gregory didn't smile. "As the dean of academics."

"Oh," she said, her smile disappearing, "Francis Plummer?"

Gregory nodded his head. "What have you heard?"

"Nothing."

Gregory nodded again. "It used to be the students couldn't talk enough about how inspired they were by him. Why the silence now? If it were any other teacher, I'd visit his classes and observe, but given his expectation that he'd be the dean of—"

"I understand," Rachel cut in. "You can't do that."

"So we have an understanding?"

"We do. If there's a problem with Francis's teaching, it's my responsibility to solve, not yours."

"Excellent! We have clarity," Gregory said.

RACHEL SAT VERY still at her desk after Gregory left. His message was supremely clear: *do your job.* She told Margaret to make an appointment with Francis in his next free period. She would start by asking him if he had fixed the problem in his freshmen class. After all, he'd promised her he would. He owed her the report.

When Francis entered her office a few minutes later, Rachel stood up and turned to meet him. She wanted to look squarely in the eye of this man she still revered, but he glanced away. Their awkwardness—

his shame and her embarrassment at witnessing it—was terrifying to both of them. She waited until he sat down in one of the chairs in the center of the office before she sat down too, facing him. It was an unconscious emphasis of her tallness, to stand above him.

He sighed and said, "Well, I guess we need to talk."

"Yes, we do," she said, relieved by his admission. "I wanted to hear how you think things are going now in your freshman class." There was a slight tremor in her voice.

He didn't answer.

"Francis?"

He shook his head as if to pronounce her question irrelevant. "Peggy thinks I never wanted the job. She thinks I was just embarrassed because everybody expected me to be appointed, including me."

"Well that would be nice, Francis—if it were true," Rachel said. It was a relief to be angry all of a sudden.

"Of course she's wrong," he said. "I wanted it all right. But she might be right about one thing." He stopped talking abruptly and looked out the French doors. Rachel waited for several heartbeats. Then he looked back at her and said, "She tells me I've been doing this too long without a break. She could be right, I guess."

"Well, that's not a sin," Rachel said. She felt the lightness already—and gratitude to Peggy—and a chain of ideas zipped through her brain like little shots of lightening: *Grant a sabbatical, starting in just three weeks with spring vacation to match Peggy's. Appoint Patience Sommers as the sub in his classes and the dorm. Surely he would come back refreshed after so long a time, his old self again. Meanwhile, the problem goes away.* "Well, Francis. Peggy should know," she said, trying not to show her excitement. "She'll be on her sabbatical, so why don't you take one too? I can arrange it for you just like that." She snapped her fingers.

Francis shuddered. "Oh, not *that* long a break!"

"No? How long then?" Rachel's worry returned, like some toxic fume she'd breathed, heavy in her chest.

"I thought that when Peggy starts her program at Columbia, I might go with her. You know, help her get settled in. That's three weeks before the two weeks of spring vacation. Five weeks total.

That's long enough. I'll start again at the beginning of the spring term."

"But you deserve a whole year."

"Yes, but I just don't happen to want one," he said testily.

Now Rachel was angry again. "All right then, I won't *force* one on you," she said, as if she could. She couldn't tell if the flush that arrived on his face at her words was anger at the very idea, or shame that he would flout her by hiding behind his clout with the alumnae. They agreed, right then—hastily to get this meeting over with, and without looking at each other's eyes—that he would take a five-week break, starting when Peggy's sabbatical began two weeks hence, ending at the end of spring vacation.

Rachel had another meeting immediately after Francis departed, and then another and another. By the time she had a few free moments to reflect on her meeting with Francis, she began to feel a little more confident. He had admitted he was tired. And who knows, maybe five weeks' rest would be enough—or maybe, with time away from school, surrounded by the excitements of New York City, he'd begin to understand how refreshing a full sabbatical would be. But why didn't he understand that now? It seemed to her that Francis was actually afraid of being away from school. At any rate, she had five whole weeks coming in which she could focus on other issues than the fate of Francis Plummer.

TWENTY-FOUR

On a morning in late March, Claire bounced through the French doors of Rachel's office waving a large, fat envelope from the Rhode Island School of Design. Rachel knew what it was right away; if it were a thin one, Claire wouldn't be bouncing. She handed it to Rachel and, like old times, went straight to the sofa and let herself fall down backwards into it the way teenagers do until they start buying their own furniture, and watched Rachel to see her reaction.

Rachel's first impulse was to jump up from the chair, bound across the room and hug her, singing, "*Congratulations!*"

Instead she stayed in her chair, opened the envelope, as if she didn't know what was inside, read the letter, then put it aside and looked up at Claire, and said nothing.

Claire's celebratory expression melted. A frown of disappointment appeared in its place and quickly became the frown of a person studying for an answer. Rachel gave her credit for that and was on the verge of telling her what the famous coach said to a player who'd celebrated in the end zone—*act like you've been there before*—when the dawning came to Claire. "Oh, I get it," she said. "This is what I was supposed to do."

"No more than that," Rachel agreed.

"No big deal?"

Rachel nodded her head.

Claire looked heartbroken. "Well, I'm sorry to bother you," she said sarcastically. She started to stand up.

Rachel waved her back down. "You're not bothering me."

Claire sat down again. Another thing Rachel gave her credit for. At her age, she would have barged right out of there. "You know what?" Rachel said. "This is like when you used to come in here and tell me things and study in here with me in the evenings. I missed you. I kept hoping you would come in here and ask me the question that I wanted you to ask, and you never did."

"What question?"

"*The* question."

Claire frowned.

"Be me, when you applied. Better yet, be Nan White in admissions. Then be you and remember what you and your dad told us and what you didn't."

"Oh, that."

"That," Rachel agreed.

Claire thought for a minute, and then she said, "All right, the question is this: would you have let me in if you had known I'd had sex with a teacher."

"Because you could," Rachel added.

"Yeah, because I could."

"Thank you," Rachel said.

Claire shrugged. "So what's the answer?"

Yes! Rachel thought. *Oh yes, in a heartbeat!* Out loud, she said, "I'll tell you in twenty years. When I know how you turn out." Claire winced. "Well, maybe fifteen is long enough."

Claire shook her head, crestfallen. "You'll know much sooner than that."

"Good," Rachel said. "Sooner is better. What did Sonja say?"

"She said congratulations and she's not surprised."

"Is that all?"

"She's going to take me out for dinner."

"That's good, Claire. And by the way, congratulations. I was just trying to make a point."

Claire managed a smile. And yet, Rachel thought she looked irritated too. "Yeah, and I got the point," Claire said, as if she'd understood all along.

"Good. When will you tell your father?"

"He's got business in New York the week after next. Then I'll visit him on the weekend. I'll tell him then."

"Yes, he can wait," Rachel said. There was no reason not to say it out loud. All he was really good for was the funding. She got up, went around her desk and reached for Claire. Claire's face brightened.

This is what she'd come for. She jumped up and put her arms out too. They hugged each other, squeezing tight. Then Claire bounced out the doors, looking as happy as when she'd come in.

It was four in the morning and Francis Plummer, waking up in Peggy's Upper West Side apartment near Columbia, came out of the dream he'd had almost every night since he and Peggy had arrived there a week ago to start Peggy's sabbatical: falling overboard from an ocean liner in the darkest hour of the night. No one heard his shouts.

He never dreamed he actually drowned because he couldn't imagine what being dead was like, but when he woke up, the terror he felt stayed with him for a while, always leaving a portion behind, adding a little more each time. Soon there would be no room left for any other feeling. He'd be just as lost wide awake on terra firma as in his ocean.

It must have been the light from the city streets pouring in the window that told him it was seven-thirty in the morning, and he was back at school where he belonged. He would have to rush to get to his eight o' clock class. He sat up, ready to jump out of bed, relieved of his fear. His classroom wasn't an endless black ocean in which he floated all alone while the ship he'd fallen from disappeared in the darkness. It was a specific, lighted space in which he was the master.

Then he remembered he was in New York. He didn't have a class to go to. Patience Sommers, now living on campus in an apartment near the Plummers' dorm, was substituting for Francis right now in his classroom and for Peggy as a dorm parent for the entirety of Peggy's fourteen-month leave of absence.

Francis lay back down and turned on his side to face Peggy lying next to him. It was then that he saw the clock on the table telling him it was only four in the morning. He tried to melt the terror that was throbbing again by imagining telling her how nice it would be today not to have to go to work. But the calm on her sleeping face and the deep, steady rhythm of her breathing caused him to feel utterly alone, and he understood that the infinite offerings of New York City to fill his day were not going to be enough to still his mounting panic. The day before him loomed as empty as his midnight ocean because he had no classes to teach—an even more terrorizing void because it was real, not dreamed.

He knew how inappropriate it would be, how unfair it would be to Patience, if he appeared in his classroom with no advance agreement and demanded his classes back days before he was expected, so he forced himself to lie still while the terror mounted. When he was a fourteen-year-old boy, he'd awakened from ether after a doctor had set an arm he'd broken, not knowing who he was, with no context for his existence. All he knew was his name. It was like that now, over forty years later. It was unbearable. So he snuck out of bed, put on his clothes, left Peggy a note promising her he'd return on the weekend, and went out of the apartment, unshaven, into a drizzling rain, heading for the parking garage where he and Peggy had left their car. She would have no need for it in New York City.

He couldn't count the times he'd told himself to turn around during his four-hour drive back to the school, that he was acting like a crazy man, but each time he kept on going, until he finally arrived a few minutes after his first-period class had started: American literature for juniors. This time of the year they'd be starting to read *Catch-22*.

It was raining harder than when he had awakened in New York, and the sky was gray and low. He could barely see the dark shapes of the maples lining the paths. He was alone because everybody else was already in class, and the only sound was the warning note of a crow cawing somewhere in the distance. Halfway across the campus, he paused, the panic at war with his common sense, just long enough to feel the emptiness he'd return to if he went back to New York, and then he walked faster, crossing the rest of the campus, entering the classroom building, and pacing down the hall.

The door to his classroom was closed. He put his hand on the knob. He heard Patience say something and then laughter, and then he opened the door to see Patience standing at the front of the room facing the students. She wore a green sweater and a red skirt and held an open paperback book in her left hand with which she was gesturing. The girls' heads turned from her to where Francis had stopped in the doorway. She turned too and saw him there, and he stepped a few feet inside.

"Francis!" she said. The paperback was still in her hand, down by her side.

"I'm sorry to interrupt," he said, looking straight at Patience and feeling the stare of the girls on his face. The very air in the room told him they'd been interested in what he had interrupted.

"Is there something you want?" Patience's tone was gentle and concerned. With her free hand, she gestured at the file cabinets beside Francis's desk and then at the bookshelves lining the wall behind her.

Francis shook his head. "I'm rested enough," he said.

"I'm glad," she said, frowning in incomprehension.

"I mean enough to start teaching again."

She stared.

"Really," he said. "I am."

"*Today?*" she asked.

He nodded, still only a few feet into his classroom.

"But—"

"Please." He heard the desperation in his voice. He kept his eyes on Patience's face. If he glanced at the girls instead, he'd catch them staring.

"Francis! I'm in the middle of—" She flushed.

"What?"

Her face got redder.

"What?" he said again, suspicion rising.

She glanced at the girls. Several of them nodded their heads. *Go ahead, tell him*, they seemed to say. Then she raised the paperback book that was still in her left hand. *The Bald Soprano*, by Eugène Ionesco.

"*The Bald Soprano*!" he said. "A French absurdist play? That's crazy. This is American literature!"

Patience's body stiffened. Her red hair gleamed. "I know what it is, Mr. Plummer. I don't need your instruction." Before he could respond, she pointed at the still-open door behind him. "And you and I need to talk." Then she stepped past him into the hall, leaving him standing alone in front of the girls.

He stood there in the blaze of their embarrassment for one or two heartbeats. Putting up both hands, palms outward, he said, "I'm sorry. I wasn't thinking." He bolted from the room.

Outside in the hall, Francis tried to apologize to Patience but she was too angry to listen. She cut him off. "The course is much too parochial," she said. "American, American, American, as if no one else ever wrote a book." Francis again tried to apologize, to confess he'd acted like a crazy man, but she cut him off again. "It's not very smart to go straight to the premise of *Catch-22* without some warm-up around the absurd," she said. "So I picked *The Bald Soprano.* Besides, it's fun. God knows they needed some of that after the way you bludgeoned them with *Death of a Salesman.*" Francis cringed. Patience's hand flew to her mouth. "Sorry," she murmured. "That was unfair."

He didn't answer. He remembered sermonizing about who Willy Loman really was and why attention must be paid. More than anything in the world right then, he'd wanted them to get it—in their hearts, not just their heads—but all they wanted to know was *Is this going to be on the test?* and he had sermonized some more in a hurt and angry voice, until one of them said, *We get it already, can we please move on?*

"I can't believe I did this," he said now to Patience. He meant both the sermonizing and his breaking in to her class. "I'm really very sorry."

Her face had softened. "I'm sorry too. I shouldn't have said what I said. I was just so *angry.*"

He shook his head. "Let's not talk about it anymore."

Patience nodded. "I won't tell anyone. This is just between you and me."

"But the girls," he said. "They will."

"I'll ask them not to."

"Thank you." He knew the girls would talk, at least some of them, despite Patience's request. He knew she knew that too, but he was grateful anyway. "I'll let you get back to your class now," he said.

"Francis, are you all right?"

"I'm fine."

"Are you sure?"

That she cared shattered him. He didn't know why. He was afraid he might start to cry right there in front of her. So he just nodded his head.

"All right, then," she said. She opened the classroom door and went in, closing it behind her; Francis stared at the closed door for a moment and turned away and headed back across campus toward his car.

He thought that maybe now he'd gotten the craziness out of his system, he'd be all right. Maybe the terror wouldn't return.

ONE MORNING, LATE in the first week of the spring term, after Francis had returned from New York and taken his classes back from Patience as planned, Margaret told Rachel that he was waiting to see her. For an instant, Rachel hoped that Francis had come to say he wanted a sabbatical after all, instead of the mere five weeks he had spent away from the school in New York with Peggy.

Then Margaret added, as if an afterthought, "And he has Patience Sommers with him," and now Rachel was worried that Francis was finding it difficult to work with Patience after so many years working with Peggy parenting their dorm. If it were not for the situations inappropriate for a male's involvement, she would not have appointed any substitute for Peggy.

Patience and Francis came through the door at the same time, squeezed together so tightly their shoulders touched, because Francis thought the lady should go first and Patience thought the elder should. They sat down on two chairs well apart from one another in the center of the office, and speaking in unison because Patience thought she should be the one to tell and Francis thought he should, they informed Rachel that Patience had found a bottle of vodka in Claire Nelson's room.

"Vodka?" Rachel said. "Claire? Really?"

Patience nodded her head. "Kettle One, no less." She looked at Rachel as if Rachel shouldn't be surprised. Francis gazed up at the ceiling.

"I wasn't trying to find something," Patience said. "Her room was a mess and I'd told her to clean it up. Then I came back to check. She'd tidied the room well enough and I told her so and was about to leave when I thought I'd better check her closet. It was still a mess: a bunch of her clothes in a jumble on the shelf. I was going to help her arrange them in her bureau, so I pulled them down. And there it was."

"Didn't she know you were going to check the closet?" Rachel said.

Patience shrugged. "Maybe she wanted to get caught."

"Maybe she thought we'd mind our own business," Francis blurted. He was still gazing up at the ceiling.

"What? Whether they drink or not isn't our business?" Patience said.

Francis looked at Rachel. She understood he wasn't about to explain to Patience what he'd explained so often in faculty meetings: nagging too much about neatness took away teachers' effectiveness in dealing with more important problems. *Yes, like under-age drinking and having sex with teachers*, Rachel thought. Besides, she wasn't sure she agreed. She wanted to get up from her chair, march across the campus to Eudora's studio, and haul Claire out of it and chew her out. She wanted Claire to know how hurt she was by her behavior, how personal an affront it was. Instead she returned Francis's gaze and waited. He looked exhausted. Clearly, he hadn't been sleeping. She asked him, "How long do you think the bottle was there?"

"Since September," Patience said.

"And last year?" Rachel asked.

"I asked her that question, and the answer is yes," Patience said. "She brought a bottle with her when she arrived last January. Evidently, she finished that one. She brought another in September. I didn't press her on whether this one that we found was the same one, or a second, or, who knows, maybe a third."

Francis wouldn't look at Rachel now. *A whole year and the two most senior teachers in the school hadn't had a clue.* "Where is Claire now?" Rachel asked.

"On the way to class, I assume," Patience answered.

"My class," Francis murmured. "I'm about to be late."

"Go teach it then," Rachel said. "And please bring Claire here when it's over. The three of us will meet with her." Francis got up from his chair, brushed past Patience, and hurried out without looking at either her or Rachel. Rachel wondered how in the world he was going to teach his class.

"I'm sorry," Patience said.

Rachel put up her hand. "I was the one who asked those questions."

"Just the same, I should have known better than answering," Patience insisted. "I was a head for ten whole years."

After the class was over, Claire arrived at Rachel's office with Patience and Francis trailing, as if she were bringing them rather than the other way around, and the first words out of anyone's mouth were hers: "I'll spend my suspension at Sonja's, not my father's in London."

"Wait a minute, Claire. We have things to talk about before we talk about that," Rachel said.

"Like what?"

"Like why you—"

"Drink? Or why I break the rules?"

"Let's do drink first," Rachel said.

"Like am I an alcoholic or not?" Claire blurted.

"All right, let's start there," Francis broke in.

"Okay," Claire said, turning to Francis. "Let's."

"Good, Claire," Francis said.

Claire's eyes were on Francis. "So? What now?"

"You tell me."

"A program, I guess."

Francis nodded. "Sonja will help you find one."

"So will Kevina Rugoff," Rachel broke back in, pointedly. "Our school counselor." Patience nodded her head, but Francis rolled his eyes. *Who needs her?* his expression said, and Rachel wondered how many times he and Peggy had chosen to take care of problems like this all by themselves without telling anyone.

"Oh, okay, I'll go see Kevina and make everybody happy," Claire pouted.

"All right, that's settled then," Rachel said, though in her heart it wasn't. The hurt of Claire's more and more choosing Sonja's mothering over her own—so obvious that Francis took it for granted—was much sharper now that Claire was in serious trouble again. And Francis responding to Claire's suggestion that she might be an alcoholic, which Rachel assumed was mere grandstanding … Rachel realized she trusted Francis to provide Claire wise advice more than she trusted Sonja. Sonja was too businesslike, too pragmatic. *If you like to drink some vodka once in a while*, she would say to Claire, *just figure out how not to ever get caught.*

But, here in her office, Rachel was the one in charge of Claire, not Sonja. "So, Claire," she said, "who is going to tell your father about this, you or me?"

"Not me," Claire said. She smirked and put an imaginary phone to her ear. "Hi, Dad, guess what: I drink. A lot." Then she put her other hand up to her other ear. "You do? Really?" Then the other hand again. "Since I was thirteen, Dad. How come you didn't know?"

"Stop blaming your dad," Rachel said. "You sound like a spoiled teenager."

"I *am* a spoiled teenager."

"Well, stop being one right now!" Patience said.

Claire didn't turn her eyes from Rachel to Patience. Her only acknowledgement of Patience was a tiny, stubborn shake of her head. Still, it was easy to see that she was surprised. This was Rachel Bickham's office, not Patience Sommers'.

Rachel pretended she didn't notice. "Okay, Claire, I'll call your father," she said.

Claire looked even more surprised. "I was only kidding. I'll call him."

But Rachel shook her head and pointed to the door. "You've made your decision. That's all for now. Get back to your classes." Patience looked approvingly at Rachel. Francis was already standing up. His face was blank. Claire turned and flounced out the door. Francis followed looking straight ahead.

Patience stayed behind. She smiled at Rachel. "You know what I hate most about events like this? Pouring perfectly good liquor down the drain." Then she left.

And Rachel reached for her phone.

"ADDICTED?" CLAIRE'S FATHER said. "An alcoholic? Are you sure?"

"No. I'm simply telling you what she implied. And I'm wondering if perhaps Claire has wanted to get caught for some time. So she used Ms. Sommers to get the message to Mr. Plummer." Rachel beat back the urge to add, *He's the closest thing to a father your daughter has.*

"I don't think she's addicted. She's being dramatic again."

"I wonder. At any rate, I'll need written confirmation of your permission for her to stay with Ms. McGarvey."

"Fine. I'll send it today."

"And for our arranging a program—"

"Wait a minute. I said I don't think she's addicted, she's just—"

"Sir, Claire's returning to us depends on it," Rachel said, deciding on the spot. "Why take chances? And anyway, whether she's addicted or not, a good long, boring rehab program might teach her a lesson."

"And just what lesson is that?"

"That being dramatic is not always the best idea."

"Oh? Well, maybe. Anyway, it can't do any harm. I'll send it today. Anything else?"

"Yes, as a matter of fact. I just thought of another reason for requiring Claire to fulfill a rehab program." It was true. She really had just thought of it.

"Which is?"

"She doesn't want to," Rachel said.

"Oh!" Claire's father said. "Now *that*'s a reason I can get behind."

TWENTY-FIVE

Two weeks later, Claire Nelson returned. At Morning Meeting she announced that she was an alcoholic. Rachel could have killed her. Claire should have just stood up there on stage looking beautiful and told the school how glad she was to be back, but no, she had to tell everybody, "My name is Claire and I'm an alcoholic."

Rachel was disinclined to think Claire was a drunk. She drank, when she did, just because she wanted to, and she wanted to especially because it was against the rules. After all, everything was much more fun when it's against the rules. Watching her on stage drawing attention to her alleged affliction was for Rachel as irritating as watching one of those dreary Eugene O'Neill plays that everyone was supposed to be uplifted by. Last summer, watching *Long Day's Journey into Night* at the Long Wharf Theater in New Haven, Rachel had turned to Bob after an hour and a half—and there was still another hour and a half to go—and she whispered loud enough for a lot of people to hear, "Why don't they just shut up, stop drinking, and go get a job so we can all go home?" She wanted to yell something just as irreverent at Claire's little drama, but she couldn't think of exactly what to say as the head of the school, so she held her tongue.

It so happened that a reporter from the *New Haven Advocate* who was researching a piece on single-sex education for girls chose that day to visit the school. She was so impressed by "the courage and forthrightness of that young woman" that she rushed back to her office right after Morning Meeting to write it up in time for the next issue. Single-sex education could wait for another day.

COURAGEOUS STUDENT CONFESSES HER ADDICTION, the headline blared, and the article went on to praise Miss Oliver's School for Girls for the progressive way it faced the truth that young people do get addicted and for embracing the young woman—whose name it revealed and whose beauty it described—when other schools would have expelled her. Rachel was sure Mitch Michaels would be all over this. Talk about grist for his mill!

At nine o'clock in the morning of the day after Claire Nelson told the world she was an alcoholic, Milton Perkins gazed out the living room window of his apartment in the River Club at the soothing sight of the Connecticut River flowing by before picking up the phone to call his colleague on the executive committee, the former president of the Alumnae Association, Jamie Carrington.

The new business manager and CFO, Mabel Walters, had reported to Milton yesterday that two hundred thousand dollars still needed to be raised by June 30 to stay on the schedule for paying down the accumulated deficit. That was not soothing news—which was why Milton was gazing at the river.

At precisely the same time that morning, as he did every morning at nine o'clock, Jamie Carrington's chauffeur refolded his boss's copy of the *New York Times* so she wouldn't know he'd read it first and carried it from the kitchen of her mansion in East Hampton to the breakfast room. He knew she read the *Times* voraciously to keep up with the news, but he was sure she never read the editorials. Why read someone else's opinion? She had her own already.

And like always, he was also carrying the *Wall Street Journal*—which he figured she read for clues as to how wealthy she was going to be on the day she died. And the *Hartford Courant* and the *New Haven Advocate*, which she'd begun to check out every morning lately for news of that school near those two cities where people sent their daughters away like they didn't love them enough to keep them around the house. He and his wife had kept their own daughter home, thank you very much, and when Mrs. Carrington had offered to pay their tuition, he'd asked for a raise instead, figuring it wouldn't cost her anywhere near as much. She'd actually thought he was joking.

She had just finished her breakfast and was picking up the phone when he arrived. On the polished dining table, it looked like two phones, the one on the bottom upside down. "Hold on, Milton," she said; then she put her hand over the receiver and turned to her chauffeur. "Good morning, Jack."

"Good morning, Mrs. C. I hope you are well today."

"I am, thank you, Jack. And you?"

"I'm fine, ma'am."

"I'm glad, Jack, and thank you," she said as he put the stack of papers on the table next to her emptied plate.

"May I clear your plate?" he asked, dutifully reaching for it, but she pushed his hand away.

"No, that's Helen's job," she said in an affronted tone, looking at him as if he'd suggested they both take off their clothes. "She's the maid. You're the chauffeur."

As if she organized the world: everything just so because she snapped her fingers. Now more than ever he wanted to see her face when she read the headline and found out that everything's not just so at that school of hers. So he picked up the *Advocate* and said, "I think you should read this one first."

"Really? Why?" she said, but she was already reaching for it. Then, "Oh! Oh. No!"

"That's why," he said—and left her there stewing and holding the phone.

"MILTON! HAVE YOU read the papers?"

"Yeah, sure. The *Times*, and the *Wall Street Journal*. Why?"

"Not the *Times*, the *Advocate*."

"The *Advocate*?" Milton laughed. "Why would I read that? I get bored just thinking about New Haven. Why would I want to read about it?"

"Milton! Listen!" Jamie read him the headline about Claire and the article.

He was silent.

"Well, you aren't joking now, are you?"

"No, I'm not. But I'm not crying either. Everybody knows kids drink."

"I'm not worried about the *newspaper*, Milton."

"Yeah, I know. More ammunition for Mitch Michaels. But the

article praises us for not hiding problems. Makes us look better than other schools. How's he going to turn that around?"

"Stop pretending you're naive, Milton. You know more than anyone, and you know this is just what he's been looking for. I was right all along. We should have kicked that girl out. But instead you listened to that woman who's young enough to be your daughter, after you went ahead and made her the head of school without even asking."

"Jamie, calm down. It's going to be all right. And I did ask."

"Yes, you asked. And then you said, *There's no one else; the year's almost over. We have no choice.*"

"Jamie, I also said she would be very good in the job."

"Well, she isn't, is she? I mean she made this great big mistake right away. It's awful. And I bet the reason you have called me is to tell me we are still behind on the deficit."

"As a matter of fact—"

"Just what I thought. With Mitch Michaels screaming, who wants to give? And now you're going to ask me to go back to the people I asked to give before and ask them for *another* gift."

Again, he didn't answer.

"You were, weren't you? And to make another gift myself? Well, I'm not going to. Not unless this thing doesn't become the disaster I know it will. If we get past this by some miracle, then I'll raise some more money and make another gift myself."

"All right, Jamie, fair enough. But—"

"No buts. It's final."

"But I have an idea you're going to love."

"I'm going to hang up now. My breakfast is getting cold."

"No, it isn't. You eat breakfast at nine o'clock. It's nine-thirty already. Now listen: there's one person we should call. Right now. And you are the person to call him."

"Who?"

"Come on, Jamie. You know."

"The kid's *father*?"

"Of course. Make him feel guilty. He owes us. Wouldn't you just love to get six figures out of him?"

"Would I? If I had a button to make him a pauper, I'd push it right now."

"Well, give it a shot, Jamie."

"By God, I will!"

"You're a star, Jamie. Always have been. I don't know what we would do without you."

"YES, I AM grateful, Mrs.—I'm sorry, your name again?"

"Carrington. And it's Ms., not Mrs., if you don't mind."

"Of course. I seem to have become somewhat English already. We are not quite so precise about such terms. Someday, I'm sure, we'll catch up. And yes, as I was about to say, I will be eternally thankful for the school's waking Claire up to what I have been told is quite an extraordinary talent."

"Oh?"

"Yes, if all goes well, she will matriculate in the Rhode Island School for Design in the fall."

"Oh really?"

"You didn't know?"

"Uh, actually—"

"I understand, Ms. Carrington. But you might go to the studio and see some of her pictures. I'm told they're remarkable."

"I will certainly do that!"

"And yes, I am also grateful, as I'm sure you were about to suggest, that the school has taken care of her alleged problem with alcohol, even arranging a program of rehabilitation for her. I would have done that myself, but being so far away—"

"You are aware she has returned?"

"She has?"

"Yes."

"How did she seem to you?"

"I was not there. I am a trustee, Mr. Nelson. I live in East Hampton."

"East Hampton! That's a lovely place."

"Yes, and, I'm sorry to report she was rather public about her addiction and it's now in the papers."

Silence.

"Mr. Nelson?"

"Really? The papers?"

"I'm afraid so."

"And what about—"

"Michaels? Not yet. But he will."

Another silence.

"Let's change the subject, Mr. Nelson. It is not what I had intended to call you about. I wanted to catch you up on our plan to—"

"Of course. Of course, Ms. Carrington. I will most certainly. What did I give last time?"

"It was fifty thousand. And it was extremely generous and—"

"I'll match it."

Silence again.

"Oh, you expected more?"

"If you could elevate to one hundred thousand, Mr. Nelson, we would be a long way toward our goal for the year to pay down the accumulated deficit. The real reason I called you is that I know you are sophisticated enough to undertake that project. There are so many who don't like to fund debt, even though, at this moment, it is critical. But your leadership will persuade others to join you."

"You are very persuasive too, Mrs. Carrington."

"Thank you," Jamie said, choosing to ignore his *Mrs.*

"And I am persuaded. You have my pledge. One hundred thousand. The check will arrive within a week."

"Thank you. I'm so glad you understand. I'll send you the pledge forms through overnight mail. They will arrive in London tomorrow," Jamie Carrington said.

But Paul Nelson had already hung up. He hadn't the slightest intention of honoring his pledge. He made it just to get her off the phone—after first having some fun with her. He'd met too many of these imperious people who were so sure they owned the world when he worked in the trust department his first years in banking. They all talked just like this one, as if they had lockjaw, in a half-British, half-Yankee accent—like Edith Wharton without the brains.

That's why he'd switched to commercial loans.

NOW, GLOWING WITH pride at her fundraising skills, and forgiveness for Rachel Bickham and Claire and her father, Jamie dialed Rachel. She couldn't wait to share her news.

"Hello, Margaret. Put Rachel on the line please."

"Good morning, Jamie. I'm afraid Rachel is just leaving now to teach her physics class."

"Don't be afraid. Tell her to wait."

Silence from Margaret.

"Well?"

"Jamie, could she call you back? She's almost late for class."

"No, Margaret, I'm busy later. And I have good news for her. I'm sure she could use some cheering up."

"But that would make her late."

"How tragic! The headmistress is a few seconds late to her class because she's talking to a trustee. The end of the world has just arrived. Please remind the headmistress, Margaret, while you are bringing her to the phone to talk with *me*, that trustees *hire* headmistresses. Sometimes they *fire* them too."

Another moment of silence, and then Margaret said, "Jamie, early in the year some of her students came late to class. Rachel made it clear that was not acceptable, so it is imperative that she never—"

"*Imperative*? The imperative is that Rachel picks up her phone. Instantly. Didn't you hear me? I have good news for her."

"Uh, Jamie, I can't bring her to the phone now. She's already all the way across the campus probably entering the Science Building. As I said, she was in a hurry not to be late."

"You mean you didn't make her stop when I called? That all this time—"

"Jamie, she'll call you the minute her class is over."

"You didn't make her stop!"

"No, I didn't make her stop," Margaret said, her voice rising angrily at last. "She was in a hurry. Shall I say it again? Yes, I'll say it again: she was in a hurry, and she'll call you."

"Well, I never! I never! Tell her not to bother. I'll tell my good news to someone else," Jamie said, and slammed the receiver down.

"Oh, it's you," Harriet Richardson said. "I thought you might call sometime."

"Yes, it's me, Harriet. Guess who I just talked with?"

"I don't know. That Bickham woman?"

"Definitely not!"

"Well, I don't have any idea then, Jamie. Milton Perkins? Has he changed his mind about her? Because if he has, then I don't have—"

"Paul Nelson."

"Who?"

"In London."

"Oh! You mean—"

"Yes, her father."

"*Her?*"

"Yes, him."

"And what did he say? Is he going to take her out of the school?"

"No, just the opposite. He said he'd give the school one hundred thousand dollars. He obviously doesn't want us to kick her out."

Silence from Harriet.

"I'm not suggesting anything. I'm just reporting. I thought you'd be interested. He was quite emphatic."

"A quid quo pro?"

"That's one way to put it."

"And the other way?"

"All depends who you are talking to."

"I understand. You can't use the word."

"No, I can't. I'm a trustee. And I'm sure you understand why I can't appear at your meeting: Trustees are supposed to support the head."

"Actually, I haven't called one. I was trying to decide."

"But now you *have* decided."

Silence.

"Haven't you, Harriet?"

"Yes. I've decided."

"Excellent. One more thing."

"I know. I didn't hear it from you."

"That's right. You heard it from what's-his-name on the radio."

"Yes, what's-his-name," Harriet said.

"Well, it's been very good talking with you, Harriet. Enjoy the rest of your day," Jamie cooed, then she hung up—and sat back in her chair, feeling very guilty. When would she ever stop being so impetuous? How would she ever be able to look Milton Perkins in the face?

THE NEXT DAY, while Mitch Michaels was half napping, his chin on his chest, because a caller-in was ranting, Mitch's studio manager, Charlie, slipped into the studio holding a newspaper in one hand. "There's an old lady who wants to talk to you after the show," he whispered.

Mitch put his hand over the mike. "Yeah? Well, tell her to beat it, okay? My back's killing me."

Charlie shook his head and handed the newspaper to Mitch.

Mitch's eyes went straight to the headline. It was circled in red ink. He sat up straight. "Tell her to wait," he said, without looking up, and read the rest of the article. Then he took his hand off the mike, leaned in, thanked the caller, and said, "Hey everybody, listen to this!"

Harriet Richardson wasn't sure what to expect as she waited on a sofa for Mitch Michaels to finish his show. An Edgar Hoover, maybe: short, fat, a perpetual expression of insolence, and skin like bread dough? Or a tired, old, petulant dinosaur in a black suit and relentless scowl like a Republican senator? Or a wild-eyed sidewalk preacher with Tourette's Syndrome? The one thing she did know was that she felt besmirched, like what she imagined a man with a conscience would feel in a brothel waiting to be serviced. It was one thing to listen to Mitch Michaels talk on the radio. *But to be in his presence!* She had half a mind to get up and leave.

But here he was in the doorway—so tall he almost had to duck. And—my goodness, handsome, sort of—in a cardigan sweater and pleated dark flannel slacks: Bing Crosby without that silly saccharine look. But this man was tired, she saw that right away.

"My name's Mitch Michaels," he said, as if she didn't know. She told him hers and lifted her hand to him. He bent over to shake it and his left hand went to the small of his back. He winced as if a knife had gone in there. *Good*, she thought. *He's vulnerable.*

"Thank you for bringing me that news," he said.

"I have more. The headmistress knew all along that girl was drinking."

"She did? Are you sure?"

"Sure? Why do I have to be sure?" she asked and then went on to explain her plan. She would call a meeting of all the parents and alumnae who agreed that the terrible things about the school he'd been saying were someday very soon going to actually be true if that ridiculous woman were not dismissed and a marvelous teacher named Francis Plummer put in her place. "I'll start the meeting by asserting that Ms. Bickham knew all along that girl was drinking, and suggest that the reason she hid this fact was because the girl's father had bribed her with a pledge to match the gift he'd already made for letting her in with an even bigger gift if she didn't kick her out."

"Just a suggestion?" he asked.

"Yes, I will have to look them in the face. But when you on the very same night announce this on the radio, you can state it as a fact to the rest of the world. It will be hard to deny. Each time she tries, it will draw attention."

"But my show goes on in the morning. I'll have to arrange for a special evening show."

"That will draw attention too, won't it?"

"I suppose it would."

"Good. So, Mr. Michaels, are you agreed?"

He grinned. He was dying to shake this strange little creature up. He said, "Does the pope defecate in the woods, Ms. Richardson? Does a bear wear a funny hat?" and watched the appalled look on her face. He wasn't tired anymore. Then he smiled and stood up. "Yes, I'm with you, one hundred percent," he said, because he really was, and then he turned back to his studio and left her sitting there.

"Do you have any idea how big an idiot you were when you got up there on the stage and said that?" Sonja asked Claire that weekend at her house.

No answer from Claire.

"Claire?"

"Yeah," Claire said finally. "I guess I do."

"You guess? Repeat after me: Monumental. Gigantic. Tremendous. Extremely large."

Claire grinned. She thought Sonja was joking.

"Say them, Claire. Or I'll drive you straight back to school right now and you'll never set foot in this house again."

"Okay, I'll get my suitcase and meet you in the car," Claire taunted.

"Fine," Sonja said. "Hurry up. I want to get back here before my dinner gets cold."

A few minutes later, in Sonja's Mercedes, while Sonja was backing out of the driveway, Claire said, "Can't I just admit I was an idiot?"

"Nope."

"Okay," Claire said. She recited, "Monumental, gigantic, tremendous."

"You left one out."

Claire sighed. "Extremely large."

Sonja stopped the car. Still in the driveway. She looked hard at Claire. "You're no more an alcoholic than I am."

"I know."

"So?"

"If you're asking why I said I was, I don't know."

"Really? Okay then." Sonja backed the rest of the way out of the driveway.

"You can't," Claire said. "You promised. You said if I said the words."

"I don't need to keep my promise to you. You just lied to me. You do know why you did it and you just said you didn't. All contracts are off." Sonja was headed down the road toward the school now, driving faster and faster.

"Well if you know I know why I did it, then you must know why I did it, so why do I have to tell you?"

"But I don't know why," Sonja said as the school came into sight. "How could I possibly know why anyone would do something so dumb?"

Claire didn't answer. Even as Sonja turned the car into the

driveway, she didn't believe this was happening. Neither of them spoke as Sonja tooled the big Mercedes up the long curving driveway and stopped in front of Claire's dorm. "Get out," she said.

Claire didn't budge. She looked straight ahead through the windshield. Sonja reached across her and opened the car door. "Get out," she said again. Claire still looked straight ahead. She started to cry. "Don't you dare pull tears on me," Sonja said. Claire turned, still crying, to look at Sonja and was stunned. There was a hardness in Sonja's expression that Claire had never seen before—not in Sonja, nor any other person. She was strangely relieved. "I don't believe your tears for one minute," Sonja said.

Claire sat very still beside the open door of the Mercedes. She put her right foot out of the car onto the pavement, while she quelled her tears. It was harder to do than the last time with her father when she'd stopped them so her schoolmates wouldn't see. Then she turned to say goodbye to Sonja and discovered that instead she was telling her how she hadn't planned to tell the school she was an alcoholic.

She hadn't known she was going say anything at all—not even that she was glad to be back—until she was actually climbing up on the stage, and even then she thought she might tell the school what had really happened and say how glad she was to be back. She'd learned a lot about addicted people and she'd made some friends among them. That's what she really wanted to talk about. That was what was really interesting and what she would have still been thinking about if she hadn't seen Rachel looking at her from where she was sitting in the audience and suddenly wanted revenge. Not revenge, exactly, when she thought about it later though. It was more complicated than that. She wanted to say to Rachel, *You can't punish me.*

"So I pretended to be addicted and everybody took me seriously," she said as Sonja started the Mercedes and headed back down the long driveway. "Getting punished is one thing, getting healed is another, and after a few meetings I began to feel like maybe I was getting over my addiction even though I didn't know quite what my addiction was. Except that it wasn't alcohol."

Claire stopped talking and started crying for real as Sonja pulled out onto the road to her house. Sonja put her right arm around Claire's shoulder and steered with her left hand. "My high school boyfriend and I used to drive around like this," she said, pulling Claire closer. Claire giggled even though she kept on crying until Sonja pulled into the driveway of her house and stopped the car, and said, "Let's you and I make dinner together."

TWENTY-SIX

On a Monday morning in the first week of May, Cary Swanson, Liz Rintoul, and Shirley Dwight, three members of Francis Plummer's celebrated Senior Honors Shakespeare class, came to Rachel's office.

"We have something to tell you," Cary said. "We asked Clark when we would get our term papers back."

For an instant Rachel forgot who Clark was.

Liz added, "As nicely as we could." And Shirley said, "But he ignored us so we asked again." They stopped right there and looked at each other.

"And?" Rachel asked.

"*When I feel like it,*" Cary said. "*When I can stomach reading them. That's when you'll get them back.*"

"He said that? Really?"

They nodded their heads. Amazement was vivid in their expressions. For what they were telling, or that they were telling, Rachel wasn't sure.

"Well, how long has he kept them?"

Shirley and Liz looked at Cary. "Since before spring vacation," Cary whispered. "Seven weeks—"

"Seven weeks?"

They nodded their heads again. Rachel could almost taste their discomfort. "He'll have them back to you by the end of the week," she said. They studied her face, unconvinced. So she said it again, "The end of the week. Count on it," and they scrambled up out of their chairs and headed for the door.

In the doorway, Liz turned. "You're not going to fire him, are you?"

"I'm just going to get your papers back for you," Rachel said.

"That's all."

"Really?"

Rachel hesitated Then she said, "Please don't worry, Liz. You did the right thing," but Liz didn't seem to hear. She just turned and fled.

Rachel asked Margaret to call Francis and ask him to come during his first free period. "No, don't ask him, tell him," she corrected.

Margaret frowned. "Trouble?"

"Big trouble." Rachel returned to her desk and waited for Francis, burning with shame. Those three kids shouldn't have had to squeal on Francis.

"I'M SO ASHAMED!" Francis said, looking terrified, an hour later in Rachel's office. "Maybe I should resign." He watched her eyes, and in the heavy silence that followed, Rachel imagined the celebration of his career, how full of glory and affection it would be. And after it, how free of worry *she* would be.

But she knew he'd said that so she would say she couldn't imagine the school without him. And, in spite of his troubles, she still couldn't. So instead, she said, "But Francis, after thirty-four years of glory, why would you sneak away in the thirty-fifth?"

The terror drained from his face. "Well, I suppose you're right."

"All right, then Francis, what should we do? After you get those papers back, that is."

"I'll get them back by the end of the week."

"Yes, you will!" she exclaimed. His face flushed with anger. He stood up from his chair. "We haven't finished yet," she said.

"I've already said I'd get them back. What else is there to say?"

"Francis, sit down!" He stared at her and she stared right back and pointed to the chair. "You know what else," she said, "and we are going to talk about it." He looked surprised. She pointed to the chair again, and the defiance melted from his face. His shoulders slumped and he sat back down. Her heart turned over. He was waiting to be saved.

"We've talked about this before, Francis, and now we are going to do it. You are going on a sabbatical starting when you've handed those papers back. It will last all the way to July first next year." She felt confident now, on firm ground, and full of regret she'd taken so long to be this forceful. The realization flooded over her: she could have saved him from shaming himself.

"A sabbatical?" he said. "Away from here?"

"Yes, and with full pay and benefits."

He shook his head, and leaned forward. "I'll stay right here. Summer vacation starts soon. That's long enough."

"No. Absolutely not. We've been over this before."

"But—"

She put up her hand. "Just think about what it would be like for you if you don't take the sabbatical and stay here teaching next year and this kind of thing keeps on happening. The first-year students already wonder why you were ever hired; next year it will be the first- *and* second-year students. That's half the school who won't know the real Francis Plummer."

He sat back in his chair and looked away.

"Francis, look at me." He turned back to her, and she saw the recognition on his face that what she'd said was true, and then she braved his eyes and said, "You need to know that if you stay and don't get all the way back to your former self, I will fire you."

"Fired?"

She saw the panic in his eyes, and understood, at last, how hard it was for him even to imagine his life without the school around him like a coat. She wondered why it had taken her so long. From the day she'd been appointed head, she'd been no different from Francis in this way. She was sure now that Francis would choose the sabbatical over the risk of being fired. The shame of that would be unimaginable, and to be cast adrift, separated from the school permanently, was a lot more terrifying for him than being unmoored for only thirteen months on a sabbatical would ever be. "Yes," she said. "Fired. Francis Plummer mustn't ever be a has-been." She was ready to add, *By then, even the alumnae would understand*, but she held back. She didn't need to diminish him any more than he already was. And anyway, she wasn't sure she was right: maybe the alumnae would be so offended that she was the one who'd go.

"All right," he said, almost in a whisper, standing up from his chair. "I'll go. I'll take the sabbatical and come back in a year."

Rachel sat still, stunned by her victory. Her desk between them was a continent. She stood to come around it, but he stepped back away and escaped out through the French doors for the second time. She watched him pass under the branches of the copper beech. This time, the buds were fat, about to burst. He stumbled once, his head bent down; then he recovered. Shoulders back, chin up, he hurried toward his classroom.

TWENTY-SEVEN

As soon as Francis was out of sight, Rachel called Milton Perkins to tell him about her decision to send Francis away on a sabbatical. The desk person at the River Club told her Mr. Perkins had left several days ago with his daughter, the older one, Mary. Yes, he had a suitcase. They had carried it for him out to her car. No, they wouldn't say where they were going. No, they didn't leave a telephone number where she could reach him. Rachel called Mary at her house. No answer. She called Mary's younger sister, Charlotte. She told Rachel, "For now it's confidential," and that she was sorry her father hadn't remembered to let Rachel know he wouldn't be available. "This is very difficult," she said, ending the conversation. "We'll let you know as soon as we can."

Seconds later, Rachel called Sonja's office, demanding to be put through to her. As vice chair, she would take Milton's place until he returned. She told Sonja first about Milton Perkins and Sonja tried to convince her not to read too much into it. Then Rachel told Sonja about Francis.

"A sabbatical?" Sonja said. "What happens if it doesn't work?" Rachel told her she'd cross that bridge when he and she got to it. They agreed Rachel should wait to inform the community about Francis's well-earned sabbatical until they knew how he would spend it.

And that the board chair Milton Perkins taking a little trip somewhere with his daughter was nobody's business.

"Hey," Bob said into the phone when Rachel called him that night. "Telepathy. I was thinking of you."

"Did I wake you up?"

"Uh uh. I'm reading."

"What? Charts? Graphs? Market share for basketballs?"

"Something like that. Not quite so interesting. What are you doing?"

"Nothing. I'm in bed." She hadn't told him she was sleeping down the hall in a single bed. She'd had a phone installed in that room.

"Can't sleep?" he asked.

"I don't know. I haven't tried yet."

"Well, how about I read you these charts? Listen to this: ratio of inventory release to shelf space has increased by 2.7 percent in March in our Chicago store and decreased by 3.1 percent here in New York, but the trouble is the New York figures are for a different month. So we extrapolate—"

"Bob?"

"Hi. Are you sleepy yet?"

"I sent Francis Plummer on a sabbatical today."

"A sabbatical. That's a good idea."

"You didn't hear me, Bob. I said *sent.* The first thing Sonja said when I told her was, *What happens if it doesn't work?*"

He laughed. "You know how many times I hear people ask that question? Besides, who cares what Sonja says? What did Perkins say?"

"That's another problem. He's gone away somewhere. His daughters won't say where. Remember I told you he almost forgot that executive committee meeting earlier in the year?"

"Yes, but I also remember you told me how well he handled that meeting for you."

"All right. I suppose I shouldn't worry."

"Of course you shouldn't. What's it like there?"

"It's nice. Spring's really come. Can you hear the frogs peeping?" Rachel held the phone toward the open window.

"Yeah, I can hear them. Horny little fellas. You run by the river today?"

"No."

"Come on, Rach. Don't just run when you're feeling good."

"All right. I'll go on a run tomorrow."

"Good. Now let's talk about something important. What are you wearing?"

Rachel giggled. "A nightgown. I said I was in bed, remember?"

"The red one?"

"No, I'm saving that one for you."

"Mmm. Yum yum. Can't wait."

"I can't either."

There was a long silence on the line, and then he said, "I love it when you call me. You know that?"

"Yeah, I know that, Bob. Thanks for listening. I feel better now."

"That's good. Now back to my charts." He laughed.

But Rachel still wasn't ready to go to sleep alone. She told her worries all over again, and this time he didn't try to persuade her not to worry. She was grateful for that. "I really do feel better, now," she said. She thanked him again and then they said goodnight, and she turned out the light and lay back down on the pillow and started to drift away. Then she thought, *Why doesn't he ever call me with his worries about his job?*

She spent what seemed like hours and hours, asking that question over and over again, until she grew so bored of it she had to think up a different one: what would it be like to forget all about being the head of Miss Oliver's School so she could become his full-time wife? It wasn't really a question; it was just a silly rhetorical image of her resentment, but it repeated itself as relentlessly as the one it replaced, until she fell asleep at last and dreamed that she was entering his tiny New York City apartment carrying a huge suitcase because she'd quit at Miss Oliver's.

"We're going to make a baby together," she announced, but he was on the phone to a buyer and paid no attention. So she went into their tiny bedroom, dragging the huge suitcase, which had suddenly lost a wheel, and got up on the bed and waited for him. And waited for him.

When her alarm clock sounded in the morning, she thought it was his. He would get up from her side and go to his huge, important, all-consuming work, and she would stay right here in their bleak apartment and wait for him.

Then she finally understood: it was *her* alarm clock that was ringing. She was still the head of Miss Oliver's School for Girls. She'd been rescued. She got out of the bed—it seemed a dangerous place—

and took a long, hot shower. She would go to the dining room this morning and eat with the girls. Their sleepy company would make the dream go away.

THE NEXT MORNING in her office, Rachel glanced through the French doors and saw Milton Perkins getting out of a car. Then she realized it wasn't his car and he was exiting from the passenger side, and she knew what he was going to tell her. She thought how strange to be surprised when what's happening was what you knew would happen all along. Before they'd even sat down, he said, "I've been forgetting things so I need to resign."

Rachel wished she had some words at the ready, but all she could do was shake her head. "I'm fine most of the time," he said. "But other times I'm not, and it is going to get worse. I don't want to embarrass myself."

Rachel sat down hard into the nearest chair, already feeling lost and lonely, wondering how in the world she was going to do her job without his guidance. He pulled up a chair close to hers and sat down too, and told her it started to happen even before she tried to persuade him he just wasn't used to not having a secretary yet.

"Remember?" he said. "We both knew then that this day was coming. Well, here it is." He shrugged his shoulders and his tone was matter of fact. "You'll be fine," he said. "You and Sonja will work well together." He paused for a second, and then he added, "Just remember, though: you'll have to manage her."

"I don't want to talk about Sonja. I want to talk about you and us."

"Can't. Don't have the time. I'm on two other boards and I want to get this over with today." He smiled and said, "Don't worry. I'll have some good days. Come see me then," and, as courtly as ever, he took both her hands in his and, standing up out of his chair, pulled her up out of hers and kissed her on the cheek, the way her father did. "I can do that now that we're just friends," he said. "I always wanted to before," and she felt his hands releasing her, his fingers slide away.

He left the way he came.

Two days later, all the windows of Francis's classroom were open and sunshine flooded in along with the smell of honeysuckle and the freshly mowed lawns as the girls of Senior Honors Shakespeare took seats around the three-sided square of tables. Then Francis went around the room, handing each girl her term paper. He'd put each in a folder with the writer's name, along with his attached critique, an essay in itself several pages long. He'd stayed up almost till dawn both nights writing them, and now he was exhausted.

Then he sat down at his desk in the front of the room, fidgeting while the girls read what he had written. Then he went around again, asking each girl to tell him whether her paper rated the expected *A*, which was already recorded, and if not, what revisions she would make, or what entirely new project she would undertake, to make that *A* an honest one.

Then, when the period was almost over, he gave them the news. "I've decided to take a sabbatical. I think you know why. Patience Sommers will be your teacher for the rest of the year." He wanted to flee then, but the bell hadn't rung. It was hard to read the girls' faces: regret and sympathy, but mostly relief. "For the first two weeks, I'll be in Italy. I've signed up for a course: Renaissance Painting in Italy. I'll be in Perugia." He didn't tell them it was an Elderhostel course. Nor that it was Peggy's idea. She'd persuaded him that what he would learn would enrich his classes when he returned. After the course was over, he'd stay with her in New York and visit her when she was in Montana. After all, his belief—he couldn't call it a faith—was more in tune with Native Americans than Peggy's would ever be. And maybe he and Sidney would canoe down the Allagash River in Maine together for two or three weeks. It was something he'd always wanted to do.

"Will you be here on graduation day to watch us get our diplomas?" the girls wanted to know.

"Absolutely! I wouldn't miss that for the world," he said, speaking the truth. "Wherever I am, I'll come back for that."

The bell rang then, and he escaped.

He taught his other three classes surprisingly well, sharing the same news with each at the end, and then, entirely spent, he went to his apartment and started to pack for Italy. He would leave tomorrow.

Mabel Walters, the newly hired business manager, had persuaded Francis to let her arrange the movement of the Plummers' furniture into storage. That was fine with Peggy. She was busy in New York, and Francis was glad to be relieved of the task. It hadn't dawned on him until Mabel broached the subject that someone else, namely Patience Sommers, the dorm parent in his absence, would occupy the apartment attached to the dorm he and Peggy had inhabited for almost thirty-five years. "We'll take notes on the exact position of everything, and have the movers put it all right back for your return a year from July," Mabel said.

Rachel asked Francis several times what he planned to do with the all the time after the Elderhostel course was completed. Each time, he put her off. She thought hanging out with Peggy in New York, and maybe Montana too, was too vague a plan. She wanted him to make a plan for refreshing himself. So to give Eudora a chance to press him on the subject, Rachel went to her studio to ask her to drive him to the airport tomorrow. She would hire a substitute to take Eudora's classes. Francis would be much more willing to take advice from a peer and friend than from a much younger head of school whose position she was sure he regretted turning down. Francis would agree with Eudora that he should make a plan, if he hadn't already.

Eudora met Rachel at the door of the studio, as if guarding it against burglars. She hated her classes to be interrupted. The smells of paint and turpentine and clay seemed especially strong today. Behind Rachel, the huge kinetic chairs gleamed in their shiny paint. Rachel whispered her request so the students wouldn't hear. Eudora shook her head. Her huge loop earrings rang like bells. "You're his boss. You should be the one. He needs the pressure."

"But I'm the last person he wants to be stuck in a car with for a whole hour," Rachel said. "He'll say, *Thank you, but I'll take Super Shuttle.*"

Eudora looked intently into Rachel's eyes. She seemed to be deciding something. Then she took Rachel's hand and pulled her into the studio. "You need to understand something," she said, her tone of voice suggesting mild reproof. "Let's talk." She headed across the studio to her office, her round, soft body rolling side to side.

She wore a white coat, like a doctor's or a waiter's, except that it came down to her ankles to protect her dress. It was many-colored with splotches of paint that didn't seem random to Rachel but part of a design. Rachel followed Eudora into her office where Eudora remained standing up. Rachel knew why: stand-up meetings went much faster. Eudora would get back to her students sooner.

"You need to be fierce with Francis," Eudora said. "I've known him for thirty-some years and I adore him. But he can act like a child sometimes."

"A child?" Rachel said. "Francis Plummer?" She wasn't as surprised as she sounded.

Eudora nodded. "Like last year when he wouldn't support Fred Kindler because he didn't agree that Marjorie Boyd should have been fired. It took him almost the whole year to grow up enough to understand that he was wrong. And by then it was too late—at least for Fred. You don't need to be imperious with most of us, but you do with Francis. You need to demand he tell you how he's going to spend the sabbatical you have given him. Not because it is in his best interest to decide, but because you want him to. He'll do the right thing in the end, whatever it is. He'll circle around it, but he'll come to it. Trust me. I know him like a book. You don't need me to give him advice from his friend. You need to give him a command from his boss." She paused for an instant. Then she added, "And the school needs you to be the person who can." She turned to the door, returning to her students, because there was nothing more that needed to be said.

The next morning, Francis met Rachel at the front door of his apartment where he had been waiting for her to drive him to the airport. He had a briefcase slung over his shoulder, several books poking out of the top, and one small suitcase which he wouldn't let her carry to her car. It seemed too small to Rachel for two whole weeks in a foreign country. "I much prefer to carry on," he said. Rachel wondered how he would know. He and Peggy never traveled.

As they pulled out of the driveway, Francis looked back at his apartment and the dormitory. He didn't turn his head forward until they went around a corner, and when they went through the gates onto the public street he looked back again until the school was out of sight.

When she asked him how he would spend all that time after Renaissance Painting in Italy was over, he answered by talking about the traffic, how there was so much more of it now, and how they never fixed the roads.

They pulled up in front of the international terminal at Bradley Airport. He put his hand on the handle of his door. It was now or never. Rachel reached across him and clamped her hand on his. "Wait a minute, Francis."

"Please don't ask me again."

"Francis, you need to decide."

"I'll decide as soon as I get back to New York with Peggy."

"Will you?"

"I said I would, didn't I?"

"And you'll let us know?"

"After I tell Peggy," he said in an offended tone, and got out of the car onto the sidewalk. Rachel got out of the car too and opened the trunk and handed him his bag and briefcase. It was clear he didn't want a hug. She put out her hand and they shook. It was noisy there at the curb: car doors slamming, horns honking, a policeman's whistle. She thought he looked like a man whose blindfold had been just taken off in place he'd never been. He dropped her hand and crossed the sidewalk to the terminal. In its doorway, he turned and waved and tried to smile and then he was gone, and she drove back to the school, wondering how Eudora would have graded her performance.

TWENTY-EIGHT

Even though meetings with Amelia Dickenson, president of the Alumnae Association and a well-regarded author, were sometimes more about Amelia Dickenson than about the Alumnae Association, Rachel was glad to find Amelia waiting in her office when she returned from the airport. The conversation would stop Rachel from seeing again and again the lost look on Francis Plummer's face as he had disappeared into the airport.

Amelia was a tall, angular woman in her forties, with a very large head of very blond hair. "I have wonderful news for you," she exclaimed, handing Rachel a galley of her latest book. "It's a collection of my essays, and I'm scheduled for the biggest book tour I've ever had with tons of interviews all over the country."

"That's wonderful!" Rachel said.

"I know. Now look at the dedication."

Rachel opened the galley and read: *To Francis Plummer, teacher extraordinaire, magician in the classroom, who gave me my career.*

"All the news releases will mention him, and the first essay is all about him and how lucky it is that he has eight years before he's sixty-five to go on teaching," Amelia said. "People like him never get old. And that's not all. I'm endowing the Francis Plummer chair. One whole salary in perpetuity. One and a half million. Yesterday, I mailed a letter to the entire Alumnae Association to tell them."

"You did!"

"Yes, you should be getting a copy of it in the mail tomorrow," she went on, oblivious of the dazed expression on Rachel's face.

"Amelia! Thank you. Nothing could be more appropriate," Rachel said.

Amelia chuckled. "I thought you would be pleased."

Rachel stood up and came around her desk, her arms out. Amelia stood also, and the two women hugged. "*Pleased* doesn't begin to express my thanks," Rachel said. She was doing the numbers in her head. One-and-a-half million, harvested annually at 4.5 percent: sixty-seven thousand, five hundred dollars. *Every year.* It wouldn't be used to reduce the accumulated deficit, but it would surely take the pressure off each year's budget from now on. "By the way," she said, "Francis is on a sabbatical."

Amelia stepped back out of the hug. "A sabbatical? Since when?"

"This morning."

"This morning! With so little left of the school year? What happened, Rachel?"

"Nothing *happened*. There was a course he very much wanted to take about Renaissance art in Italy, and it starts the day after tomorrow."

"Oh." Amelia looked relieved.

"I can't think of any teacher in any school in the whole world who deserves a sabbatical more than Francis does, can you? So when he asked for this, I didn't think about it for one second. I just said yes." Rachel didn't feel the slightest bit guilty for lying. "And to tell you the truth, I'm amazed that this school has been going on for years without a sabbatical program," she said, warming to the subject.

"You know, you're right. We should be ashamed of ourselves."

"And you know what: he'll be even more brilliant when he comes back," Rachel added.

Amelia nodded her head. "Yes. Francis Plummer is the embodiment of this school."

A few minutes later, Amelia hurried off to another appointment, and Rachel called Sonja to tell her the news. They agreed that wherever Francis was, he should return to school on graduation day to receive this honor in person from Amelia. In the next few hours, Sonja set up a conference call with the executive committee of the board in which it was agreed the optimal time to announce the gift would be graduation day.

FRANCIS FELT A pulse of excitement when, looking down as the plane glided in over Rome, he saw a brown ribbon below him and realized it was the Tiber. The excitement carried him through the drudgery of customs and onto the bus to the Termini, where, looking out the window at Rome's exotic streets, he was amazed to realize this place he'd read and taught about so much was real and he was actually here. By the time the bus arrived at the Termini where he'd board the train to Perugia, he had decided to stay at least a week in Rome after the Elderhostel course. The first thing he'd do was go to the Forum and stand on the place Antony stood when he made the speech at Caesar's funeral, and the next time he and his Senior Honors Shakespeare students studied that speech together, he'd be able to say, *I've been there.* He would tell them what it felt like to stand on the exact spot imagining himself as Antony starting a civil war, and that famous Shakespearean moment would be real to them.

A few minutes later on the platform for the train to Perugia, he saw a knot of people shaking hands, and understood they were there for the same reason he was. Then he saw by the way they stood together and introduced themselves in pairs that they were a group of couples, and, without Peggy, he wished instantly to be elsewhere. And then he saw that all of them were old! Of course. *Elderhostel! Fifty-five and older.* Why was he surprised? He fought off an impulse to turn around and go right back to the airport. Instead, pretending not to notice them, he scooted down the platform to board the furthest car away. He took the last seat but one by the window, and when the train began to move, he thought he'd be all right. He needed time to gird his loins before he mixed with strangers.

Then he heard a hiss of air at the head of the car and the door opened and a handsome woman in a smart blue dress came down the aisle. She had a little dewlap above a modest necklace. He scrunched himself against the window, wishing he had the *New York Times* to hide behind. She smiled at him and sat down and put a book in the seatback pocket in front of her, nesting for the trip. "Are you by any chance with the Elderhostel course?"

She introduced herself as Clara Beecher. From Cleveland. She had three grown children, two of whom were married with children, the third, she made a point of emphasizing, was gay and living with a partner. He understood she told him this as a test to see if they could be friends. Satisfied, she went gently on to say her husband had died six years ago. "We were both only fifty-five, it seemed unfair," she said. "I'm finally getting used to being alone."

She waited for him to return the introduction with equal detail, but when he only said his name and made sure she knew he *wasn't* retired, she said, "You must have flown all night too. We'll talk later." She patted his arm. "Get some sleep." She reached for her book; he laid his head on the window. All the way to Perugia, he watched Italy go by and pretended to sleep.

THE NEXT MORNING in the museum, Clara Beecher walked beside Francis Plummer as the lovely Elena Sensi, their art historian, led them from painting to painting. Clara and Francis both knew that if there were three unattached people in the group, there would be three bodies pressed together each time the group had to cluster tightly before a painting to hear Elena talk. But there were just the two of them. Three or two, Clara didn't care. The world was beautiful to her that morning; she was happy in her years, and one more friendship to remember two weeks from now would be icing on the cake. She borrowed Francis's pen, a fancy one Peggy had bought for him on impulse, to take some notes.

Francis was terrified handing her the pen. It was as if some pact had been made with a stranger in an alien land where there were no boundaries, no schedule to structure time. For release, he focused on the beauty of the lovely Elena Sensi, remembering exotic stories of love affairs in foreign lands: Grace Kelly lunching with Cary Grant in an open sports car, the blue Mediterranean spread below them. *What will you have, a leg or a breast?* Behind Elena, framed on the wall, were Jesus dying on the cross, Sebastian full of arrows, and the Baptist's severed head.

Just before the lunch break he pretended to need the men's room and escaped. He exited the museum through a side door and hurried through the narrow winding streets and tourist crowds to what he thought was a distant café, where he bought the *International Herald Tribune* to hide behind and sat down at an outdoor table in the fierce Italian sun.

But when he looked around to make sure he was safe, he saw

the museum only a hundred yards away across the square, and was just distraught enough to believe for an instant that it had put on wheels and followed him, though the truth of the matter was that the serpentine alley he had trotted almost a half mile on so frantically had led him unerringly from the museum's side door back around to near its front door—out of which at that precise moment he saw Clara Beecher emerging.

He watched her start to cross the square in a pale green dress. A waiter appeared and hovered impatiently while Francis watched and prayed she wouldn't see him. "Pasta?" the waiter said. "Zuppa?"

"Oh God, please, not here," Francis murmured, and the waiter, misinterpreting, stomped away, and as if she'd heard Francis's prayer, Clara headed for another café fifty meters away.

Hungry now and wondering where the hell the waiter had gone, Francis breathed in a relieved breath, but before he let it out he saw how the sun lit the sides of the ancient buildings. He heard the lively voices of the diners around him—Italian, Spanish, English, German—and saw how the many-colored clothes of the tourists moved and swirled in the square. It was all there for the taking, but not for him, and caught off guard by this awareness, he was overwhelmed by sadness. So, not to redeem his discourtesy, nor to be kind, but for strictly selfish reasons, he left his café and headed for the pale green dress.

"Oh," she said. "I thought you wanted to be alone."

"You mean you saw me?"

She smiled to show she understood—or didn't care, he wasn't sure which. Just then the waiter arrived and she switched her focus to the menu. She asked the waiter a lot of questions, sought translations. It interested him that she cared so much about a lunch. He ordered a beer and sandwich from the top of the menu that he could have bought in New York.

They were silent for a moment after the waiter left. Then she said, "I'm glad you followed me. Now when all those married people see us together every day, we won't be a fifth wheel anymore; maybe they'll actually talk to us."

"Every day?" Involuntarily, he leaned back, away from her. He hadn't heard her playful tone.

She stared at him, moving her hand from the table and putting it to her mouth.

"Oh my God!" he said. "I didn't mean—"

"You thought I meant like married people? The same room?"

"No!" he said, too loud. "I didn't mean that at all." The diners at the tables near them went silent. They turned to look.

"Well, what did you mean, then? You moved back as if I had a disease!" She was standing already, rummaging through her purse.

"Oh, don't go away," he begged. "Stay. Eat your lunch. You already ordered it."

She pulled out a fistful of euros and flung them on the table. Right away, the breeze began to scatter them. Then she marched away.

He had no time to watch her go. The euros were migrating too fast. He scooted in and out among the tables retrieving them, and, to cover his embarrassment, began to make a big show of stuffing them in his pockets while his audience watched and began to giggle. Then with a flourish he put twenty of his own and twenty of Clara's on the table and was taken completely by surprise by his rush of anger at Peggy for being so happy to study anthropology in New York City and Montana and for persuading him to come to Italy. Just as the waiter arrived with his and Clara's lunches, he turned to the diners and made a stylish bow, a comedian making his exit. It was exactly the kind of effective goofiness the girls had loved in his teaching. Everyone clapped as he left.

CLARA BEECHER CUT through the crowd like the bow of a ship through water to put as much distance as she could, as fast as she could, between herself and that tired old man she'd been trying to cheer up. She grew even angrier as she felt again how quickly he'd leaned away from her. "Look in the mirror!" she said out loud as if he were there to hear her, "Who do you think you are, Clark Gable?" The people in her way parted even more quickly.

Then, just as she began to ask herself if maybe she *had* been making a pass at Francis, she passed a sidewalk café and remembered she was hungry. Her appetite had been stirred when she'd ordered lunch from that gorgeous waiter who'd been so friendly. Well, good, there was plenty of time before the afternoon session. She'd have a nice big lunch and a glass of wine, sit in the sun, and enjoy herself. So she sat down at a little table, near a young couple. She smiled at them. The girl smiled back, the boy hardly looked at her. He was wearing one of those awful sleeveless shirts. What in the world did the girl see in him? She was accosted out of the blue by the old question: whether her husband's death by cancer had been his way of escaping her. She'd sought help and made this craziness go away years ago, but here it was again—because an old man she hardly knew had been repulsed by just the idea she and he might grow close.

"Well, I'll have none of *that*!" she said aloud, tossing her head. She smiled at the young couple, glad they were speaking Italian. She didn't want tourists, she wanted Italy, as much of it as she could get. She broadened her smile at the boy and, sure he couldn't understand English, said, "Buy yourself a shirt, young man; those black hairs under your arms could ruin my appetite." The boy smiled back. Clara was happy again.

As the waiter approached, she remembered she'd left her credit card in the safe at the hotel, but never mind, she had lots of cash. And then she remembered what she'd done with her cash. "Oh my goodness!" she exclaimed and the sleeveless boy looked worriedly at her, ready to help. But then she remembered she did have her ATM card. The waiter handed her the menu. "ATM?" she asked. He pointed across the street. Relieved, because by now she was famished, she ordered the same dish she'd ordered in the other café and two glasses of wine. So she'd lost some money, who cares? Her husband had left her tons of it. She headed across the street.

She didn't see the man who followed her. Later, she realized he must have trailed her a long way, figuring her for an easy mark, a crazy old lady who pushed people out of the way, making speeches about cables. She took the crisp new bills out of the machine, remembering how she loved it that her granddaughter thought this was all you had to do to have enough money. She put them in her purse and turned to return to her lunch. Then she felt the tug. Someone was pulling her purse away.

She put her other hand on it and held and pulled too. There was a red spot on his tie where he'd spilled something. Tomato sauce, she thought and then saw his face, the surprised look at how strong she was, and then she kicked him right there where her husband had told her to if she ever were mugged, and he was bending over and she was swinging her big purse over her head and down on his head over and over again. He had both hands over his head now and she kicked him again but she missed that place because he was kneeling now and she got him in the ribs instead. "Ugh," he said. "Ugh."

"I can't even get a lunch!" she yelled, and the man squirmed away, like a little cockroach, she thought, so she missed him with her purse and hit herself on the leg. The man tried to run, but a crowd had gathered. She thought she heard them cheering her. They delayed his fleeing. And then the police arrived.

And arrested both of them.

ON HIS RELUCTANT way back to the museum, Francis was overwhelmed by embarrassment. He started to walk faster so he could catch up to Clara and apologize. Then he heard the commotion and saw the police cars arriving, and quickened his step still more to see what was happening and arrived as the police were ushering the purse snatcher into one of the cars. It was while he was making the observation to himself that Italian cops put bad people in the backs of police cars the same way as they do on American TV—as if their biggest worry in life was that the crook would bump his head—that he saw Clara's green dress. A second policeman was holding her elbow and leading her toward the other police car. Francis pushed through the crowd to her side. "Clara! What's happening?" She didn't answer, wouldn't even look at him. "Are you all right? Are you all right?" and she still pretended he wasn't there. The policeman, who seemed almost as young as Francis's seniors, kept one hand on Clara's elbow and with the other pushed firmly on Francis's shoulder for him to get out of the way. "They're *arresting* you?" Francis said. She looked at him then for an instant. He saw how humiliated she was and jumped ahead to the police car and blocked the way. The policeman frowned, made a gesture for Francis to get out of the way. "Please!" Francis said. "Please. Per favore, I know this woman."

The young policeman hesitated. It must have been hard to believe this lady was the attacker in spite of the report on his radio. "Lui la conosce," someone said in the crowd, translating. "He knows her."

The policeman turned to Clara. "Vero?" he asked her.

"Falso," Clara replied. "I've never seen this man in my life."

The policeman looked disappointed; he shrugged, ushered Clara gently into the backseat of his police car, and carried her off.

Francis looked around frantically for a taxi. There were none in sight. Then he realized he didn't know how to say *follow that car* in Italian anyway, and started running in the direction the police cars had gone. After several blocks, he came to a hill and labored up it through the narrow street. It seemed that everyone else in Perugia was coming down the street and he had to snake his way through them while a movie played in his head in which a burly police woman ordered Clara to strip, handed her an orange jumpsuit, and shoved her into a cell full of women in spiked heels and short dresses. He finally reached the top where there was a little piazza with a fountain in the middle. "Policía!" he shouted, so distraught he didn't realize he was speaking Spanish now. "Dondé está la policía?"

Several people pointed across the piazza to a building with a cluster of police cars in front. Francis dashed toward it, a spray of pigeons lifting before him, and burst into the police station. There in the center of a dingy anteroom were Clara and her young captor standing side by side in front of an ugly gray metal desk, behind which sat a large policeman with braids on his shoulders. He had dark stubble on his face and seemed to be exasperated. Clara turned to the door as Francis burst in. "Oh, it's you again!" she said, but he could see that she was relieved.

"Clara, I came to help."

"Well, bully for you! Can you speak Italian?"

"No."

"Oh damn! No one here speaks English." Clara looked back and forth between her young captor and the man with the braids behind the desk. They both smiled sheepishly.

"I'll be right back," Francis said, and moved to the door.

"Where are you going? Don't leave me."

"To find someone who speaks English and Italian," he called over his shoulder and ran through the door into the street. Almost immediately, he saw a man coming out of a store on the other side of the street. There was a display of silk ties and elegant shirts in the window. Francis ran across the street. "Do you speak English?" he asked. The man was about Francis's age, tall and portly; he wore an expensive linen jacket, a yellow tie, and crisp gray trousers.

"Yes. I'm from New York."

"And Italian too?"

"That too. I have an import business. What may I do for you?"

Francis explained Clara's predicament.

"Oh, your poor wife! Of course I will help. My name is Alfred."

"My name is Francis, and thank you, but she's not my wife. She's just an acquaintance," Francis said.

Inside, the police station, Alfred translated while Francis told Clara's story: that she was from Cleveland and had three children and lots of grandchildren and that she was in an Elderhostel course. He explained what *Elderhostel* meant and was about to announce that Clara was his sister when the large policeman waved his hand and interrupted. "Basta!" he said, the Italian word for *enough*. He stood, came from behind his desk, and pumped Alfred's hand. Then he turned to Francis. "Grazie," he said solemnly, and then faced Clara and bowed to her. "Mi dispiace," he said.

The young policeman, smiling happily, moved to the door and opened it for the three Americans. On her way through it, Clara stopped and gave him a motherly kiss on his cheek, and then—free at last!—she was standing outside in the sunshine.

Alfred gazed at Clara. "Have you two had lunch?"

"Have we had lunch!" Clara rolled her eyes at Francis. "But we're both still famished, aren't we, Francis?"

"I am too, rather," said Alfred, who'd completed a sumptuous and lonely lunch just before he'd gone into the store to buy a tie. He kept his gaze on Clara. "In fact, I'm starved."

"Wonderful!" Clara said. She loved being looked at like that! She put one hand through Francis's arm, the other through Alfred's, and squeezed them both to her side. "I know just the place."

With Clara in the middle, they headed down the hill toward the restaurant where the purse snatcher had prevented Clara's lunch. Clara's waiter saw them coming. He rushed out onto the sidewalk to greet them. "Bravo! Bravo!" he cried, taking Clara by her hand and leading her to a table. He pulled a chair out for her and seated her, then zipped around the table to pull two other chairs out for Francis and Alfred, while the other waiters and the owner came to the table too and surrounded it. They all talked at once and smiled and laughed and waved their hands. Then Clara's waiter turned to the other diners. "Silenzio! Silenzio!" he shouted and told the story of how he watched in awe, while across the street this nice old lady here beat the shit out of the scum, the pus of the earth, the purse snatcher. He pointed to Clara's huge purse, which lay on the table, and swung his hands through the air, demonstrating how she'd done it, and when he'd finished some of the diners stood up and clapped.

When the waiter and his colleagues had left them, Francis spoke across the huge purse to Clara. "You're amazing! I would have given him everything."

She shook her head, a little gesture: that's not what she wanted to talk about. "You followed me. That's what I'll remember."

Francis felt a rush of shyness. "What was it like?" he asked to change the subject.

"Wonderful!"

Francis frowned. "Really?"

"Well, what would you expect?"

Alfred reached and touched Clara's hand. "I think Francis means, what was it like when you were hitting the man?"

"Oh, I thought you meant when you followed me," Clara's voice trailed off.

"Well, anyway, thank you for feeling wonderful," Francis said.

"So, what about when you were hitting the man?" Alfred persisted.

Clara pondered. "You know, I've never hit anyone in my whole life. All of a sudden I was bashing him over the head. If I'd had a weapon instead of my purse, I'd be in jail."

"Well, you're not in jail," Francis said. "And if you were, Alfred and I would get you out."

"Absolutely," Alfred agreed. "It's clear we excel at such heroics." He was still touching her hand.

After they finished, they tried to pay and were refused. The waiters and the owner surrounded them once more to say goodbye. It was then that Alfred wondered aloud if the Elderhostel leader would let him join the tour. "I've always wanted to learn about Renaissance art," he said, though his late wife, an art historian, had told him more than he'd ever wanted to know about every kind of art.

"Wonderful!" Clara said. "Now I don't have to suggest it."

Alfred moved out of his hotel and into the Elderhostel's that afternoon. He took a room just down the hall from Clara.

AT ABOUT THE same time that Francis and his new friends were eating their celebratory lunch in Perugia, Rachel happened to glance out the French doors of her office while dictating to Margaret and saw Sonja McGarvey rushing toward her across the lawn. "Oh boy, she's loaded for bear," Margaret murmured, her gaze following Rachel's. "You better get ready."

Seconds later, Sonja barged through the doors, waving a sheet of paper. Harriet Richardson had written a letter to the parents and alumnae. "That bitch! I'm going to destroy her."

Margaret jumped to her feet. "Sonja McGarvey!"

"You're right, Margaret: that's a word we never use here. I'm sorry," Sonja continued, somehow looking sheepish and angry at the same time, and Margaret nodded her head, picked up her notebook, and started to leave the office. Sonja said, "But I'm still going to destroy her," addressing Margaret's back as she exited through the door, and then Sonja turned to Rachel, holding up the letter. "We should have known Harriet Richardson would rise from the grave. I'd love to know who she sent the letter to and who she didn't. Somebody sent me this anonymously so I would know what's going on. Listen to this!"

She read from the letter, sarcastically imitating the tremulo in an ancient woman's voice:

I am writing you to report that I have reliable information that our recently appointed headmistress knew all along that the young woman whose name was flaunted in all the newspapers was an alcoholic. Moreover, there is reason to suspect that perhaps she was persuaded not to expel the young woman by the belief a very large gift would be forthcoming from a not-disinterested person as a reward for retaining her. If you would like to discuss this further, please call me.

"Let me see it," Rachel said, grabbing the letter out of Sonja's hand, as if her reading it would make it say something else. She remembered this Richardson woman was the one Milton was wary of—the one who didn't like her "tan"—and the muscles along the back of her shoulders tightened as she read the same words Sonja had.

Sonja watched Rachel read, studying her face. Then, when Rachel had finished, Sonja said, "Don't worry, we're going to shut her up." She put her hands on the edge of Rachel's desk and leaned over Rachel as Mitch Michaels had months before. The difference was that Michaels's ferocity had made him ugly while Sonja's rendered her more beautiful than ever. "I'll write a letter from the board calling a meeting of all the alumnae and parents to address the lies Harriet Richardson has published," Sonja said. "Every single board member will show up. I'll stand up and ask her, did she really think a girl couldn't hide a bottle of vodka if she wanted to? I'll say that *she* certainly could since she's so good at writing letters about people behind their backs."

"Sonja, take it easy. Calm down," Rachel said. She was still feeling vulnerable, unprotected, and, now in Sonja's fierce presence, unsure of herself without Milton Perkins's guidance, and she remembered his warning that she would have to manage Sonja. She hungered for retribution as ardently as Sonja, but she said, proud of herself already for her calm, "This isn't really between Ms. Richardson and me. It isn't personal."

"Not personal? Of course it's personal. Everything is always personal. I guarantee you'll take it personally if she manages to get you fired and Francis Plummer put in your place. I'm going to say, *Did Mitch Michaels con you into this, or did you just make it up?*"

"Sonja, sit down, okay? Let's talk about this."

Sonja looked surprised. Like a preacher whose sermon has been interrupted by a disbeliever in the back pew. But then she smiled and sat down. "You're right. No more ranting. Just strategizing."

"She won't just talk to people on the phone, right?" Rachel said. "So let her call a meeting, not us."

Sonja looked intrigued. "Of the people who've been listening to Mitch Michaels?"

"Yes. They'll finally have a place to go."

"I get it," Sonja said, nodding her head. "You'll show up at it. So will the whole board of trustees. That'll fix her wagon."

Rachel shook her head again. "Not if the trustees come, it won't."

Sonja frowned. "Because it would make you look as if you needed us?"

"That's right. It would play right into her hands."

"You know, I think you're right."

"I'd look weak," Rachel said.

Sonja smiled, shaking her head—as if the very idea of Rachel looking weak was beyond imagination, and, even at that moment, Rachel couldn't help remembering how weak she'd been in handling Francis Plummer. She felt like an imposter in Sonja's presence. "So who *will* you take?" Sonja asked. "Even if it's just for moral support."

"Gregory van Buren. And it will be for more than moral support."

"Well, I'll be damned! Gregory van Buren. We're really are moving on, aren't we? Good for you. No wonder that old lady's pissed."

"I think I'll take the president of the Alumnae Association too. She has a lot of clout around here now, don't you think?"

Sonja shook her head and frowned. "No way. We don't know whether she'd be on your side or Harriet Richardson's."

"She's on my side, believe me," Rachel said. "I just know it. She knows I wouldn't look the other way when I knew a kid was getting herself in trouble with alcohol, and she knows for sure I wouldn't ever take a bribe."

Sonja looked doubtful. "You just know?"

"Trust me. I do. We had a good talk. Besides, her gift honors teaching. She knows Francis's talent is for teaching, not running things. I wish I'd figured that out sooner."

"Suppose you're wrong?"

Rachel shrugged and raised her hands, palms up. "I trust my instinct, so I'll take the chance."

"Don't," Sonja said.

Rachel raised her eyebrows at Sonja and shook her head and said, very calmly, "Sorry, Sonja, but I'm going to."

"Suppose I tell you not to?"

Rachel grinned.

"Oh, never mind," Sonja said. "I remember what you said last time a board member asked that question."

"Right," Rachel said. "And I'm going to ask Amelia to call up Ms. Richardson to find out when and where the meeting will be. It will be very hard to refuse the president of the Alumnae Association, don't you think?"

A hint of a smile appeared in Sonja's worried expression. "I have to admit, I like it when you get feisty like this."

"I do too," Rachel said. She was on the verge of admitting to Sonja that she wished she'd been feisty like this with Francis Plummer. But she drew back. It didn't feel like the kind of thing you should confess to a person who needed to be managed.

"Well, all right then." Sonja stood up, ready to go. "I've said my piece. It's your call." She left the rest unsaid: *it's your headship too.* But Rachel heard it loud and clear. "Good luck. You'll be on your own."

Then, the decision made, and businesslike as usual, Sonja said goodbye and left, and Rachel picked up her phone and called Amelia Dickenson.

Amelia sounded wary. "I was about to call you," she said.

"Really?" Rachel heard Sonja's warning again.

"Yes, there's a letter going around."

"I know. I've read it."

"Oh? She sent it to *you* too?"

"Of course not. Sonja showed it to me."

"How'd *she* get it? Surely she wasn't supposed to."

"Someone forwarded her a copy."

"Anonymously?"

"Yes."

"Why wouldn't she say who she was? Why be so cagey?"

"How do you know it was a she?" Rachel blurted and immediately regretted her words. If only she had waited. Then if Amelia did call her to warn her about the letter, she would absolutely know she could trust her and that Sonja was wrong.

"I'm just assuming," Amelia said, clearly offended. "This *is* a girls' school, last I heard."

"I'm sorry, I didn't mean—"

"That it was me, playing it safe—not showing my hand until I see who wins? That would be like me asking you if Harriet Richardson is telling the truth."

"I apologize," Rachel said. "I'm really very sorry."

"*Did* you take a bribe from Michaels?"

"I'm not going to answer that, Amelia. Let's start all over again."

Amelia sighed. "Okay, let's. What a mess! You and I have to feel each other out. Harriet Richardson thinks the president of the Alumni Association will believe that the head of school would take a bribe. How dysfunctional can things get?"

"She's going to call a meeting to convince a lot of people that I already have taken a bribe," Rachel said.

"I suppose so."

"Well, I intend to go to it."

"You do?"

"Wouldn't you?"

"Me?" Amelia processed that for a split second. "Yes, I guess I would, if I were you. Yes, come to think of it, I would."

"I want you to come with me."

Silence for a few seconds, then, "All right, I will."

"As president of the Alumnae Association, not as a board member. A lot of the people there will be alumnae. Maybe you could even take over."

"Maybe I could," Amelia said, sounding very pleased with herself. "That way I could facilitate things, couldn't I? Make them come out the way we want. Yes, I can do that."

"We need to find out when and where the meeting's going to

be."

"I'll ask her."

"Thanks, Amelia. I really do appreciate this."

"We'll figure out how to silence Harriet, and then everybody will appreciate it."

"And then maybe we can figure out how to silence Mitch Michaels." Rachel's trust in Amelia had fully returned.

"We won't have to. He'll do that for us. He'll self-destruct."

"You think so?"

"Of course. His kind always does. Don't worry, Rachel. You'll come out of this just fine. I've got to go now. Bye."

TWENTY-NINE

Soon after Sonja left, Milton Perkins's daughter Mary called: "He's having a good day. Can you come for lunch?" Rachel told her of course she could.

Mary met Rachel at the door of her eighteenth-century house in Essex, looking like a younger female version of her father, in a dress the color of her sun-drenched lawn, stockings, and a pearl necklace. She'd graduated from Miss Oliver's early in the tenure of Marjorie Boyd, Fred Kindler's predecessor, and her daughters had graduated almost a decade before it ended. Mary had kept her maiden name when she got married—not at all unusual for alumnae of Miss Oliver's School for Girls.

She took Rachel's hand and pulled her into her house and shut the door as if there were neighbors near enough to overhear. "It's Alzheimer's," she whispered in the big front hall by the mirror. "I'm sure you've already guessed."

Rachel nodded. "How bad?" She whispered too, assuming Milton was near them in the living room. It opened from the hall.

Mary shook her head. "It's early. No one will tell us how fast—" She cut herself off, tugging on Rachel's hand again, and Rachel followed her through the house, glancing into the living room as they passed it. Milton wasn't there. "He's been looking forward to this since the minute he woke up this morning," Mary said, no longer whispering. They passed through the kitchen and out through the sliding doors at the back of the house into the sunshine again where an old man, sitting with his back to them at a table already set for lunch, gazed down over a sloping lawn to the river. "Dad, Rachel's here," Mary said.

Milton turned slowly. Rachel guessed he was reluctant to stop his dreaming, or maybe he was afraid he wouldn't know who *Rachel* was. Indeed, there was a moment when he peered at her before his face lighted up, and then he stood up, looking like the commodore of a yacht club in his blue blazer, yellow polo shirt, and khaki trousers with sharp creases. "You're right on time!"

"For you I always will be on time," she said, running across the lawn to him. She gave him a quick peck on his cheek, as she did with her father, returning the one he'd given her when he told her he was resigning. Why not? He wasn't her boss anymore and she loved him. He was clearly taken aback though, surprised, not sure he approved, and so she knew he wasn't remembering he wasn't the chair anymore, but as graceful as ever, he erased the moment by pulling out a chair for her at the table where there were just two places set. Mary crossed the patio and stood next to her father, her hand on his shoulder, and told Rachel her dad will have his martini now and asked her what she could bring for her. Rachel told her water would be fine.

"That's right, water," Milton Perkins explained. "It's not Friday, like last time. She'll have to get back to school. We only have an hour. And lots to cover." Mary and Rachel exchanged glances. "Let's see your list," Milton said opening his hand for Rachel to put it in, as Mary left to fetch the martini and the water.

"Oh my goodness, I left it in the office," Rachel said.

"Who cares? I never knew why you brought a list, anyway. If it's not important enough to stick in your mind without a list, why would you bother me with it?" he said, and she remembered that one of the symptoms of Alzheimer's was crankiness.

By the time, Mary returned with the martini and the water, Rachel had told him about Amelia Dickenson's gift and he had made astute suggestions about which of the school's fund managers it should be invested with. Then she told him about Francis and he wondered aloud why Francis would want to study Renaissance art. "He's a literary man, so why didn't he go to Oxford, maybe, and study James Joyce or something?" It went on like that for a few minutes as she caught him up with all the news—except what worried her most: Ms. Richardson's letter, and the long way still to go to meet the schedule for paying down the accumulated deficit. Why bother him with stuff like that? In the meantime, Mary, wearing an apron that said, *Kiss me if you want seconds*, brought an omelet and then a salad.

"Well, that's all I have," Rachel said at last. He nodded his head as if to say, *That's enough for now, I'm tired.* He didn't speak. He seemed to be trying to remember something. Rachel filled the silence by telling him how lucky they both were to live beside a river, and then she went on to report that she'd read in the *Hartford Courant* about a whale that had been spotted near the mouth of it.

He perked up. "It must be lost," he said. "Whales don't ever come into Long Island Sound."

Mary brought dessert: bowls of cut-up fruit smothered in yogurt, and her homemade cookies. She put the bowls and the cookies down in front of them and then went behind her father and mouthed, *Keep talking.*

So Rachel described her family's place on Martha's Vineyard, going on and on in detail. He interrupted once to say he'd love to visit her there sometime and she told him how much her father would love to have his company, and how alike they were—easy to say because it was true. She started to tell him about her brother, but it became clear by the appalled expression on his face that he'd just remembered he wasn't the chair of the board anymore. Rachel kept on talking, hoping that he'd already forgot that he'd been acting as if he still was, but she could see by the stricken look he was trying to hide that he knew what they had been both doing for the last hour and a half, so she finished her dessert as quickly as she could, then looked at her watch and remembered aloud she had an appointment.

"Well, then you better go," he said gently and stood up.

She stood too and they shook hands and said goodbye. Then she started across the patio. Mary was watching them through the kitchen window. She and Rachel exchanged their stricken looks.

"Rachel." It was Milton's voice behind her. She turned. "I apologize," he said.

"Oh, please don't," she said. "I owe you the world!"

He smiled, his old self for at least that moment. So he knew how much she loved him. Rachel went inside. Mary and she embraced in the kitchen. Then Rachel walked through the house and out the front door.

WHILE RACHEL WAS driving back to school, the phone rang in Harriet Richardson's kitchen just as she was about to go upstairs and take her after-luncheon nap. She was so sleepy she would not have answered it if she were not sure it was another shocked parent or alumna calling about her letter. She crossed the kitchen toward the phone's insistent ringing, admitting to herself that it was her breakfast sherry that made her so sleepy in the mornings. Back to orange juice, she resolved right then and there. The delicate business she had on her plate demanded alertness. She must keep her wits about her every minute until the business was done.

"Ms. Richardson?"

"Yes, this is Ms. Richardson."

"This is Amelia Dickenson."

A wary silence.

"I called to see if you received—"

"I did, Ms. Dickenson. The galley came yesterday. I meant to call to thank you, but I've been very busy."

"Yes, and I appreciate what you have been busy about. I really do. Very much. Very, very, very much, as a matter of fact. Did you get a chance to glance at the dedication?"

"I confess I haven't, but I will very soon, Amelia. I may call you Amelia, mayn't I?"

"Of course you may, Harriet. Thank you. I think you will be touched by the dedication. May I read it to you?" Without waiting for an answer, Amelia read: "To Francis Plummer, teacher extraordinaire, magician in the classroom, who gave me my career."

Harriet didn't speak. She was overcome by the rightness of what she'd just heard—and by her relief that the risk she had taken by including Amelia among those to whom she'd sent her letter was justified. She'd gone back and forth with herself about that, and finally just sent it. Now she knew: anyone who felt so strongly for Francis Plummer would agree that he should be the head, not that Bickham woman. "Superb, Amelia. Superb!" she said, finding her voice at last. "I am touched. Every woman who has been taught by that man will agree. You speak for all of them. He's the heart of that school."

"Thank you, Harriet. I treasure your opinion. I'm wondering if when the book comes out, you might write a review in the alumnae magazine."

"I would be delighted," Harriet said, her spirits soaring. "In fact, Smith's and Wellesley's alumnae magazines might welcome a review from me. As you know, I served both of those institutions in my time."

"Oh, I didn't think of that. I'd be grateful for it. Thank you. We speak from the same position," Amelia said. She paused to let that point reverberate, and for transition's sake, then went on. "So now that I know you received the galley, I would like to chat for a moment about that other matter you've been so busy about."

"I thought you might," Harriet said.

"What do you think we should do about it?"

"I have decided to call a meeting. I do hope you will attend."

"Of course I will."

"Excellent. To have your participation as president of the Alumnae—I can't begin to—"

"Yes, I do think it will lend credence. Can I help you arrange the meeting?"

"It is already arranged, thank you. It will be on May twenty-seventh at the Women's Scholars Club in the city, seven o'clock."

"The Women's Scholars Club! That's impressive."

"Yes, I've been a member for years."

"That does the club much credit, Harriet. Thank you for caring so much for the school. We'll get to the bottom of this. You can count on me." Then she thanked Harriet again, said goodbye, and hung up.

Seconds later, she was on the phone to Rachel. "You were right. There will be a meeting. It will be at seven on May twenty-seven at the Women's Scholars Club."

"The Women's Scholars Club. That's hard to get into, isn't? Are you a member?"

"Not on your life! I'd die of boredom. What would I talk about, footnotes?"

"Somehow, I think if you were a member it would give us leverage over the situation. They'd be so glad to get a famous author they'd let you in in a heartbeat."

"Well, maybe," Amelia said, sounding more interested than her words implied. "I'll think about it."

Immediately after she had thanked Amelia and said goodbye, Rachel walked into Gregory van Buren's new office and handed him Harriet Richardson's letter. "I'm going to need your help with this." She sat down in a chair near his desk and watched his face as he read it.

He kept his eyes down on the letter for a long moment, obviously reading it more than once. Then he looked up at Rachel. "How disappointing!" he murmured. "How sad! There's so much healing we have to do."

She stared at him. She saw the sadness in his eyes. She had expected anger, surprise, outrage at treachery, the desire to protect her. "That's not the reaction I expected from you," she said. "But it's the right one. Suddenly I feel—actually, I don't know how I feel. Like a child? All I wanted was to win."

"Of course."

"And keep my job!"

"Yes, but fighting back is a right reaction too. Sometimes we have to do that first," he said.

She didn't answer. She didn't want to think about how to counter Harriet Richardson's threat right now. That in itself was a surprise. She wanted to think about healing, about the sadness that had arrived on Gregory's face when she had expected anger and outrage and protectiveness. She had understood that healing the hurt that had been laid on the school by its fraught dissentions was a part of her job, inextricably allied to all the other parts. But it had been a distant understanding. Now it was upon her, a whole new dimension.

"I don't think we can just ignore this and hope that nothing comes of it," Gregory said. "Besides, that strategy is too passive." He smiled and added, "That's not you. So let's make a plan."

"I already have," Rachel said. She told him about the meeting Harriet Richardson had called and that she, Amelia Dickenson, and he were going to surprise Harriet by attending it.

"To contradict her assertion and explain to the secret listeners our decision to keep Claire?" he said. "Our word against hers?"

"Yes. I'm sure we can. We'll be telling the truth, and she will be lying. It will be obvious."

"But how do we know Amelia is on your side? What if she is just pretending? Think of the harm she could do once the meeting starts."

"Trust me," Rachel said. "She knows better than to want Francis doing stuff like this instead of teaching. And if I'm wrong, you'll think of something."

"Like what?"

"A curare dart." Rachel mimed bringing a tube to her mouth and blowing. "*Pew.*"

Gregory smiled in spite of his worry. "She's a big target," he admitted. "I couldn't miss." He hesitated and his smile disappeared. "But I do hope that you are right and I don't have to."

"You won't have to. You can count on that," Rachel said, standing up and heading for the door to leave.

But Gregory still looked worried.

THIRTY

That evening in Perugia, Clara, Alfred, and Francis had dinner together and lingered late into the night reliving their escapade over lots of wine and laughter. At last Clara announced she was going to bed. "I want to be awake and alert for tomorrow's pictures." Alfred managed a yawn to show he agreed and stood up to go. So Francis did too.

The message light on the phone in Francis's room was flashing when he arrived. He was instantly nervous: something had happened to Peggy. But when he picked up the phone, it was Rachel's recorded voice: "Francis, I have wonderful news for you. Call me." He couldn't imagine any wonderful news except that she'd changed her mind about his sabbatical and wanted him to return in September, but he knew she wasn't *that* indecisive, and he realized he dreaded going back only a little bit less than he dreaded staying away. It was a surprise, and it frightened him. He dialed the direct line to her office because it was only six o'clock where she was and he knew she'd still be there.

"You have news for me?" he said.

"Yes. Just listen to this," Rachel said. She read the announcement that would be made at the graduation ceremony of Amelia's gift in his honor.

He didn't get it at first. He was in Perugia in a hotel room. He'd just helped someone get out of jail. "Amelia Dickenson?" he said. "An endowment? Would you read that again?"

Rachel read the announcement again. This time he thought he heard her pumping enthusiasm into the words. When she finished, he didn't know what to say. *Thank you very much? Oh my god? Really? Me?* He realized he'd been sublimating the expectation of some such honor for years. So why did it feel like it was coming from Mars?

"This has been a long time coming, and you deserve it," Rachel said, and he still didn't answer, and she told him the gift would be announced at the graduation ceremony and asked him to keep it a secret until then—"except from Peggy whom we've already told, of course."

"All right," he said. "That's fine with me."

"That's all you're going to say?" Rachel said.

"I don't know how I feel about it yet," he admitted. "I'm going to have to think about it."

"Well then, don't think about this year. Think about all those other ones. Because when the announcement's made, everybody is going to stand up and cheer. They'll feel how right it is."

"All right, that's how I'll think about it," he said.

"Promise me you will?"

"I promise."

"Good. I'll let you go now, so you can get on the phone with Peggy before she goes to bed. She'll help you think about it right. You can celebrate with her."

"Goodnight then, Rachel."

"Goodnight. And Francis?"

"What?"

"You deserve it. You just have to believe that. Because it's true." Then she hung up and he was left holding the receiver, wondering if Amelia would have named her gift for him if she knew what Rachel knew. There was no way he'd talk to Peggy tonight, feeling the way he did. He'd call her in the morning. Maybe in the sunshine, after a good night's sleep, he'd feel proud and jubilant—vindicated for all those years, as Rachel said—before he'd shamed himself. He put the receiver down.

Then, sitting very still on the edge of the bed, he realized how free of himself he had been that day in his adventures with Clara and Alfred, how liberated into a world where colors had grown vivid again.

So this was a lesson, he told himself, bending over now to untie his shoes: Engage with others. Marry life! Maybe it wasn't only terror of being fired that had motivated him to choose the sabbatical over staying home; maybe it was his instinct to reach for the light. Well, he'd find out. Starting tomorrow morning, he would get to know the others the way he had Clara and Alfred, and he would open himself to what Elena Sensi saw in the art she loved. He'd take her passion and her knowledge into himself and use it in his teaching when he returned after the sabbatical to Miss Oliver's School for Girls. That was the path back to being the real Francis Plummer, the one who'd earned the honor of an endowment's being named for him.

Thus decided, he got undressed and climbed into bed and turned out the light, expecting that he would sleep well for the first time in months. Instead, he dreamt again that he was floating all alone in an ocean in the middle of the blackest night. This time, he actually started to go under and he woke up terrorized, holding his breath. It seemed forever before his breathing steadied. When it did, he turned on the light, got out of bed, went to the bathroom to drink a glass of water. Then he returned to bed and turned out the light again, and finally, just before dawn, he fell asleep.

Nevertheless, he was still determined to engage with the world that morning as he dressed for breakfast. So what if he felt a little dizzy and weak in the legs? He picked up the phone to dial Peggy. Then he remembered it was two in the morning in New York City. He'd call her tonight.

He joined Clara and Alfred at their table. Almost immediately another couple, members of the tour whom he had barely noticed before, arrived and sat down too, on Alfred's left. She was pretty, soft blue eyes, her hair dyed black; he was small, with a severe expression, his brown hair parted exactly in the center of his head. Francis's immediate reaction was to wonder what she saw in him. Money, he joked to himself: her first husband ran away with all of it, and she was desperate. "We're Martha and Stuart Bush," the husband announced, reaching to shake Alfred's hand. "No relation to the president," he added, though it was obvious by his expression he was proud of sharing the president's name.

"Well, that's a relief!" Francis murmured. Stuart Bush's face went red. Clara kicked his foot under the table. "Because we won't be surrounded by secret police," Francis said, trying to joke his way out. Martha Bush was giggling aloud.

"Oh no," she said. "That's not what you meant at all. You just said what came to your head. I do it all the time."

Francis smiled at her. A compatriot! He felt a surge of joy. If he could only think of something smart to say now—something that would make her husband so mad he'd jump up from the table. Maybe even run out onto the street and get run over by a Vespa. He knew he was having some sort of crack-up, but the release it provided him felt too good to pass up. Clara sent him a warning look, but he paid her no attention. She was much more interesting when she was bashing crooks over the head than when she was trying to keep the peace.

He was still struggling to find the exactly right juvenile thing to say when Stuart Bush's eyes lifted from Francis to a space behind him, and his face lighted up. Francis turned around to see what Stuart was looking at. And there was Elena Sensi approaching.

Radiant in a white summer dress that revealed her slim arms and the heartbreaking shape of her body, she smiled at them as she approached. She was the only young person in the room. Stuart Bush stood and pulled a chair out for her with a gallant flourish, and as Elena leaned forward, seating herself, Francis saw the top of her breasts. He watched her, trying not to seem to stare, wondering if, next to him, Clara could sense how stirred he was. Elena was even fuller in the breasts than Peggy, taller, rounder in the hips. And much more frankly sexual, Francis thought—though maybe only here where, surrounded by the elderly, she felt safe. With that thought came a surge of resentment, surprising in its force, followed quickly by another dose of longing, and then a scene, vague and fleeting, in which he made love to Elena in a room where the curtains by the ancient casement windows floated in and out like flowers opening and closing, and on the heels of this fantasy, which shamed him even as it melted, came a still higher tide of resentment at Peggy for not being there, and for not being as eager a lover in their real life as Elena in his fantasy while he watched her in the here and now.

In the storm of all these feelings, he heard Elena reminding them where they would spend the day and what pictures they would see. "Oh God, not more Jesus pictures!" he blurted. Elena stopped talking. Everyone was looking at him now, Clara with alarm, Alfred with curiosity, Stuart Bush with contempt. Martha Bush was smiling politely.

"Yes, other clients of mine have expressed the same fatigue with so much Christianity," Elena said, coming gracefully to his rescue. She kept her beautiful dark eyes exclusively on him, inviting his reply, and the next thing he knew he had launched himself into a long monologue about how markets control art's subject matter.

"Then it was religion, now it is materialism. So we get hot towel racks in the Museum of Modern Art, installations that a drunk could improve on," he announced and went on and on, only dimly aware that no one responded to his invitation to speculate on how much greater the range would have been for Elena to show them if it hadn't been the church that did all the buying. He continued for another several minutes, so hungry to regain his former self, the brilliant teacher who, at the drop of a hat, could launch a riff to mesmerize a class, that he refused to acknowledge the vacant looks of his listeners, until at last, he knew it was time to stop. "Just think," he said in closing, already afraid of his listeners' reaction if he actually said what he knew he was going to say: "If someone like Peggy Guggenheim had been around to stimulate the market, Elena here would only have to show us one or two instead of a million pictures of Saint Sebastian full of arrows while looking like he was having the best wet dream of his life."

Now there was an embarrassed silence. No one would look at him. He thought he might get up from his chair and slink away.

"But why take it out on the paintings?" Martha Bush asked, looking straight across the table at him to rescue him. Everyone else looked up from their plates to hear his answer. "Why?" Martha asked again. "I really do want to know."

Stuart Bush leaned into the table toward Francis and said, "So professor, you don't have the answer for us?"

Francis didn't answer.

"Come on. We're waiting."

"Stuart, don't," Martha said.

"Why not? We're hanging on his words, aren't we, everybody?" Stuart looked around the table. "I mean, why listen to our art historian here"—he pointed to Elena—"when we have the professor?"

Martha moved her eyes from her husband to Francis. "Don't pay any attention to him," she said.

"What?" Stuart said, turning on his wife. "What did you say?"

"Oh, keep quiet, Stuart," she said. "Please, please, just keep quiet!"

Stuart froze in his seat. A thin smile appeared on his face. *See, she's just joking*, it seemed to say. Martha shook her head. Stuart threw his napkin down on the table, stood up so fast he knocked his chair down with a clatter, and walked away.

Elena began her talk about the pictures they would see that morning, gracefully filling the silence which still contained the clatter of Stuart's retreating footsteps. While she talked, Francis smiled a thank you across to Martha, who looked to him now as if she regretted her put-down of her husband and might follow him to apologize. He shook his head to tell her not to. *Let him go*, he said with his eyes. She returned his glance for just an instant, then looked away, retreating from any further complicity with him, and he was suddenly furious.

The waiter arrived. While he was putting the plates down at each place, Elena stopped talking and in the silence, Francis's anger transmogrified, first to sadness and then to a paralyzing fear. He sat very still, wholly aware there was nothing in the room that could kill him, but it was hard to breathe and sweat oozed out of his armpits and his heart was banging in his chest. He couldn't have been more terrified even if someone were holding a gun to his head.

Elena finished talking and Martha Bush excused herself and left. Then everyone else left too, except Clara and Alfred. Francis was too paralyzed to move. Besides, he couldn't think of where to go. His room? The bus? They offered no retreat to him.

"Are you all right?" Clara asked.

He shook his head and didn't look at her.

"I'll leave you two alone," Alfred said. "I'll save seats for both of you on the bus." He rose from the table and left.

"Francis, look at me," Clara said. "It's a panic attack. I can tell by just looking at you. Your unconscious is trying to tell you something you really need to understand. You'll have more before you're through. You can't die from them. I know. I've had them too."

That's it! he thought. *And I know what it is it's trying to tell me: I'm in the wrong place. I'm supposed to be teaching.* "I'm leaving!" he blurted, the words flying out of him, his panic lifting with them. The decision arrived simultaneously with the words. He moved his chair back from the table so he could begin his journey.

"Well, I'll go with you," Clara said. She thought he meant he was leaving the table and the dining room. She wasn't about to let him be alone in the middle of a panic attack. She stood and reached to help him up.

"Come with me? You're crazy!" He yanked his hand away and stood up by himself. "Why would you want to?"

"That's a good question," Clara said, insulted and hurt. "Why would anyone? All the way across the street to the bus, for goodness sake! It's at least a million miles."

Francis was patting his pockets and holding his breath. "Oh Jesus, where did I leave it?"

"What in the world are you looking for?"

"My passport."

"Well, the hotel has it, dummy."

"Of course." Francis let out his breath with his relief. "I can't remember anything anymore."

"Nobody can after they're a hundred years old," she said. "But what do you want it for, we don't need—Francis! You're not—"

"I told you I was leaving."

"Oh, Francis, that's really dumb!"

Francis didn't answer. He was thinking that he'd go straight to the airport to find the first flight home instead of calling ahead. American Airlines, British Airways, he didn't care, whichever left the earliest.

"Francis, the course has just started. Give it a chance."

"No. I have to get my job back before it's too late." He felt a sweet nostalgia for his time with her and Alfred. "Thank you for everything," he said, reaching his arms to hug her goodbye.

She had no desire to accept his hug. Not while the insult of his yanking his hand away from hers—repulsed by her a second time—still reverberated. She reached her arms to him anyway, too proud to be ungraceful at such a time. They parted then and she hurried to join Alfred on the bus. She couldn't wait to sit beside him.

THAT MORNING, IN Connecticut, Gregory van Buren, all dressed up for spring in his brand-new Haspel lightweight suit, sauntered right past Margaret into Rachel's office. It was all Margaret could do not to jump out of her chair and bar the way. For years, right up until the moment Gregory became the dean of academics, also known as second in command, he'd made appointments with the head at least a week in advance. Now he and Rachel were in and out of each other's offices several times a day. It was confirming for Rachel that she'd made the right decision to see what Gregory's new job did for his pent-up talent. There was a new bounce in his step, a new breezy confidence, even more sartorial splendor, and even though he had retained his full teaching load, he was still co-parenting his dorm with a young female teacher, plus still advising the school newspaper. Rachel hoped that school vacations brought him the pleasures he didn't have time for the rest of the year. She fantasized his rendezvousing with a teacher who did nothing but work and sleep small hours in some other boarding school with the same vacations. An ex-debutante, maybe, in high-end clothes with a taste for theater, poetry, good wine, and romance.

Gregory continued his saunter toward Rachel's sofa, where he seated himself with the air of a clubman about to order a vassal to bring him his cigars, and informed her that he'd made a decision that she "perhaps should know about."

Rachel smiled. "Only perhaps?"

He nodded. "There'll be reverberations."

"Reverberations," she repeated. "Really? We've just sold the library to Grover Norquist? We've admitted boys?"

Gregory's chuckle was on the verge of irritating. "Nothing quite so drastic. Only that we've eliminated Plummer's Senior Honors Shakespeare class."

"Eliminated?"

"For next year. We'll see what happens after that," Gregory said. He wasn't chuckling now.

"Whose idea was this? Yours or Patience's?"

"Mine. Why should she teach someone else's course? I told her she could teach it if she wanted to, but if she didn't, she could design her own. The girls get a ton of Shakespeare in their other courses. Senior Honors should be as exciting for the teacher as for the students. She leaped at the idea when I told her this. She hadn't thought she had the right to ask."

"Well, there'll be reverberations, all right," Rachel said.

"Maybe not. Take a look at this." He handed her a folder. She felt his eyes on her while she read Patience's as yet unfinished first rough draft notes of her design: *The Great Gatsby*, *Death of A Salesman*, *An American Tragedy* and its film version, *A Place in the Sun*, not as separate stories but one story about an old culture, archetypal dreams written on the tabula rasa of an empty continent. The collected letters of women pioneers. *Call it Sleep* for the immigrant experience. Plus assigned interviews with immigrants, preferably elderly in nursing homes, also of illegal immigrants and write-ups of their stories. A biography of Frederick Douglas. The poetry of Countee Cullen, W.E.B. Du Bois. James Baldwin, maybe. Something from Faulkner, probably from *Go Down, Moses*, and W.P. Cash's *The Mind of the South*, along with an inquiry of why he killed himself after he wrote it. A cross-class with the Art Department on jazz and gospel. A note at the end to Gregory: *All I have time for now. More, much more, about how these dots connect when—*

"There was some consternation when I asked the English Department how they felt about canceling Francis's course," Gregory said.

"What did you tell them?"

"That we were going to cancel it anyway. They seemed relieved."

It was then that Rachel admitted to herself how much brighter the atmosphere had become when Francis Plummer's absence had begun—as if a fog had melted to reveal a bright blue sky.

THIRTY-ONE

The limo from the airport brought Francis to the front door of his apartment early in the morning of the next day. Home again among the arching maple trees and white clapboard buildings, he felt the optimism of a returning lover. He'd shower and put on clean clothes and then telephone Rachel to agree on a place they could meet without being seen. At his front door, he fished in his pocket for the key. It was forever before he remembered emptying his pockets of metal at the Rome airport. He'd put it in his suitcase. So he laid his suitcase down on the stoop and unzipped it. If he couldn't find the key, he would have to go to the maintenance office and get a duplicate. The idea of having to explain why he was back on campus without first having settled it with Rachel that he was canceling his sabbatical horrified him. He'd bust a window, if he had to, to get inside his house. He began to pull things out of his suitcase to get at the key, strewing dirty underwear and shirts helter-skelter on the front stoop.

On the other side of the door, Patience Sommers was concentrating too hard correcting essays to hear the strange sounds at her front door. She was so delighted to have been ensconced in her new home days before she expected that she hadn't been able to sleep and had got up before the sun. So what if it would be her home for only a year? She knew enough to celebrate a bird in the hand.

But the noise persisted and she finally got up and sneaked a look through a front window and saw a small man whose face she couldn't see because his back was to her, kneeling over a suitcase whose contents he was spreading over her front stoop. She thought maybe he was looking for a gun and was about to call 911. But then why would a robber bring a suitcase full of clothes? And besides, he didn't look at all dangerous. There was something so vulnerable and lost in the set of his shoulders, so distraught in his pawing through his suitcase, that she had a sudden urge to weep. She thought of people who wander away from asylums for the insane, she thought of Alzheimer's too, and just as he fished the key out of his suitcase, she opened the door to him.

"May I help you?" she said, and then he turned and there was Francis Plummer. "Francis, what are you doing here? You're in Italy." She took a backward step into her house, then held her ground.

All he could think of to say was, "Not anymore. I came home." He took one step forward, matching the one she'd taken backward, and now he could see all the way into the foyer and the living room. All his and Peggy's furniture gone! "I see," he said. "I see." His suitcase was still behind him on the stoop, his clothes still strewn there. A wind could carry them away. "I feel ridiculous," he said.

He turned back to the stoop and put his clothes back in the suitcase. She watched him, wanting to help because he seemed so fragile, but of course she couldn't. He closed the suitcase and carried it with his left hand into the house and put it down lightly in the foyer. He still had the key in his other hand. He put it in his pocket.

"Didn't Rachel tell you?" Patience asked. She was still holding her ground in the foyer.

He nodded. "I just didn't think it would happen so fast." He looked past her. At the end of the hall the black rotary phone was where it had always been in its niche under the stairway. "I need to make a call," he said.

She frowned. "To Rachel?"

"No. A cab. I'll catch the night owl back to Rome. I'd rather Rachel didn't know."

Patience's frown melted. "I'm sorry, I thought for a moment you were going to ask her for—" Her voice trailed off.

He shook his head. "I was, but now I'm not. It was crazy, I know. I'm sorry too. Please don't tell anyone."

"I won't. I promise."

"Thank you." He moved past her, deeper into the house toward the niche in the stairwell.

"Francis?"

He turned around.

"It is only for a year," she said.

He turned back toward the phone without responding.

It was impossible not to feel that Peggy and Sidney were somewhere in the house, or maybe Peggy was in the dorm visiting with the girls, and that he was about to go to his classroom and teach his classes. But when he finished his call and stood up, turning from the phone, he saw into the living room where, on the opposite wall, a full-length mirror showed him a not-quite-elderly, burnt-out man. He had to take a step away from the phone and see the stranger take a step too, before he was sure he was seeing himself. Then he turned to see across the hall Patience's desk in the middle of his study, and at last he understood that his unconscious in the panic attack had been trying to tell him his career at Miss Oliver's School for Girls was done. For thirty-five years his desk had been against the wall!

Patience followed his gaze to the desk. The papers she'd been correcting made four piles on it. "Don't you love seeing how they think!" she said.

He tried to smile and said, "I remember the feeling."

"*Remember?* You'll have it again after your sabbatical."

He shook his head, and moved back to the foyer, and handed Patience his key. "Duplicate in case you lose yours," he said. She tried to give it back, still not understanding, so he closed her hand around it. Then he moved past her and stood just inside the front door where he could wait for the cab without being seen.

IT WAS WARM and sunny that afternoon at Miss Oliver's School for Girls, the maples leafed out, the lawns as green as Ireland, shad running in the river, and Gregory van Buren in Rachel's office again, pestering her to do something about the way the girls were allowed to dress. He had just informed her, "Even Gypsy Rose Lee wouldn't reveal as much of herself as our girls do the minute the weather gets warm," and she had laughed and asked, "How do you know, were you really old enough to have watched her strip?" when Margaret entered and said Bob was on the line. Rachel was instantly nervous. He never called during business hours. Courteous as ever, Gregory stepped out into Margaret's office.

"Bob, what's wrong?"

"Nothing. I just wanted to hear your voice."

Her husband stopping work just to say hello? Sometimes he didn't stop even to eat. He could go till ten o'clock at night before he discovered he was hungry and realized he hadn't eaten since breakfast—and he'd eaten that standing up.

"Only two more weekends and we'll be together again," he said.

"I wish it were this weekend so we wouldn't have to wait so long, but I have a dinner with the Boston Area Alumnae Club on Saturday night."

"I know, you told me, and anyway I have to go to Chicago."

"What for?"

"A speech."

"You're going all the way to Chicago to hear a speech? Have someone tape it." He didn't answer, and she thought maybe for once he was considering her advice, but he still didn't answer and she finally caught on. "Oh, you mean you're—"

"Yeah, that's right, I'm making it."

"Well, why didn't you tell me?" she asked. "Hold on a minute." She put down the receiver, releasing herself to the sudden joyous impulse, and stepped into Margaret's office. Gregory was still there. "How would you like to be me at the Boston Area Alumnae Club dinner?"

"Me?"

"You."

He thought for a second or two. "I'd love it."

"Good. You're on."

Then she went back into her office and picked up the phone. "Tell your secretary you need another ticket on the flight to Chicago," she said. "Make sure she knows it's for your wife." She hung up and went back to Margaret's office. Gregory was still there. "They'll ask you to make a few remarks," she told him. "Promise me you'll keep them short? After five minutes their minds wander, you know. They'll want to get back to reminiscing with each other."

"I'll promise if you'll promise to think some more about a dress code."

"All right, I promise," she said, and he rolled his eyes and left.

"That's two promises that will never be kept," Margaret said, looking very happy.

Bob talked that Friday evening at his alma mater, Northwestern, to the people who would receive their master's degree in business administration in the morning. They had used the founding and successful growth of Best Sports, Incorporated as a case study and wanted to hear from its president and founder. Bob talked for forty-five minutes and kept their attention all the way through. He told them how Best Sports had been going nowhere until he realized he was acting like the owner. "I'd started it so it was mine," he said. "Then I woke up and started delegating, giving it away." There was more to his speech, but that was the gist.

He glanced Rachel's way several times to see how she was doing. *Just fine*, she signaled with her eyes, *thank you very much. I'm watching a soul mate in action.* It was dawning on her that she couldn't ever stay married to a person who wasn't the kind who took the helm and lived on the edge. And he couldn't either! It was a revelation. It was like taking their vows all over again.

And she was also learning how fine it was, sometimes, to be the least important person in the room.

That night they wanted to make love, but they were in the guest room of the dean's house on campus, and who knew how thin the walls were? Instead, they put their arms around each other and Bob described, one by one, each of the three people he had delegated to when he'd had his epiphany. For the third, the one who had killed himself, whom she had failed to ask about, he described the wake, how there was no food served, no drinks, not even water, to distract from the meaning of a good man's life. How the corpse in the open casket declared the inescapable news: *I didn't want to be here anymore.* And how the next morning in the church, the daughter read what Jesus said about feeding the hungry and caring for the sick and visiting people when they're in prison, and the son spoke a simple eulogy about the father he still loved, and the priest in his sermon told the congregation to be brave and believe. Then Bob told Rachel how beautiful the music was, and fell asleep.

They left early Saturday afternoon, right after the graduation ceremony, arriving at LaGuardia just in time to decide on the spur of the moment that there really wasn't anything that couldn't wait until Monday in his office or her school, and they got the last two seats on a Cape Air flight to Martha's Vineyard. They arrived at the cottage just as her brother and sister and father were sitting down to dinner. They had come that morning to prepare the cottage for the June renters, but the day had been so lovely they'd spent it walking the beach. Her family jumped up from the table, delighted and surprised, and told Bob and Rachel how great they looked while Bags, twice as big now, smelling like the dead fish he'd just rolled in, wagged his tail so hard it almost knocked the bridge lamps down.

After dinner, they turned off the lights in the cottage and the five of them went outside and lay down side by side on beach blankets so they could look straight up and see the stars. Rachel's father lay in the middle, her brother and sister with Bags between them to his left, Bob and Rachel to his right. All the neighboring cottages were dark, it being so early in the season, nor was there any moon, just the thousands of stars in the black dome above them, the smell of the ocean, the sound of waves, and a distant, repetitive foghorn. Deep in his contentment, in the bosom of his family, the father was the first to fall asleep.

When Rachel awoke, everyone but Bob had gone inside. They had thrown beach blankets over them. It was warm and snuggly under them. Rachel counted the shooting stars while she waited for Bob to stir. *What better place than this to be conceived?* she would ask him, but she didn't have to because, just then, he opened his eyes and said, "Ah, you're awake!" And she opened herself to him. Like flowers to the sun.

The next morning they got up early to make up for the lost time and vacuumed the rugs and swept the floors, scrubbed the bathrooms and kitchen and washed the windows and took the covers off the wicker furniture. They caught the last ferry back to the mainland. The sun set as they reached the dock at Woods Hole where Rachel rented a car. Her brother drove Bob back to the city.

BACK AT SCHOOL the next morning, Rachel was so happy with her certitude that she'd conceived, she jumped out of bed at six-thirty, put on her running clothes, and headed out into the June sunshine, coasting loosely and easily down the long slope of the dew-soaked lawns to the river trail. She ran and ran, breathing in, breathing out, pure mindless joy along the bluff above the river, then, flying, down the slope to where the trail ran beside the river, past where Gregory and she had watched the deer, and then some more and more and more. She was a hunter-gatherer loping through the veldt. She was a person who never sat in chairs. She turned back after she had run farther downstream than she ever had before and headed home thinking it should be against the law for every school-age kid not to do this every day.

On the hill up to the bluff, she only slowed a little bit and then sprinted along the bluff and onto the campus where she slowed to a jog and then a walk. And then she stopped and stared at the white clapboard sidings of the campus buildings gleaming in the sun, the maples arching their branches over the girls in their bright dresses walking to breakfast on the paths. A revelation for the second time: this was where she belonged. No place on earth more beautiful to her than this.

Just before Rachel went into the Head's House to change her clothes, she saw a Mercedes pull into the driveway of the Plummers' dorm, now parented by Patience Sommers. Claire got out of the car, glanced at Rachel, and looked quickly away. So, taking the hint, and because she had no desire to stop and talk with Claire's father, whom she assumed was delivering Claire from their weekend together in Vermont, Rachel kept on walking. But then not Claire's father but Sonja got out of the car and opened the trunk. Claire pulled out her backpack and then she and Claire embraced, and Claire, still not looking at Rachel, went into the dorm.

As soon as Claire was out of sight, Sonja and Rachel approached each other. Sonja explained. "The son of a bitch brought his new girlfriend with him."

"No!" Rachel said. "He didn't!"

Sonja didn't answer. She stared at the door through which Claire had disappeared. She was on the verge of crying. Sonja, crying? Rachel wanted to explain that Claire had gotten over needing her father. She invited Sonja into the house. They'd have breakfast together before they went to work.

Rachel was pouring sweat, her T-shirt soaked through, sticking to her skin, and it was cool in her cavernous downstairs. So she asked Sonja to wait while she went upstairs, showered, and dressed. When she came back down, Sonja had set the table. "My goodness," Rachel said, wondering how Sonja had found everything. "When did you get to be so domestic?"

"Since I've been taking care of Claire."

They made the breakfast together: granola, yogurt, and fruit. Rachel cut up the fruit and Sonja made the coffee.

"Claire met his plane," Sonja said when they had sat down at the table. "Got there just as he picked up the bags at the baggage claim. She didn't notice the lady who walked beside him as she ran to him. She'd made up her mind she was going to be nice to her dad, for a change. Just the two of them together. '*Hi, Claire, my name's Deborah*,' the lady said, but Claire didn't speak. In the rental car the lady tried to sit in the back, but Claire beat her to it. All the way to Vermont her father and the stranger sat talking beside each other, Claire staring at their backs. The next day the lady tried her best to include Claire, but Claire wouldn't have it. She called me and I drove right up."

"Her father just let her go?"

"He and the lady were taking a walk. Claire left her a note: *Dear Deborah, he's all yours.*"

They finished their breakfast. Sonja cleared the table and Rachel loaded the dishwasher. Then Rachel walked Sonja to her car. "I hope Claire comes and tells me about it," she said.

"She will," Sonja said.

THIRTY-TWO

It was warm and cloudless, New England springtime at its best, when Francis Plummer, returning from Italy after the conclusion of Renaissance Painting in Italy, got out of the cab early in the morning in front of Peggy's apartment building near Columbia. There was even a slight breeze from the west, bearing the fresh primeval scent of the Hudson. But what Francis smelled was the garbage in the shiny black plastic bags waiting along the sidewalk for pick-up. He was overwhelmed by homesickness for the campus of Miss Oliver's School for Girls.

Yesterday, right after the celebratory lunch that concluded Renaissance Painting in Italy, Clara and Alfred and Francis had retreated to a bar to be together one last time before they parted. They'd become even better friends since Francis had returned to Perugia and discovered that Martha Bush was no longer with the group. She and her husband had disappeared without paying their hotel bill. The authorities were trying to track them down. Francis had been imagining telling Martha how amazing it was to be surrounded with Patience's furniture in the place he and his wife had been living for nearly thirty-five years. He was sure her husband had dragged her away because she had shamed him in front of everybody. He wanted to believe she didn't know her husband hadn't paid the bill.

Alfred and Clara were delighted that he'd returned. He told them he'd changed his mind about canceling his sabbatical on the flight back to the states, and had turned around as soon as he could. It was just too complicated to explain what really happened. "See, I'm not so crazy, after all," he'd said. He didn't tell them he was through at Miss Oliver's School for Girls. It would be wrong to tell them before he told Peggy and Rachel, in that order; and it seemed only right to wait to tell Peggy until he would be face to face with her.

Over snifters of brandy, Alfred told him that Clara and he were going to live together. "We very much wanted you to know," he said in his gravest tone, and Clara, wearing the same green dress in which she'd been arrested, told Francis how grateful to him they both were for bringing them together. He told them he was happy for them, refraining from pointing out that he'd brought Alfred into Clara's company to get her out of jail, and then they informed him they were going to travel through Europe for a couple of months together, maybe more, before returning first to her place in Ohio, then his in New York, where they hoped he'd visit them. He'd told them he would. It wasn't that far, Fieldington, Connecticut, to New York City.

Now he was lugging his suitcase up the barren stairway to Peggy's apartment, tired after flying all night. At the tiny platform that was the fifth floor, lit from above by a dirt-encrusted skylight, he had to stop and think for a few seconds before he remembered which of the three doors was the one to Peggy's apartment.

He knew it was unreasonable to resent her for being here, but that didn't make the pain any less. He rang her doorbell instead of opening it with his key so she would have to greet him outside in neutral territory. There was no answer. He rang again. Maybe she was in the bathroom. He counted to ninety and pushed the doorbell button again, harder and longer, leaning on his finger, and there was still no sound of her footsteps coming to the door. He was surprised she'd leave for Columbia so early. He unlocked the door with his key and walked in.

She'd left a note in the tiny kitchen: *Welcome home, you prize-winning man! So proud of you! Goodies in the fridge.* He wasn't hungry. He left his suitcase in the kitchen, went into the tiny bedroom, climbed up on the bed, where the pillow smelled like her shampoo when he put his head on it, and fell asleep.

He awoke in late afternoon, with a startling suddenness, realizing that when Peggy came home, he would tell her he had decided to resign. He'd been pushing this necessity out of his mind, stubbornly refusing to think about it, but the minute she came in the door he'd be face to face with her. It had to be done.

He sat up in bed terrified, as if he were about to confess an irredeemable sin, and trying to convince himself that what he was about to tell her would be as easy as when he'd gone to a strip club years ago in a moment of weakness and came home feeling so guilty he confessed to her and swore he'd never do that again. Her response had been a hurt, sarcastic, "Thank you for sharing," but a few minutes later she'd started to laugh. The thought of Francis raptly staring at naked dancers was just so funny she couldn't help it. He found that reaction slightly insulting, but he'd never visited a strip club since.

He didn't think he should get right to the point. He needed first to tell her what had happened in Perugia—at least some of it. But most important of all, he would tell her about the dream he'd been having.

He heard her key in the door. He got off the bed, was halfway toward the door when she came through it, carrying a paper bag. "Hi," she said, as if they'd parted just this morning.

"Hi," he said, still standing where he'd stopped.

"Look what I've got." She pulled a bottle of red wine out of the paper bag and showed it to him, then put it on the counter. "And this." She reached into the bag again and pulled out a steak. "Homecoming celebration," she said. "Yum." Then she stepped toward him and hugged him.

"How are you?" she asked.

"I'm fine. How are you?"

"Oh, Francis, it's so interesting! I'm learning so much! I can't wait to tell you about it."

"Well then, do."

She shook her head. "No, you first. You've been all the way to Italy." She pointed to the wine bottle for him to open it, then pulled an apron out of a drawer and tied it on.

He pretended to be occupied by opening the bottle. "Where do you keep your wine glasses?" he asked to delay some more.

She smiled. "Does having an endowment named after you ruin your eyesight? They're right there in front of you."

"Oh, so they are." He poured the wine. His heart was pounding. He handed her a glass, then picked up his own. "Cheers."

"Cheers." She took a sip, then turned away to light the broiler for the steak.

"I've been having this dream," he said. It was easier to say it to her back. He described how it felt to be treading water, holding his chin up above the waves in the dark.

She turned back away from the stove and cut holes in the steak to fit the garlic slices in. She looked worried. He was glad. "Maybe you ought to talk to someone," she said.

"I am. I'm talking to *you*." He was suddenly angry—which was exactly how he didn't want to feel. Finally he was actually telling her what was going on inside himself and she wanted him to tell a shrink instead. To punish her, he blurted it out, instead of describing what happened in Perugia first so she would understand. "I'm resigning."

"Resigning?"

"Yes."

"From what?"

"From school. What did you think?"

"From school?"

"What else is there to resign from, Peggy?"

She put the knife down on the counter, looked up from her work and stared at him. She wasn't taking it in. The smells of the garlic and the raw steak and red wine filled the kitchen, reminding him of happier times. "What's happening, Francis? What's going on?"

Her voice had gone soft, and he heard how ardently she wanted to know what was really going on inside of him. "Oh Peg!" he said. He took her hand, and led her away from the counter to the tiny plastic dining table where they sat down across from each other and he told the whole story. When he got to the funny part, Clara's arrest and his and Alfred's rescuing her and the lunch afterward when the waiter told the other diners how Clara had beat the shit out of the crook with her purse, Peggy looked relieved. He could see her thinking that whatever was happening to him wasn't all that serious. It would go away and he would change his mind. When he described his crazy rant at the breakfast table, about Peggy Guggenheim and Saint Sebastian having the best wet dream of his life, he could see she didn't quite know whether that was funny or sad, but when he got to the part where Patience met him at the door, he saw the revelation on her face, and when he told her how amazed he was to find Patience's desk in the middle of the room, she started to cry.

He got up from the table and lighted the broiler and put the steak in the oven, and Peggy stopped crying, and he made the salad. When the steak was done, he brought the food and the bottle of wine to the table.

Peggy said, "I wish I'd been there to hold your hand."

They ate their dinner in silence. When they didn't need their left hands to cut the steak, they reached them across the table to each other. They weren't ready yet to ask whether they should both move off campus and live together, letting Peggy commute to the school. Or should Francis move off campus, and Peggy stay in their apartment and continue parenting the dorm?

They cleaned up after the dinner; then, holding hands on the sofa, they watched the evening news. Afterward, neither of them could remember any of it. Then, finally, Peggy said, "Promise me you won't tell Rachel until you've had more time to think about this." She pointed out that Rachel wouldn't need a lot of time. All she would have to do, if Francis insisted on not returning after his sabbatical, was change Patience Sommers's status from substitute to permanent.

"I promise," he said, though he wasn't the one who needed more time.

"Good, Francis," she said, patting his hand. "There's no need to rush."

AMELIA DICKENSON, GREGORY van Buren, and Rachel Bickham took the early afternoon train to New York on May twenty-seventh, the day of Harriet Richardson's meeting with the secret listeners at the Women's Scholars Club. As Rachel had suggested, Amelia had applied to the Club, hinting she would join the Century Club if not admitted right away. The very next day the Women's Scholars Club's board voted her in at a special meeting and then sent a celebratory announcement to the members and a news release to the media.

Amelia insisted on paying for the taxi ride from Grand Central to the green awning that stretched from the club's front door to the street. Then she led the way into the hushed atmosphere of the big anteroom as if she'd been a member for years. There was a vague scent of lavender. The floor was in red tile, the oaken walls hung with portraits of elegant women, a few middle aged and beautiful, most of them elderly and handsome—and, Rachel noticed, one-hundred-percent white. The elderly white-haired gentleman who greeted them behind a large desk was black, however. He wore a blue serge suit and expressed surprise when Amelia, after introducing Rachel and Gregory as her guests, announced they were here for the meeting two hours before it would begin "to make sure the arrangements are correct."

"But it is Ms. Richardson's meeting," he said.

"Yes, but Ms. Richardson has asked me to facilitate it," Amelia lied. The man looked doubtful. "As president of the Alumnae Association," Amelia added.

Now he looked a little less doubtful. He glanced at Rachel. She returned his gaze, nodding her head. "Ms. Dickenson is an outstanding facilitator of meetings."

"All right then," the deskman said. Who was he to argue with a famous author? Besides, he was outnumbered. "The meeting will be held in the Blue Room." He stood and led them across the anteroom to two big oak doors and pushed them open to reveal a podium standing on the opposite side of a very large blue-walled room. The chairs were in rows facing it.

"Oh, this certainly won't do!" Amelia said. "We need a circle of chairs. This is going to be a discussion, not a speech."

"But Ms. Richardson expressly ordered rows," the deskman said, "and there's nobody around to rearrange them."

"That's not a problem, sir," Gregory told the deskman. "Ms. Richardson expressly told us she has changed her mind, and we can do it ourselves." Rachel couldn't tell by his tone if he was still suspicious of Amelia's intentions. Maybe he was playing along, waiting for a chance to smoke them out. She remembered her joke about the curare dart. It didn't seem funny now in the actual place where the climactic moment was about to happen. She wondered why she had been so sure of Amelia. She pushed the question aside. It was too late to change direction.

Rearranging several hundred chairs into a circle that reached almost to the walls, leaving a gap for the podium, was a big job;

it also required that they move the refreshment table to another part of the room. Rachel worried they wouldn't finish on time—until Amelia explained there were two other reasons for the change besides facilitating discussion. "One, so we can recruit the people to help us finish rearranging them, which will give them something to do to get over discovering *you* here. It might even get them involved and put them on our team. The second reason is that it will make Ms. Richardson angry to have her orders contradicted, and that will be fun."

As the participants started to arrive, Amelia and Gregory stepped forward to shake hands with them, thank them for coming, and introduce "our new school head, Rachel Bickham, whom you may not have met." The surprise of Rachel's tall presence, combined with the requirement of actually shaking her hand, brought instant confusion and wariness and the flush of guilt to their expressions, which Gregory and Amelia especially pretended not to notice. Rachel felt a surge of joy at their discomfort as she told them how glad she was to meet them, thanking them for coming "to this important discussion," and then inviting them to help finish putting the chairs in circles. As Amelia had predicted, they were obviously relieved to escape from Rachel and have a task to complete.

At precisely five minutes to seven, Gregory nudged Rachel's elbow. "Here she comes." Rachel had never laid eyes on Harriet Richardson before and so had asked Gregory to identify her. All she knew was that Ms. Richardson was elderly, virginal, very small, and spoke with a quavering voice.

But it turned out she didn't need Gregory to identify Ms. Richardson. Everyone's eyes were on her as she came through the door, and even from across the room, Rachel saw the red flush come over her cheeks and her tiny body quiver with anger as she saw what had been done with the chairs—and in fact was still being done. Then she recognized Rachel—from her picture, Rachel supposed—or was it because she happened to be the only African American in the crowd? Surprise blossomed on Harriet Richardson's face, and then comprehension, and then disgust, and the next thing Rachel knew she was approaching Ms. Richardson with the purpose of announcing in a very loud voice that she better get ready to apologize in front of all these people for telling a lie about her and going behind her back to do it. Ms. Richardson turned away, but Rachel reached and touched her on the shoulder. Ms. Richardson whirled around, her blue eyes blazing. "What?" she said. "You have something to say to me?"

Rachel didn't answer. She was regaining enough self-control just in time to realize that everybody in the room was watching a tall, young black lady towering like a prize fighter over an ancient white one with a dowager's hump. One intemperate word out of her and she was toast.

Then Amelia Dickenson was beside Rachel, reaching for Ms. Richardson's hand. And Gregory van Buren on Rachel's other side, his hand on her elbow. "Ms. Richardson! How lovely to see you," Amelia sang. "Thanks so much for coming. Wouldn't you like some coffee?" She put her arm through Ms. Richardson's and led her toward the back of the room. "There are wonderful cookies too. Oh, and by the way: since many of the people here are alumnae, I thought I should facilitate the meeting—as their president. I'm sure you agree."

And Gregory led Rachel away. "Now, listen," he said, sotto voce, but more fiercely than she'd ever heard him before. "You're going to get control of yourself. Understand? Otherwise we'd have been better off with Sonja Testosterone McGarvey here. Who do you think you are to make this personal?"

"I thought you didn't trust Amelia," Rachel whispered.

"I don't have any choice now," he whispered even more quietly. "It's too late to change tactics, don't you think? Just be watchful and ready to counter."

"Seats, everybody, please," Amelia said a little while later from behind the podium. The buzz of conversation stopped. There was the sound of chair legs squeaking against the floor. Otherwise the silence was enormous. Gregory and Rachel took seats beside the podium. Across the circle, facing them, Ms. Richardson had already sat down. She looked like a fierce little bird.

Amelia introduced herself as president of the Alumnae Association—a fact as well known as that she was a famous author—and thanked everyone for coming and then turned to look at Rachel.

"Rachel, will you address us, please?" Rachel stood up, feeling the weight of everyone's eyes. As the head of school, she was already used to that. She understood it's when everyone looks away that you know your tenure's gone. But she wasn't used to being managed. She expected Amelia to step aside, but Amelia stayed right beside her. Indeed, she leaned into the microphone and said, "There is no question that it appears that the school knew about and ignored the student's drinking."

Rachel turned away from the audience to Amelia and stared. Behind her, she was sure Gregory was rising from his chair. She heard Sonja's *don't*. She was about put her hand on Amelia's shoulder to push her away from the mike, but then Amelia added, "We can absolutely understand why one could draw that conclusion, but I happen to know that was not the case, because I've had several long conversations with Rachel, and she told me it wasn't true." She paused, nodding her head to show her conviction—though there had been no such conversation. There was a throbbing silence for several heartbeats while the audience was deciding whether they too believed Rachel wouldn't lie. Rachel had no idea whether Amelia was being sarcastic, or not. And then Amelia said, her voice ringing with faith, "And I just can't believe the dorm parents, Francis and Peggy Plummer, knew. *They* never would have allowed a cover-up."

The audience sighed. People nodded their heads. Then every eye turned to Harriet Richardson. She was staring at Amelia.

Say something, Rachel told herself. *Right now, before she does.* She was almost dizzy with relief and it was hard to think of the right thing to say. Everyone in the room seemed to be turning their heads back and forth to look at Ms. Richardson and then back to her, as if they were watching a tennis match. And then, suddenly, Rachel knew exactly what to do: *talk philosophy. Like a head of school.* She let her breath out and said, "But we should have known that a student was drinking." She paused, looking contrite and judicious at the same time. She added, "And I'll take the blame for not realizing that we have too large a tendency to respect privacy at the expense of our duty to supervise and protect young people from drugs and alcohol and all the other dangers kids are vulnerable to."

"How interesting!" Amelia said, still standing next to Rachel.

She paused. Rachel was sure she was deciding how to finish Ms. Richardson off. A bright light came on in Amelia's expression. Clearly an idea had arrived. She sent a gleeful look at Rachel that seemed to say, *Watch what happens now*, and then she turned to the audience. "How many of you actually search your children's rooms when they are home?"

On Rachel's left, Louisa Hazard's hand shot up—her daughter Diane was a junior—and beside her, two women whom Rachel didn't know raised theirs tentatively, like students not sure of the answer. Everyone looked at them, some with admiration, some as if these they were visitors from an exotic culture. Others shook their heads. The two mothers next to Louisa Hazard looked around the circle, and took their hands down when they saw they were so few, but Louisa stood up. She was short, wore big glasses, and had long, blond hair. "How do you know what your daughters are doing if you don't search their rooms once in a while?" she asked in a defensive tone.

There was a little silence and then someone called, "We trust our daughters." Rachel didn't see who it was because she was watching Louisa.

"Well, I *love* mine!" Louisa said, and sat down hard and stared at Rachel.

Then Rachel promised that from now on the faculty would balance the two, privacy and protection, and supervise more rigorously. It was easy to say because she knew it was right. They would become brazen invaders of that privacy when they suspected drugs or alcohol, and, yes, boys smuggled into dorms. They would learn never to apologize. The audience nodded their heads and sent Rachel approving looks.

And then Amelia invited the parents to join Rachel in a rich discussion about parenting—until at nine-thirty she said, "Rachel, I think it is time we let these people go home, don't you?"

Ms. Richardson was the first to leave. She hadn't said a word. The big oaken doors at the back wouldn't budge when she tried to open them, until the person behind her reached over her head and pushed them open for her. "The poor thing," Gregory murmured. Amelia was surrounded by people, basking in their praise.

THREE MINUTES BEFORE he was to go on air, Mitch Michaels still didn't know how he was going to tell his audience that Rachel Bickham took a bribe from Claire Nelson's father. Yes, there would be thousands more people listening tonight, all of them expecting sensational news because of all the fanfare about the different time slot, but he'd think of something. He always did. It was when the first word out of his mouth was a surprise that he was most able to empty himself of his anger. When that happened he achieved a serenity that sometimes lasted for hours.

He kept his mind blank until the minute hand on the clock reached twelve and then he leaned into the mike and started to weep. That was his first surprise. The second was his sudden lightness. The third was that he'd never done this before. "I haven't always been honest with you," he blurted through his sobs. "Well, tonight I'm going to be. You know that girl I've been telling you about? She stood right up in front of a reporter and admitted she was an alcoholic. So now it's time for me to tell you that I'm a painkiller addict. Yes, I'm addicted to painkillers. I've had a bad back for years. That's been my excuse. But no more. Lots of people hurt just as bad, but they don't take that escape. So I'm not trying to set an example here. I'm a radio guy, not a role model. I'm doing this for myself." Mitch paused here to quell his sobs. He'd cried about the right amount. Any more would be a turn-off. Besides, the silence was dramatic.

Then he took a big breath and went on. "Some of you have heard rumors that the headmistress knew all along that the girl was an alcoholic and took a bribe in the form of a gift to the school from the father not to kick her out. Well, that might be true, but what I *know* is true is I've been bribing the ladies who clean my apartment in New York and my house in Connecticut for years. They'd have to be blind not to know about my addiction. The tips I give them are bigger than their fees, and I give them Christmas presents and there's a timeshare in Florida they love to go to with their families in the wintertime."

Mitch paused again to let that sink in. "So I'm going to check myself in at a treatment center. While I'm gone, you'll be listening to Abigail Winters. She's the one who took my place when I went to England, remember? I hope you don't like her so much that you'll want to keep on listening to her instead of me when I get back. And don't worry about me when I'm gone. The treatment center is in Hawaii. See what you get for being rich? When I'm not rehabbing, I'll be on the beach. So goodbye for now."

Charlie was smiling and nodding his head when Mitch passed him on the way to the exit. "You're not surprised?" Mitch said.

"Surprised! Are you kidding? I was worried to death about you."

Now Mitch was surprised again. "Charlie, thank you!" If he wasn't careful he'd start to cry again.

Charlie shrugged.

"See ya later, Charlie."

"Yeah, see ya later, Mitch. You really have a timeshare in Florida?"

"Nah, I just made that part up," Mitch said and then headed for the door. He had a lot of arranging to do before he left for Hawaii.

THIRTY-THREE

The news that Harriet Richardson had been defeated, humiliated, and silenced, plus the surprise revelation of Mitch Michaels reduced to confessional tears, brought Jamie Carrington a wondrous relief. She actually felt lighter. She would have no more nightmares in which she stood nude (except for her shoes and a New York Yankees baseball hat) on the Miss Oliver's auditorium stage, confessing her sin while the girls stared at her and Milton Perkins, in the front row, dressed in a judge's black robe and an absurd English barrister's snow-white wig, laughed and laughed and laughed.

But the news that Paul Nelson's pledged one hundred thousand dollars was long overdue made her angry. She understood now that he'd been toying with her. She would make him pay for that. One way or another, she would get that money for the school.

It didn't take her long to decide that the way to that money was through Eudora Easter, Claire's teacher. He had said she should go to Eudora's studio and look at Claire's painting because he had heard they were "quite remarkable." Well, that's how she would start. Jack, her chauffeur, would drive her to the school in the morning and she would look at the paintings that he, her own father, had never seen, and then she'd telephone him and make him feel guilty for ignoring his daughter's accomplishments; and if that didn't work to induce him to honor his pledge, she would let him know how disappointed his daughter would be to learn that he'd reneged on a promise—because, with a father like him, no wonder she was an alcoholic.

Jamie sat for four hours on the lush leather backseat of her Mercedes the next morning, staring at the back of Jack's head and replaying her transatlantic phone conversation with Paul Nelson while her embarrassment and anger heated. Why hadn't she heard the contempt in his voice?

Everyone was in the dining room at lunch when she arrived at the school. She told Jack to get himself something to eat in Fieldington and to be back in an hour, and then she wandered through the empty Art Building. When she had graduated in 1948, the arts were taught in one small, temporary building, which this one had replaced, and which she had helped to fund. Which of these rooms would interest her the most if she were a student now?

In the ceramics studio where the air smelled like dried earth and the floor was gritty, she put her fingertips on the flared lip of a vase that waited with others, like soldiers in a line, for its time in the kiln, and wished she were fifteen years old, her fingers on cool, wet, malleable clay, innocently making a vase. It was a sudden, surprising rush of emotion. She thought she might actually weep. Instead, she fled from the ceramics studio as if escaping a danger, promising herself that when she got home this evening, she'd figure out what the moment had meant. Right now, she was pretty sure it had something to do with how she was supposed to spend the rest of her life—and that it had nothing to do with ceramics.

In the anteroom she rubbed her hand over the hard, shiny surface of the Humpty Dumpty chair and remembered some words: *cracked and crazed enamel.* She'd been fifteen years old, a freshman reading Robert Frost, and now she was accosted once again with a desire to weep—which she had absolutely no intention to do.

So, to change the atmosphere, she sat down in "The Star-Spangled Banner" chair and listened to the whole damn thing. When it started all over again, she jumped up to stop it. How she would have preferred "America the Beautiful"! She'd had enough of inane macho nonsense about bombs bursting in air and flags waving, and some idiot who wondered if it was still there. "How can anyone listen to such drivel, let alone stand up for it?" she wondered aloud in the new silence, then heard someone giggling, and turned around, and there was Eudora Easter standing beside a tall, black-haired, very pretty young woman. She looked more like an actress playing the part than an actual student. "Claire Nelson?" Jamie guessed out loud, and when Claire nodded, looking surprised and curious, Jamie said, "I've come to see your paintings."

Claire and Eudora both looked even more surprised and maybe, Jamie thought, a bit suspicious too. But when she explained that she had been talking to Claire's father, asking for a contribution, and he had proudly urged her to go see his daughter's work, Eudora led her into the studio. Displayed on a wall in the front were Claire's painting of two girls on a beach, and a black-and-white etching of the same tree whose image hung in Rachel Bickham's office, but this one was of the tree in the wintertime at night. At its feet two small people looked up through the naked branches at a black, oppressive sky. Claire said, "I left the stars out."

Jamie shivered. No one spoke. And then Jamie turned to Eudora, and said, "I wish you had been teaching here when I was a student. I would have become an art collector."

"It's not too late," Eudora said.

"Oh. Is this for sale?" Pointing to the two girls on the beach.

Claire shook her head.

"Claire's going to give it to her dad on graduation day," Eudora explained.

"On graduation day. Really?"

"Yes, a kind of reverse graduation present."

"Well, what about this one then?" Pointing to the tree.

Claire frowned. She didn't answer.

"Claire?" Eudora said.

"I don't know. I thought I'd just leave it here when I leave."

"A gift to the school?" Jamie asked.

Claire shook her head. "More like a thank you," she said. "And I never thought about selling."

"Well it's time you started, young lady," Jamie said. "Tell you what. I'll buy it from the school and leave it here myself. How's that for an idea?"

"Really?" Claire said.

"Oh honey, don't act surprised when people want to buy your work. It's not good marketing," Jamie said. "Now if you don't mind, I'd like to speak to Ms. Easter."

A moment later, in the privacy of Eudora's studio, Jamie cut Eudora off before Eudora finished thanking her and explained her mission. She asked Eudora to join her in the call to Claire's father.

"Two against one," she said. "We'll gang up. Besides, how can he possibly say no to you?"

Eudora agreed that it would be difficult, given what she had done for his daughter, and suggested that they not announce who they were—just that it was Miss Oliver's calling with some very important news about his daughter. "Otherwise he might not come to the phone."

The ruse worked. Paul Nelson's secretary said, "Just a minute, please," and a few seconds later, Paul Nelson said warily, "Hello?"

"Hello, Mr. Nelson. This is Eudora Easter."

"Yes?"

"Your daughter's art teacher."

"Oh? What's happened? Is she in trouble again?"

"Absolutely not, Mr. Nelson. Quite the contrary. She has just sold one of her paintings. I thought you'd like to know. This is the very first time in the history of the school."

"Really? Thanks for telling me. How nice of you to take the trouble to call me. How much?"

"Well, I think I should let the purchaser tell you," Eudora said, grinning madly at Jamie. "She's a very famous art collector. Would you like to talk to her?"

"Of course."

"Good. Here she is." With one hand over her mouth to stifle her giggle, Eudora handed the phone to Jamie.

"Hello, Mr. Nelson. This is Jamie Carrington. Remember me?"

"Who?"

"Jamie Carrington, Mr. Nelson. From East Hampton."

Silence.

"You do remember me now, don't you?"

"Uh—yes, actually, I do."

"Good," Jamie said then stopped talking. There was another silence. It lasted forever. Eudora giggled again, out loud this time.

At last, Jamie broke the silence. "I believe I heard you say you would like to know what I paid for it,"

"Well—yes—I did."

"Guess."

"I have no idea."

"A very familiar number, Mr. Nelson. At least it is to me. Shall I remind you?"

"I don't understand." A sharp intake of breath followed. "Oh! Oh, no. You're not serious."

"I am, Mr. Nelson. And so is Ms. Easter. We have discussed your situation at great length and have agreed to be deadly serious. As soon as we hang up, we intend to tell your daughter—"

"You wouldn't do that to her."

"Let me finish, please. We will tell her that you have made a very generous gift of one hundred thousand dollars to the school out of gratitude for—well, you know what for, Mr. Nelson—and we will remind her to call you up and thank you. Please think about how that will make you feel before you decide."

"Well, I'll be damned!" he said. "I'll be—"

"We never know," Jamie said. "You might not be." Then she hung up.

"We are not going to do that!" Eudora said.

"Of course we won't. He'll write the check before we have to. Then Claire can thank him if she wants."

THREE DAYS LATER Paul Nelson's check arrived. Just to be sure, Mabel Walters waited for it to clear before she informed Rachel. "We made it!" she exclaimed, bursting triumphantly into Rachel's office. "Four hundred thousand for paying down the deficit. Our goal for the year." She held up a thumb: "One hundred thousand from Sonja, her first installment"—then a forefinger—"one hundred from the alumnae's match."

"But that's only two hundred thousand," Rachel said.

Mabel raised her eyebrows. "Yes, but look at these." She slapped two more checks down on Rachel's desk.

Rachel stared at the checks, one signed by Paul Nelson, the other by Jamie Carrington.

"They're real," Mabel said. Then she explained: "Mrs. Carrington bought a picture from Claire and then gave it to the school. Who knows what it will be worth someday?"

"Oh my goodness! What will I say to Jamie Carrington?"

Mabel frowned. She looked mystified. "Why not just tell her thanks?"

"Yes, why not," Rachel murmured, reaching for her phone.

THIRTY-FOUR

On the evening of Friday, June eleventh, just four weeks since they'd made love on the beach on Martha's Vineyard, Rachel and Bob were getting ready for the Senior Dinner, which always took place the night before graduation and always outside in the back garden of the Head's House, because it never rained on graduation weekend at Miss Oliver's School for Girls. Rachel, whose obstetrician had just that morning confirmed that she was pregnant, came out of the shower with nothing on and her hair all wet. Bob was naked too, about to step into the shower. On the way, he stopped and placed his hand on her belly. She put her hand over his and together they caressed the new life inside her. Then he put his arms around her. She returned his hug, and they clung to each other.

Then the front doorbell rang.

He let her go. She crossed to the window and leaned her head out, careful to hide the rest of herself. "Yes, what is it?"

The president of the junior class stepped backward from the front steps into view. "The hat."

"What hat?" Bob asked behind Rachel.

"Oh my God!" Rachel exclaimed, turning back to him. "Daniel Webster's."

"Daniel Webster's!"

"I don't have time to explain," Rachel said. "I have to find it." And then, calling down to the president of the junior class, "Don't worry, I'll bring it down when I come."

"Please hurry," the president called back up. "We have to put the names in it."

Bob gazed at the window as if the person on its other side had lost her mind.

"It's a tradition," Rachel explained.

"What, looking for Daniel Webster's hat?"

"No, putting the names in it. The president of the junior class puts a blindfold on during Senior Dinner and pulls them out, and that's how we know what order the seniors will receive their diplomas in tomorrow."

"Oh," he said, grinning now. "Have you thought of teaching them the alphabet?"

"Please! Help me, I have no idea where Fred Kindler put it."

"Maybe he took it with him if it's Daniel Webster's hat. Maybe he's a collector." By now, Bob was laughing so hard he had to sit down on the edge of the bed while, still naked, Rachel started rummaging through the closets for Daniel Webster's hat.

In a minute the laughter behind her subsided to a giggle. She felt Bob's hand on her shoulder and turned around. He was wearing a huge sombrero she'd bought for him on their honeymoon in Mexico. It came down to his eyebrows. Otherwise, he was still naked.

She pounded her fists on his bare chest. "Will you just please take this seriously!"

"I am," he said. "We'll tell them it's Daniel Webster's other hat."

So she got dressed and hurried downstairs and told the president of the junior class that this huge sombrero was Daniel Webster's other hat, "and it's time we used it."

Around eight-thirty, while the seniors still lingered at the tables, the kitchen crew arrived to clear the detritus of the dinner away. Bob helped them. Rachel was just as worried as he about how long these faithful people had already worked that day, and would have helped too, but the girls didn't want this evening to end. They trooped into the Head's House as if it were their own and Rachel went with them. Who knew how long before they would meet again?

When Bob had finished helping the kitchen crew, he stepped into the living room, thanked the girls for including him in their dinner, congratulated them for graduating, assured them tomorrow was going to be sunny, and said goodnight. He and Rachel exchanged glances as he started up the stairs. He would wait up for her. The sun was just setting on the long June evening.

Around eleven, Rachel told the girls it was time to get back to their dorms. "I bet most of you haven't even started packing yet," she said, though it didn't really make any difference when they got back to their dorms. They would stay up most of the night wherever they were, too excited and nostalgic already to sleep. As the girls said goodnight and started to leave, Rachel wondered if Claire would stay back for just the two of them to be together, but she trooped out with all the rest.

Rachel was halfway up the stairs when there was a knock on the front door. She thought Claire must have changed her mind and returned to talk, but with the first step upward, all her focus had switched to being with Bob in bed, and now she didn't want to talk to Claire. She stopped climbing, but didn't turn around. Maybe Claire would get the message and go away. She waited a few seconds and took another step upward, feeling slightly guilty, but then there was another knock, a little louder. It seemed urgent and tentative at the same time, not Claire's signature at all, and she wondered who it could be. It really didn't make any difference though. If you were the head of a boarding school and someone knocked *twice* on your door in the middle of the night, you answered it.

It was Francis Plummer. She was too surprised to speak. It flashed on her that he must have been watching the house, waiting for the girls to leave. "I hope you don't mind," he said.

She managed to say, "No, Francis, come on in," though alarms were going off in her head. She hadn't seen him since she had said goodbye at the airport when he flew to Italy. Eudora had told her he would spend the night in her apartment so he wouldn't have to rush in the morning to be on time for graduation.

Rachel ushered Francis into the living room, and he sat down on the sofa, and she chose a chair on the opposite side of the coffee table. She would need the distance when she told him, *No! You can't cancel your sabbatical.*

He waited, watching her closely as she settled in her chair. He smiled a rueful smile and shook his head. "Don't worry, Rachel, I'm resigning. I wanted you to know before tomorrow."

Once again she was too surprised to speak.

He said, "I began to know when I saw all our furniture was

gone." She frowned in incomprehension and he went on to tell her the whole story of what happened in Perugia and his aborted return, leaving nothing out. "Peggy told me to wait to tell you in case I would reconsider, but I knew I wouldn't. And then, tonight, I couldn't sleep, worrying that, after being honored tomorrow, I'd change my mind. So I got up out of bed and put on my clothes, and here I am." He paused, glancing sideways at the stairs. It was past midnight. Then he looked back at her and said, "I hope you won't offer me more time to reconsider. That would be a mistake, don't you think?"

Rachel struggled to think of what to say. Yes, she thought, it would be a terrible mistake—one more in a long list of them.

"Answer me, Rachel. Just say it. I need to know I am right. And you need to be part of this."

Once again, an arrow in her heart. "All right," she said. "It would be a mistake."

He nodded his head. "There. It's done." There was silence. Again she tried to think of the right thing to say, and couldn't.

"But I don't want anyone else to know tomorrow," he said. "It would take the focus away from the graduating girls. Just you and me. We both should have known how stale I'd grown before I didn't get those papers back."

"Yes, especially me," she said. Because now she did know what to say. "That's my job."

He nodded again and said, "We both failed." It was a categorical statement, made in a neutral tone. It struck her that he'd never looked at her so directly in her eyes before, nor for so long a moment.

Then he said, "Now I've kept you long enough," glancing at the stairs again. "Get some sleep. Tomorrow's a big day for you." His tone was fatherly now.

She thought she might weep. So she stood up. The last thing he needed was for her to fall apart right then. She came around the table, and he stood too, and they walked beside each other to the door. She opened it and the scent of honeysuckle rushed in. He said, "I hope you don't mind my telling you so much that is so personal."

"Dear Francis," she said. "I've never been so honored."

He smiled. "When I got back to Perugia, I was going to explain that what amazed me so was that Peggy and I had lived in that apartment for thirty-four, almost thirty-five years, but I never did."

"But Clara would surely understand—"

"Not Clara. Martha Bush. You're surprised?" He shrugged. "But anyway, she wasn't there, that's why I never told. She and her husband had disappeared. They stiffed the hotel, didn't pay their bill. Isn't that something?"

Rachel agreed that it was, and he nodded, satisfied. "Well, good night then, Rachel."

"Good night, Francis. I'll see you tomorrow." She watched him disappear into the dark under bright stars. Then she closed the door. But the smell of the honeysuckle still lingered as she climbed the stairs.

At the top of the stairs, she stopped, struck by a question. Shouldn't Patience have told her about Francis's sudden appearance? What if Francis had changed his mind and decided not to resign? Wouldn't the head of school want to know he'd been behaving so strangely? She wanted to ask Bob: who *should* Patience be loyal to? But it was too complicated, so late at night.

And anyway, he was fast asleep.

THIRTY-FIVE

"You're not a substitute anymore," Rachel said to Patience the next morning an hour before the graduation ceremony would begin. "You are now permanent."

"Oh? Francis told you what happened?"

Rachel nodded. "Last night."

"At last! Now I don't have to keep it inside me anymore. I hated knowing when you didn't. I didn't like that between us."

Rachel didn't answer. She let the silence speak for their need to stay with this a little longer.

"He didn't have to ask me," Patience said. "I just knew how much I wouldn't want anyone else to know, and so I promised."

The contrition in Patience's tone seemed wrong to Rachel now. She didn't want to hear it anymore.

"So I'm forgiven?" Patience asked.

"I have nothing to forgive," Rachel said. She was hearing Eudora again, predicting Francis would do the right thing in the end. "It wasn't your secret to reveal to me. It was Francis's, and he did. You preserved his dignity and he did the rest."

"Thank you," Patience murmured. "Even if I didn't think it through."

Rachel sensed there was something else that had happened between Patience and Francis that Patience was holding back. But she didn't need to know. Nor did she feel like a novice anymore in the presence of her elder. It was time to change the subject. "And here's another thing. I can say it to you because you've been a head. I'm relieved. I'm sad too. But more relieved than sad. And that makes me even sadder."

"Well, it *is* sad," Patience said.

AS THE FACULTY were assembling in the faculty room for the graduation ceremony, Rachel noticed Patience and Francis step outside together. Right then and there, she had an idea she hoped would be a small step toward her redemption. She gave them enough time for Francis to tell Patience that, last night, he had informed Rachel he was resigning and for Patience to reply that Rachel had informed her of that just minutes before, and then for him to thank Patience again for not telling Rachel that he'd rushed home thinking he would cancel his sabbatical. Then Rachel went outside and told Francis she thought he should make the graduation speech instead of her.

"Oh, Francis, do!" Patience said. "You're the only person I know who can think of the right thing to say and say it perfectly with no preparation."

His eyes lighted up. "Thank you! I will."

Five minutes later the faculty and staff marched out into the sun. The graduating class was already seated in their white dresses in the honored position to the left of the dais, and the weather was perfect. Exactly as the clock in the library steeple struck noon, Francis Plummer strode to the microphone, jaunty, confident, young again, Clark Kent disguised as a small, almost elderly teacher of English. First he had to lower the microphone because it had been set for Rachel. He started by telling why Peggy wasn't there.

"Every minute of her day in Montana is critical to what she is learning," he explained. "Just think how much new insight and understanding she will bring to enrich our curriculum from her sabbatical." Then, in less than four minutes, he summarized the history of the school's dedication to the empowerment of young women from its founding by its first headmistress, Miss Edith Oliver in 1928, to—with a nod toward where Rachel sat in the front row—"its present brilliant young head of school who will be with us for many more years."

Also in the front row, Gregory van Buren knew he would use that summary in his rhetoric class in the fall. It would serve as a brilliant example of how effectiveness and brevity are one in the same.

In closing Francis said, "I've had the same dream, over and over, for thirty-five years: Peggy and I have just been appointed to our positions here at Miss Oliver's School for Girls, but we can't accept them because for some perverse reason we don't understand, we have accepted positions and are already on the faculty of another school. Sometimes that school's in a big city, sometimes in France, sometimes on a lake, and once I didn't know where it was, only that there were a lot of round towers made of stone the color of tomato soup and dirty snow that never melted. I'm always crushed. We've thrown away our lives. And then either I dream I wake up and Peggy tells me it isn't so, or I really do wake up and Peggy really does tell me, I never know. Either way, it is always she who rescues me. Such a surge of joy, such a ride of delight, to know we are here, the most beautiful place on earth to us, doing what we were meant to do!"

Later, everybody would understand he was saying goodbye. They couldn't know why Patience was crying. Rachel managed not to fall apart. Her husband sat beside her, squeezing her hand.

Francis said thank you, as if the audience had given this gift to him, rather than the other way around, and left the dais. Everybody leaped to her feet. The applause went on and on and on until he'd crossed to his seat and sat back down.

Amelia climbed up on the dais then, her blond hair like a miniature field of wheat in the noonday sun, and called to Francis to return. Francis came tentatively forward. The audience was quiet. A dog barked somewhere in the distance, and then Francis stood beside Amelia, looking very short. Amelia abandoned her prepared speech—she'd caught Francis's brevity like a happy contagion—and announced in just one sentence the Francis Plummer Chair. Instantly, the audience was on its feet again. Francis returned to his seat, holding the embossed leather folder inside of which in intense legalese was the stipulation that the endowment's harvest would match his salary until he retired, and after that his successor's, and after that in perpetuity.

Cary Swanson, Liz Rintoul, and Shirley Dwight had chosen Francis to be the teacher who conferred their diplomas. Such classy kids! They were the ones who'd had the courage to report Francis to Rachel for not returning their papers. Rachel wondered if they'd also had the courage to tell him they were the ones. For each, while their parents' faces glowed, Francis told them who they were as freshmen and then sophomores and then juniors, and who they were now, ready to try to make the world a place that worked for everybody, naming every hurdle and leap.

Eudora Easter, resplendent in a huge red hat and red slippers with toes pointed skyward like a genie's, made sure the audience understood that this was a certificate of extraordinary artistic accomplishment she was conferring on Claire Nelson, not a diploma—"because I did that last year." It was the excuse Claire's father offered for not being present.

For the second year in a row, Gregory van Buren was the last to confer a diploma upon a senior. But this year the poem he read about her was not indecipherable, and when he hugged her he didn't bend his middle away from her, sticking his butt out behind as if he were wearing a bustle. This year, he lifted his senior right off her feet.

A FEW HOURS later, as the graduation luncheon was winding down, Claire Nelson came up to Rachel. "Sonja told you about the weekend with my dad, so I didn't," she said. "I know you wanted to know."

There was a spot of whipped cream from the strawberry shortcake on Claire's lip. Without thinking, Rachel reached with her finger and wiped it away. "I'm glad you and Sonja are such good friends."

"I'm spending the summer with her, not in England with my dad."

"That will make her very happy. She needs you as much as you need her, you know."

"I know. I'm kind of like a daughter."

"I'm glad you understand that, Claire," Rachel said. She reached to hug Claire and kissed her on the forehead. She would have loved right then to tell Claire she was going to have a baby, but Claire would learn soon enough. Over her shoulder, she saw Sonja waiting to take Claire home.

Then Rachel said her goodbyes to the last lingering guests, except Amy Michaels and her mother, who remained seated at their table, clearly waiting for Rachel to be alone with them. The summer holidays for St. Agnes School on Lake Windermere had started earlier and Amy had returned to see her friends, particularly Claire.

Rachel sat down with them, already feeling the deflation as the school emptied after the day's excitement. In the hot sun, yellowjackets buzzed around the little mounds of strawberry shortcake left on the plates. The noise of the bus leaving for the airport and of car doors shutting sounded as if they were coming from miles away.

"Amy has something to tell you," her mother said. Jenifer Michaels was an attractive woman, pushing fifty, just a little bit stout.

"I've decided to stay at St. Agnes. I love it there. I'm on the sailing team and I'm a delegate to the Round Square Conference and I've made a lot of friends, and there's a wonderful headmaster," Amy said. Her tone was unapologetic. She smiled at her mother. "And my mom's moving over there to be near me."

Rachel nodded her head vigorously up and down to show them she approved, that she wasn't surprised. "It must be a wonderful school. I'd like to visit it someday."

"Oh, I hope you will!" Amy said.

"But you do know that your father has stopped saying bad things about us, don't you?" Rachel asked.

Amy shrugged. "Sure."

"Amy asked her father to stop," her mother said, looking proudly at her daughter.

Amy looked surprised. "When did he tell you that?"

"When I told him we were staying in England," Jenifer said. She turned to Rachel to explain. "I don't hang up on him when he calls me anymore. I've cut him a little slack about what he says on the radio. He has a right to his own philosophy." Then she smiled and said, "Besides, if I never talked to him, how would he know where to send the alimony?"

Amy stared at her mother. "He just made that up, Mom. I didn't ask him. We never talked."

"You didn't?"

Amy shook her head.

"How sad!" Jenifer said.

"Yeah," Amy said. "It is. And it's not a philosophy, Mom."

"What is it then?"

"A personality disorder," Amy said.

Rachel thought, *Out of the mouth of babes!*

On the quiet empty paths to her house, Rachel reflected on Amy's remark. She was surprised by how ardently she hoped Mitch Michaels would conquer his afflictions and get it right with his daughter. He was never a danger—just a media storm, all sound and fury outside the gates. The real danger had come from within—from what it was in her that had allowed her to look the other way when Francis Plummer was collapsing. He had saved her by resigning.

But had he saved himself? Would he regain his true self in some other school? Would there be new goals, new hopes, fresh sunlight rushing in, as there were for Gregory van Buren? Or was it too late? Would Francis always be the not-quite-elderly, burnt-out man he'd seen in the mirror?

The question seemed unbearable, but it was hers to bear. And so was the understanding that if she had moved on Francis earlier, she would have saved him from shaming himself in what should have been his most glorious year. She carried her questions and her understanding, and her sadness for Francis Plummer, which she knew would be enduring—as she also carried the new life inside her—into her house, and into the arms of her husband.

He was waiting for her just inside the door.

WEST MARGIN PRESS

Book Club Guide

No Ivory Tower

Stephen Davenport

Discussion questions for *No Ivory Tower*:

1. Consider the role Rachel Bickham plays in her first year as the head of Miss Oliver's School for Girls. What are some of the strengths she brings to the position? What are some immediate obstacles standing in the way for her? For new heads, some schools hire a coach who is an experienced professional (often a former head of school) to provide advice behind the scenes. If you were that coach, what advice would you give Rachel?

2. In the first faculty meeting before school begins, one faculty member says that all the assistant dorm parents wanted to see Rachel together, to which Rachel responds, "I never meet people in groups." What does Rachel accomplish in that scene? Why did Gregory van Buren approve of her response?

3. Boarding schools serve many purposes, with just one of them being education. What are some reasons why Claire Nelson enrolled into Miss Oliver's? What about Amy Michaels? How does a boarding school impact friendships and relationships among classmates and with teachers?

4. Claire's past with Mr. Alford of her previous school provokes difficult discussions with varying perspectives among the adults of the book. What is the law's position on this, and how does that position compare to the viewpoints of Rachel, Claire, and Claire's father? Why do you think the adults' views differ from Claire's classmates' views? Keeping in mind that the novel takes place in the early 1990s, do you think society has changed its perspective on this subject?

5. Though storied in his legacy and legendary as a figure in the school, what did Francis Plummer need from the school throughout his career than he never got? How did his time abroad in Italy affect his mindset of where his place was at Miss Oliver's?

6. Contrast Francis Plummer to Gregory van Buren. What was his standing at the start of the novel among the school faculty and teachers, and how did it change? Why do you think his working relationship with Rachel is so different from Francis's relationship with her?

7. Arguably one of the most controversial characters in this novel is Amy's father, Mitch Michaels. Thinking of his role as a radio show host and as a father, do you have any sympathy for Mitch? Does he have any admirable characteristics? What motivates him to range an attack on Claire, even after meeting her and learning she is his daughter's best friend?
8. Aside from school politics, Rachel struggles with her long-distance relationship with her husband. Why do you think that distance changes relationships between spouses? How does that relationship compare to relationships between students and their teachers, like Claire and her father, or Amy and her parents?
9. Ms. Richardson secretly arranges a meeting that Rachel discovers and attends, to everyone's surprise. What was the impact of Rachel's presence and Amelia's support of her? In what ways did it alter the course of the conversation and change the attitudes of the people at the meeting?

Keep reading for the first chapter from
Saving Miss Oliver's
by Stephen Davenport

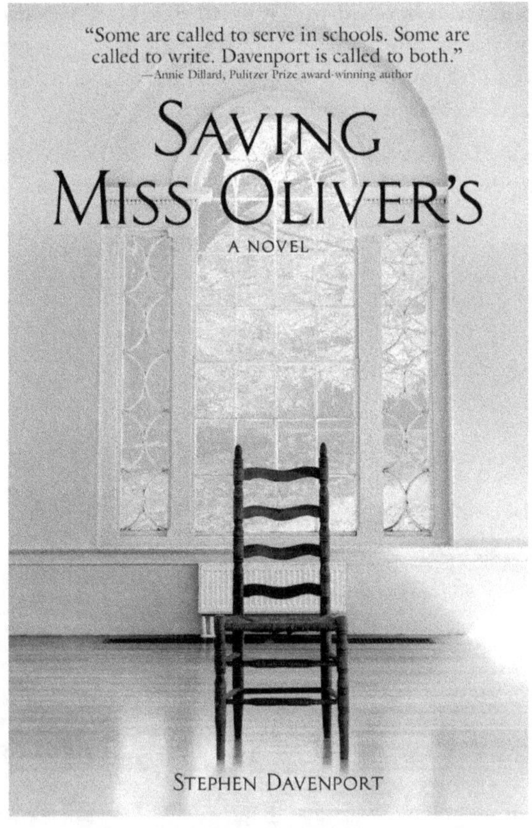

Excerpt from *Saving Miss Oliver's*

ONE

Even in that last year of her reign, Marjorie Boyd had insisted that the graduation exercise take place *exactly* at noon.

"When the sun is at the top of the sky!" she declared—as she had every year for the thirty-five years she had been headmistress of Miss Oliver's School for Girls. "Time stands still for just a little instant right then. And people notice things. They *see!* And what they see is the graduation of young women! Females! From a school founded by a woman, designed by women, run by a woman, with a curriculum that focuses on the way *women* learn! I want this celebration to take place exactly at noon, in the bright spangle of the June sunshine, so the world can see the superiority of the result!" Marjorie demanded once again, still dominant at the very end in spite of her dismissal. She would be the headmistress till July 1, when her contract expired. Until then, her will would prevail.

Even her opponents understood that it was Marjorie's vivid leadership that had made the school into a community so beloved of its students and alumnae (who were taking their seats now in the audience as the noon hour neared) that it had to be saved from the flaws of the very woman who had made it what it was. Founded by Miss Edith Oliver in 1928 and standing on ground once occupied by a Pequot Indian village in Fieldington, Connecticut, a complacent suburb twenty miles south of Hartford on the Connecticut River, the school that Marjorie created was a boarding school, a world apart, whose intense culture of academic and artistic richness was celebrated in idiosyncratic rituals sacred to its members.

"But it will be too hot at noon," the more practical-minded members of the faculty had objected once again in an argument that for senior faculty members Francis and Peggy Plummer had become an old refrain. They were like theatergoers watching a play whose ending they had memorized.

"No, it won't," Marjorie replied.

"How do you know it won't?"

"I just do," she said, standing up to end the meeting. For meetings always ended when Marjorie stood up—and began instantly when she sat down. Francis and Peggy understood that what Marjorie meant was that she would push the weather to be perfect for their beloved young women by the sheer power of her will. The weather had always been perfect for each of the thirty-three graduation ceremonies in which Peggy and Francis had been on the faculty—and that day, June 10, 1991, was no exception.

Now the clock in the library's steeple chimed the noon hour, and Marjorie Boyd was standing. She strode across the dais to the microphone. The graduating class sat in the honored position to the left of the dais, their white dresses glistening in the sunshine. The sky was an ethereal blue, cloudless, and under it the green lawns swept to the edge of the acres of forest that lined the river. Behind the dais a huge three-hundred-year-old maple spread its branches, and Francis imagined a family of Pequot Indians sitting in its shade. The scent of clipped grass rose. In the audience the mothers wore big multicolored hats against the sun, and behind them the gleaming white clapboards of the campus buildings formed an embracing circle.

Standing at the microphone, Marjorie didn't look much older to Peggy and Francis than when she had first hired them thirty-three years ago immediately after their marriage—Peggy as the school's librarian, and Francis as a teacher of math and soon after also of

English—assigning them too as dorm parents in what was then a brand-new dormitory. Marjorie still wore her long brown hair, now streaked with gray, in a schoolmarmish bun at the back of her neck. Her reading glasses still rested on her bosom, suspended from a black string around her neck. "You *were* Oliver girls," they heard Marjorie say, and Francis reached to hold Peggy's hand. They knew what she was going to say next, and when she said it—"Now you are Oliver *women*!"—giving the word a glory, Peggy started to cry. She was surprised at her sudden melting. For up to this moment she had managed to assuage her grief over Marjorie's dismissal by reminding herself that she agreed with the board's decision.

But Francis wasn't crying! He was too angry to cry, wouldn't give his new enemies the satisfaction—for that's how he thought of those colleagues, old friends, whom he suspected of optimism over the dismissal of his beloved leader. He gripped Peggy's hand, squeezed hard, made her wince. *It's her school!* he wanted to shout. *Marjorie's! Not theirs!* He didn't want Peggy to cry; he wanted her to be angry, to be obstreperous at every opportunity, to express disgust at the notion that schools bore any resemblance to businesses, as he did; he wanted her to say rebellious things in faculty meetings, the way he'd been doing, surprising everyone, including himself, by seeming out of control.

Still sobbing, Peggy yanked her hand away. She'd been over this so many times before! *You can be loyal without being stupid*, she wanted to yell. *She was your boss, not your daddy.* But of course she didn't. It wasn't the time to tell her husband that maybe his ardent following of Marjorie was his way of escaping the dominance of a father who couldn't have been more different from Marjorie—he would have fired her years before this! She kept her mouth shut. It was bad enough that people saw her sobbing.

Marjorie sat quietly after exactly four minutes during which she told her audience that now *they* must take care of the school. All of her thirty-five graduation speeches had been exactly four minutes long. She practiced them, first in her bathroom. "I love to hear the words bouncing off the tile," she told Francis and Peggy every year when she started working on her speech weeks before the event. Francis and Peggy knew that she timed herself with the same stopwatch she brought to the track meets so that she could congratulate any girl who had improved her time. In this last year of her reign she had been taking the stopwatch to faculty meetings so she could time the windy ruminations of Gregory van Buren, head of the English Department, who, second in seniority only to Peggy and Francis, sat that day immediately to Peggy's right in the front row of the graduation audience, smirking as if he had discovered a grammatical error in Marjorie's speech. Gregory didn't even try anymore to disguise his joy at what he loved to call "Marjorie's expulsion"—or the "demise of the monarchy at Miss Oliver's School for Girls."

There was a second of silence after Marjorie sat, and then, simultaneously, Francis and the graduating class stood up. In an instant Peggy was up too, taller than her husband. The audience rose. Their applause swelled. The block of undergraduates sitting right behind the faculty chanted, "Yay, Marjorie! Yay, Marjorie!" On the dais, the trustees stood too, their board chair, Alan Travelers, looking uncomfortable.

To Peggy's right, Gregory rose too slowly. She turned to him, grabbed his elbow, pulled him upward. "Stand straight, windbag!" she whispered through her sobbing. "Stand straight and clap!"

Gregory was too smart; he didn't even turn his head to her. He was gazing up over the podium as if he were watching a bird, his hands coming together so softly they didn't make a sound, and Peggy was amazed to hear herself hissing: "Louder, you *politician*! Louder! Or I swear to God I'll poke out both your eyes right here in front of everybody!"

For an instant as the words flew out, she felt wonderful, a prisoner released. But then stupid. This wasn't her. She didn't insult people, she had never been involved in the school's politics. And she didn't have Francis's talent for effective goofiness. She thought maybe she was going to lose control permanently, wondered if everything was falling apart: Marjorie's leaving and the resultant division in the faculty, and equally pressing, Francis's leaving the next day on a trip that would last all summer, the first time in their thirty-three-year marriage they would be apart for more than a week. It was the final straw. So she made up her mind: she'd stay in control. Not just for herself. For Francis too—until he was able to control himself again.

Gregory still didn't turn his face to her. He stared straight ahead, placed his right hand on Peggy's, lifted her hand from his elbow, placed it at her side as if he were putting something back in a drawer, and whispered: "I thought you understood, unlike your husband, who only understands the past. Actually, I *know* you understand."

Gregory was right. She did understand. It had been the newer members of the board who forced the issue. The era has passed, they had pointed out, when being a great educator is enough. No longer do certain kinds of families automatically send their children away to boarding school; and besides, just as boarding school grows too expensive for many families, single-sex education for women seems to be losing its allure. So pay more attention to the business side: to marketing scenarios, strategic plans, financial projections. That's the road to survival.

Peggy had tried hard to persuade her friend to pay attention; and when rumors began to fly that the school was so strapped that it might have to make the one decision no one could even dare imagine, the one that would destroy the reason for the school's existence—namely, to admit *boys*—to survive, she had barged right in to Marjorie's office and told her that if she, Peggy Plummer, the school's librarian for the past thirty-three years, were on the board, she would vote for Marjorie's dismissal in spite of their ancient friendship unless Marjorie changed her ways and started to act as if her profession, for all it was a calling, were a business too. But nobody gave Marjorie advice. It was the other way around. So Peggy hadn't been surprised when six months later the board, whose chair, Alan Travelers, was the first male board chair in the school's history, screwed its courage to the sticking place and demanded Marjorie's resignation.

Peggy stopped crying by the time she and her friend Eudora Easter, chair of the Art Department, had to go up front and confer the diploma on the first student. The order had been determined the night before when the president of the junior class picked the graduates' names out of the tall silk hat that was brought out of safekeeping once a year, according to ritual. The hat was rumored to have belonged to Daniel Webster. At Miss Oliver's it was a sign of loyalty to believe myths that lesser schools would scorn.

Facing the audience beside Eudora, Peggy was calm again. She was tall, slim, full breasted, her short black hair not covered by a hat, and she wore a trim business suit—librarian's clothes. Eudora was much shorter than Peggy, very round, her beautiful African features shadowed under a huge red hat, and her red slippers were pointed upward at the toes like a genie's. The students cheered her costume.

The ceremony went on for several hours. For the graduates the teachers recited poems, sang songs, performed dances, even put on little skits. Francis conferred the diploma on several girls by himself, and he and Peggy together did so for three girls who lived in their dorm. For each, Francis spun the amazing tale of their blossoming, thus blessing their parents. Gregory van Buren's one girl got a long poem that nobody understood. She tried hard not to show her disappointment. When Gregory hugged her, he bent his middle away from her, sticking his butt out behind as if he were wearing a bustle.

LATER THAT DAY in the desolate silence that overcame the school, when the last girl had left for the summer, Peggy roamed her empty dormitory. For the past four years at exactly this time, their son, Sidney, would return from college and she and Francis would focus on him all summer, feasting on his presence. But Siddy, who had finished college a year ago in June, left for Europe in September to wander for an indeterminate time. *He's figuring out who he is, what he wants to do with his life*, Peggy told herself over and over, seeking comfort. *All the young ones do that these days.* The mantra brought her no more comfort than knowing that young people didn't bother getting married anymore before they lived with each other. To Peggy, whose school was a home away from home for three hundred and forty-five students, wandering was anathema.

So, she asked herself, why did her husband insist on this trip that he would start tomorrow, the first day of summer vacation? He would be away not only from her for the entire summer but also from the new head who needed the senior teacher's help in getting acclimated—and had every right to expect it. Francis had a big responsibility to fulfill right here this summer, one that he could fulfill better than anyone. So why did he choose to wander? *He* was not just out of college; he was fifty-five, for goodness sake!

She knew Francis's response would be that he wouldn't be wandering. He'd be chaperoning a group of students from schools all over the East on an archaeological dig in California—what was wrong with that? Wasn't Miss Oliver's School famous for its anthropology courses; wasn't that what made them different from all those other schools? "If our girls can learn to look objectively at other cultures," he had reminded her, "then they can look at their own with open eyes, instead of the way they have been indoctrinated to see—by men. That's how we change the world! We're going to live in a reconstructed Ohlone Indian village on the shoulder of Mount Alma while we do the dig to find the real village they lived in," he had told her—as if she hadn't known!

If he would just admit to himself the real reason, that he wanted to be like an Indian, she could object—and remind him that Indians made their vision quests when they were fourteen years old! For that's what Francis and his students were trying to do: be like Indians. Otherwise, why not just live in tents?

But chaperoning an exercise in anthropology? How could Peggy argue against that? She was the one who, thirty years ago, had started the tradition of cultural relativism that made Miss Oliver's unique. It was she who had discovered the jumble of Pequot Indian artifacts in a closet of the little house that then served as the school's library, and it was she who had persuaded Marjorie to raise the funds for a new library in which the Pequot artifacts, and several small bones of a young Pequot woman unearthed when the library's foundation was dug, were now respectfully displayed. It was lost on no one that the library—which many of the faculty thought of as Peggy's Library—was situated exactly at the center of the campus.

Peggy walked slowly down the hall of her dormitory, entering each girl's room as if it were ten-thirty in the middle of the school year and she were saying goodnight. Even though she knew the girls wouldn't be in their rooms to turn their faces to her as she stood in the door, she was surprised to discover how lonely she felt in the sudden barrenness where the sound of her footsteps echoed off the walls.

She moved from room to room. It didn't surprise her that Rebecca Burley had left the poster of Jimi Hendrix on the wall; she and Francis had told each other more than once that this kid needed to try on lots of different coats before it was too late, but further down the hall, when she discovered a well-used bong sitting squarely in the middle of the desk of Tracy Danforth—who had just graduated and was president of the Honor Council—she wanted to get Francis, bring him here to show him how Tracy had been trying to show them who she really was. But she didn't get Francis. Because he was too busy. Packing for his trip.

She thought: *He can't possibly pack for a whole summer without my help, he's helpless about such things, doesn't know where anything is, he'll go off with no underwear and ten pairs of pants.* She turned away from the empty dorm.

SHE FOUND FRANCIS in their bedroom. He was on the other side of the bed from where she stopped in the doorway the instant she saw him putting a big duffel bag on the bed. He was holding his hiking boots in his hands, about to stuff them in.

"Oh!" she said. "I've never seen those before."

"They're new."

"When'd you buy them?" They were ugly, she hated them.

He shrugged. "The other day."

"Oh!" she said again. She took one step back, almost out the door. Why did seeing him pack disturb her so? She wondered if she were going to cry for the second time that day.

He noticed the movement and stopped packing, his attention full on her. "I got them at Le Target." He pronounced it "targay," looking for her smile.

It didn't work. But his little joke did stop her retreat. "Maybe you should pack later, Francis," she said, taking several steps back into the room. "The reception for the new headmaster starts in half an hour." She knew it was dumb to think he'd change his plans and stay home where he belonged if he deferred packing until after the reception. Nevertheless, the thought flashed.

"I'm not going to the new head's reception," he said.

"Say that again." She was standing perfectly still now.

"I'm not going," he said again. But already he was beginning to relent. He knew how foolish it was to stay away, how churlish it would seem. But in Marjorie's house! *It's her home*, he wanted to say, *no one else's*. But of course it wasn't her house; it was the school's.

"Yes, you are, Francis," Peggy said. "You're going. You're not childish enough to stay away," and immediately she regretted using that word.

He dropped his gaze to the bed. Now he was tossing in his shaving things and his toothbrush and toothpaste. Loose. All jumbled up with everything else.

"Oh, for goodness sake!" she said. "You can't pack like this!" She reached in, pulled out a wad of shirts, tossed them over her shoulder. "Or this!" she said, tossing a crumpled pair of chinos in another direction. "Or this!" Three big paperback books went flying, their pages fluttering. She put her hand back in the bag again. She was going to empty the whole damn thing. She knew perfectly well she wasn't helping him pack, she was *un*packing him, and she was crying now, his clothes flying all over the room.

"Peg! I said I'll go!" He was gripping both her wrists now, one in each hand.

She let him hold her, keeping her hands still, and forced herself to stop crying. "You know," she said, "sometimes I think we're as married to the school as we are to each other." It was the first time she'd dared to put the thought into words.

"No," he said. "No way, Peg."

"So when you risk your place here, I wonder what other seams will start to tear."

"Peggy, I said I will go."

She felt a huge relief growing, as if maybe she didn't have so much to worry about after all. "You know, he's been very considerate," she said, speaking of the new head. She was looking at Francis again because now, with victory, she couldn't resist explaining her point. "He refused the invitation to speak at graduation."

"I know all about it," Francis said

She saw Francis trying not to look irritated and persisted anyway. She wanted so much to convince! "He said it was inappropriate. He said it was Marjorie's moment, not the new head's. That's pretty nice, you know."

"I don't want to talk about him," Francis said. "I'm not going to his reception for him. I'm going for you." She realized that the other part of her relief was that of the mourner who doesn't want the wake to end because then she'd be alone.

FIVE MINUTES BEFORE they left for the reception, Francis stood in front of the mirror above his bureau, putting on his tie. Peggy came up beside him, kissed him on the cheek. Leaning against him, she felt his body soften. "Indians don't wear ties," she said, trying for a joke. Right away she wished she could take the joke back when she felt his shoulders stiffen. He turned his head just slightly away so that her kiss didn't linger, and she stepped back, feeling her anger flame. *Why right now?* she suddenly wanted to ask again. To hell with jokes. On top of everything else! *Don't you know we're too old to believe in different things?* Francis moved away, leaving her framed in the mirror, and for an instant she didn't recognize the tense woman who stared back at her.

Francis still thought he was going on an archaeological dig, the face in the mirror told her. He's not ready to admit he's going on a vision quest. It's much too far out for Francis, too over the top, too *embarrassing*, to imagine himself, a middle-class white man in a tweed sports coat, a boarding school teacher, for goodness sake! chasing Indian visions. In California too, where everybody's weird! But that's what was happening. And she had thought for years that her vision and his were the same. She'd known almost from the day they met that Francis was a spiritual man. That was the deepest of the reasons she loved him so much. So it wasn't hard to believe that the reason he had asked her to join in his family's staunch Episcopal faith when they were married was that he believed in it. He thought so too, she understood, for the force of that belief was so strong in the family that he couldn't believe he was different enough not to share it. But what she knew now, better than he did, was that the real reason he had asked her this favor was that he couldn't imagine explaining to his father that he cared so little for his religion that he wouldn't ask his wife to join it. Even though she had none of her own to relinquish if she did.

I've been hoodwinked, she wanted to say, *hoodwinked and deserted*, thinking of how much she'd been rescued from the barrenness of her own disbelief by the religion she'd joined and now was nurtured by, how much she'd come to love her father-in-law for the belief she shared with him, how much she'd missed him since his death five years ago. *When you don't resolve things with your father, you live with his shadow until you die too*, she wanted to lecture Francis. *It makes you crazy.* She didn't say that either.

AT THE FRONT door of Marjorie's house, Francis hesitated. "This is Marjorie's house," he said. He'd walked through this door hundreds of times.

"It's the headmistress's house," she reminded him. Then corrected herself: "The headmaster's."

He turned to her then, gave her a look as if she has just slapped his face.

"Sorry."

"I can't," he said. "No way. Not in her house."

She took his hand, tugged it. "Come on, Fran, let's go."

He resisted.

"Grow up!" she said, tugging at his hand. "It's time."

When he still resisted, she dropped his hand, turned from him, went through the door. He hesitated, then, surrendering, followed her. He always stayed close to her at parties, using her vivacity as a cover for his shyness, but this time they moved to separate rooms in Marjorie's big house, which was loud with people talking.

Francis moved through the people in the foyer into the living room. It seemed bigger somehow, empty of something he couldn't put his finger on. He stopped walking. A surprising fear of the new largeness of Marjorie's living room rose in him. While anxiety took hold of him, Marcia Holmes, his young friend in the History Department, moved across the rug to him.

Smiling, she told him how much she liked hearing what he'd said about the girls he graduated. "You tell such wonderful stories," she told him, and went on to say how much she wished more girls liked her enough to invite her to graduate them, and suddenly, while part of him told her not to worry because next year would be easier, the second year always was, and another part of him watched her face, still another part watched the scene that suddenly appeared inside his head for the second or third time that week while he began to sweat and went on talking to this lovely young woman in her sexy summer dress as if everything were normal: the stern of a ship was moving away, he saw the froth by the propeller, going away from him, no one had seen him fall overboard, no one heard his shouts. Marjorie's big sofa was missing, he realized, coming back fully to his young friend, and the top three shelves of her bookcase were empty, and that was what he pointed out to her, as if it were a discovery of some amazing new scientific fact, interrupting her as she told him of her summer plans, and there was a funny look on her face—part worry and part a question, as if she were hoping that he was telling her a joke she didn't understand. "She's started to move out already," he said in a very matter-of-fact way.

"Yes," Marcia said. She was waiting for a punch line, but he couldn't think of anything else to say. She patted his arm—he couldn't tell if it was sympathy or just her way of excusing herself—and moved away.

FRED KINDLER, THE new headmaster, was standing by the fireplace in the center of Marjorie's living room. Marjorie stood next to him, a good six inches taller. They were talking calmly together—as if nothing had happened, as if everything was the same, and Francis remembered Marjorie telling him of her resolve to hide her bitterness. "These people, who wouldn't even have a school to be on the board of if it weren't for me, want me to pretend I yearn for retirement," she had told him. "Well, I'd rather yearn for death. But all this is for your ears only," she went on after a pause. "The last bitter statement I'm going to make. I'll take their advice. I'll say I want the time to take up—what, golf? My grandsons? You know, the truth of the matter is I'm not remotely interested in my grandsons," she murmured, speaking half to herself and half to Francis as if she'd just discovered this about herself. "This school is what interests me."

Francis was surprised again at the new head's red hair, the big red mustache, and the short, stocky, powerful body. For an instant, Francis, in his mind's eye, observed his own short, almost pudgy body, as if in a mirror, his round mild, unobtrusive face. He couldn't resist staring across the room at Kindler. *He's so* male! Francis thought, and then registered what he had seen instantly when he first saw Kindler standing next to Marjorie: that he was wearing the same brown polyester suit that he'd worn during his interviews. *Polyester!* Francis thought, shocked at himself that he even noticed. He'd always been proud that in the world of preppydom of which it was a part, Miss Oliver's School for Girls was studiously unpreppy, so why did he care what the man wore?

Kindler and Marjorie both noticed him. Francis saw Marjorie put her hand lightly on Kindler's wrist and Kindler move across the room toward him. He had an awkward gait; his feet pointed outward like Charley Chaplin's. For an instant, Francis felt sorry for him, imagined girls imitating that walk, every girl on campus walking like that everywhere they went, day after day, until the poor man had to leave.

Kindler's right hand was out. His left hand patted Francis on the shoulder. All Francis could see was the red of Kindler's hair and mustache. "Come see me tomorrow," Kindler said. "I'm here all day. Mrs. Boyd's lending me her office. I need all the advice I can get, and I want to start with the senior teacher. Want to collect the best ideas and get a running start when I come back."

Francis was appalled at the boyishness. He felt suddenly like a tutor. That's not what he wanted—parenting his own boss. "I'm leaving for the summer dig project tomorrow. Six a.m.," he said.

A waiter from the caterers came by with a tray of drinks. Francis plucked a glass of white wine. Without taking his eyes off Francis, frowning slightly, Kindler murmured to the waiter, "No, thank you," and then to Francis: "Oh? That so? You're going on that dig? Somebody told me that one of the teachers was going. I didn't realize it was you."

"I signed up way back in February," Francis said. He almost added *before you were appointed*, but he didn't feel like explaining himself.

"Well," said Kindler, "I could have used you around here this summer. But that's the way it has to be." His face brightened. "California, right?" Francis had the impression that the man had changed his expression on purpose to make him more comfortable.

Francis sensed Peggy watching him from across the room. "Right, California." He took a sip of his drink, noticed that several people were watching him and Kindler. *We're on stage*, he thought. *It's a big scene*, and now he was seeing himself as some kind of fulcrum. Took another sip, his hand was shaking, spilled some wine on his shirt, felt its cold.

Kindler handed him a napkin. "Mount Alma, right?"

"Yes," said Francis. "Mount Alma." He saw himself driving out across the flat Midwest, lonely without Peggy in the car. Then he saw the mountains, felt a little surge of joy, but his hand was still shaking, and he spilled some more.

"You all right?" Kindler asked.

For an instant, thinking the question was sardonic, the new head's first spear thrust, and Francis was relieved. Then looking at the man's too youthful face, he realized the question was sincere, uncomplicated, devoid of subtlety, and he was panic-stricken. "I'm all right," he managed. By now he was sure everybody was watching them.

"Look," Kindler said. "I understand." He was talking now very quietly so no one else could hear. "Why wouldn't you feel that way? You've served her for years. I've admired her too—just from a greater distance. Just the same, I'm sure we can work together."

"Well, as long as you don't change anything," Francis blurted. Then he realized what he'd said, how dumb it was. He managed a grin, a little chuckle, as if he'd been joking, as if he hadn't meant exactly what had come out of his mouth.

His camouflage seemed to work. Fred Kindler smiled. Francis saw the red mustache move. "Good," said Kindler. "I look forward to working with you." Then he moved away to mix with the others.

THERE! FRANCIS THOUGHT, *I've managed to get through it. Now I can go home!* He looked for Peggy, saw her across the room, stared at her back until she turned. He signaled her with his eyes that he wanted to leave. But she turned her back to him to show she was engaged in the conversation. He felt empty, moved across the room to leave the house.

He figured if he could just get out the door . . .

But on the way, he overheard Milton Perkins telling one of his Polish jokes to a circle of uncomfortable-looking faculty members. Perkins, the recently retired president of one of the biggest insurance companies in the state, had been on the board a long time. Francis found himself slowing down on his way to the door, listening to the joke. He'd heard it before. Perkins was seldom able to resist baiting the faculty's liberalism and being politically incorrect in a loud voice whenever he got an audience of teachers. Francis had always forgiven the man, understanding that underneath, Perkins had a deep respect for the school and the people who taught in it—which he had shown by years of generosity. To Francis, who, if pressed, would admit he liked to make derogatory generalizations about businessmen, Perkins was merely a gambler in a fancy suit who was just smart enough to sense the inferiority of his vocation to that of teaching. So why should Francis be bothered by the old man's backwardness?

But now, listening to the story, knowing exactly how it would build to the punch line in rhythmic stupidities, Francis stopped walking toward the door, turned, stepped back toward Perkins and his group of embarrassed listeners. Francis knew what he was doing, knew he shouldn't, discovered that he'd been holding back these feelings for years in order to make things work for Marjorie, realized also that Perkins probably had been instrumental in Marjorie's dismissal. He took another step toward Perkins and his group of listeners and saw Rachel Bickham, the chair of the Science Department and director of Athletics, whom he admired, looking at him hard. She shook her head, an unobtrusive gesture meant just for him. *Don't*, she seemed to warn. *Just don't*. But he loved the release he was about to get. The room was very bright to him now, all its colors vivid.

"Why don't you shut up?" he heard himself saying to Perkins. "Why don't you just clam it?"

That's exactly what Perkins did—for an instant. He turned to face Francis. He clearly didn't know what to do. He was certainly not going to apologize! So he just turned his back on Francis and went on telling his story. That's what enraged Francis so—the dismissal! After all those years! He tapped Perkins on the shoulder, and when the man turned around, his face flaming, Francis told the same story back to him, substituting *Republican* for *Polack*. The group of teachers to whom Perkins had been telling his story glided away, so it was just Perkins now, and Francis, in the center of the room. Francis was pronouncing the name *Perkins* with the same clowning sarcasm with which Perkins had emphasized the final syllable *ski* of the Polish person in the joke.

They were center stage. Francis glimpsed Marjorie, who was still standing by her fireplace, staring across the room at him. Her expression was begging him to stop. Father Michael Woodward, the local Episcopal priest and part-time chaplain, one of Francis's and Peggy's best friends, was standing by the opposite wall making slicing motions at his throat.

Francis didn't see Peggy. He went on and on, building a vastly more complex story than Perkins's joke, a fantasy of ineptitude in which the absurdly Anglo-Saxon main character reached mythical idiocy. When a few of the people in the room couldn't resist laughing, he was even more inspired, felt the lovely release, and went on some more—until he realized that Eudora Easter was standing at his right side and Father Woodward at his left. Their hands were on his elbows. He shut up.

"Jeeeezus!" said Perkins into the sudden silence. "What in hell was *that* all about?"

Nobody answered because Eudora and Father Woodward were escorting Francis from the scene of the crime.

CPSIA information can be obtained
at www.ICGtesting.com
Printed in the USA
BVHW050048150319
542743BV00002B/2/P

9 781513 262024